Dedication

This one is for my devoted Hellhounds, who remind me often how much they miss the Road to Hell characters. Without your prodding, I'd have never finished Royal Partnerships. I'm glad y'all continued to pester me. Love all y'all to pieces!

Thanks to Tamika McCaskie for naming my dark and sexy incubus...Aramayis.

Thanks Megan Marie McGehee for naming the monsters...Indra and Khoal.

Thanks Ginnie Hutto for loaning me your name to use for one of my new characters, which is a Baltic paranormal creature.

Cast of Characters

Madison Wescott—Mother of Amos, wife to Micah. Called "Mads" by Nix Birmingham. Is a Lynx succubus.

Usha—The demonic name of Madison's demon.

Amos Wescott—Son of Madison and Micah. Part angel, succubus, and human.

Micah Dominus—Is a fallen archangel. Angelic name is Beliel. Is one of the Four Kings of Hell. Husband to Madison and father of Amos.

Phoenix "Nix" Birmingham—A Sherlock dedicated to hunting down and killing monsters. Is the Ark of Heaven and an heir of Jesus Christ. Has many of the same special powers as Jesus. Is in love with Madison.

Zennyo Ryuo—Nicknamed Zen by Madison. An immortal dedicated to keeping the balance between humanity and the paranormal.

Petralegija (Petra)—Daughter to Micah, half-sister of Amos, and a centuries-old succubus demon. Assisted with the murder of Nix's parents.

Elias—Is a fallen archangel. Angelic name is Eliel. Micah is his twin. One of the Four Kings of Hell. Assisted with the murder of Nix's parents.

Raguel—Is a fallen archangel. One of the Four Kings of Hell.

Lucifer/Hielel—Is a fallen archangel. Angelic name is Hielel. One of the Four Kings of Hell.

Gage Birmingham—Sherlock and cousin to Nix Birmingham.

Zoe—Sherlock and girlfriend to Gage.

Georgie Birmingham—Aunt to Nix Birmingham and a psychic. Married to James Birmingham and the mother of Gage Birmingham.

James Birmingham—Sherlock. Husband to Georgie, father of Gage Birmingham, and uncle to Nix Birmingham.

Alessa/Alessandra—Nicknamed "Lucky" by Nix because when he visited her nothing bad ever happened, so was his lucky charm. Was saved by Nix from her Werewolf husband. Became fast friends with Madison after Nix went to Hell. Helped Madison save Nix from Hell. Owns a horse ranch.

Lasso—Alessa's dog.

Kur—Dragon Madison freed from Hell and now commands.

Cael—Dragon Madison freed from Hell and now

commands.

Celeste—Madison's mother and a succubus demon.

FiFi—A Hellhound Madison brought to earth from Hell.

Devlin—A Hellhound Madison brought to earth from Hell.

Taz—A mini-dragon Madison brought to life by accident from a picture drawn by Amos.

Glossary of Terms

Archangels—The most elite angels created by God; they are warrior angels.

Four Kings of Hell—The fallen archangel's responsible for building the hellish empire.

Ichnaday—A term in the royal demon dialect used by the Kings of Hell to command those of a lower caste. If this word is used, a demon cannot disobey.

Ichnay—A command from the royal demon dialect used by the Queen of Hell to control those of a lower caste. If this word is used, a demon cannot disobey.

Lynx—The rarest breed of succubus that feeds off supernatural powers.

Messian—Magic produced by Nix Birmingham. Gives

him the ability to heal and bring people back from the dead.

Neko—A hellish cat, easily as big as a small vehicle.

Nephilim—A child born to a fallen angel and mankind.

Scroll of Cursed Souls—A scroll created by Zennyo Ryuo for trapping creatures in Hell. There are five Scrolls, each trapping a different creature. Madison wears one like a tattoo on her lower back and because of it, she is able to command the dragons.

Seraph—Magic produced by Micah and other angels.

Succubus—A demonic female creation that will die without feeding on sexual energy.

Incubus—A demonic male creature that will die without feeding on sexual energy.

The Word—God directly speaking to a person.

zkihtak—Xapil word for brother.

Xapil—The name of the demon dialect.

Scepter of Spirits—A spiritual sword given to Micah as the lead Archangel. It allows him to slay other angels and he can reap them to whatever plane of his choosing.

Esdras—Fire angels. Used to destroy with fire. The same angels that killed Madison in Genesis Queen.

Azura Stones—Stones that all demons have. They're tied to their genetics and each set only works for a specific demon. They're prophetic stones, giving guidance for the demon who owns them.

Sterillium— Prismatic seeds of destruction that

when ingested are toxic to all supernatural creatures, and cause a graphically painful death.

Angelfire —Special fire, blue in color, used to trap angels. The fire itself doesn't harm an Archangel, but will kill a lesser angel. If trapped within a ring of Angelfire, if an angel does not escape prior to it burning out, they'll die.

Casket —It is a goblet that ensures true and total death of any supernatural creature.

Madison's Sigil

Micah's Sigil

Royal Partnerships

What Happened then on the Road to Hell...

MADISON'S LIFE LESSONS

Caught in an abusive household she can't escape, at fifteen Madison meets Micah on Christmas morning at her father's church. Through a series of events he digs his way into her life, becoming the hero she needed to better her life.

She marries him at eighteen, endures her parents' death a few years later, and delivers Micah a son at age twenty. But her marriage isn't perfect. He rules her with an iron fist, and his outbursts of violence toward others frighten her. Neither can she relax enough to enjoy the marital bed, which obviously frustrates her husband.

Then after a beautiful evening when she almost allows herself to relax enough to enjoy her husband sexually—until her father's abusive words echo through her head—he leaves for work the next morning and never returns.

PANDORA'S BOX

Madison has exhausted all routes to aid her son, Amos, who has been murdering the family pets and attacking her. Her last source of help arrives in the form of a cocky, yet attractive, Sherlock, Nix Birmingham, and his family. Although Madison's husband walked out on her three years ago, he's back now and he's got a new face. He's a King of Hell, on a mission to reclaim his family for Hell's purpose.

Madison and Amos travel the United States, avoiding Micah and taking out demons one at a time, while learning about the supernatural world they've been plunged into. Along the way they add Zen to their list of allies, as well as Micah's succubus daughter, Petra.

With a false supernatural lead, Micah captures Nix, Gage, and Zoe. After having Gage and Zoe killed, he reveals his trump card...Nix is the Ark of Heaven and can bring his family back to life. Micah will show him how to wield his power to save Gage and Zoe, but Nix must sacrifice his lineage to the King in a blood covenant and join him in Hell. With no other viable option, Nix accepts the terms.

Intent on saving Nix from Micah's deal, Madison confronts them, but makes the mistake of thinking if she opens Pandora's Box, she can use the power against her husband. Instead, the entity in the box ravages Madison from the inside out, determined to seek her own revenge. Zen comes to the rescue and leads Micah to believe he's killed Madison in order to keep the King from ruling the world.

HELL'S PHOENIX

Madison has a plan to save Nix from her husband's control, and she's going to do it by infiltrating Hell

2

with Nix's lucky charm—Alessa. Before she can get the other woman into the fiery realm with her, she must sell her soul to Madison.

On the Road to Hell, nothing ever goes as planned. In Hell, Nix has become Micah's lover and is enjoying his demonic side. Once they discover Madison is alive, they set a trap to lure her out of hiding. Again Zen saves her, but they send in Micah's twin, Elias, to bring her to Hell.

The only chance Madison has of surviving Hell is to accept her demonic DNA. But she's not the average succubus. She's a Lynx, the most powerful of all the breeds and magic-hungry, too. After she goes demonic, she and her Lynx succubus kill the entity inside Pandora's Box and claim the ancient power as their own.

Just barely managing to save Nix from Hell with the aid of dragons, Madison is left in Hell with a dragon blade that's toxic to angels. Her mission is to kill her husband. But during their warfare, her heart isn't in the fight. She does stab Micah in the chest—but only to save her son from his father's plans for the future.

Confused by her sadness that she might've killed her husband, Madison returns to earth on the dragon's arm. She wants to return to Hell where she feels at home, but knows she cannot, for her son's welfare. Hours after returning to earth, Madison is pulled back to Hell by Micah, who survived her attempt at murder.

GENESIS QUEEN

Lines between what's right and wrong blur.

After a night of passion with Nix, Micah pulls Madison back to Hell. She's excited to discover he survived her attempt at murdering him, but now the Four Kings of Hell don't trust her even though she's claimed her demon fully. With her loyalties torn and Hell's power diminishing her humanity, she submits to being anchored to Hell and covenants with Micah to return to Hell with Amos to prove her loyalty. And since it's a covenant she cannot renege on the deal.

Before she can be fully anchored to Hell, Amos and Nix jerk her back to Earth with a spell. Madison demands they demon lock her and then explains the covenant she made with Micah to return to Hell with Amos.

Thinking the Angel Lock will keep Micah out since he won't willingly lock himself into one place, they're surprised when Micah presents himself to speak with her. He tells her the Azura stones predict death for her and Amos. He wants them to return to the safety of Hell. She refuses, but reluctantly agrees to his protection when Zen thinks it's their wisest option at keeping them safe.

Trapped in the home with Micah doesn't come with the protection they'd anticipated. Esdras Angels have found a way to trap her, incapacitate Zen, and keep the aid of the dragons away. Both Micah and Elias are trapped in *Angelfire*, Nix is knocked out, and Amos used against her. They order Madison to commit suicide by eating *Sterillium* seeds or they'll kill Amos. With no other options, and hoping her dragons will instigate a surprise rescue, she eats the seeds even though Micah objects to their ingestion. The third one kills her and Micah collapses because their lives are covenanted to one another.

Zen is able to fight free of his incapacitation, severing himself from his Creator's divine presence, Falling from God's grace, and he ultimately saves his adopted family. Nix is awakened and he uses his Messianic magic to bring Madison back to life, but her death extinguished her life-covenant with Micah.

Madison discovers she can create life when a picture Amos drew of a mini-dragon comes to life and allows Nix to name the creature Taz. She discovers Kur and the dragons were an accidental creation from the mixture of Micah and Zen's magic during the time when they were allies.

Then danger from the most unlikely source

4

comes...Elias kidnaps Madison and secures her inside a cave in Hell. Now that her life is no longer bound to Micah's, and she can die without her death killing Beliel/Micah, Elias is determined to break her for Hell's service or kill her. He vowed to his brother he'd help her break whatever the cost and it's his time to fulfill his promise.

Elias tortures Madison physically. When she impresses him and holds out, he mentally tortures her into making her think she's killed Amos and Nix. When she fails to claim her hellish seat of power, he offers her a drink from the *Casket*, which is a goblet that ensures true and total death. But Elias lies to her and tells her drinking from it will give her the ability to bring either Amos or Nix back to life.

Micah, Kur, and Nix save Madison from Elias, and Micah plans to kill his twin until he learns Madison drank from the *Casket*. In order to live, Madison must decide if she's willing to claim her destiny as Queen of Hell or reject the seat her husband offers.

With death staring her in the face, the only chance she has to fight off the *Casket's* spell is to accept her destiny as the Queen of Hell.

Saved and now officially seated on her throne, Madison admits she's in love with both Nix and Micah. Choosing between them is impossible, especially after Zen delivers the news that the *Esdras* angels attempted to sway him into joining their cause to kill her because she's pregnant with Nix's baby. A child that is part demon, part heir of Christ, a child that can open the doors to Heaven and create havoc, and an abomination in the eyes of the angels.

Madison chooses to forge her own destiny, with both Nix and Micah at her side, as her lovers and husbands.

Chapter 1

THIS IS THE real *definition of Hell.*

Hoodwinked into tagging along for the "family meeting" was an injustice to the King of Hell. The Birminghams weren't even Micah's family, but he strode into the den beside his kitten to divulge the scandalous news that Madison would enter into a relationship with him and Phoenix.

I'm acting like a fucking domestic poodle. Or he'd hit rock bottom. At this point, both were viable options.

The coming confession might warrant some entertainment though and served as the only reason he hadn't balked at the not-so-quaint assembly. Of course, he'd gone along to protect Madison, too, because he expected the news to go over as well as Mother Theresa applying for Queen status in Hell. In other words, not a chance in hell of the outcome being peaceful.

Family. *Bah!* He had family. These mortals weren't even close to being classified as kin. His brothers, Madison, and Amos were his dynasty. And he guessed he could call the Ark of Heaven a kissing cousin of sorts since they were now tied to the same woman. Not

6

that categorization mattered in the long scheme of immortality. What mattered was whom he would die to protect.

He knew how the Birminghams felt about him without any mind reading necessary. Zoe feared him, not that he blamed her. Beliel *had* coldly ordered her execution. Without hesitation, he'd make the same call again if it would serve his needs. Gage hated him and wanted revenge for what he deemed misdeeds committed against his gal. Micah respected the mortal's emotions and could relate to them, but his family came first.

Either way, he'd never met a mortal more closed off and unturnable than Gage Birmingham. Color Micah impressed because humans without at least one crack in their defenses were rare.

James disliked Micah as much as Gage. Not that Micah lost any sleep over their hatred.

Georgie was just as leery of him, and she'd never forgive him for how he'd had her precious son, Gage, killed in such a blasé manner. Or how he'd used Phoenix against Madison. All had been actions necessary to drag his lovely bride out of hiding, and he would never apologize or regret his choices.

Dirtying his hands to kill mortals wasn't his style. Never had been and he wasn't likely to start. He preferred to leave that nasty business to Elias, Petra, or other demons. Instead, Micah liked to corrupt them with their very human flaws. Wasn't much of a challenge really, and sometimes he grew bored with the ease of humanity's Fall.

Micah reclined in a chair, and Madison perched on the arm of the seat. The shrewd Birminghams would recognize his claim of ownership when he rested his hand on her hip. She surprised and pleased him when she laced her fingers with his. Solidarity in one little move.

Yeah, take that, Birminghams.

For a split second, he caught the gaze of each member of the Ark's family. They all noticed. Good, let them stew on what their joined hands signified.

James's Adam's apple bobbed when he swallowed. A nervous tick Micah had discovered not long ago. The elder Birmingham's gaze honed in on his nephew. "Nix, care to explain what's going on?"

"Shouldn't *he* be gone by now?" Gage nodded at Micah, his animosity blazing from dark brown eyes.

The puppy amused Micah.

Phoenix held his arm out toward Madison, and with her free hand she took his. All eyes riveted on the joined hands.

By their panicky glimpses at one another, Micah predicted none of them missed she held both of their hands.

The Ark notched his head at a challenging angle. "Mads is remaining with both of us."

"You cannot be fucking serious." Gage crossed his arms over his chest and widened his stance.

"Very serious, Gage. I don't expect any of you to understand or approve. I'm telling you how things are going to be. Feel free to walk if you can't deal with my choice at happiness."

Blessed silence lasted for about twenty seconds before James spoke. "Demons killed your parents."

"Elias killed them," Phoenix corrected. "Petra was there, too, toying with them." Micah's daughter had been the one to turn the bat on Phoenix. "Elias performed the actual murders."

"When did you realize?" Micah didn't know the Ark had ever grasped who'd slaughtered his family.

"In Hell." He thought the man squeezed Madison's hand. "It's one of the main reasons I'll never like Petra, Mads. I tolerate her only for you and Amos, baby."

Micah let Nix's vow of hatred toward his daughter slide.

"This isn't what I've foretold for you, Nix." Georgie clutched her hands in her lap and rocked back and forth. It would be entertaining if she broke out in an insane cackle, but Micah predicated Phoenix wouldn't find it as amusing as he would.

"Are you sure what you saw didn't have Micah in it?" He waited a heartbeat before asking, "Did you see a kid in our future?"

The prophet frowned. "No, of course not. You know that."

"Mads is pregnant with my baby."

Zoe collapsed into the chair situated behind her, tears welling in her eyes. Gage looked horrified, mouth parted and eyes rounded. Georgie and James's expressions both held varying degrees of emotion, as if they couldn't decide whether to be happy or as disturbed as their son.

"You're keeping it?" And they called Micah the uncouth one. Gage was doing a damn fine job of showing his boorishness. "A demon baby?"

Tensing, Micah let his angel flame in his eyes. "Careful, pup, be very cautious of the next words out of your mouth." Beliel met Phoenix's glance over Madison's shoulder. Anyone maligning the King's woman or her unborn child would not be tolerated.

"I know you mean well, cousin, but I can't believe you asked me that question or referred to my baby as a demon." Phoenix's shoulders tensed, but his voice remained placid. "Of course we're keeping it. A baby is a blessing, not a curse."

"It is a demon, son." James paced a small path behind Georgie's chair. "Madison is part demon. I— I...." His hands covered his face as he shook his head.

Madison is full demon, not part. Micah held his tongue because to argue would cause further unnecessary drama.

Gage took up where his daddy left off. "Not only is getting pregnant irresponsible, but—what did you say you are...the Ark or some shit like that? A man of God is having a baby with a *demon!*"

"Gage!" Georgie rotated her fingertips against her temples as if she suffered a headache.

"Mom, it's true."

"Don't." Madison squeezed Micah's hand and shot him a commanding look. He bit the inside of his mouth to maintain his silence. That he allowed her to dictate his quietness verified he'd been pussy-whipped. "Gage, I'm sorry you feel that way. While I planned neither of my children, I already love this one"—she laid her palm over her flat tummy—"as much as I do Amos. And just because my child has demonic connections doesn't mean it'll become evil or worse, the Antichrist."

"No." Gage glared at Madison, fine lines fanning from the corners of his eyes. "That was Amos's role, right? Might still be if you allow *him* into your world." He indicated Micah with a slash of his hand.

Madison tensed. Micah whispered in her head, *Don't*, even though he wanted very much to rip the other man's tongue out. She tossed him a cagey scowl. *If I have to play nice, so do you, kitten.* Her frown intensified, and he winked at her.

"She's with me because she's *my* family. Don't forget it, cousin." The Ark of Heaven spoke with grit in his voice. "Do not malign her, Amos, or our child. Got it?"

Cousins glared at one another a long while, the tension in the room growing denser as the seconds lapsed off the clock. Micah waited on them to come to blows. Then Gage trashed his anticipation.

"Fine." But Gage appeared anything but fine, his glower as disagreeable as the Neko cats in Hell. "We all know the Sherlock lifestyle is no place to raise a child."

"I'm no longer a Sherlock." Phoenix's calm statement delivered a quiet so profound it made Micah's ears ring. Now the hits would come. He leaned forward anticipating the brawl.

Mute tears rolled down Georgie's cheeks. Turning her head aside, she swiped them away with her fingertips. To his exasperation she seemed to collect herself after several deep breaths.

"Nix is right." James rubbed his eyes with his finger and thumb, before locking sights on his nephew. "A child is a blessing."

'In normal circumstances' is what Micah heard at the end of that sentence. Just because the other man bit the words back, didn't mean he wasn't thinking them.

"Congratulations to...both of you," Georgie said through a bevy of sniffles. Micah couldn't gauge if the new addition, or Nix's rejection of his Sherlock upbringing, caused her unhappiness.

And damn it he still wanted a Birmingham fistfight.

"I don't get how you can justify this situation when you know demons killed your parents." The Ark's uncle placed his hand on his wife's shoulder, an obvious show of comfort.

"I'm in love with Mads. She had nothing to do with their deaths and neither did Micah. I don't understand why you think I should leave them when they had nothing to do with their deaths."

"Don't understand—he's a goddamn King of Hell!" Gage motioned to Micah, then toward Madison. "Not only is she a fucking succubus demon, but the Queen of Hell too. Neither fit in our life unless we're murdering them. You used to agree."

No longer willing to take the placid stance, Micah rose to his feet. "Trust me," he said by way of assuring Phoenix and Madison of his honorable intentions before leveling his focus on the Birminghams. "The way I see it, you have two very simple choices. Either accept Phoenix's decision or get the fuck out of his life. If you choose the latter, I'll wipe your memories clean. You chose the first option, you'll be granted safety from *my* demons only."

"Go back to Hell, you bastard! We don't make deals with the devil, and you don't get to dictate options on how we deal with family." Gage apparently lacked the aptitude for knowing when to back down.

"You *mortals* aren't allowed to dictate how *my* family lives either. As of thirty minutes ago, Phoenix became a part of mine. So suck up your pride and make a goddamn choice. You have three months to decide." He offered his hand to Madison and when she accepted, he pulled her to her feet.

"And if we refuse?" The inherent challenge in James's question made Micah want to rise to the bait.

"I'll be happy to make it for you, father Birmingham."

"You're on board with this ultimatum, Nix?" Gage's expression and tone implied he couldn't believe Phoenix would tolerate Micah's highhanded tactics.

The Ark of Heaven's straightforward regard should've made them proud of him because he stood up for his choices. Instead they were all too busy wallowing in their own misery to grasp Phoenix's wisdom. "What other choice have you left me, Gage?"

Phoenix's cousin clenched his hands into fists. His jaw locked, and the glare he directed toward the Ark hinted Gage wanted to burn the walls down around them. His cousin wouldn't let it go. "If we say fuck you all, he might erase our memory, but you'll still become our target."

"Good luck locating us." Micah held Gage's glower. "Puppy, if I don't want to be found, I'm invisible even if I'm standing next to you. Do you honestly believe the same wouldn't be true for my family if I willed it?"

"If—*if* we accept this situation and took your first offer, you would tolerate us Sherlocking even though we're killing demons?" Georgie rose to her feet, her expression blank as she stared at him while clenching her hands together.

"Yes. So long as you're not slaughtering mine or Madison's demons."

"I don't have any demons." His kitten gave him a confused expression.

"Of course you do." He tweaked her nose. "They were my wedding gift to you when we married. Five hundred thousand of them to be exact."

She gaped at him.

Phoenix swiped his fingers through his spiky hair. Clearly, Madison possessing demons rattled him. Evidence the other man continued to struggle at accepting Madison's status as Queen of Hell.

"Nix." Zoe placed her hand on the Ark's arm, halting his departure from the room. "May I talk with you a moment?" She glanced at Madison and Micah. "Alone."

"No, Zo." Phoenix squeezed her hand. "I cannot ride the fence on this. No amount of family discussions is going to change my mind. Mads is my future, our baby a blessing. I want my family to be a part of all of it, but I cannot serve two paths. You guys have a decision to make, and I won't listen to any arguments against my choice. My mind's made up." He kissed her cheek and exited the room with Micah and Madison.

The Ark had drawn the proverbial line in the sand. Felt like a victory to Micah, so he blasted the Birminghams with a grin over his shoulder. He'd attained everything he wanted, plus more than he'd bargained for, with a slight modification on his Earthly plans.

Chapter 2

MADISON OWNED DEMONS. Five hundred thousand of them to be exact. What was she to do with them?

Together we can think of something fun. A wicked edge darkened Lynx's voice.

Murder and mayhem is off the list, Madison shot back at her demon, as she walked ahead of the guys. But...she rather liked the idea of having them. Made her feel like she joined Hell with a little something extra in her pocket other than her Lynx firepower.

"Jesus Christ, Micah. She owns demons?" Nix demanded the moment they exited the den. "You didn't think that was relevant information before now?"

"She's a demon, Phoenix. Why wouldn't I spot her a few?"

Madison shivered at Micah's words. As a demon, she'd never felt freer than the moment she accepted her genetics. At the entrance to the kitchen, she stopped and turned toward her men, who continued to deliberate over her demonic acquisitions.

"All the Kings have demons at their command."
Micah peered at Madison as if to measure her mood.
When she only stared at him, he went on. "The Queen
should as well. As for relevance...they were on a need-
to-know basis until she accepted her hellish status."
Micah shrugged and ran his fingers through his hair.
Telling her before now would've been ammunition she
could've used against him. "I'm really not seeing the
problem. It's not like it's the end of the world."

Nothing to add to his monologue, she went to work
undoing his tie.

He glanced down, twin lines forming between his
eyes. "Kitten, what are you doing?"

"I want you in something else other than a suit and
tie."

"Why?"

She ignored him and pulled his cravat off his neck.
"Get comfortable—"

"I am comfortable."

"—wiggle your ass into some jeans and a T-shirt."
She released the top buttons on his shirt. "Always
wearing a suit makes you seem uptight, Micah, and we
three know you're not. Might help the Birminghams
accept you a little better if you look more
approachable."

He grinned. "You don't care what the Birminghams
think of me, you just want to see my ass in a pair of
jeans."

She returned his smile. "Busted." She pressed the
tie into his hand. "Now you two run along and do
something fun. I'm gonna cook something special for
tonight."

"Not that I'm complaining, but what's the occasion,
baby?" Nix braced his forearm against the wall to her
right, infiltrating her personal space. He smelled so
good, she and her Lynx considered rubbing up against
him.

15

"My son is safe, I have my two favorite men, and a baby on the way. And it's our first night together as a family. Do I need more reasons?"

"You could've said 'because', and I'd have been convinced." Nix cupped the back of her neck and tugged her in for a lingering kiss.

"Will I ever not feel jealous when you kiss her?" Micah bitched, but in a good-natured tone.

"I sure as hell hope not." Nix Eskimo kissed her, his eyes twinkling with devilry. To her he whispered, "Needling him is entertaining."

"Don't antagonize him, Nix." She gave Micah a kiss so he wouldn't feel left out and then shooed them both away. "I want to surprise y'all, so go do something while I cook."

"You want to know my favorite dishes, kitten?" Micah's incorrigible grin was contagious.

"Mads is my favorite dish," Nix said deadpan.

"That's a given," her demon King made a 'duh' face at Nix.

Hands on their chests, she nudged them both through the kitchen's doorway and walked away from them.

She heard Micah say, "You think that's a subtle hint to get lost?"

"Not all that subtle, if you ask me."

An hour later Madison was knuckle deep in kneading dough when one of her dragons entered her domain. Cael's waist-length hair was secured at his nape.

He strolled into the room and leaned against the island where she worked. "Hi, sexy Q."

She shook her head at his quirky nickname that was an abbreviation for 'sexy Queen'. "Hey, Cael."

This dragon flirted worse than Kur and often toed the line of preserving respect. But as Kur's right-hand man, that meant she trusted him to keep her safe.

"What are you making?" He nodded at the dough she kneaded.

"Biscuits."

"Mmm...love your biscuits." As if to prove his point, he licked his lips.

"Want to help roll some out?"

"Putting me to work, eh?"

"A dragon's gotta earn his keep somehow," she teased.

"For the record, I prefer stud services." He winked.

"There's still a one-way ticket back to Hell for you."

Unfazed by her threat, he laughed. He washed his hands in the sink before stepping up beside her. "Show me what to do."

"Watch." Madison pinched off a portion of dough and rolled it between her hands. "That's it," she said when she exposed the ball in the center of her palm.

Cael took over the biscuit rolling as she retrieved a baking sheet and prepped it with non-stick spray. "Put the biscuit balls on that about two inches apart."

"Got it, sexy Q."

She shot him a look. "I know very little about you, Cael."

He shrugged. "Not much to tell."

"Everyone has a story."

The dragon glanced at her. "I'll die for you."

"Only because I hold the Scroll to your freedom."

Zen had placed the Scroll of Cursed Souls on her body right before she went into Hell so she'd have an edge against Micah. This particular scrollwork gave her control over a million dragons. One hell of a powerful army if she did say so herself. They were her servants, slaves without the power to gainsay her, and even though the demon side of her loved owning souls, her practical side recognized the unfairness of their relationship.

17

"We have always supported someone." Even though she suspected he endeavored to sound uncaring one way or another, there was a tenseness about him that suggested he was less than honest with her. "You are better than all of our prior masters."

Madison flinched. "You'd rather be free."

Anyone would rather be liberated. She'd fought for freedom from Micah's plans for her life, so she understood his desire for independence.

Cael stiffened, his hands stilling on the dough. She watched him for a moment as he slowly placed the prepared yeast on the baking sheet. Golden all over, with hair the same shade as his skin, even his eyes held a golden hue and tinted the tips of his eyelashes with a glittery like cast. Built like a linebacker and over six-five, his size dwarfed everyone she knew. Sparring against him tested her skills and demonstrated several of her weaknesses.

He finally lowered his gaze to her. "You have granted us freedom. We were trapped before, now we have mobility."

It wasn't enough. Not for him. She could sense it. Kur was happy with the status quo. He had purpose so long as he served her, but Cael desired more. She could sense the restlessness in him.

"I grant you freedom to come and go as you please, Cael." Had she thought he was motionless before? He went even more stagnant now as she spoke. "I want to be your friend. I want to inspire your loyalty because of that friendship. I could remove the Scroll tomorrow and Kur would remain steadfast. Kur has that same loyalty from you. I want the same loyalty from you, and I don't have a problem earning it any way I can."

That startled him enough his gaze jerked around to seal upon her. "I can't have true freedom with the Scroll on you."

Madison crossed her arms over her chest. "My understanding is I can decree whatever I want with the Scroll. I dictate freedom for you. There are rules of course." She went back to rolling biscuits since he'd

18

stopped. She gave him a shoulder bump. "Don't look so surprised. I understand craving freedom. You knock up a human, I'll castrate you and lock you back up in Hell."

"I've never fucked a human." He sounded bemused. "Too docile for my tastes."

"Then that rule won't be an issue." She made two more balls before she added another rule. "Can't expose your dragon to humans, either. That's for your protection, not theirs. Can't go after any demons without my permission."

He nudged her aside and took over the biscuit making. "What if I prefer to remain with you?"

"I'm not kicking you out, Cael. I'm giving you choices. Now...tell me about your life. Do you have a significant other in your life?"

"No. There aren't many female dragons, and all of them are mated. Most babies born are male."

"That sucks."

"Succubi are plentiful and fun to play with." Her grin seemed to encourage him to keep sharing. "They would sneak between cracks that we couldn't squeeze through. It's how we met Petralegija."

"Why does Kur hate her so much?"

"He didn't tell you?"

She explained what he'd said about Petra killing their prior dragon-chieftain.

Cael snorted. "Only part of what happened."

"Why don't you fill in the holes?"

"An order or a choice?"

"Choice." She shrugged as if she cared little, when she really sought the entire truth.

"Petra and Kur were...lovers I guess is what you'd call them. Many dragons speculated they'd mate. We thought they were in love. I know Kur loved Petra. None knew she fucked around with our chieftain. She played Kur against him—"

"What was his name?"

"I don't remember. Once one of us dies, we forget their name."

"Why?" That seemed tragic in so many ways to Madison.

"I don't know. It's just the way it's always been. Want me to go on?" She nodded, and he continued. "I can't recall the falling out Kur had with our chieftain, but I know it was over Petra. You'd have to ask Kur for all the intricate details, but Petra killed our chieftain with his very own scale, a stab through his spinal cortex. He was a goner before he collapsed. Only a coward sneaks up and kills from behind."

Madison nodded, ruminating over the specifics of what Kur shared and matching them up with what Cael detailed. "Kur told me Petra had a right to kill your chieftain."

He shrugged. "Can't say. Like I said, you'd have to ask Kur for the intricate details. He hasn't shared them with anyone. He was next in line for chieftain, and he stepped into the role without hesitating. He's hated Petra ever since."

Madison felt Georgie's presence before she announced herself by clearing her throat. "I'm sorry to interrupt."

"Would you like for me to leave, sexy Q?" The dragon beside her went from relaxed to tense the moment Georgie entered.

"I prefer you stayed." Madison had been enjoying their conversation and had no intention of letting Georgie ruin that. She glanced at Cael and giggled when she spotted the streak of white flour along his cheek. "You have flour on your cheek."

"Your fault," he teased.

"Guilty as charged." She dampened a paper towel and showed it to him. "May I?"

He nodded and leaned down so she could spiff him up.

As she wiped the dust off Cael's cheek, Madison said, "Feel free to just say what's on your mind, Georgie."

The woman had never held back before, no point in starting now.

"I'm not sure what to say." The matriarch of the Birmingham family rubbed her nape. "We're packing so we can head out before Gage does something stupid."

Good to know Gage was a loose cannon, but which part bothered them the most? That Madison had become Queen of Hell or that she'd decided to remain with both men instead of picking one? She hoped they thought of Nix before they made the rash decision to depart his life permanently. They meant a lot to him, and she'd hate to see him lose them. As callous as it sounded, if it came down to Madison losing Nix or him losing his family, she'd boot his family out the door herself. Nix wasn't vacating her life, not if she could help it.

As if he disengaged from the conversation, the dragon beside her stepped back to lean against the counter.

Madison tossed the paper towel in the garbage. "While you're making a decision, remember Nix would be heartbroken to lose y'all."

That agitated Georgie if the twisting of her fingers together was any indication. Madison couldn't recall ever seeing the woman this frazzled.

"Nix is all I've been thinking of since your announcement a bit ago. I'm so disappointed—"

"I *won't* apologize for making any of my choices." The Birmingham matriarch treaded dangerous territory, and her approval or disappointment meant nothing to Madison. "When you walk a mile in my shoes, *only* then are you welcome to judge me."

Georgie flattened her palms on the island countertop. "That attitude is part of the problem. A year ago—even two months ago—you were fighting against Micah's plans for you. You were willing to sacrifice your life so you wouldn't go demonic. Now you're happy to accept it like you would a new haircut."

"Some plans are unavoidable."

"Fate is a fickle bitch." Cael put that out there, surprising Madison.

"Bullshit." Georgie's curse startled Madison, and she elevated her eyebrows. The woman rarely swore, and she went on without noting Madison's shock. "What happened to you in Hell that made you give up?"

Madison slowly rolled her head from side to side as memories of what transpired in Hell flitted through her mind. None could handle the truth of Elias's torture. If she slept, she'd have nightmares of the torture he carried out against her. The pain had been minimal compared to her misconception that she'd been forced to kill Nix and Amos. That belief caused her unimaginable suffering she never wanted to relive.

She met Georgie's gaze. "We were wrong to believe I could escape my fate."

"Cop-out."

"No." She rinsed her hands and dried them on a towel. "You said Nix was my fate. Amos says Nix and Micah both are, and we know his track record compared to yours." Since he'd begun prophesizing the future, Amos had only ever been wrong once. Georgie's visions couldn't claim such accuracy. "Neither of you ever saw that I'd escape my hellish seat of power. Not one single time did either of you *see* that outcome. That says something, Georgie. So what would you have me do, accept only the fate *you* approve? The one that makes *you* comfortable."

They stared at one another as the clock on the wall ticked the seconds off, as loud as any death toll in the cheesy horror flicks she watched with Amos.

The creak of Cael's boots permeated the room as he shifted from one foot to the other.

Madison counted to two hundred and nine before Georgie looked away and spoke again. "I cannot help but feel I led Nix to this outcome when I sent him to aid you."

"Without him, I'd have Fallen sooner, Micah would've eventually found him and used his lineage for a very different outcome." That new trinity plan had at least been axed, which gave humanity a chance at survival.

"Madison, if you really love Nix, you should leave him. Or force him to go. For once, do what's best for him."

Fuck you, Usha snarled.

"No," Madison said between gritted teeth.

"Your demon King will destroy the righteous man Nix is if you don't walk away."

"No." Twice Madison had glimpsed a side of Nix in Hell that his family couldn't fathom. His righteousness was already ruined. He'd enjoyed helping Micah get her off in the vat full of blood, a pool that'd been filled with the suffering of Nix's victims. She'd felt his desire as he watched Micah fuck her in Hell, and she'd enjoyed him taking her in the hellish shower later while Micah waited his turn. There was a darkness inside of Nix that had *nothing* to do with her or the King of Hell. His family needed to open their eyes, accept that, and move on.

"Won't you just think—"

Voice hard and uncompromising, Madison said, "*Li.*" Realizing too late she'd transitioned into Xapil, she repeated the word in English. "No." Patience worn thin, Madison tucked hair behind her ear. "I'm having his baby. He wouldn't walk away even if I forbid him to stay with me."

"Once the child is born you could give it to Nix to see that it's raised...right." The Birmingham matriarch winced and glanced about as if indirect eye contact would soften the blow of her words.

A low growl of what Madison interpreted as displeasure came from the dragon beside her. Georgie fired a hesitant glance at him.

Bad choice of words. Her Lynx tensed, causing her muscles to strain for immediate action.

For several long seconds all her focus shifted to keeping her demon from gaining freedom. "Are you implying I cannot raise a child without corrupting it for evil?"

"I ah...fear you won't be able to help but—"

"Tread very cautiously, Georgie." She had to actively work at keeping her demon contained.

Whatever expression she wore, it caused the older woman to take a step back. Or maybe Cael's steady growling caused the retreat. Either way, it was a wise choice because it seemed to coddle her demon a smidge.

Georgie gulped, her throat jerking with the action. "The baby's why the angels killed you?"

Topic change. Smart move, Usha cooed, sizing the other woman up as she fantasized about ripping her spleen out and forcing her to eat it.

Just barely containing her Lynx, Madison forced a jagged feeling nod. The child could open the Gates of Heaven, which endangered the saintly inhabitants. In Micah's hands a year ago, it'd have been a disastrous outcome. He was happy to just be with her now, have her as his Queen and continue on with collecting human souls and warring against his Father.

I hope.

Don't delude yourself, Usha chided, *our King will always want more.*

Yeah, the real question was how long would he be satisfied with the status quo? She'd handle that problem when it was presented.

"A descendent of Jesus and part demon. I'm still trying to wrap my brain around Nix's genealogy." The prophet rubbed her forehead. "But I know that makes the baby a heavenly abomination. Kind of blasphemous."

Her Lynx lurched to the forefront again, and she startled when Cael's hands settled on her shoulders.

"Killing her will not go over well with your dragon-marked male."

Madison nodded to let him know she understood Nix would be very displeased if she harmed his aunt. "That's my child you're slurring, Georgie. Nix's child. *Your* niece or nephew."

Georgie increased the distance between them. "Your demon is showing in your eyes."

"I'm aware." Anytime her succubus was out, her eyes went pink. At the moment, she bet they were lit up like a meteor entering the atmosphere. "I'm having a hard time containing my Lynx. Slurs against my family have a way of bringing out the worst in me."

"None of this will end well."

"Seen that in a vision, Georgie?"

The psychic sighed and rubbed her eyes with her fingertips. "Sherlocks will come for all of you."

Madison laughed. Those uptight fuckers were the least of her worries.

"Don't underestimate them." Georgie crossed her arms over her chest. *A defensive gesture...does she think I'll attack?* "They're worth worrying over, Madison."

"Assuming I can't take out a Sherlock...." There were many that resided with her that could kill one of the hunters with ease, including her son. "Do you really believe Micah or Zen couldn't handle them with little to no effort? Did you forget about the dragons? Or Petra? None of y'all even know how to stop a King of Hell. How do you imagine I'll be any easier to kill now that I'm a Queen?" She wouldn't get into how territorial her hellhounds and Taz were. "And what of Nix? He might not want to harm a Sherlock, but if they pushed him to pick between them or his family, you know he'll put the hunter down."

"You've gone darker than I expected if you would kill an innocent Sherlock?"

A dark laugh erupted from Madison's lungs. "None of them are innocent. Anything or anyone that comes for my children will *die.*" She'd learned her lesson with the angels.

"Sexy Q, your children have the protection of the dragons," Cael said.

Madison found comfort not only in his declaration, but that she'd given him freedom and he still sought to talk her down. "Georgie, it'd be prudent for you to warn the Sherlocks to keep their distance from us. Any sign of aggression will be taken as an act of war." Not that she'd ever met a hunter that evaded a creature they felt needed killing. They were a proactive bunch.

"You asked us to think about what side we're going to stand on. You think about letting Nix go."

"*That* conversation is over." She shrugged out of Cael's light grasp, retrieved a knife and cutting board, and began to dice carrots. "You'd be wise not to bring it up again."

Put the blade to her throat, I bet that'll shut the meddling bitch up.

Ignoring her demon, Madison took out her frustrations on the vegetable instead. They weren't acting out that scenario no matter how enticing it sounded for the sheer joy of terrorizing the woman for her racism toward her children.

"You would forfeit Phoenix's happiness to settle your unease?" At the unexpectedness of Zen's question, Madison looked up. He sauntered into the kitchen with his usual easy grace that often reminded her of an apex predator. He leaned against the island and gawked at Nix's aunt. "I didn't take you for the selfish type, Georgie."

Have I mentioned lately how much I love your crystal genie? Usha purred her approval, and Madison just barely stopped herself from rolling her eyes. She did catch the slight smirk that hit Zen's lips, which meant he'd intercepted her demon's comment.

The Birmingham matriarch squared her shoulders and met Zen's stare. "This situation is about more than my happiness or Nix's. None of us matter when there's a rogue succubus determined to do things her way."

"The '*rogue succubus*' in question"—he inclined his head in Madison's direction but maintained his focus on Georgie—"is under my guidance and protection. I thought I'd proven where my loyalties lie?"

"You sure have." Georgie nodded at Madison. "With that rogue succubus, who has also become the Queen of Hell."

"So you're questioning my loyalties to humanity, as well?"

"I—I wouldn't say that."

"Then what are you implying?"

They stared at one another. Zen's countenance impassive, giving nothing away, but Madison knew what it was like to *try* and win a standoff with him. Sure enough, seconds later Georgie averted her gaze. "We should've taken her up on her offer after she saved Nix from Hell and killed her then."

Madison stopped chopping and palmed the blade for battle before she realized her intent.

Zen snagged a diced carrot, and tapped it on the cutting board, drawing Madison's gaze to him. He shook his head, a subtle request to relax, before flicking a glance to the dragon.

He popped the vegetable in his mouth. As he chewed, he turned away from Madison and Cael to ponder Nix's aunt. "Micah gave you an ultimatum."

"I cannot believe you're suddenly friends with him."

"I understood friends respect one another?" He gave Madison a questioning glance, and she nodded her head to confirm his definition of the word. "Classify us however you like, Georgie. I'm not big on titles, but I *do* support the ultimatum he presented to your family. You were given three months." He snagged another carrot. "I'd suggest you use the time wisely to consider your decision sensibly."

Chapter 3

ARGUING WITH HIS family grew tedious. Nix suspected Micah managed to withhold his opinion by the sheer skin of his teeth. But the King held his tongue, while perusing the local newspaper—an oddity as far as Nix was concerned.

Nix wished his family would try and see things his way. No longer an immature youth, he'd weighed the pros and cons. A relationship with Mads invited complications, but he loved her enough to sacrifice everything and risk even his soul.

Listening to his uncle detail every reason he should reconsider his decision, proved his family saw him as an adult only when it came to Sherlocking. Lifelong decisions apparently were out of Nix's scope of maturity. Yeah, he could understand their hesitation, but after they'd known Mads for so long, and known she was his fated woman, he'd thought—hoped like hell—they'd be more understanding.

Evidently pie-in-the-sky bullshit.

Becoming a daddy was a big deal to him, and he wouldn't shirk his duty no matter what they felt was best. Uncle James should fathom the enormity of the gift Nix'd been given. Instead James offered justification and explanation, and even went as far as to suggest Nix leave Mads after the baby was born, and raise the child without her. Like he could do that to her or that she'd *let* him remove their offspring from her care. He'd known his uncle could be a cold motherfucker, but he hadn't realized he could be this callous.

Nix could feel Micah's agitation and his control slipping. It was a wonder the fallen angel managed to restrain himself this long.

"Not a demon," Micah muttered, rattling the paper with a finger tap to an article. Nix expected an explosion from the King, not a random comment. "Something supernatural. Lots of weird stuff going around in this city."

"Does *he* have to be here?" Uncle James motioned to Micah.

Nix massaged the back of his neck. "Any reason why he should go?"

"I don't like him, don't trust him, he killed Gage and Zoe, used you against Madison for his own benefit, *and* he irritates me."

"All the more reason to stay." Micah cast James a derisive grin. A moment later his eyes lit up, glowing like the embers of Hell. "A human after my heart." He tossed the newspaper on the coffee table and pressed his thumb over the black and white typed-words. A blue-white light exploded beneath his touch. "Must offer this one a lucrative deal."

"There are other things to life than spreading sadism and murder, Micah."

"You wound me, father Birmingham, with your limited insight into my objectives." Mads's husband leaned back in his seat and crossed one ankle over a knee, his focus primed on Nix's uncle.

Now he'll make the killing shot.

"If all I wanted was to spread murder and sadism...I wouldn't need humans to do that. Not when I could flick my finger"—he demonstrated by swishing his index back and forth—"and I'd have an orgy of sadism and murder. Too easy. No fun."

James shot Nix a nervous glance. "What do you want, then?"

"Humanity's Fall from grace." Delivered in a cool concise tone, Micah's statement elicited a sharp inhalation from James. "At last count, we're over halfway there."

Silence struck like a heavyweight boxer delivering a right-hook. His uncle held the demon King's stare, James's shock very noticeable in his wide-eyed gape, while Micah preened at delivering said jolt.

"What do you get out of this idiotic relationship with my nephew?"

Micah laughed. "You're mistaken if you believe I must explain myself to you. Madison gave Phoenix the choice, he chose her. He could've walked away. He chose not to. That should tell you all you need to know."

Translation the way Nix saw it: The fallen angel got nothing out of Nix staying with Mads. He allowed the threesome because she requested it and because he was a kinky bastard anyway.

"Madison has embraced her demon, she's not thinking straight." That elucidated how little James understood Mads.

Nix had never seen her thinking as straight as she was now, despite her demon's presence.

"She was a demon when she returned from Hell. You welcomed her home, told her you owed her one. She was a demon when Phoenix knocked her up!" Micah launched to his feet.

"And now she's become your Queen of sins and lies." James faced off against the King, demonstrating the courage Nix grew up idolizing. "That does not make her a righteous woman."

Micah snorted. "You're goddamn delusional if you believe your nephew is righteous. I could give you sordid details of the many things he performed *and* enjoyed while in Hell. Those details won't even skirt the myriad wickedness he executed *on* Earth *to humans.*"

"That happened while you had your claws in him. Before Madison saved him. He wouldn't have been like that before he accepted your deal."

"It was much more than a deal. It was a blood covenant, and it gave him choices. He could've elected to deny *his* demons. Where there is righteousness and honesty, there is *always* evil, too. *That* is humanity's weakness." The glimmer in Micah's eyes detailed how close to the surface his angel patrolled. "Falling to his baser inclinations eased him toward the path of revenge. He did not do that for me, for himself, or because he was weak, but because he loves Madison, and he felt compelled to prove it. You wish to blame someone, then look to your nephew, because he alone made his choices."

"Pardon me if I don't believe the King of lies." Sometimes James's tact left a lot to be desired.

"Micah's right," Nix said. That silenced his uncle and extracted a smirk from Micah. "I chose to Fall and become the monster that committed atrocities against humanity."

I'd do it again for Mads.

"So what're you saying, Nix? That an honest and civilized man has given up? That you're happy to have bedded down with a Queen and King of Hell, pleased that you gave her a spawn and—"

"Enough!" Micah's eyes blazed with his anger. "That's my wife you criticize and her child. Get the fuck out of my presence before I retract the *choice* I gave *you.*"

"Nix—"

"Thirty minutes, father Birmingham. You have thirty minutes to get the fuck out of my face or I'll eliminate your options."

James peered between Micah and Nix. His uncle rarely conceded to anyone. That the ultimatum came from Beliel further complicated his dilemma.

Nix shook his head, silently telling him to drop the argument and just walk away. Frankly he was relieved Micah silenced his uncle. He grew weary arguing. "I agree with him, James. You should respect my decision, and be satisfied that I'm happy. If you can't...well, then I guess that's all the answer I need."

"You *cannot* expect us to cozy up to this monster." James swung his arm in the direction of Micah.

"Charming. We've upgraded to name-calling." Micah's sarcasm couldn't go unnoticed. "Wrap this conversation up, Phoenix." The King of Hell gave Nix a pointed stare before portaling out of the room.

"Don't tell me you can't grasp the ignorance of this situation. Do you really want to start a relationship with Hell's royalty?"

He'd already had an intimate one with the demon King once before. Not that he planned for things to go that far this time around. This relationship was about Mads, not his former bi- one with Micah.

Nix shrugged. "I had an intimate liaison with him while in Hell. It wasn't so bad."

James stuttered over that confession. As if planned, Micah portaled back into the room, his hand on both Gage and Zo. He dumped them in the center of the room and executed another hasty departure.

"What the fuck?" Gage bellowed, face blood red, as Beliel disappeared.

"We were packing, and he just showed up out of nowhere, grabbed my arm and dragged me to Gage." Zo explained, while rubbing the chill bumps on her arms, clearly freaked out by the suddenness of what'd transpired. "Once he had his hands on both of us, he brought us here."

Before Nix could respond, Micah returned with Georgie. She looked just as frazzled as Zo.

"You'll find your clothes packed and in your vehicles." Micah zeroed his gaze on James. "You've got thirty seconds to get the fuck out."

A direct and impolite demand to leave, but James still opened his mouth to argue. Beliel started counting, causing Nix's uncle's teeth to snap together. "Twenty-nine, twenty-eight, twenty-seven...tick tock, Birminghams. Tick-fucking-tock. Twenty-one...."

Nix's family finally took the hint. James shot him a turbulent glance, but nudged Gage forward toward the door. "Go Zoe and Georgie."

"Dad—"

"Shut up, Gage," James snapped out. "Just leave for now."

Nix read between the lines. His uncle would retreat, but only because he intended to be prepared for the next battle.

"Is your family going to always be that big a pain in my ass?" Mads's husband demanded the moment the door shut behind them.

"Even if they agree to accept my decision, I don't think they'll ever like you."

"You think I care?"

He knew Micah didn't. "No."

"Good. I'd rather spend the day with our woman. You with me?"

"Definitely."

Chapter 4

A WEEK LATER Micah found his woman in the kitchen. The scent of frying pork chops invaded his nostrils. His mouth salivated to dive into the fare. Diving into her sounded like an even better idea. Now that'd he'd tasted her sexually and she enjoyed the sex, he wanted to gorge himself on her.

Keeping his tread ghoulishly silent, he entered the room and leaned a hip against the table. Phoenix snagged a beer out of the fridge, noticed Micah's presence, and motioned to his bottle with a finger. Beliel shook his head, declining the offer.

Music pulsed from a Bluetooth mini-speaker resting on the counter. Mads wore a pair of black running shorts that molded to every curve she possessed and a red top that didn't meet the hip-hugging shorts. Flat abs attested to the athlete in her, hard hours of sparring with Zennyo Ryuo, and who knew what else. Since the rise of the dragons, even Kur and Cael often were involved in the fray, double teaming her and forcing her skills to a new level. Even Micah tested her limits, always cheating so he could watch the determination to defeat him bloom in her eyes.

"Come on, angel, give it a try. Follow my movements." Madison demonstrated some hip rolling action that hit the fast beat of the music.

Amos shook his head. "Momma, it ain't normal for you to move like that."

"Not true. Everyone can dance. Just let the music guide ya'." She flipped the pork chops and they sizzled.

In Micah's estimation, Madison's version of dancing served as heavy reminders of epic sex.

"Okay, how about this?" Amos jigged about twitching his head. The moves reminded Micah of a seizure rather than any dance move he'd ever seen. Madison pealed with laughter, as did Phoenix and Petra.

The Ark of Heaven planted a kiss on her shoulder. Not long ago he'd have been jealous of Phoenix's affection toward her. Jealousy served no purpose in their relationship, but hindered it instead.

"Amos, Mads has *mad* dance skills, and we all would benefit from taking a lesson or two from her." Phoenix kissed her temple, and she grinned at him.

Madison has other mad *skills too, but I won't comment on them.* As if he sent the thought to her, his gorgeous wife peeked at him beneath her lashes and sent him a small smile.

"She could be a stripper." Petra popped open a *Gangster* energy drink.

"Um...no thanks." Madison grimaced and shook her head. "I don't get naked in front of my mirror, so a definite no-go on the stripper occupation."

Phoenix whispered in her ear, but Micah couldn't catch what the other man said. Her eyes widened, and she jerked her head to gape at Jesus's heir. Whatever passed between them, the Ark gave her a devilish grin and delivered a non-sexual kiss to the corner of her mouth before strolling to the table. Phoenix pulled out a chair and slumped into the seat with a smile still tugging at the corners of his mouth.

A deep breath lifted Madison's shoulders, and she exhaled as she turned toward them. A rosy flush gave her cheeks color.

What'd he say? Micah sent the telepathy.

Madison's teeth toyed with her bottom lip as she replied. *He wants me to dance naked for the two of you.*

Fantastic idea.

Her flush deepened.

What was it about her blushes that made him hotter for her? As a succubus she was built for sex, but even as the most powerful of them all, intimacy remained difficult for her. He and Phoenix both had been inside her almost every way imaginable—except anal sex, but that would come. All sex demons enjoyed anal sex, and he held no doubt she would, too. They'd just have to ease her into the act—or rush her instead, he couldn't decide which tactic would be best with her. Either way would require eliminating her reservations. Or dominating her, which meant taking what he wanted.

There was no rush for any of it. He'd gone a decade before he could claim her as his woman. Waiting to introduce her to the seedier side of sex wasn't that big of an issue.

"Daddy, you think you could work with me and Petra tomorrow on my power?" Amos grabbed his soda off the counter and climbed onto one of the stools at the island.

"Why not tonight after dinner?"

"We're watching a marathon of *Nightmare on Elm Street.*"

Micah glanced at Petra, who shrugged in response. What a mundane, very human pastime. He'd watched one of the movies with his son recently and had been surprised when he'd enjoyed it immensely. There was something gratifying about watching a nightmare murder defenseless mortals in their dreams. What he'd discovered was that these ordinary moments were what he'd missed the most since walking out of his wife and son's lives. The normal day-to-day events that *made* them family.

"I'm lucky Madison gave me a second chance, and now I have all of my family."

Micah didn't realize he'd spoken the thought aloud until Amos grinned and said, "I saw it happen. Just didn't know how."

Madison gave him a soft smile as her reply filtered into his head, *I love you, Micah—you'll always be my white knight riding in on a black Porsche.*

That was part of the vow she'd made to him at their wedding. The impact of those words was staggering, informed him she forgave him all his transgressions. Without thought, Micah walked straight to her and dragged her into his arms. A surprised expression flickered across her face right before he planted a kiss on her mouth.

He broke the kiss off when Kur cleared his throat. Micah leaned his forehead against hers, for the simple pleasure of ingesting her aura into his senses. After millennia of living, he finally felt fulfilled. No...no. He couldn't allow this feeling of rightness take root until he sought revenge for his woman and rammed the *Scepter of Spirits* through Elias's traitorous heart. She was his to protect, and he'd failed by entrusting her safety to his sibling. His brother *must* die. Yet...a sentimental side of him rebelled at the idea.

That makes me weak.

"I'm sure it's safe to bet you have more family than you ever wanted." Phoenix drew her out of Micah's arms and challenged him to object with the sharp jut of his jaw. "Let the woman cook. I'm starving."

"It *is* kinda weird that my sister is older than my mom." Amos slurped loudly on his soda. "She's the coolest sis ever though. You think the baby will think I'm cool like Petra?"

Madison smiled at Amos's comment. "Yeah. Why wouldn't it?"

Emotions too volatile, Micah shifted his focus off his wife before he dragged her from the kitchen and made love to her again. He wrapped his arm around Petra's shoulders, and felt her tense. She was uneasy around him, and he regretted that. She'd made a choice, his son and wife over him, and once he'd been angered by that decision, but no longer. In time, he hoped she could relax around him.

I could've been a better father to you, Petralegija. Forgive me? Not a full-blown apology, but the best she'd ever receive because apologizing showed weakness.

Madison glanced at Micah as if surprised. Had she heard his telepathy to his daughter? Unconcerned if she had, he added, *I love you, daughter. I have always loved you. I'm proud of the succubus you've become, and the choices you've made.*

Petra gaped at him.

I've missed you. He kissed the top of Petra's head, and felt her relax against him, her arms going around his waist in a loose hug.

Even while thinking she'd betrayed him, he could've called her home at any time. But he'd left her with them, knowing she protected them when he couldn't.

He faced the rest of his eclectic family—Phoenix, the dragons, and even Zen. The Ark turned up his beer, while standing beside their soon-to-be joint wife, watching her fry pork chops. Not long ago he'd only have displayed this level of emotion as a tactic to trick someone. But honesty came easy when they shared similar commonality.

One by one the kitchen became overcrowded with his new 'family'. Kur sat at the table, his legs stretched out. As a product of his and Zennyo Ryuo's magic, Micah should feel more affinity toward Kur since he was technically one of Micah's offspring. He'd used the dragons for selfish gains, but had never really thought of them as children. They were helpful to Madison and her unborn child's safety, because with the Ark of Heaven's offspring in her womb, there'd be others that would come for them. Yet, for the first time since the dragons' creation, Micah recognized his familial relationship with them.

His gaze shifted to Zennyo Ryuo, and the immortal tipped him a nod. Strange how life came full circle, he and the immortal had worked side-by-side eons ago at Father's request. Until his Fall, since then the other man had tried to kill him more than once. Had come close at least a dozen times. After thousands of years of animosity, they were united again. It was a nice feeling. Yeah, the uptight immortal would hinder any nefarious plans against humanity, but Micah knew how to subtly play mankind to acquire his objectives. Demons were his biggest asset in any strategy.

"Dinner's ready." Madison set food on the table. After guiding Petra to a chair, his beautiful wife captured his hand and pulled him close, whispering, "That was sweet what you said to Petra."

"Keeping it honest is all." He could almost read her mind. If she thought he let some of his former angelic ways shine through she couldn't be further from the truth. *There is nothing angelic about me.* "Kitten, don't pretend I'm suddenly an upstanding citizen."

She touched his cheek, and her thumb traced his jaw. "I wouldn't be happy if you were. I *see* you. Sit." Micah could sense her sudden unease as she motioned to the chair on her right. Curious at her unexpected nervousness, he pulled out the seat she'd indicated. Zen sat at the head of the table, with the rest of the group fanned out around.

"You going to join us, Mads?" Nix toyed with her fingers when she remained standing between him and Micah.

Kur stopped heaping food onto his plate to peer at her. "Trying to get up the nerve to break the news to your guys that you're ditching them for me?"

"You got it wrong, Kur, it's me Sexy Q prefers," Cael teased, throwing a wink Madison's way.

"Sit down and shut up, dragons," Micah said between clenched teeth, his disposition for the their tomfoolery low given Madison's apprehension. "What is it, kitten?"

Madison cleared her throat. "I want our ceremony soon. I need us"—she flicked her finger between the three of them—"to be official. I want to be able to call y'all mine."

That was all? He'd been a smidge worried. Now he could breathe easier knowing she only requested a commitment, but why'd she bring it up in front of everyone. "We're already yours. A ceremony doesn't change that."

"I know, but this is important to me, Micah."

"Anything you want, baby. Right, Micah?" Nix gave him a glare that defied him to disagree.

Beliel smirked at the Ark. He could give the man lessons on how to spoil a succubus. "Yep, what Phoenix said, anything you want, kitten."

She beamed a smile at them. "Amos, will you give me away to Nix and your dad?"

"Heck, yeah!"

She grinned at Amos's enthusiasm. "Zen will officiate."

That unsettled Micah. This was his former enemy. "Raguel solemnized our marriage. My brother." *Someone I trust.* "I'd be more comfortable if he performed this one also."

"That was our marriage, with all your misguided attempts at trickery. I don't want Raguel presiding over this one, a reminder of the bad blood between us. I want a clean start, without any mementos of your former deception. This ceremony is about the three of us, not just you and what makes you feel more comfortable. It's *my* time to be selfish. Zen is *my* brother, and my best friend."

Micah held her gaze, and decided her friend list could use some heavy tweaking. "More years than not, he was my enemy, not my friend."

"Still not your friend," Zen said in his bland-as-fuck voice.

From the corner of his eye, he noticed Phoenix settle a little deeper into his chair. The Ark trailed a finger along her hip. "This is my ceremony too. Don't I get a vote?" Before Micah could respond, Phoenix said, "I'm good with Zenny. It's not often a man gets to brag his wife's crystal genie officiated their marriage."

The immortal grunted his displeasure at Phoenix's ridiculous nickname, which improved Micah's mood and eradicated the tension in one quick hit of humor.

Madison laughed, but smacked the Ark on his shoulder. "Stop calling him that."

"Fine." Micah could make concessions. This one was minor. Their marriage remained valid anyway, the vows just as relevant as the day they were spoken. This go round she'd be making oaths to him knowing the truth of his lineage. And hers. She came into it with open eyes and a willing heart. "I'll grant you this boon and agree to permit Zennyo Ryuo to preside over the ceremony."

"I knew you would." She gave him a look that was all haughty Queen, testing his boundaries and her influence. "That's why I already asked him, and he already agreed."

I'll make her pay for that later.

Phoenix ran his finger along her pinkie finger. "I can't wait to call you *wife.*" He stood, clasped her face between his palms, and Eskimo kissed her. She melted into him with a little purr. The gentleness Phoenix showed her was the sweetest fucking thing Micah'd ever seen. But Beliel understood her succubus's requirements better than the heir of Christ. A firm hand fed her a different type of nourishment and reduced her aggression, but it was evident she craved the Ark's tenderness too.

When he'd agreed to this arrangement he'd foreseen Phoenix as a pet, something they'd keep around until she tired of him. Yeah, he realized Madison loved the Ark, but in this moment he admitted to himself how deeply she was in love with the former Sherlock. This wasn't just a passing fancy for her.

The Sherlock raked the fingers of one hand through her hair as he gave her a soft, non-sexual kiss. Together they balanced out her Lynx. It was a combination that benefitted them all.

Kur cleared his throat. "The personal display of affection is interfering with my appetite."

The hand in Madison's hair subtly shifted, and Phoenix shot the dragon the middle finger salute from her glossy locks. Amos giggled, while Taz squawked, making his sudden presence known, along with his displeasure over Phoenix touching *his* woman.

Chapter 5

NIX LEANED AGAINST his red 1968 Dodge Charger with his ankles crossed, waiting for Alessa to join him. He swatted a fly away as he hit the send button on his phone and put the device to his ear. On this sweltering summer day in the South, cicadas made a weird buzzing sound in the air.

Just as Nix was about to disconnect his call, Zo picked up with a whispered, "Hang on."

He thought he heard the opening and shutting of a door. Best guess, she vacated Gage's presence so she could talk to him freely without being overheard. That need for privacy stung.

"Nix, how are you?" Zo's voice came a little louder, even if she sounded cautious.

"All right." Devlin the hellhound romped around the lawn with his ugly sister FiFi. From the beginning he'd doubted the beasts could make submissive pets, but despite his reluctance and their classic fatal behavior, they obeyed Mads. "Zo, I won't make this any more awkward than it already is for you so I'll get right to the point."

She snorted her disagreement, but reaching out to her put her in a precarious situation with his family. That she felt it necessary to sneak out to chat with him proved it.

"I'm marrying Mads on Saturday. Wanted to extend an official invite."

Total silence. He could imagine she quirked her lips like she always did when she pondered a difficult situation. Getting married had never been on his bucket list. Hell, he hadn't expected to *ever* wed, much less find a woman, but he would've never anticipated having to ask his family to be there. Nope. If he'd ever fantasized about that moment, his entire family would've been eager to be a part of the festivities.

After a moment, Zo stuttered out, "Um...yeah...I— I'll let them know. See what I can...um...do."

He shouldn't have called. Pipe dreams hoping his family would come through for him. He could pretend their behavior didn't hurt, but it hurt worse than he could have ever imagined.

Planting his foot on the tire, he pushed away from the vehicle and swiped the fingers of his other hand through his hair. The humidity had sweat trickling down his spine.

"Nix, please try to understand their—"

"Understand this...I'll be damned if I'll beg my family to be a part of my life. I shouldn't have to. None of you should expect it. 'Family first' that's what Uncle James preached to me." Bitterness burned his gut like cheap whiskey. Watching Alessa exit the house and approach him, Nix cleared the scratchiness from his throat and attempted to wrangle his temper under some semblance of control. "Hypocritical words, because they mean shit to my family unless they approve of my choices. Come or don't, Zo, I don't give a damn anymore."

"You don't mean that."

Of course he didn't. The fact he'd reached out to her verified he cared very much, but a man's pride could only take so much rejection.

44

"They think you need help, Nix. I'm not talking about intervention, but there's been some discussion that maybe you're holy possessed instead of demonically possessed. I don't know. None of it makes any sense."

They're having meetings about me? Had he stepped into the *Twilight Zone?*

"Are you fucking with me?" The evening he acquired his gifts he hadn't felt anything enter him, except the coin Micah stuck to his head. During his time in Hell, he'd learned Micah never lied to him, not once. To lie in Hell was a sin. Go figure. So he knew he wasn't possessed. "It's fine by me if you all want to fool yourself about who and what I am. It's fucked up, but it's okay. At least Alessa's here for me. Thank fuck someone has a sense of family loyalty."

"Nix—"

"Not in the mood for excuses, Zoe." He hung up and crammed the cell in his front jean pocket.

Alessa halted in front of him, eyeing him while she pursed her lips. "You got that pissed off look about you. Like you'd rather shoot first and ask questions later."

"No, I don't." He was so far beyond pissed off, he couldn't express the depth of his fury...and he was hurt beyond what he'd ever believed possible.

"What's your saying?" She tapped her temple and quirked her head to the side as if she gave her question some serious thought. "'Can't bullshit a bullshitter,' right, Nix?"

Unexpected humor ripped from him, and he chuckled. Not only was she right, but she'd also managed to lighten his mood. "Ready to go, Lucky?"

"Yep."

They'd met when he saved her from her werewolf husband, bonded over her near-death, and became fast friends. He'd given her the nickname Lucky because she'd been like his lucky charm. When he visited her horse ranch in Oregon, nothing bad ever happened. And even though they'd once had a friends-with-benefits type of relationship, she was one of the few people he thought of as a real friend.

After snapping their seatbelts into place, Alessa ruminated as he drove out of the driveway. "The last time I went to meet up with Vela, I was with Madison. We got ambushed. You know, the time you and angel-jelly trapped her and used me against her."

"I remember." Wondering where she was going with this line of conversation, he sent her a sideways glance as he hit the interstate. At the time, Mads and Alessa had thought he was a reluctant citizen of Hell, while he and Micah had believed Mads was dead. Erroneous assumptions all around. The ambush had been used to verify Nix's belief that Mads still lived. "You do realize angel-jelly is a ridiculous name for Micah?"

"It's dead-on accurate, Nix. From what I hear, you weren't impartial to his hotness either."

"Can't some shit be private?"

"Puh-lease."

He suspected she rolled her eyes, but he kept his focus on the road and bit back a grin at her sarcastic tone.

"This is me you're talking to, Nix Birmingham, your longest-running friend. I *know* you. The second I saw you and Micah together at that bar, I *knew* you were fucking each other. Only Madison is delusional to your depravities."

He laughed, reached over, and snagged her hand, lacing their fingers together. As he squeezed, he said, "I think Mads understands better than you give her credit."

"You do realize that kind of proves the validity of my nickname for that hellish god, right?"

"Even when we were fucking, I never once thought of him as angel-jelly. Only your brain works that way."

"You might have a point." Alessa shrugged. "My brain works in weird ways. It's a coping mechanism."

He knew all about those coping mechanisms.

An easy silence fell between them as he drove.

When she spoke again, it wasn't what he expected. "Do you think we're walking into another trap? This one hosted by Vela for real this time?"

Nix's first inclination was to lie to protect her, but that wasn't his way. "I'd say chances are pretty high. You'll be safe since you're human." Sherlocks had a strict 'no harm' policy when it came to mortals.

"You know I'm not worried about me."

He looked at her. "I've got my lucky charm with me. What bad could possibly happen to me with you by my side?"

She *did* roll her eyes at him that time. He grinned and concentrated on the roadway again. Nix took the exit and executed a few turns before he rolled to a stop in the café parking lot.

Sherlocks milled about the parking lot. He'd anticipated the reception, but not in this number. "You should probably wait for me in the car."

"In what screwed-up world do you think that's going to happen? Did Hell fry your brain cells?" She not only managed to sound offended, but looked it too.

Better question: *In what messed-up world does my best friend stand by my side, but my family won't?*

Tossing him a rebellious frown, Alessa shoved her door open so hard it banged against the vehicle next to them. Nix cringed at the possible damage to his Charger.

"Something for them to remember me by," she said, and then she was out of the vehicle.

Nix took care not to hit the car next to him when he opened his door. He strode around to the front of the hood where Alessa joined him. He wrapped his arm around her shoulders, drawing her tight to his side. He kissed the side of her head, a subtle *if you fuck with her, you're fucking with me* kind of message to those present that might not be as moral about the human thing as he'd like. Lucky wasn't an acceptable loss.

"What happened with your succubus bitch?" Mac, a former ally, asked as he approached them, eyeing

Alessa too closely for Nix's peace of mind.

"Where's Vela?" Shooting the shit wasn't on his agenda. Only because of his prior relationship with Vela had he agreed to meet her. Otherwise they could all piss off.

"Gots to pat ya' down first, Nix. Can't let ya' harm Vela."

"If I wanted to harm her, I wouldn't need weapons." The straight-up truth. He saw five in the parking lot that'd been present at the bar the day they ambushed Mads and Alessa not six months ago. He'd shot three of them with his golden bullets, and then healed all three when Mads demanded it. No weapon needed then, or now. "If Alessa has any weapons, you're not taking hers."

The crunch of booted feet against the crushed gravel heralded a new arrival. Genovela "Vela" Maxwell, appeared, red hair pulled back into a ponytail, her brown eyes smeared with heavy makeup. "Nix. Alessa."

"Long time no see, Vela." Alessa hugged the other woman, while Nix held back, unsure if his affection would be welcomed.

Lucky wasn't tall by any means, but she was a good four inches taller than the petite Vela.

"You look great," Alessa told Vela. "Did you do something different?"

She looked the same as always to Nix.

"Yeah?" Vela beamed at her. "It must be the eye shadow. It's new."

"Definitely the eye shadow."

Nix shot Alessa an inquisitive glance, but she seemed serious enough.

"But those boots...only a true friend would tell you this. I hate them. And as only a good friend would do, I'll sacrifice myself by taking them off your hands...or feet."

Vela giggled at Lucky's teasing, then went straight-faced a moment later. "You too shady to hug me, Nixy?"

"I hate that fucking nickname," he bitched good-naturedly. As he embraced the shorter woman, he said, "I'm still the same man, even if I'm no longer a hunter."

With her palms resting on his arms, she peered up at him. "I still owe you for saving my life, too."

"Don't owe me a damn thing." She'd been possessed by a hundred demons, and he'd managed to evict them all. It'd been his job back then, but he'd have done it willingly since he knew what it was like to house a hellish spawn. "I'd kill those demons tomorrow if they hijacked you again." If Micah objected, he'd tell him to go fuck himself.

Nix held Vela's stare as she studied him for several heartbeats. "Why don't we go inside and take a load off?"

"Sure."

"I could've set a trap."

Roping his arm around Vela's waist, he led her toward the café as he leaned in and said, "I'm pretty fucking sure you've got some scheme going on, Vela. I know you. That's your style, sweetheart." He pushed open the door, guided her in and over to the only vacant table. There were such a vast number of hunters present, it was like a Sherlock reunion and would've been a demon's wet dream. Scoping out the Sherlocks in attendance, he recognized most of them and knew their fighting style and their preferred weapon of choice. Not a single one of them would fight with honor. He pulled out a chair and sat with his back to the room to prove he held zero fear of his former friends. "I'm not your enemy. Neither am I a hunter's enemy."

"From what I hear, you shot them with magical bullets. Sounds like an enemy." Vela poured liquor into three shot glasses and pushed them toward him and Alessa. She held hers up and said, "To old acquaintances."

Nix held his glass up, and then downed the

49

contents. The way Vela watched him, he suspected the spirits were laced with holy water. "I was under the influence of Hell."

Eyeing him, she fiddled with a red ringlet, coiling it around her finger and letting it go, then repeating the process. "You're having a baby with the enemy."

"Word gets around fast." He relaxed into his chair, but he wondered who'd spilled the beans about the baby?

"If you all think Madison is the enemy, you might want to get to know her first because your attitude will change real quick." Alessa held up her glass. "Give me another shot."

"Right, because demons aren't known for deception." Vela uncapped the vodka bottle.

"Yeah, Madison's a demon. So what? Her main focus is on saving humanity. She's already diverted one apocalypse, not that you Sherlocks give a damn." As always, Alessa's bravado amused him and reminded him of himself more often than not.

Vela refilled Alessa's shot glass to the rim. "What apocalypse was that?"

"Doesn't matter." Nix propped his ankle on his opposite knee. "She sacrificed her humanity for you all, that's what matters."

"The way Gage explains it, she did that for you. That's a long cry from humanity."

"I'm not here to debate Mads's integrity." Because she *had* given up her humanity for him and him alone, but the results for mankind had been the same. "I came in good faith to meet you because of our friendship and no other reason."

They held one another's stare, neither of them blinking. Vela finally nodded her head. "There *is* that." She executed an almost imperceptible head nod, but confused him with her next words. "It's because of our friendship and no other reason, we're giving you a chance to redeem yourself."

A metallic click to the right testified to one of the Sherlocks priming a firearm.

Nix turned his head and sure enough, Johnny had placed the barrel of a gun to the back of Alessa's head. Alessa's wink verified she trusted him and had faith in his ability to handle the situation. Even bring her back to life if Johnny did the unthinkable and pulled the trigger. At least, he hoped that's what the wink indicated.

"Fuck you, Vela. Fuck all of you and your misguided opportunity of redemption." Sitting forward, he placed his forearms on the table and leaned even further forward. "Go ahead and shoot her." *I'll just revive her.*

Vela blinked, clearly not anticipating his response.

He gave Johnny his attention and leveled his voice. "If you're going to shoot her, do it already. Time's ticking, and I got other stuff to do."

Several seconds lapsed. A quiet tenseness decimated the café. He could feel their unease, a metallic taste on the back of his tongue, and prickles staging a protest on his nape.

"Here's the problem with Sherlocks...." Deciding Vela was the one calling the shots and Johnny wasn't going to shoot Alessa without Vela's instruction, Nix faced the woman again. "They see the world as black and white, good versus bad, humanity against monsters, but not all monsters need killing. Some help mankind survive."

Vela notched her chin in clear dispute. "Name one."

Mads. He declined to offer the reminder that they owed Mads for discarding Micah's original plans for humanity, so he named another monster. "Zennyo Ryuo."

"He sides with Madison, pardon me if that clearly defines him as a monster."

"He is an agent of God, Vela. *Clearly* that defines him as a *good* monster. Unless Sherlocks think they're wiser than God now? If that's the case, then I'd say you all are the new monsters in town." Nix elevated to his feet, leaving his hands on the table and shoving the chair back with his foot. "If you don't lower your weapon, Johnny, I'll break your goddamn arm." His glare remained on Vela. Without waiting to see if Johnny complied, he said to Vela, "Ever raise a weapon against Lucky or have someone do it again, friendship or not, and you'll regret it, Vela."

"That a promise or threat, Nixy?"

Vela could take it however she wanted. "Do we understand one another?"

Wearing a slight smirk, the redhead inclined her head. "I'll ruminate over what you said."

That was code for she understood everything and not just his threat about Alessa. She'd consider his arguments, but being a woman with her own mind, she'd draw her own conclusions.

With a nod, Nix faced Alessa, only slightly mollified that Johnny had wisely lowered his weapon. Nix wouldn't have been responsible for his actions had Johnny not complied with his demand. One look at Lucky's face while Johnny preened behind her, and anger charged through his system. Zero thought went into his arm snapping forward and nailing the Sherlock in the nose with his fist. The other male went down with a loud cry, and several hunters pulling their weapons.

"You okay, Lucky?" He asked as he shook out his hand.

"Peachy."

He grinned at her. *That's my girl, ballsy to the very end.*

As he assisted Alessa from her chair, he glared down at Johnny. "That's for putting a gun to her head, you fucking bastard."

Nix roped his arm around Alessa's shoulders and turned them to face the door. An army of Sherlocks barred their departure. "Stand aside."

"I can't let you walk out of here, Nix. We're on a mission to fix you."

"Nothing is wrong with me." He ground his teeth together. Alessa must've sensed his rising temper because she wrapped her arm around his waist and squeezed his side.

"You'll thank us for it later," Vela said in a singsong voice. "We've got this new technique that'll eject the—"

"*Stand aside.*" If anything, his command had his former allies shuffling closer together, creating a solid wall of muscle and determination.

"Nix, be reasonable. We're trying to help you evict the monster out of you. You'd do the same for us. You said so yourself earlier that you'd kick the demons out of me again."

Was Vela off her meds?

Nix removed his arm from Alessa's shoulders and stepped in front of her, but remained facing her. The stance put his back to the Sherlocks, placing him in a vulnerable position, but his sole concern was Lucky's safety. He met Vela's stare dead-on over Lucky's head. "I don't have a demon inside me."

"Wrong, Nixy. I want to return the favor and save you like you did me."

"I don't need saving."

She indicated the hunters. "The ones you shot with those gold colored bullets testify to the inaccuracy of that claim. You're a good hunter, one of the best, it's why we're willing to save you instead of kill you."

"I'm the heir of Christ. The power I hold comes from my genetics."

She *tsked* him, unmistakably not believing him. "Nixy, Nixy, Nixy...I understand—"

Nix had heard enough. Done listening, he cupped the back of Alessa's head with his palm to pull her into his safety net and slammed power from his feet into the earth below him. He guided the magic up into the table in front of Vela. Bracing him and Alessa with a bubble of power, he protected them from any possible attack or gunshot wounds.

A second later the wood furniture exploded into a million pieces. Vela screamed and crouched low, covering her head. Instead of the shards turning into projectiles, he controlled them, and contained them in the space where the table sat turning them into a mini-wooden tornado.

"The blood of Christ runs through my veins, Vela." She peeked at him from her crouched position. "Nothing else. I drank your holy water in the liquor a minute ago. That should prove to all of you I'm not housing a demon. I see the Demon and Angel Locks on the ceiling, and when I walk out that door I'll confirm all over again that it's just me in my skin."

He suddenly released the wood fragments and they collapsed to the floor with a thud.

Nix grasped Alessa's hand, and turned and guided her straight toward the line of hunters. They parted like the Red Sea in Noah's wake. He shoved the door open and strode out with Lucky in tow. Opening the passenger door to the car first, Nix waited as Alessa slid into the vehicle while he kept an eye on the hunters milling about the parking lot. None seemed inclined to approach them, but they all observed.

Shutting her door, he strode around his Charger and climbed inside. He shoved the key in the ignition and turned the engine, relieved when the rumble of the machine came to life.

"You okay, Nix?" Lucky asked when they pulled out of the parking lot.

He glanced at her. Her expression detailed her worry. At least someone he thought of as family still cared about him. "You talking about that back there?"

She nodded.

"I expected that Sherlock reception." He eased into traffic with a right-hand turn. "Went better than I anticipated. Figured they'd try to kill me. Never thought they'd try to save me or let me walk away after what I did to some of them in the bar a while back."

He'd been sure those he'd shot with his magic bullets would want recompense in blood. None had sought it, but instead had threatened Lucky and offered salvation hunter style with an exorcism that wouldn't help him.

"You think this is over?"

54

"Doubtful." Nix rubbed his forehead with his fingertips. "You know Sherlocks never give up easily."

"Yeah." Alessa slumped into her seat.

They drove in silence for at least a good thirty minutes. Nix kept his eye on his rear view mirror but detected no tail. He couldn't get it off his mind that Zo said the family thought he was possessed and now, Vela was accusing him of the same thing.

With a sharp yank, he pulled off the road and threw the car in park.

"Something wrong?" Alessa turned in her seat and peered through the rear window.

"We're not being followed. Just give me a second, and we'll get back on the road." He pulled out his cell, called Zo, and waited for her to pick up. The moment she did, he demanded, "Did any of you put Vela up to this bullshit?"

"No clue what you're yammering about," Zo shot back.

Nix believed her, and he took a few seconds to give her the short version of what transpired.

"Holy shit," Zo whistled low. "You okay, Nix?"

"We got out without a scratch."

"I'll find out if Gage or James put them up to it. I know Georgie didn't. And I didn't. I'll get back with you." The fire in her voice let him know she'd ferret out the truth if one of his family was behind the Vela-ambush.

An hour later he got the news he expected. Uncle James was the guilty party. Nix tried to convince himself his Uncle meant well, but he felt more betrayed than ever.

Chapter 6

ZEN WATCHED AS everyone engaged in a game of Monopoly. They'd livened up the game by having Amos craft various supernatural creatures as game pieces from dragon scales using hellfire. Instead of buying Boardwalk, they purchased real estate in Hell, Heaven, or Earth. His eclectic family—minus Micah and Phoenix because they weren't his family, but were Madison's kin—was loud, obnoxious, and the biggest cheaters he'd ever come across. He was highly entertained.

He peered out the window and recalled his first family. Created from the breath of God when He first visited Earth. They'd been a peaceful race, not oral because they communicated telepathically and could read minds, so they were open and honest in all things. None had anything to hide. Each had been given a spouse to love, but...he pondered Phoenix in the reflection of the windowpane. He hadn't loved his spouse as much as the Ark of Heaven did Madison. The Sherlock sacrificed everything for her, his humanity, and maybe even his blood family.

My emotions were subpar for my wife compared

to Phoenix and Micah's feelings for Madison.

Yes, he'd cared for her, would've died for her, but he'd lacked passion for her. She'd been akin to his best friend moving through life as his companion. Only recently had he realized how lacking his life had been then. How devoid his life had been of the basic emotion of *real* love for a woman.

I only really loved my children.

He'd believed the Creator took everything from him when he lost his first family. Despite his pain and anger, it'd been incomparable to what Madison's soon to be husbands endured when the Esdras angels murdered her, and Elias kidnapped, tortured, and tried to kill her.

After the slaughter of his race, the Father had breathed into Zen's lungs, giving him life once more, but with a new focus...to keep the balance among humanity and paranormal factions.

Zen had never looked back. Instead, he'd stepped into his new role with gusto, pleased to have a purpose. He'd missed his "family", but what he'd really been missing was his peaceful, non-violent lifestyle, and companionship. Madison and Amos had taught him the real meaning of family. He would do anything for the two of them. His adopted sister and nephew weren't perfect, but their passion for life and kin was enviable. Her love for her men, and theirs for her, had shown him the truth of what it meant to be 'in love'.

Tomorrow he would officiate their wedding, while Amos 'gave her away'. Both were strange traditions to him, but he understood the significance behind the ceremony.

"That's Queen Boulevard, Nix, you owe me one hundred souls." Madison held her hand out, palm up. "Cough it up."

"I don't have a hundred souls." Phoenix counted out his fake-bills that they'd re-crafted to suit their twisted board game. "I'll give you the fifty I have, along with Twisted Street"—*their game is twisted*—"and Bloody

Fingers Lane."

"Don't do it, kitten. It's a bad deal. Neither of those properties hold much soul-value."

"Giving advice is cheatin', Daddy," Amos chided.

"That's friendly advice, son. A big difference." Micah tossed the boy a grin.

Petra piped up, "Cheating would be something along the lines of, make him sign a covenant, Madison."

"Ooo...I like that idea." Madison's eyes lit up.

Amos laughed. Zen grinned.

"That's my girl, trained her right." Micah winked at his daughter.

Phoenix grunted. "All of you are swindlers. I expected more out of you, baby."

Just like the Ark expected more out of his family. And he should. Zen's family had taught him to always have one another's back.

Convene, the voice slammed into his mind so hard, Zen swayed forward until his forehead bumped against the windowpane. It was a voice he'd never thought to hear again.

You okay, Zen, Madison asked, and he wondered what notified her of his immediate disquiet.

Peary. He gazed into the darkness beyond and perceived no one.

A moment later, Madison jerked him out of his reverie by placing her hand on his arm. "The saying is 'peachy', not 'peary', but you're not peachy. What's wrong?"

He leaned his forehead against hers, and realized he only felt comfortable demonstrating the truth of his emotions with her. The small contact settled his unease in a single breath. *Someone from my past contacted me just now. I must assemble with him. I cannot rebuff his invitation.*

That's no invitation then.

Zen said nothing to her interpretation of the fact.

Her hand slid down his arm until she squeezed his hand. A show of support, solidarity, and affection in one move. Not even his wife had made him feel so cherished as this succubus did.

Then go, but be careful. Maybe take a dragon with you, because I know you'd never agree to take Micah.

Phoenix would be a better champion in this scenario, but he withheld that information. *I'll take extra precautions.* Zen kissed her forehead, and just in case this was the last time he saw her, *I love you, my sister.*

one move. Not even his wife had made him feel so cherished as this succubus did.

Madison smiled, as she drew back to meet his silver gaze. She should tell him 'sis' was a better nickname, but the formality of 'my sister' fit Zen's personality so much better. On the tip of her tongue were the words, 'come back to us, Zen,' but to utter them verbally or telepathically felt like a giant jinx. He teleported from the room before the next breath could fill her lungs and before she could decide to utter those words.

The look in his eyes concerned her because the individual who contacted him had obviously rattled him. And worry on a man that showed little to no emotion, was cause for even more apprehension. She hadn't asked for the contactor's identity. Zen hoarded secrets like Hell hoarded souls.

"It's a good thing I'm not jealous of Zennyo Ryuo's affections for you, otherwise his oddly out of character public display of affection toward you just now would've riled me."

Madison tilted her head back to discover Micah standing behind her. She hadn't even heard him approach.

His palm locked around the base of her neck. "Tell me."

"I only know he had someone demand a meeting, and he couldn't decline," she confessed as Micah shifted to her side.

Nix took the opportunity to align his chest to her back, his arms encircling her waist so he could palm her belly like he often did of late. "I heard the voice, and all he said was 'convene'. Pilfer the voice from my head, Micah, and maybe you will recognize his identity."

"I think Uncle Z will be okay." Amos stacked the wad of 'souls' into the box with the rest of the game. "I didn't hear the voice like Daddy-Nix, but I don't sense anything will happen to Uncle Z."

"I didn't hear it either." Madison leaned back and drew comfort from Nix's strength, nuzzling her forehead against his jaw. "But I felt his alarm."

"He was scared," Amos agreed. "No danger approaches us."

Unexpected tears burned her eyes, and Madison closed her lids to obtain control over her emotions. Micah kissed her, surprising her, and her eyes snapped open.

"I know the voice," he said against her mouth, the chill in his eyes terrifying her. "I still have a trail of Zen's teleport. It's fading, but I can follow him and secure his safety. Go to lockdown until I return." The eyes of a King elevated to focus on Nix. "Keep our woman safe, Phoenix." The portal shimmered behind him. He gave her another hard kiss. "Stay safe until I return. Don't do anything stupid."

"You know me—"

"That's why I said don't do anything stupid, kitten." He stepped to the edge of the doorway and gave her a look that she couldn't quite decipher. *You're our twin flame, be safe, kitten, or the consequences will be catastrophic for Earth,* he nodded toward Nix to pinpoint who he meant when he said 'our' in that sentence.

"Micah," she fisted his shirt and tugged him away from the portal. "*Who* contacted Zen?" *Maybe you shouldn't go if this individual poses enough danger to warrant a recommendation from you on my behavior.*

Nix kissed the side of her head as Micah ran a finger down her cheek. "Phoenix, Petra will take you to Hell. Don't depart from there until I return."

She felt Nix's head move beside hers, so she guessed he nodded at Micah's instructions.

"When I return with more answers, I'll give you all the details." Micah blew her a mental kiss and disappeared through the portal before she had a chance to call him back.

Stunned by his sudden departure and tormented expression, she gave Petra not a smidge of her focus when she grabbed her hand. "Already dropped Amos in Hell. It's your turn, Mommy Dearest."

"He'll be fine, baby." Phoenix turned her in his arms and hugged her the moment they were on Hell's soil. "Think of all the years you rallied against him and still lost."

Worry would eat at her until she knew Micah and Zen were safe. Being stuck in Hell unable to aid them would make her stir-crazy if she focused on it. So, she latched onto Nix's words and rubbed her face against his chest. "You do know I won, right? Kinda hard to consider myself a loser when I have the two hottest guys in all of creation in love with me."

Nix grinned, dimples blazing. "That's my girl."

She nipped his jaw. "Distract me from the worry, Nix."

"With pleasure," he said moments before his mouth descended upon hers.

Chapter 7

ZEN CAME OUT of the teleport at the Roof of the World, the Himalayas. The air was thin, and oxygen couldn't saturate his lungs. The noise of the whipping wind soothed him and made this location his favorite place for meditation. It was also the same place the Esdras angel imparted the news of Madison's pregnancy right before the angels sought her death.

The Messiah stood at the edge of a sharp cliff. The wind lashed his coal-black hair into his face. His dark complexion seemed even darker against the contrasting white of his shirt. He would blend among any middle-Eastern race.

It has been a long time, my friend. The Lamb of God remained facing away from Zen while acknowledging his presence.

I won't betray her, Zen said as he neared the holy man, his steps guarded.

That is not the reason for my visit.

He couldn't recall the last time Jesus visited the human side of life. As the right hand of God, his counsel was more effective in Heaven, his purpose on Earth already served. Instead of engaging, Zen waited for the savior of mankind to get to his purpose.

Zen halted beside him, laced his fingers behind his back in a casual stance. He felt anything but casual, his muscles tense and ready for battle even though he'd lose against this particular adversary. The Messiah only required words to annihilate Zen.

He stared at the inky horizon without seeing the terrain. The wind howled around them. At this elevation, and on these peaks, he could almost escape the noise of mankind's thoughts.

I was surprised you and Micah are once again allies. I never anticipated that outcome.

Zen sent a sidelong glance in the Messiah's direction, but the other man's blank expression gave nothing away. *I've no desire to ally with Micah. I asked for guidance and received none from the Word.*

Father did not condone the Esdras attack on Madison.

I know. But He'd allowed it to happen anyway, which resulted in Zen's Fall from grace.

Speaking of your Fall, the Lamb of God said, proving he knew Zen's thoughts just as the Creator always had, *it was freewill.*

Freewill was never mine before. So why now grant him the privilege? He'd killed children for God because they were monsters. But leaving Madison and Amos in the hands of the Esdras, knowing they planned their deaths, that'd been too much for him to turn a blind eye.

The Messiah faced him, his features utter perfection, wrinkle free, and unmarred by any indication of age. The green of his eyes contrasted against his tanned skin tone and black hair. Those eyes were the only genetic trait he'd passed down to Phoenix. In the sense of visible traits, that was.

Freewill has always been yours. You never cared enough to use it before. Millennia ago Father presumed your race lacked empathy. That you cared enough to Fall for the succubus is the only reason

Father has allowed her to live.

Unsure how to reply, Zen remained silent.

When you showed compassion and did not kill Madison as an infant, Father became intrigued by your choices.

Zen suspected that was why the Word had come to him so seldom since stumbling upon Madison. *Why'd the Creator let Micah's actions go unchecked so long if He disapproved of Madison's creation?*

Not our business to question Him. A vague reply from Jesus and not an unexpected response either. *While I do not comprehend His love, Micah was always one of His favorites. He once told me Beliel was His brightest archangel and often surprised Him, taking the path less chosen, and designing fate in a way He had not foreseen, almost as if Beliel held foresight.*

Zen nodded. *You must realize Micah will never seek redemption.*

His redemption is in Father's acceptance of Hell. Redemption was also granted when He elected not to punish Beliel for his blasphemy at dabbling in creation. Father's judgment is absolute, never to be faulted. While I do not understand His decisions or agree with them, I am ever faithful He knows best.

Startled by the bitterness in the holy man's voice, Zen glanced at Jesus sharply. By the time the Lamb of God spoke again, all evidence of any possible resentment was gone, and Zen doubted what he'd heard.

Phoenix has my power to give life to what was once dead.

He'd revived Zoe, Gage, and Madison.

Madison's genetics are also in creation-magic.

Madison had given life to Taz, and when she thrust her magic into a plant, it served as Miracle-Gro. As she'd told him, in an apocalypse, no one she loved would starve.

Her particular style of magic is why the Lynx goo was trapped in the Pyxis and stored in safekeeping.

64

Their particular magic combined is the only reason she conceived. Zen mulled over that for a moment during Jesus's brief silence. The Messiah continued before Zen could reply. *Madison's ability to conceive was dead until Phoenix planted his seed inside her. Her magic must have innately took charge from there, crafting Phoenix's seed into an embryo.*

It'd been thought only God could create life in any form except for that which He deemed permissible. That Micah had experimented in it, and now Madison bore blasphemous offspring, proved that thought a myth. Maybe suggested a heightened state of evolution...or a new species entirely.

The humans call it science, and Father calls it a phenomenon not of His making. It is offensive to me, a desecration of all that is holy and pure, and I would kill all involved given my choice, but I follow Father's directives. Despite Madison being an abomination, He wants her to live, a boon to you and your years of service. The words 'for now' were implied even though Jesus didn't utter them.

And now they were back to the reason for the meeting.

It is not Amos who has the potential to be the anti-Christ but the abomination growing in Madison's womb. All of their future offspring have the same potential.

That startled Zen. *But Micah is the King of Hell, and Amos his offspring.*

She carries twins.

I'm aware. This news wasn't a surprise to Zen. *I'm already in communication with them.*

They are a combination of Heaven and Hell.

Amos is the same combination.

No, you are incorrect, my friend. Madison was human at Amos's conception. That makes him a Nephilim with demonic and angelic possibilities. Madison was full demon when the twins were conceived.

Zen rubbed his forehead. Sounded like a complicated mess of inconsistencies to him.

I do not acknowledge the unborn children as my kin. If they ever open the Gates of Heaven, I will kill them. Jesus sighed as if he was weary of his role as God's sire. *Humanity continues to shun Father at an alarming rate. He has decided you are in charge of humanity. Millenniums can lapse before Armageddon transpires, or the end can happen in a few short years. It is your choice and your job to manage.*

The Creator plans to just walk away and desert the human race? That was a mindbender because He'd loved the humans best.

He still loves them over all His creation. You've lived among them just as I have and Micah has. You understand them and—

I rarely understand them.

You understand their compassion, their weaknesses, and their ability to love beyond their need to survive. I died for humanity because of my love for them.

No, Zen shook his head. *You were sacrificed because the Creator asked it of you.*

Semantics. The holy man shrugged. *Father has chosen you as Earth's savior because of your interference in Madison's life. Because of your influence, she was able to halt Micah's plans for the new trinity. How much have you heard, brother?* Jesus turned away from Zen, and Zen followed the Messiah's gaze. Micah stood nearby. He hadn't even sensed Beliel's arrival. *I hid his presence from you,* the Lamb of God confirmed.

Micah's jaw was locked, his gaze honed in the way Zen only saw when he prepared for battle. "I heard all of it."

Speak telepathically, Beliel.

"I'll speak however I choose without a solitary give-a-fuck for your preference."

Jesus tilted his head to the side, ogling Beliel. While the Prince of Peace held sway over Zen's actions, he'd never been given that control over Micah. *Ever the rebellious one, Micah. Nothing has altered, not even your unfathomed anger toward our Father.*

"I rebelled against Father, not you, as to everything else...go fuck yourself."

Eloquent words, Beliel. You rebelled because of Father's love for humanity, and now you speak like one of them.

Micah smiled, a slow predator-ish type of grin that failed to reach his eyes. "With that assessment you prove you know *nothing* of my quarrel with Father."

A stilted pause ensued. Even though Jesus's expression wore no emotion, Zen could feel his doubt, while Micah wore a very obvious gloat. Zen wondered if maybe Jesus didn't have all the facts, but neither did Zen if that were the case. He too had believed Micah Fell only because God had demanded he place humanity above all creatures.

The fate of humanity rests in your hands, my friend. Choose your allies wisely, and implement sage decisions because it only takes one wrong move, and the world will burn. One word of advice...Phoenix needs his family in his life. Without them it is a game changer. Even as he spoke to Zen, he continued to stare at Micah. *Father will be pleased to have glimpsed you through my eyes.*

"Tell our father, I said—"

The Messiah was gone before Micah could finish.

The King stared at him, and Zen held his glower. Finally, Beliel dragged his fingers through his hair and inhaled deeply. "You must know everything in me wants to fuck you over so you fuck up Father's decree."

"Armageddon hurts you, too."

Micah executed a sharp nod. That put the King of Hell in a moral dilemma. "Madison worried for your safety."

"Return to her, and alleviate her unease while I speak with the Birminghams." Zen teleported.

The Birminghams had been on Zen's radar since their departure, so he knew the exact location to teleport. He arrived outside their hotel door in an effort not to frighten them with an abrupt appearance. After a sharp knock on the chipped wood, he waited for someone to greet him.

"Zen..." James peered over Zen's shoulder as if he expected to find someone else behind him. The mortal's reception was cool, his thoughts even icier, but Zen had anticipated this unwelcome greeting.

"I'm alone. May we converse?"

The Sherlock stepped aside and motioned with his hand for Zen to enter. Gage and Zoe reclined on one double bed. Zoe made notes in a notebook, while Gage cleaned his weapons. Georgie sat with her back to the headboard, book in hand, but her focus shifted to Zen when he entered.

"Evening," Zen addressed them with a quick onceover.

"Hey, Zen," Zoe said cheerily, with a small finger wave.

"Didn't realize you knew our location." James scratched his jaw, leaving the door open so he could force Zen out in a hurry if needed. Why the man saw Zen as a threat confused him, but he kept his knowledge of the other man's thoughts to himself.

"I know where you are at all times." Zen caught Gage's hard glance in his dad's direction, his thoughts like petals falling off a stem into Zen's mind. That he could track them unsettled the younger Birmingham. "No spell will aid you. I'm immune to them. I offer none of you any danger."

"That you can read our minds represents danger to us," Gage's tone came out casual, but Zen caught the tensing of the muscles in his shoulders even as he blocked the other man's thoughts.

"If I wanted you dead, you'd all be dead already."
Strangely that gave them no comfort. It should have,
it'd been his idea of a peace offering.

"You protect Madison and Amos." The Birmingham
father figure crossed his arms over his chest. A clear
defensive gesture. "They are a threat to mankind."

She's already damned Nix's soul. Zen glared at
James as the other male's thought filtered into his
mind.

"They *are* both demons, Zen." Gage dragged his
hunting knife across the whetstone.

"By your definition, even Phoenix is a monster. *The
only good monster is a dead one.* Your exact thoughts,
James," Zen said to the man, turning his attention to
him and away from Gage. The other man's eyes
widened a fraction. "Phoenix is immortal, hardly
damned. Nothing prevents me from reading any of
your thoughts, not even that talisman you wear." He
nodded at the charm on the chain around James's
neck. "Your monster handbook requires an update. I
fit your classification as well."

"Who says you're not a monster?" Gage rested the
blade across his thighs, his nostrils flaring wide, and a
challenge in his brown eyes.

"God." The silence in the room was shocking,
especially since even their thoughts staggered over his
declaration. "I understand you're angry, disappointed,
and hurt by Phoenix's choices. Suck on it—"

I hope he means suck it up, Zoe's confused thoughts
hit him.

"—Yes, I mean suck it up. Thank you, Zoe." He
inclined his head at her, and she gave him a weak
smile, realizing he'd heard her, which had a way of
unnerving most mortals. It had even unsettled
Madison in the beginning. "Suck it up and deal with it,
support Phoenix like a family should. You taught your
nephew that." He looked James Birmingham straight
in the eyes. "You taught him to be loyal to family. You
taught him to stand up for what he believes in. He's

standing up for what he believes in, and you're shunning him for it. To walk away from him now would make you a hypocrite, James."

Gage opened his mouth to defend his dad, but Zen heard his arguments before he could speak, so he cut him off. "Quiet. I came to talk. You will listen." He swept the Birmingham clan with a scowl. "Madison may have been born from hellish plans, but her genetics aren't inherently evil. Their orientation came from the Creator. Elias is an angel, and he is unadulterated wickedness. His father—God—made him that way. There are many angels that are viler than Madison could ever bring herself to become. I know what's in her heart, and at the root of who she is, is the same woman all of you came to respect...love, compassion, and a need for acceptance. She still craves to resist immorality, and she nixed Micah's original plans for her, creating a net of safety for humanity. At any given time, the lines between good and bad are shadowy in the best scenario."

"The lines between good and bad are blurred." Zoe corrected him, but gave Gage an unapologetic shrug when he shot an exasperated glare in her direction.

"Yes. Thank you." Zen offered her a small smile. "I have met *many* Sherlocks that are monsters, and yet none of you would raise a hand against a fellow human except in self-defense. You think your war is against evil, but you're deceiving yourselves. You kill anything that is supernatural, regardless of alignment between what you deem good or bad. Gage wanted to kill me when we first met." Phoenix's cousin flinched in surprise. "You felt I was a threat if I was uncontrollable. That is a dangerous line to toe, Gage." Zen thought about the war the Sherlocks engaged in. "More times than not, I discover evil in humanity more than in the paranormal community."

Zen let those words sink in, waiting a moment. "Phoenix has made the *only* choice fate designed for him. You know this is true, Georgie. You saw Madison in a vision before he met her. Amos knew Phoenix would become his second daddy and, unlike you, his record is more precise. Gage," he shifted his attention to the man, "Phoenix has not betrayed you or what he stood for. You're betraying your core values. Family first, monsters last." Zen rounded on James. "You are his second father. Act like one. Accept him for the man he's become, not the man you wanted him to be. And Zoe..." he swiped the hair off his forehead and shook his head. "I am baffled. You aren't his blood relation, but you're the only one eager to stand beside him. I respect you and your loyalty to those you call family."

"Thanks." Zoe grinned. "He's kinda like my kid brother."

"Micah murdered Gage." James slammed his fist down on the dresser next to him. The lamp rattled on the wood.

"And Zoe," Gage said between clenched teeth. The snapshots of her death flashed through Gage's mind, giving Zen a peek into the horrific moment.

A demon held Zoe with an arm around her waist and a knife pressing into the skin of her throat, a busted lip the least of her injuries. Her arm rested at an odd angle, the chalky white of her bone piercing the flesh of her bicep. Wincing at her ashen skin tone and eyes glassy from pain, Gage prayed she'd pass out to alleviate her agony. She'd given the demon hell before suffering defeat, and he'd tried to defend her, but they'd all been easily subdued.

Micah stepped up to Nix. "Let me introduce myself." His voice lowered so only Nix could hear him. Nix's awed expression confused Gage, but all he cared about was the pain Zoe was in. "Each time I meet you, I'm disappointed, Phoenix." The blue demon sucked on his teeth, and Gage wondered when his cousin had met this particular demon before. He'd certainly never mentioned him. "After all your exploits, I expected more from you."

Me too. We're here because Nix insisted on

checking out the signs. *He and Zoe had wanted to blow them off since they hadn't been classic demonic insignias.*

"I would say I'm sorry to disappoint, but you have to know it'd be a lie," Nix said with a curl of hatred on his upper lip.

Gage wanted to scream at his cousin to cower and beg and maybe they'd survive this. Ballsy to the very end wasn't the way to go in this instance. Not with Zoe's life on the line. Angering him wasn't the best path to follow, certainly Nix knew that!

"Slice her throat," Micah said, voice cool.

"No!" Gage screamed as the demon dragged the blade across Zoe's neck slowly—his best guess for maximum suffering. Blood bloomed, ran like paint splashed against a wall, and Zoe gurgled, choking on the fluid.

Gage fought the demon holding him with everything he had, but they were stronger than him. They wouldn't even let him go to Zoe to console her during her dying minutes.

"Oooo..." Beliel shivered in delight. "The gurgle of death...a composition vastly more beautiful than anything Bach could compose."

"I'll kill you, motherfucker," Nix promised.

Gage sobbed, choking out Zoe's name over and over, a eulogy to the woman he adored and loved more than his life. Nix was to blame. Nix had insisted they come here because he'd been bored and antsy to see Madison. Gage should've—

Zen yanked himself out of the memory, blocking out Gage so he couldn't accidentally become caught up in another one of these horrid memories.

"Yes," Zen blew out a weary breath, closing his eyes at what he'd witnessed. Graphic memories that would've undoubtedly made him as angry as it had Gage. "I came to defend Phoenix's choices, not Micah's. One thing I can tell you, Gage, it's not Nix's fault Zoe died at his hands. Neither is it Madison's."

"Nix brought us back to life. Me first," Zoe reminded her boyfriend.

"After he sold his soul to the motherfucker!" Gage yelled at her. "Damned his soul for a goddamn demon."

"That goddamn demon got him his soul back," Zoe said, her tone reasonable. Gage shot to his feet, one fist balled, the other curled around the hilt of the knife, but before he could speak she had more to say. "Without her trickery he'd still be Micah's pawn."

"Tell me how he's not still Micah's pawn," James asked. "Wanting to marry Madison, while she marries Micah too. Having her cake and eating it too. Just like a demon."

"You're guilty of the same, James Birmingham." Zen held James's hostile glare. "You only want a relationship so long as Phoenix does what you want. And Gage, I just witnessed your emotions, your rage over Zoe's death, so I know the answer to my question, but would you have done any differently had the roles been reversed? How far would you have gone to save your woman? Think on that while you unjustly judge Phoenix."

Zen teleported out of the hotel.

Chapter 8

"**QUIT YOUR BELLYACHING**, mortal, I'm demonstrating mercy." Micah yanked on the human's finger. The bone gave way with a harsh crack, and the man shrieked. "Man up. That was minimal discomfort. I could do worse." Had done worse. He favored flaunting his crueler side but held himself in check since he dealt with a living, breathing person rather than a soul that could take much, *much* harsher abuse.

"*Lots* worse." Petra stood at his side, with her head angled at a cant, watching him work on his victim.

His quarry blacked out from the pain, irritating Micah enough his claws almost ejected before he contained them. This mission *had* to work. In a few hours he would remarry his woman. Giving her Elias's head on a platter as a wedding gift would be invaluable and would demonstrate his dedication to her.

With time limited, and working fast being his immediate goal, Micah slammed power into the mortal, jerking him back to sharp awareness. The young male panted when he spied them, his chest rumbling as sobs ripped upward from his lungs to bless them with his agony and fear.

Petralegija licked her lollipop. "He doesn't scream right."

"His vocal chords are busted."

"Oh." She sounded like a fascinated, young and innocent child instead of an ancient succubus demon who'd proven time and time again she mastered torture as well as any King of Hell. Her fabricated sweetness had felled more than one mortal. "I could enthrall him and make this go faster."

"Please!" The supplication in the mortal's eyes disgusted Micah. At this stage in the interrogation, with all ten fingers broken to the point they'd require surgery to repair, Micah suspected the human would do just about anything to ease the agony.

Right where I want him. That's when individuals usually became compliant.

"Don't want it to go faster." The man wept so hard at Micah's comment he choked on the snot running from his nose.

Micah studied the male without pity. Mid-twenties, wearing expensive clothes, manicured fingernails, and a hundred dollar haircut had Micah questioning Elias's interest in the human. "Slow torture vents my frustration."

The man's sobs increased.

A month without a bead on his twin increased Micah's anger. To the human, he asked once again, "Where's Elias?"

"I told you I don't know who that is."

Petra tsked at Dumbfuck—as she'd named him two minutes into the interrogation.

"Remember that time we castrated the human and forced him to eat his cock?" she reminisced, and Dumbfuck's eyes grew wide.

The stench of piss hit his nostrils, and Micah glanced at the human's crotch. Piss stained his slacks, and urine leaked from the mortal's pant leg and puddled on the floor beneath his chair.

Weak. Humans are disgustingly weak.

"Indeed." He glanced at his daughter, proud of her despite her defection from his camp. Felt like old times working with her again. "I was proud of your ingenious idea to dismember that mortal with a plastic butter knife. You sawed and sawed until you hacked off his dick."

She sighed, eyes glazing over in fond memory. "His screams *were* the best jingle."

"I don't know an Elias!" the mortal screamed...or tried with his busted vocal chords.

Petra put her knee into his groin and ground down. "Don't yell at my daddy."

Dumbfuck would've puked, but she clamped her hands over his mouth, choking him on his bile.

"Show some respect." She stepped away and picked at her nail polish, as the mortal coughed. "He's a King."

Micah missed tormenting souls with his offspring. Her sickening flair for mayhem never failed to impress him.

"Please...I have a family," their victim rasped out.

Pathetic. Mortals always resorted to begging. He'd heard every excuse in the book, and pleading was ineffective because few in the paranormal community empathized with the weak species. Not even his angelic siblings that were governed by his father commiserated with humanity.

"Don't care." Micah tempered the ejection of his talons from his fingertips for maximum mental-effect on his quarry. "My family takes precedence over yours."

"You carry Elias's scent, so we know—"

"What are you doing?" His wife's uptight immortal friend demanded in his haughtiest tone to date.

A fraction of a second before Zennyo Ryuo teleported into the warehouse, Micah sensed him. With his abrupt arrival, the human wept like a dramatic teen. Micah's patience took a direct hit.

Maintaining his focus on his victim, Beliel ran his index-talon along Dumbfuck's arm, and was satisfied with the way the mortal's flesh twitched at his touch. "He has information on Elias I *will* get from him."

"I cannot tolerate this behavior."

"I don't require your tolerance." For the first time since the immortal's arrival, Micah lifted his gaze to Zennyo Ryuo. Micah fed a challenge into his stare. Hopefully the other male recognized it in the power he allowed to bristle along his frame. "Neither do I answer to *you*."

Stare-to-stare they squared off.

"You do answer to Madison."

The cool, crisp declaration irritated Micah and he laughed, even though he felt no real mirth. That the immortal attempted to micromanage him through Madison's influence rankled his tolerance. She was his wife, not his keeper, and she held no delusions about his real temperament. A tame King of Hell would result in the domain's downfall. Even though Earth served as a battle zone between Heaven and Hell, allowing anyone to temper his behavior diminished his supremacy among demons and angels alike.

Instead of engaging in a pissing contest with the self-righteous immortal, he said, "He sold his soul to Elias."

He knew that tidbit of information would put an entirely different spin on Zennyo Ryuo's principles. Knowing the mortal had bartered away his spirit should negate the immortal's need to safeguard him. As Micah suspected, a new gleam entered the Zennyo Ryuo's eyes, and he turned his focus on Dumbfuck.

"That was a drunk hallucination." The human gaped at them, eyes wide with fear.

"That happened for *realz*, Dumbfuck." Petra twirled her sucker in her mouth and smacked loudly when she withdrew the sugary treat. "All for the cash to purchase another round of whiskey for you and your friends. That makes you a fool too stupid to live."

"I—he..." Dumbfuck dropped his chin to his chest and shook his head. "I don't remember him telling me his name."

For Elias to solidify the deal names had to be exchanged. But while the mortal felt compelled to spew his knowledge, Micah glowered at him and held his tongue.

"Man, you have to understand. I was high on blow and liquor. We were celebrating passing the Bar exam. I"—his voice cracked—"thought it was a dream. But I think he had talons like yours." He glanced at Micah's hands, fear causing his chin to tremble. "I'm telling you the truth. I didn't remember until she said something about selling my soul. It's all a foggy memory. I can't be held to contracts made under the influence."

"Incorrect. Substandard mortal laws do not apply when bartering with a demon King."

Dumbfuck finally realized how damned he was. His Adam's apple bobbed with his gulp.

Micah ran a hand through his hair and met the immortal's eyes. "I can't jack his thoughts like a normal human because Elias owns him. I have a plan. I invite you to leave so I may implement it."

Arms crossed over his chest, Zennyo Ryuo shook his head.

He bet a quarter of his souls the immortal would grow squeamish once he discovered the full extent of Micah's strategy. "Consider yourself warned, my friend."

"Not your friend, Beliel."

They were allies with a common interest, Madison the merger between their divergent scruples. Zennyo Ryuo couldn't argue that. But quibbling over useless disagreements served no purpose, so Micah dropped the topic.

Petra rolled her eyes. "It's an expression, Zen. Five years hanging out with us and you still haven't gotten the nuances of the English language. You're hopeless."

The immortal flicked his glance in her direction. "Half of the spoken words are prevarications or misrepresentations. Listening to thoughts is a more reliable form of communication. What are you doing, Beliel?"

Micah slapped his palm over the human's mouth and carved his sigil into the mortal's chest directly over where the soul was located. "Binding his soul to his body."

"How does that assist us?"

The King of Hell met Zennyo Ryuo's eyes, removed his hold on the human, and held up his arm. Micah twisted his hand, and Dumbfuck's neck made a satisfying crack.

Dead, the former mortal slumped against his restraints. His soul a silver glob that lingered nearby.

Anger flashed through the immortal's features so fast Micah would've missed the emotion if he hadn't been watching. Before Zennyo Ryuo could speak, Beliel said, "His death will draw Elias out to retrieve his property. We're currently waiting for his arrival."

"For future reference I'm not comfortable being an accessory to the murder of humans."

"Don't be a scrupulous fucker and bitch when his soul was bound for Hell anyway." The sooner the immortal realized he would do *anything* to avenge his woman, the better. "Do tell, Zennyo Ryuo, how many defenseless humans did Father command you to kill? Or better yet, confess how many Madison killed while under *your* sanctimonious watch?"

"Can you two measure dicks later when we're not waiting to nab Uncle Eli?" Petra smiled when they both looked at her. She casually tossed her lollipop stick aside. "Just sayin'...now's not the best time."

Micah winked at his daughter, as Zennyo Ryuo said with a stiff upper-lip, "We will have words over this infraction, Beliel."

"Fuck you, Zennyo Ryuo. Fuck you hard." Micah morphed into his angel skin, the *Scepter of Souls* itching to eject from his palm. He fantasized about how it would feel when he thrust the sword into his brother's chest, the way the steel would tug when it pierced Elias's heart. He'd watch on as Elias perished, placated to know his face, his anger, and his hatred were the last thing his twin would see. The contentment Micah would feel, knowing he'd avenged his wife, would surely be analogous of the moment when Madison claimed her seat in Hell.

"Going old school, *zkihtak*." *Brother.* "I expected something with a little more flair from you." Elias strolled into the warehouse as if he held not a care in the world. His shoes created dull thuds against the concrete. "Let's discuss this. A war between us hinders Hell."

He'd expected loyalty from his sibling, only to be betrayed by him at one of the most crucial moments in Hell's history. Not interested in hearing Elias's lame excuses for why he'd instigated brutality against Madison, Micah wasn't predisposed to engage in conversation. He wanted blood. That was all. "You've been ousted from Hell's power."

Elias's features hardened. "An uncalled for action when I honored our agreement."

"You *know* your actions were wrong! Went against my desires." Micah glanced at Petra, and his temper soothed a fraction. "I'm not discussing this."

"I can understand upholding your end of the bargain." Zen's even voice contradicted the power coalescing around him in pastel rainbow colors. Those orbs gave him a tame appearance, but Beliel knew firsthand how deceptive they were. They packed one hell of a punch. "You would've killed her had Micah not intervened. His plans for her required life."

Micah's twin scoffed. "He would've figured out a way to bring her back. He's resourceful that way. Or just brought Phoenix into the equation. His Jesus-toy is his fail-safe."

"Bullshit, Uncle Eli," Petra called his bluff. "You know drinking from the *Casket* invites oblivion. Nix can't fix that."

Which meant there was no coming back from that. Ever. Micah suspected Madison had only survived because she hadn't willingly committed to death. All the previous drinkers had sought extinction.

Elias blew out a weary breath. "Think long and hard if you really want to scratch me with that tinker-toy, Micah."

I'm going to do more than scratch you.

"We're twins. You'll regret this choice."

Micah slowly shook his head. "I thought you of all people were above begging. But then I also thought you were trustworthy."

Beliel portaled, but his brother executed the same move. Micah spun around and found Elias near Petra. She went for Eliel, and he slammed her against the wall, trapping her with magic. Because she was no match for any of the Kings, Micah had anticipated Petra's nullification.

Eliel canted his head toward Zen. "Shall we keep this just between us, brother?"

Micah nodded.

His twin portaled from the warehouse. Micah followed him through the traces of his magic. Beliel landed in the middle of an outcropping in the Grand Canyon. They circled one another as the wind swirled around them, blowing Micah's hair in his face.

Elias held his hands out to the sides. "I did not anticipate this extreme of a reaction from you."

"Proof you don't know or understand me. I love Madison. Draw your weapon." Micah's muscles trembled with eagerness to stab his brother into oblivion.

"I won't draw on you, Beliel."

"Don't expect me to show the same honor. I *will* fucking kill you." *And enjoy it.*

"Listen to yourself. You would kill your twin for the love of a woman." Eliel snorted. "No woman is worth this division between us."

Those words proved Elias failed to comprehend Micah's devotion to Madison.

"We've lived through eons fighting by one another's

sides. I've had your back against everyone, including Father! I *Fell* for you, Beliel!" Elias's voice softened and he continued, "Only because of you. I would do anything for you, but even for you I refuse to break a covenant. I'm sickened you expected that from me. More repulsed that you expected me to do it for a goddamn woman who was too chicken shit to claim her seat of power."

Micah's jaw locked, anger causing his hand to vibrate. "Draw. Your. Goddamn. Weapon."

"What would you have done had you been in my shoes, *zkihtak*? Would *you* have reneged on our deal to do *anything* to force her to accept her rank?"

Considering his sibling's words, Micah glanced at the landscape. With all honesty he couldn't say what he would've done. But he knew with certainty Eliel had relished torturing Micah's love, and had looked for ways for years to get his hands on her so he could make her scream.

Micah swiped his fingers through his hair. He gripped the *Scepter* in his other hand so tight his knuckles ached. Ready to spring into action at any moment, he met Elias's gaze. "I would've broken our deal because she meant everything to you."

"You're a pussy-whipped liar." Eliel's upper lip curled, exhibiting his rancor. "Delusional too. She's turned you into half the King you were."

"No. She's made me stronger, given me a reason to make Hell a more viable powerhouse." Micah launched at his brother, and their swords clashed. He punched Eliel in the face and slashed with his sword hand, but his twin portaled away to the edge of the cliff.

"I forgive you your momentary lapse of mental illness for a pussy that's not even yours, *zkihtak*."

Micah wasn't sure he heard Eliel's words right. They made no sense given the fact Madison was very much his woman.

"I'll be your devoted brother again when you've come to your senses. *Puc Taqq'j mifak voexa cio ulx taam cio juwa el hta elhakep.*" *May Hell's power guide you and keep you safe in the interim.* His twin disappeared through a portal over the side of the cliff.

Micah seeded his power along the seams of the opening, but couldn't find the trail to follow his twin.

"*Eliel...you coward!*"

The words echoed back to him off the bluffs. Clicking mentally through everything that had led to this moment, he admitted he'd made a few mistakes that'd allowed his sibling to escape. He should've drafted an angel lock around the warehouse, caging his brother so he couldn't run. Zen could've released Micah after Elias's demise. Or he should've laid a trap for his twin in a different locale. Grafting the Angel Lock into the landscape, taking the lead, and having his brother follow him instead would've been a better plan.

Next time I'll be smarter with my trap.

Chapter 9

IN A FEW hours Nix would wed Mads. He alternated between being nervous and antsy to take his vows. Disappointment over his family missing the ceremony lingered on the fringes of his conscience, which annoyed him. He wanted nothing to interfere with today's joy. But he couldn't help his discontent either. Relatives were supposed to *want* to attend the big day. Too bad he couldn't dismiss his hurt in the same cavalier manner they'd scorned him.

He'd told Mads they'd seen weirder when she expressed concern over their reaction to him remaining with her and Micah. At the time, he'd believed that.

I should've known they'd sing a different tune with Micah involved, and Mads the official Queen of Hell. And my baby... He closed his eyes and released a heavy sigh. *God my baby had been their biggest objection.*

He swiped his fingers through his hair and focused on his excitement instead of his disgruntlement. Watching Mads scurry around getting ready for the ceremony infected him with a dollop of her enthusiasm.

Micah was in the wind. He assumed Petra must be tagging along with him because her whereabouts were unknown too.

Nix's personal she-demon, Mads, sauntered into the room wearing jeans and a T-shirt. He couldn't wait to see what she'd picked out for the ceremony.

Lucky was at her side and appeared frazzled with stray hair strands escaping her ponytail. "Whew! That dragon of hers—"

"Which one?" Nix asked.

"Kur," Alessa clarified.

At the time he tattooed the dragon on his back and shoulder, he hadn't given much thought to whether he'd like them or not. He'd just been memorializing a creature that was supposed to save him. Kur *had* saved him and become attached to his woman at the same time. It was bittersweet. He didn't exactly begrudge Mads their protection since they *had* helped defeat the Esdras angels that had attacked and killed her. "What's he done now?"

Alessa leaned in as if she'd whisper a national secret to him, but spoke in her normal voice, "He took me flying." She plopped into the seat nearest him. "God, that was fun. Thought it'd be scary, but it was exhilarating." The flush in her cheeks testified to the thrill she'd endured on the back of the dragon. "He said I could ride him anytime I wanted."

Nix almost choked on that. He tossed Alessa a grin. "I'm sure he did."

"Scrub your dirty mind. He didn't mean it that way."

"Yeah, he *did*, Alessa." Mads's fingernails scraped over Nix's scalp, teasing scratches as she plowed her fingers through the back of his hair.

He smirked at Lucky. She childishly poked her tongue out at him.

"What'cha doing?" Mads leaned in, her breath heavy in his ear.

His libido took instant notice, and his voice came out gruff. "Tweaking my vows."

Her tongue slid over his cartilage. "You want me to peek at it and give you some pointers?"

"Not a chance in hell, baby." Twisting slightly, he caught her about the waist and pulled her down on his lap.

Mads smoothed her palms up his chest before wrapping her arms around his neck. She Eskimo kissed him. "Just a tiny peek."

He flipped the paper over so she couldn't steal a look-see. She gave him a smooch that had his fingers curling into her hips to hold her in place.

"Cut that crap out, you hussy." Alessa smacked Nix on the arm. "Save it for the honeymoon."

Mads giggled and slid off his lap. "Jealousy doesn't suit—hey! Dragon, come back here with that." The doorbell rang while she yelled at Kur and hurried to the door. "Will one of you see who's at the door so I can find out why that dragon has my wedding cake?"

Just that quick his woman took off.

"I'll get the door. Probably just a delivery anyway. I mean who has tuxes delivered for hellhounds? For that matter, who in their right mind forces hellhounds into tuxes and a doggie dress?"

"My crazy woman." Nix winked at Lucky.

She laughed. "Good point. God love her."

"More like Hell loves her."

"Yeah...well, I say Heaven's loss to that." Nix chuckled at Alessa's spin on it. Right before she walked out of the room, she threw out over her shoulder, "Get those vows right or I'll be too embarrassed to call you my former fuck-buddy."

A few minutes later someone cleared a throat behind him. Nix turned sideways in his seat and discovered his family in the room.

"Not quite the delivery I was expecting." Alessa stood behind them and just slightly to the left of James. She twisted her fingers together in a nervous fashion. "I'll be in my room if you need me, Nix."

Zo rushed him as he gained his footing, wrapping him up in a tight hug. As he returned her affections, he warily met his family's gaze over her head. Unsure what their sudden arrival indicated, he wouldn't jump to conclusions only to be disappointed later.

Gage said nothing, just strode toward them, his long-legged stride eating up the distance between them. Once he had Zo sandwiched between them, he caught Nix's nape with his hand and rested his forehead against Nix's. "I'm sorry. You're more than my cousin. You're my brother, and I should've supported you. Doesn't mean I have to like your choice, or agree with it. I damn sure don't understand it. I can't ever forgive that fucking King for what he did to Zoe."

Nix cleared the thickness from his throat. "I get it. I'd never forgive anyone that put Mads in an early grave. I don't ask that of you. If I could turn back the clock and change that night, I would."

"I know." Gage released him as if he'd been pulled away.

Maybe he had been because his fierce, petite aunt stood beside them with her arms wide open. Without any hesitation, he engulfed her in a hug, lifting her off her feet with a growl.

"I love you, Nix. Didn't mean to make you think we wouldn't be there for you, but these knuckleheads had to come to their own decision," his aunt confessed.

"I love you, too, Aunt Georgie." He could say he understood, but that'd be a lie. "What matters is that you're all here now."

Next he came face-to-face with his Uncle James. He was a hard man at times, usually forgiving unless family had been wronged, so Nix wasn't sure if his uncle was along for the ride or truly supportive.

"I don't like your choice, but a wise man reminded me that having kids isn't about agreeing or disagreeing with them. It's about being there for your boys when it matters. If you'll forgive an ornery old man, I'd be honored to be a part of your child's life."

"Uncle James"—he rarely used their titles, but it felt appropriate in this moment—"my child will be better for knowing you."

Micah portaled into their home and paused to take stock of the pungent aroma in the air. The ripe scent of humanity testified to the Birmingham family's presence. Just his damned luck they'd chosen Phoenix, even though he'd hoped they'd select the other option. Sure it was selfish of him, but so what. He felt what he felt. Meddling relatives wasn't to his taste. The only positive was they'd all be dead and out of his hair in under a century. He could tolerate anyone for that long.

Modifying his direction, he followed his nose to the living room. Decked out in fancy attire, the entire Birmingham clan—minus Phoenix—reclined on various seats.

The room went silent the moment he entered.

"Look who took their time making the right choice." He actually was a little surprised they'd made the decision so quickly or *this* particular one at all. Crickets. None of them responded, but instead just gaped at him. "How many Sherlocks did you give the whereabouts or other details of Madison and Amos?"

"None," James replied, jutting his chin at a mutinous angle. "I'm insulted you'd accuse us of selling them out."

"Live with it."

Gage spoke up next. "You should know the Sherlocks have already heard Madison became Hell's Queen. I don't know if it's just speculation on their part or if someone or *something* they captured told them."

Micah pondered that information. It was likely a

demon spilled the information, but he knew it wasn't any of his demons because all of them were in Hell. His brother remained free, so he could be guilty.

Facing Zen who stood at the entrance to the room, he asked, "Do they speak true, Zennyo Ryuo?" Because there was no way the immortal hadn't already wormed through their minds.

"Yes."

He nodded and faced the Birmingham clan once again. "You must verbally say you accept my offer for the deal to be sealed."

"Which one would that be?" Gage might seem calm with his arm casually draped over Zoe's shoulders, but Micah could feel the mortal's tension.

He spoke to James rather than Gage. "The one where you're granted safety from mine and Madison's demons, and you agree to not go after any of them either. You'll also not feed the Sherlocks any information about any of us, that includes Madison, Amos, Phoenix, Zennyo Ryuo, Petra, the dragons, basically *anyone* associated with us."

"What if your demons attack us first?"

Darkness slithered through his mind. Just a few months ago, he'd have said none of his demons were stupid enough to go against him, but then Celeste had done the unthinkable and helped Elias kidnap, terrorize, and torture Madison. "You'll defend yourself, but leave them for me to punish."

Woe to the demon that crosses me.

"I'd like to add a clause." Gage removed his arm from Zoe's shoulders and leaned forward in his seat, placing his forearms along his thighs. "*All* Sherlocks are to be protected from you, Madison, and your demons."

"This isn't a negotiation, puppy. You can choose to accept the offer as is or I'll wipe your memory. Make your decision fast because if you remain for the ceremony, I'll consider that an acceptance of the deal offered. To default on a deal with a King bears huge reprisals." Without any further words, he strode from the room. *Please let them leave now...*but in his heart, he knew they'd remain.

"What's wrong?" Phoenix asked when Micah entered their bedroom.

"Saw your family is in attendance. Congratulations." *Fuck my luck.*

"Yeah, I was surprised they came. Where were you?"

Noting the Ark of Heaven's fancy attire, Micah pinched the bridge of his nose. They were to marry their woman in under an hour. "I had a bead on Elias." His twin's death would've been the perfect wedding present. At Phoenix's hopeful look, Micah shook his head. "He got away."

"There'll be a next time. Probably best you're not coming to the ceremony with blood on your hands."

Beliel shrugged aside the comment and studied the other man. Nix cleaned up nice, and finery fit him like tailor-made clothing. "Good thing Madison was in charge of your wardrobe for the ceremony. Probably best you didn't come to the ceremony in your worn-out, holey jeans."

The former Sherlock shot him the bird before getting back to work on his tie.

Micah was about to rib him some more about his attire, when Madison burst into the room. Eyes shining bright pink, she demanded, "Where the hell have you been, Micah? It's thirty minutes until the wedding, and you've been off gallivanting who knows where."

Why'd he find her sexier when she was pissed off?

"Had a time sensitive lead on Elias." No point in detailing their run-in as it'd cause her to worry.

"Our wedding is time sensitive." She poked him in the chest, and he bit back the reminder they were already married.

Let her have her new day. He could be gracious enough for that...and spoiling her felt right. "Consider me chastised, kitten."

She gave a tight, frustrated groan. He might've backed off from his original plan of world domination, but there were many things he couldn't just accept and alter. Protecting her was his first priority. Seeking recompense against his twin was as much for her as it was for him.

Phoenix curled his palm around her nape and slowly drew her against him. "Can't believe I'm saying this, but cut him some slack, baby. He's on time, and all spiffed up for you."

"*And,*" Micah added with a devilish grin. "I was defending your honor."

She snorted, calling his bluff. Micah could lie to anyone except Madison and his siblings. A mistruth would burn his tongue hard enough he'd cringe from the pain, which would out him as a liar. Likewise she couldn't fib to him. Because he didn't recoil she knew he spoke the truth. "You are defending your pride."

Yeah, he could admit to that truth too. But demons held a different code of honor, and if he allowed this slight to go undefended, he'd lose their respect. "I told you to let it go, Micah. Nothing good will come from revenge against your brother."

"Satisfaction." He felt his eyes ignite with his passion and knew they saw the kingly reddish-orange. "I *need* the satisfaction of revenging the wrongs he's committed against you. I cannot just let it go. *He must pay.*"

Madison released a weary sounding sigh, but he saw the flash of pink in her eyes. "I don't want to argue with you about this. Not today."

"If he doesn't do this, baby," Phoenix said against her hair. "He'll lose respect among demons."

He'd have thanked the Ark of Heaven, but before he could, she said, "So this is about peer pressure?"

The King of Hell bristled at the catty term. Fuck peer pressure, he did what he pleased, when he pleased, and how he pleased, but showing weakness even to one of his angelic-siblings could incite a rebellion.

"No," the former Sherlock shook her just a little. "Baby, come on, let's bust his balls another day. Blood and revenge shouldn't be on the agenda today." He shot Micah a hard glare. Micah shrugged, and Phoenix kept talking. "Today is about our commitment to one another."

"I've already shown my commitment to Madison."

"This isn't a competition, Micah." The look all over Phoenix's face clearly asked him to drop it.

"You'd lose if it was." Less than certain of that outcome, he'd never admit to defeat graciously.

Madison smacked him on the chest. "Enough."

Loving it when she got heavy-handed with him, he grinned and gave her a hard kiss.

"I picked both of you," she said, voice rough, after he pulled away. "That's what matters. Now, let's not keep the guests waiting, and let's get hitched."

"Again," Micah pointed out. "First time still counts for us."

He caught Phoenix's eye-roll. "You're as high-maintenance as some women, Micah. Not you, baby, but other high-maintenance women."

Madison huffed. "Be glad you're hot enough to eat, Micah Dominus, or I might boot you out of this marriage."

Not a chance in Hell of that happening, but he kept that thought to himself. She loved him despite his 'evil' ways—her view, not his. Some might disagree with his assessment, but he'd been created by the purest source...God. Micah'd birthed Madison from the vilest lot of Father's divine goo, but in spite of her conception, she remained good-hearted in a way he'd never been. The only one of them capable of true evil was Madison, since she was a demon at heart.

That is a reality I have trouble comprehending.

Born to do bad things, she'd overcome her base instincts and chose her own destiny. For that reason alone, he'd fallen in love with her. Yes, he'd loved her during their marriage, but in a way an individual loved

92

a pet or possession. It was her spitfire and gumption to gainsay him, that'd had him fall for her in a way no other angel—fallen or otherwise—ever had.

Chapter 10

NIX WAITED BESIDE Micah for Mads to join them. Shifting from foot to foot, he wondered what could be taking her so long. Only his family, Alessa, Petra, and the two dragons were in attendance. Other than Zenny, of course, but he would officiate the ceremony.

He spied Mads in the doorway. His soon-to-be wife was always gorgeous, but this concoction devastated him. The red silk of her dress hung straight to her ankles. It slashed low in the front exposing ample cleavage and skin. Tonight he saw no point in removing the strappy matching stilettos belted on her feet with tiny hooks.

Beliel cupped his shoulder and murmured, "We're lucky fuckers."

The King of Hell had never been more right. She pushed her long blonde hair over her shoulder, baring the creamy exposed expanse of her skin. God, she looked amazing.

With his head held high, Amos waltzed her down the aisle decked out in his finery. By the way he held his head high, Nix deduced the boy took his job

94

seriously. The hellhounds trailed them decked out in doggie finery. Watching her wrangle the hellish canines into those clothes had been entertaining. Somehow the red bows Mads attached to FiFi's ears stayed in place, but instead of dolling up the fur-baby, it gave her a creepier appearance.

Out of the clear blue and to Nix's surprise, Petra started to sing in a pure, angelic sounding voice that was unexpected for a succubus...."Here comes the Queen, All dressed in red, Wickedly sexy for her men of might, Enthralling me, Gliding to thee, Evil love joined for eternity."

Mads laughed at the twisted reworded rendition of *Here Comes the Bride*. Micah grinned and shot his daughter a wink. Nix settled on shaking his head, while mentally contradicting the 'evil love' portion of the song. The King of Hell could be considered evil, but despite Mads's DNA, she was anything but diabolical.

When she halted in front of them, she glanced between him and Micah, and Nix realized the high-heels placed her on Nix's eye-level. That would make it all the easier to fuck her standing up against the wall.

"Who gives this woman to these men?" Zenny asked, his voice clear and loud enough everyone in the room should have no problem hearing him.

"I do...and Taz." Amos indicated the mini-dragon that was wrapped around the boy's free arm, a sulky, growly-purr noise emitting from his scaly body.

"Taz is ticked off Amos is holding him and not me," Mads confessed sending the petulant creature mock pity in the form of a raspberry. The little monster loved being draped around her neck like a scarf. Nix could understand Taz's obsession with Mads, but his possessiveness went to the extreme at times. Like now.

"Same as the first time, I give myself to Madison," Micah said, confusing Nix, but it brought forth a smile on Mads's face, so she apparently understood his reference.

She kissed Amos on the cheek and murmured something to him.

"Love you, Momma." The boy gave her a hug before stepping away and taking his place at the front of the guests in attendance, next to Alessa.

Nix got an eyeful of the slit that ran up the entire length of Mads's leg. Strapped to her exposed thigh was the knife he'd given her for her thirtieth birthday.

Nix chuckled and pulled her against him for a quick kiss. "Love the blade accessory," he said against her mouth. "Sexy."

"Thought you might approve."

"Gorgeous as always, kitten." Micah kissed her shoulder.

It was a blur after that. They progressed through the ceremony, each speaking their "I do's" and "I will's" at the appropriate moments. When it came time to speak their vows, Mads stepped right up and proudly declared hers.

"Nix," she said as she whipped out her blade and cut her finger, smearing the small bead of blood on the two tree-like crystals that were manifestations of her souls. One-half human, the other demon. The red smear disappeared into the crystals, and she held them both up. "You're my true north, that guiding star that never lets me down and keeps me on track. Despite my monster, you love without judgment, see *me*, not the evil of my genetics. No one has ever accepted me the way you have, totally and without reservation. I see you too, the good and the bad. I love your demons, but most of all I love you even more for what you've sacrificed for me because you surrendered to your feelings without asking me to be someone I'm not...someone I can't be."

Stepping closer, her breasts brushed against his chest. "You smell good." She inhaled as her arms slid around his neck. Her fingers were soft glances against his skin as she secured the necklace on him. Meeting his gaze, she said, "I bind myself to you by giving you my demon-soul, a spot of my blood provides you with an open pathway to me. Grasp it and say my name, and you'll be taken directly to me."

Nix ran his fingers along her cheek, sliding them to the back of her neck. He brushed his lips across hers. "You're my sunshine, the center of my universe, Mads. I was a dead man walking, viewing the world through a black and white lens, with no goals in life except revenge, killing monsters, and hungering for peace. I accepted my fate, expected to die young and bloody because I had nothing and no one to live for. Then you crashed into my world and brought techno-color and excitement into my life, somehow calmed the bloodlust of my hatred, and taught me to love without restrictions. Gave me love without judgment." He slid a dragon-scale-crafted ring onto her finger. It blazed on her finger like lava. "You are my breath, my sole reason for living, and more than I ever dreamed for my life."

She rubbed the ring with her fingers, her voice gruff with emotion. "I feel your magic in it."

"You gave me part of you, so I had Amos use his magic to help me shove a piece of my soul into your ring while sealing it inside with hellfire. But, you gotta know, baby, that you already own all of my heart and soul."

She palmed his cheek and mouthed, "Love you, my Sherlock, so very much."

"With this kiss, I wed you, Mads," Nix breathed the words against her mouth right before hauling her against him and sealing their lips together in a kiss he hoped burned her as much as it did him.

"That's *my* line," Zenny grumbled.

Micah elbowed Nix out of the way and presented his ring to Mads, holding it up to the light so she could see the way he'd captured his angel dust into one solid band. The sparkly blue material was almost blinding. "No diamonds this time, kitten, instead I'm giving you *me* like Phoenix gave you part of him."

"Wait...me first." She held up the other crystal, the

one Micah had worn until she removed it when she stabbed him in Hell. "Micah, you were once my knight in shining armor, saving me from hellish parents. I loved you then not because you rescued me, but because you were the first to teach me to love myself. I've been infatuated with you since I was a child, loved you since I was fifteen, but I fell *in love* with you only recently. Thank you for adapting and learning to love *me* and not the monster you wanted."

Nix rubbed her back, relishing her bared skin against his palm, as she secured her soul around Micah's neck.

"Madison, nothing has changed since the first time we wed. You're still the master of my universe, my heaven, and my salvation. I crafted you because I was lost and craved a different future. Before you I only existed, blind to what it really meant to live, ignorant of what I truly wanted and needed out of eternity." Tears shimmered in Mads's eyes, but Micah went on. "You taught me how to really love someone, wholly, and without reservations. I would sacrifice everything I am for you."

Expression soft and shining with love, she traced her fingertips along the King's jaw. "I wouldn't really love you if I asked that of you."

Micah kissed her wrist. "I love you enough to make the offer, kitten."

"I love you, too. You're still the King of my heart..." she slid a glance at Nix. "Okay, you're co-King of my heart."

Beliel chuckled and kissed her forehead. "I don't deserve you or a joint relationship with Phoenix, but I vow to you I'll be a better husband this time around, and I'll forever support, cherish, and love you in good times and bad. Your wants, desires, and safety will take precedent over mine."

With a twisted smile, she leaned in and whispered, "You're too selfish to keep that vow, but I love that it's a genuine pledge. *That* is what matters." She smoothed away the frown lines that drenched Micah's forehead.

"Don't fret. Crazy as it might sound, part of why I love you is because of your selfishness. I love Nix because of his sacrificing nature. Without those traits, y'all wouldn't be you."

She squeezed both their hands, as her crystal genie pronounced them husbands and wife.

The reception afterward overflowed with alcohol and food, and his family surprised him by embracing the festivities. Not that the newlyweds were around long enough to participate because within half an hour Micah shoved them through a portal from the ceremony straight into Hell.

Chapter 11

MADISON LAUGHED WHEN they landed in Hell. "You're impatient, husband." Impatient like he wasn't already making love to her night after night.

"More than is decent." The King of Hell yanked off his jacket and tie before slowly working the first button on his dress shirt through the hole. "Phoenix bears your sigil, I wish to wear it."

Her demon's response could only be described as a satisfied purr. Marked with her sigil would verify he belonged to her demon, and while it wouldn't hold the same meaning on Micah as on Nix, Usha recognized the significance of his request.

Her Sherlock licked down her spine, causing goose flesh to erupt along her skin and set her libido into overdrive.

Two buttons undone on Micah's shirt, Madison took the single step necessary to be in his personal space. She knocked his hands aside, and their gazes met. After curling her fingers around the lapels of his shirt, she yanked hard. The skin-stitched floor cried out as buttons pinged and skidded along the surface.

Flattening her palms on his pectorals, she ran them

along his shoulders and down his arms to remove the garment. The material caught on his wrists and bunched up, shackling him in a flimsy hold.

"Use your hellfire to brand me, kitten. Right over my heart."

She tapped the area where she'd stabbed him with the dragon blade in Hell. "Here?"

He nodded.

Madison pushed him backward until his legs hit a chair. "Sit," she ordered with a slight nudge against his chest.

Micah complied, with his hands still restrained behind his back.

She inched her dress up until she could climb up and straddle him. Wanting Nix to be a part of the branding, she twisted to reach out to him to draw him closer, but he'd followed. He cupped the back of her head and leaned down to kiss her, while his other hand circled and cupped her breast through the silky fabric.

With his thumb swishing back and forth along her nipple, her Sherlock lifted his head and nodded toward Micah. "Get on with it, baby, so we can make love to you."

While Nix toyed with one nipple through the fabric of her dress, he pushed his free hand inside the dress to cup the other breast. He licked the outer shell of her ear as her finger heated up with her hellfire. As she lowered her hand to sear her sigil into Micah's chest, Nix sucked her earlobe into his mouth.

Madison sat back when she completed the sigil.

He looks finer than sin with our symbol of power.

A-freakin'-men, she agreed with her Lynx.

When it was over, her King kissed her until her toes curled, and she buried her fingernails in his shoulders. A ripping sound rent the air, and his arms lifted to indicate he'd torn the fabric of his shirt. The material vanished a moment later in a brief burst of flames. Micah kissed along her cheek as he dragged a finger down the center of her body over her dress.

"Za vila," *Be gone*, he uttered in Xapil, and her outfit vanished in another eruption of hellfire.

Micah set her on her feet, and Nix cuddled against her back, placing moist kisses along her shoulder. The composition of her Sherlock's suit contrasted against her nakedness. Even Micah still wore his slacks, and her sigil burned like coals on his chest.

As she watched, her King shifted into his angel persona, his wings rising high over his head to flank both sides of his body. He showered her and Nix with angel dust.

"Fuck," Nix buried his face in the hair at her nape. Angel dust amped up his libido and in Nix's words, made him harder and hornier than was humanely normal.

Holding Micah's gaze, Mads reached back and cupped the back of Nix's head, while circling her nipple with one of her free fingers and raking angel dust off the tight peak. Micah's eyes blazed with fire. She popped the digit into her mouth and sucked off his angel dust, moaning at the sweet elixir that incited a hum from her succubus.

Micah smiled and moved down her body using his mouth, tongue, and teeth on her. As her King of Hell rolled a nipple through his teeth, Nix angled her head to the side and fucked her mouth with his tongue as his hand suddenly slid between her thighs, pressing angel-dust-laden fingers inside her without any forewarning.

Even though she was already wet for them, Madison gasped at the sudden penetration.

Micah suddenly shifted downward, placing ticklish licks against her belly, leaving her shuddering in Nix's arms, and gasping for oxygen as the angel dust shocked her nervous system worse than any known manmade narcotic.

"Pretty demon eyes," Nix said staring at her.

Micah dragged his teeth along her thigh, causing her pussy to clench in response. "Give me your Queen flames."

Every time they entered Hell he wanted her coated in her flames. Practice, he explained the first time. The more she engaged her magic, the more connected she felt with the fiery realm, and the practice increased her proficiency.

Noaal wqupaj...Queen flames, she thought, and blue fire erupted along her flesh and power streamlined into her.

Flames consumed Micah's head when he licked her thigh neighboring the area Nix continued to slowly pump his finger into her channel. Immune to her flames, he rubbed his face against her, while extending his mojo to protect Nix from harm.

Welcome back, Raguel said in her head. *As much as I'd like to watch, your Ark of Heaven wouldn't appreciate the peek.*

Hielel acknowledged her with a nod and a firm mental door shutting in her face.

Elias gave only a slight ping on her radar, but she could locate him if she wanted.

"Are my brothers out of your head?" Micah mouthed the sensitive flesh just about her pubic region.

"Yes."

Good, he telepathed as he clenched the edge of her panties between his teeth and dragged them down her thighs. His palm landed on the inside of her ankle, and his hand skimmed upward until he could join Nix and press a finger inside her.

The fuller penetration extracted a moan from her, and she turned her face into Nix's neck. She rocked her hips into their touch as they pumped into her together.

"Phoenix, remember your *first* time after your Fall?"

"Yes." He sucked on her earlobe.

"That happens tonight."

Nix stopped sucking on her ear, and Madison frowned, trying to process his sudden disquiet she sensed. "Are you sure she's ready?"

"Ready for what?" Madison buried her hand in Micah's hair and held his head steady so she could stare into his eyes.

"Trust me." Beliel flicked a finger over her clit, and her hips jerked at the unexpected contact.

Trust wasn't an issue, but the way his eyes glowed with apprehension sent a squirrel of doubt twisting through her belly. Micah plotted something even Nix expressed concern over.

"You won't do perverted things to me, Micah."

The King of Hell mocked her with a grin. He removed his finger from her pussy and licked her arousal off.

Nix chuckled and said what Micah's grin implied. "Mads, baby, we already do perverted things to you." He dragged his mouth along her throat and whispered straight into her ear, "And you're wet for the perverted things you know are about to come. *You* included are about to come." She shivered at the double meaning. They always made her come more than once. He took a couple of steps backward, drawing her with him. "Maybe we should start by me licking your pussy while you suck Micah's dick."

They came up dead to the edge of the mattress. Nix moved out from behind her to stand in front of her, while Micah removed his pants. She held Micah's stare a long while until he elevated his eyebrows. She recognized that look. It indicated he wanted *her* to present herself for his feasting.

Micah wrapped his hand around the base of his cock and stroked. He could climax five times back to back and still keep going. His stamina eclipsed hers and Nix's, but just a taste of angel dust and they would join him again.

She sat on the edge of the bed and would've scooted to the middle if Micah hadn't axed her plans. "No. Roll over and crawl to the center of the bed."

She ignored his bossiness in the bedroom because his proclivity to fuck her hard doggy-style, delivered mind-blowing orgasms.

He gives us mind-blowing orgasms in every position. Usha made her case with flashbacks of previous exploits.

As Madison rose and faced the bed, she told her demon, *Nix isn't a lightweight.*

Never said he was.

Once she was positioned on her hands and knees, Nix cupped her mound and pressed two digits into her core. She whimpered, but knew this served as the warm up, and anything to follow would only be better.

A slow couple of pumps, and then Nix instructed, "Move to the center."

With Nix's fingers inside her, she crawled to the center of the bed. Each shift of her body adjusted his digits filling her just enough to tease her. Once she reached her destination, she felt the bed dip near her feet and knew Micah joined them. She twisted to look at them over her shoulder.

Both her men knelt on either side of her near her ass. Only Nix remained dressed. Micah was clothed in his angel. When he caught her eye, he doused her in angel dust again, lightly coating Nix as well.

"Stop that shit," her Sherlock shot a glare at her King.

"Quit your bitching, Ark, you know you'll thank me later."

"*I'll* thank you later." *Me too*, her demon piped in.

"I'll hold you to that, kitten." Micah nipped her ass and slithered his tongue where Nix's fingers probed her body.

"Mmm...." she moaned, indulging in the sweet feel of penetration and being tongued. Her men drove her mindless in bed. Micah had a tendency to piss her off and push her limits in and out of bed, but she guessed—

She jerked when he rimmed her ass. He touched her there frequently and each time was a shock. Her demon wanted him to push her further, but Madison elected to remain with the status quo of no ass play.

Nix pumped his fingers slow as Micah swirled his tongue against her backdoor. "Stay ass up, baby, and relax your head and shoulders on the bed."

She went into position and groaned at the deeper penetration the angle lent. Micah spread the cheeks of her bottom and dug his tongue in deeper. Pleasure morphed from her belly and heated her body. Madison strangled on a moan.

"Trust me?" Nix asked.

"Yes." And she did, with everything. Her life, her body, her heart, and even the piece of her soul she'd given him.

"Trust Micah?"

She stuttered. "Y-yes." A slight sting hit her tongue, which ousted her as a liar. "I don't trust him to not push my limits."

A slight shift of the mattress, but from her angle she couldn't discern Nix's movements.

"Focus on trusting me, Mads."

Micah bit her ass-cheek again and swirled his tongue over the sting. When he spoke, his mouth moved against her flesh. "You wound me, kitten."

She could feel the slight curve of his mouth, so she knew he teased.

"Taste her, Micah." Nix removed his fingers and slicked them along her anus.

Micah rimmed her again. She fisted the sheets and turned her face into the mattress, stifling her moans. That felt way better than she was comfortable admitting.

"I want my mouth between her legs," Nix said, and the eager tinge to his voice had her demon so giddy she practically cartwheeled in Madison's head. He'd been the one to teach her how good oral sex could be.

Micah shifted his weight, and Nix settled between her legs beneath her. Madison bowed her back so she could peek at him and reached a hand down to run her fingers through his hair. He slanted his head back just enough that their gazes caught. From this view she could see and feel Micah straddling Nix's chest.

"Hold on, baby." No other forewarning, Nix just wrapped his hands around her thighs and pulled her pussy down, snug to his mouth.

Madison cried out at the first lap of his tongue through her folds. A thumb entered her core—had to be Micah because Nix's hands remained tight on her legs—and then the thumb shifted upward to spread her arousal over her ass. Micah licked the moisture away and repeated the steps over and over again, just as Nix repeated his swipes against her clit until her belly began to clench and her pussy throb.

"If you don't stop I'm gonna come, Nix."

Nix kept going. If anything, his sucks and licks grew more focused. As heat spiraled from her core, Micah's thumb penetrated her pussy, delved deep and exited her body. She whimpered at the loss of penetration.

"Phoenix," Micah said. "Now would be a good time."

For what? Nix's response was to suck hard on her clit.

"Oh, gawd," she moaned and would've humped his face if they hadn't trapped her in position.

Micah's thumb pressed into her ass.

Madison gasped at the sudden invasion and pushed up, but the slight sting set off her climax like a lightning strike, and she went limp. While moaning her release, her demon latched onto them to force their climaxes.

"No!" Micah clamped his hand on the back of her neck. "We're not joining you in release. *Fuck!*" He bellowed the final word when her demon wrenched harder, determined to see their climaxes.

He curled his hand around her throat and yanked her upward to her knees. His thumb remained inside her ass, wedging a little deeper at this new position. Nix circled her opening with the tip of his tongue, lapping up her release.

She peered down at her Sherlock, his green eyes

locked on her as he ate her out. Her clit twitched wanting more of that action.

The slight burn in her bottom reminded her where her husband had gone without permission. Although it hadn't hurt the way she'd anticipated. "Remove your finger from my body, Micah."

"You like the way it feels." He pumped it slow.

Yes! She ignored her demon.

"No." Burning hit her tongue, and she cringed a little at the sting.

"Liar."

Some days she despised her inability to lie to him. "I don't think—"

"Stop your goddamn thinking." Harsh words whispered against her ear. "No more holding back. You're going to release your demon. All of it."

Usha was giddy with the possibility of being set free. Madison only allowed her out in small doses, never *all* at once because she must maintain total control.

"That's dangerous." Madison had no idea what would happen if she granted Micah's request.

"Not in Hell. If you're going to give up control this is where it should be tested. Tonight's a special night. We're solemnizing our marriage and giving all of ourselves to one another."

Anal sex is damn sure all of me, she griped at her demon.

I want it. You want it. Stop pretending and let go. Usha scratched at the flimsy wall that Madison trapped her behind.

Nix circled her clitoris, and she jerked at the flirty caress.

"I might lose myself, not be able to get back or know what she does when she's in total control." A valid fear, at least she thought so.

"Madison, you'll always be in the driver's seat. Stop fearing your demon. It's a matter of simply letting go, setting yourself free to be you. I'll protect you, draw you back if needed. I doubt you will. But you'll never know if you don't try." All through his words, his thumb continued to move in and out of her ass.

She hated it and loved it. The duality of her reactions, shame over her pleasure, and the slight sting that morphed to bliss, discomforted her, and her first thought was to run like always.

The temptation to give in to what he wanted was strong too. Curiosity at what it'd be like to allow her demon full access, to feel all of her at the forefront instead of just increments of her, served as a strong enticement to give Micah and Nix what they asked for. Usha came in handy, made her stronger, but she dominated her demon out of fear of the "what ifs" and "could'ves".

Beliel kissed her shoulder as Nix drove his tongue into her pussy. "Let go totally, and trust us to guide you back. I promise, you won't need us to guide you back." He nipped her ear. "Besides, when have I ever been wrong about what your succubus needs? Trust me when I tell you your succubus *needs* what I'm going to do to you."

Her breath hitched. She *knew* what he intended. "Anal sex."

"Yes." Micah licked the shell of her ear. "But more. So much more. As I feed you my cock, I'll feed you my seraph, my love, and Phoenix will give you the same. I'll wrap you up tight in King magic. How much bigger do you think these flames will become when we're connected?" The flames shrouding her were only a small buzz of fire. "You think we can make them change colors? Make them spark?" His hand relocated off her throat and slid down her body until his fingertips pressed against her clit and circled slow as Nix fucked her with his tongue. "We'll penetrate you together after you're comfortable with me inside your ass. Slow increments, kitten." He pushed his thumb deep into her bottom and circled it. "Does that hurt?"

"No."

"Phoenix, undress so we can make love to our

woman. See if we can make her demon submit to us and give us what we wish."

"She'll never be submissive, Micah," Madison said as Nix wiggled out from underneath her.

Micah's teeth scraped across the column of her neck as the swishing sound of Nix removing his clothing hit the air. "I know a thing or two about succubi. In the bedroom, I'll own her."

He sounds so sure of himself.

"We'll own her." Nix flung his shirt over his shoulder and kicked aside his jeans. She watched him as he retrieved a bottle of lube and climbed onto the bed to converge with them in the middle.

"I've not agreed to anything, Nix." She gave the bottle a pointed glare.

He squirted the clear liquid into his palm. "You're not saying no and that's as good as a yes."

"Madison, release Usha." Micah ambushed her with another dousing of angel dust.

He never plays fair. She groaned as he applied a dollop straight over her clit.

"My turn, Micah." Nix tossed the bottle onto the mattress beside them and shuffled into her personal space.

She met his green gaze. "Ni—"

He cut her off with a kiss, driving her head back to rest on Micah's chest. With their tongues roping together, she decided her men were so smooth they must've seduced others together a time or two. Instead of irritating her, their seduction enthralled her.

Nix thrust his hand to her bottom as Micah removed his thumb from her rear. But only a few seconds lapsed before Nix was filling her forbidden hole with a slippery finger. She groaned into his mouth as he pumped into her.

"I'm scared," she muttered against his lips when he gave her a moment to breathe. "What if it hurts?"

That's so lame, you're not scared, you're freaking out because you're excited, and you think it's wrong. Like Micah, Usha never pulled any punches.

Micah fumbled with the lube, but the way he moved against her back she assumed he slicked his dick. "Kitten, you're a succubus. Sex is part of who you are. How you feed. Do you think your demon would let you hurt? Much less us?"

"I hear some people like pain."

Nix scraped his scruffy jaw along hers. She tried to nip his chin, but he pulled away with a teasing grin. His finger went deep. "If it hurts say stop."

She felt Micah tense behind her. "It'll never be repeated if you don't like it." He pushed her hair off her nape and pressed a moist kiss there. That spot was as sensitive as her clit. "Trust us and release your demon, kitten."

"If it hurts, I'll make you both bleed."

"I like that shit so you're welcome to make me bleed all you want anyway."

Madison dropped her head back against Micah's shoulder and laughed. *Kinky bastard.*

Nix added a second finger, her breath stuttered out, and she shot a glance in his direction.

"Hurt, baby?" Despite his question, he kept thrusting as if already knew the answer.

Usha snorted. *You're practically coming with his fingers in our ass. Yeah he already knows the answer.*

"No." She sounded breathy to her own ears, but right or wrong no longer hit her moral meter. Pleasure was all that mattered. She reached back and trailed a fingertip along Micah's jaw. "You wanted my demon. Here she is."

Madison lowered her shield and let her demon free. The black and white tendrils of magic burst into her vision, detailing Hell's power.

Nix pumped his fingers into her ass quicker. She grabbed his nape in a hard grip.

Micah curled an arm around her waist, and his hand dove between her legs. One of his fingers entered her pussy and together he and Nix pumped...one in her cunt, and two in her bottom.

"Madison, you *are* your demon."

That was something she hadn't really gotten until this moment. She chatted with her other half as if Usha existed as a separate entity, while keeping her mojo caged until she required its usage. With her Lynx on top even now, she realized she remained in control. She regulated herself, while her magic shrouded her and lent clout among other paranormal creatures.

"Usha's just your demonic name," Beliel went on, "the one that gives followers power, in exchange for you owning them. Embrace her and free yourself."

"Do wicked things to me." And she meant it. She craved for them to teach her the joy of all things sensual.

She gasped when Nix scissored his fingers.

"Hurt, baby?" He watched her face as if he attempted to gauge her reaction.

"No."

Micah circled her clit a few times, before feeding her pussy two of his fingers. Sandwiched between her men, the King caught her mouth with his and stole her whimpers of pleasure. They pumped into her, giving her a small taste of what was to come, while teaching her to crave the debauchery.

Another orgasm was in reach when Micah removed his fingers and instructed Nix to lie down, with her on top of him. Nerves tripping over one another, she bit back the request to halt. She wanted to experience everything with her men, show them she feared nothing, not even a little thing like anal sex. That Usha bit her tongue and threatened to mentally abuse her if she chickened out now probably went a long way in staving off the request too.

Her Sherlock pulled her into position, anchoring a hand on her lower back, with his cock butting against the entrance to her cunt. His other palm cupped the back of her neck and added slight pressure until their gazes locked. "Relax. He'll go slow. Trust us to give you nothing but pleasure, baby."

"I trust you, Nix," she said, her heart tripping as she

felt Micah's thighs snuggle against the back of her legs. "Last chance to say no, kitten." The head of Micah's cock wedged against her backdoor.

"Bull." She'd have tossed a glance over her shoulder, but couldn't with the way Nix held her positioned. "You'll stop if I ask even if you're halfway in."

Micah's only reply was a clench of his hand on her hip, and the forward press of his cock into her forbidden channel. Madison's fingers curled into the skin-fabric of the bed linens, and she held her breath.

"Relax," Nix mouthed, his eyes dilating, as Micah pushed into her. His excitement bled into her like her skin soaked up his seed. It fed her demon just as good too.

Beliel's advancement caused her vision to blur and her toes to curl.

"Goddamn," Micah grunted out, halting his advancement as he ran his palm along her spine. "You feel good, kitten."

Fuck yes, Usha drawled in a thick voice. *Feels so goddamn good.*

Madison couldn't disagree, so she closed her eyes and remained silent as she processed the foreign invasion as he went back to inching into her. Her breath returned when his hips snuggled against her ass. Micah pulled back just a fraction and then shoved forward with a hard nudge.

She gasped, and her eyes flew open.

Nix kissed her the moment their gazes sealed.

When they broke apart, Micah leaned over her back and whispered against her ear, "Knew you'd take me without a twitch of pain. A human couldn't have done it the first time, Madison." He executed short, but sharp pumps, his pelvis banging against her ass, as his cock speared her. "Your succubus feeds on sexual deviance."

Before she could formulate a reply, Micah clamped a hand on her shoulder and began to drive into her, long, slow pumps where it felt as if his head reached the tight ring of her bottom before driving back inside her as deep as he could go. Madison became lost in sensation as Micah rode her, and Nix kissed her non-stop, devouring her whimpers and cries.

Her pussy was throbbing when Micah stopped, pulled out completely, and invited Nix to join them. Madison never questioned his command, or felt renewed fear that she was about to be double penetrated.

No one said anything as Nix clutched her hips between his palms, and wedged his crown tight against her opening. "Look at me, Mads."

Only with the request did she realize she'd closed her eyes in an effort to savor every little nuance of sensation. She met his stare as he thrust up into her. Micah leaned over her back, caught her wrists between his hands and pushed her arms up and over her head. With her structure of support removed, she was forced to stretch out flat on Nix's chest. While she held her Sherlock's gaze, his breath panted against her lips as one of his arms circled around her back to anchor on the opposite side of her waist. His other hand curled over her ass, and he flexed his hips to thrust into her a few times.

When he halted deep inside her, she felt Micah pushing against her backdoor again. Once he had his head hooked inside her, he entered her in one forward thrust. Madison cried out, the unbelievable pleasure of being penetrated by both of her husbands staggering even to her succubus. Micah cuffed her shoulder with a palm, and tangled the fingers of his other hand in her hair, pulling enough her scalp stung. The position forced her to stare into Nix's eyes.

They rode her in unison then, one pushing deep as the other pulled almost all the way out. Their timing was perfect, proof they'd achieved the mastery of their lovemaking during Nix's Fall.

The orgasm struck Madison by surprise, and she screamed her release. Somehow her demon kept her wits about her without hijacking Nix and Micah's climax to glutton on their pleasure. They continued to pump into her, Micah raining angel dust over them, and Nix cursing as he was coated in the light blue material.

Their lovemaking seemed to go on forever, Nix was red in the face from fighting off his release, so when he came, he was loud, and spurting hard inside her. Madison fell over the edge with him, crying out again as she climaxed.

"Goddamn," Micah mumbled just before he groaned and gave up his orgasm too.

They all collapsed in one big sandwich. *A MicMadNix sandwich.* In her head Usha giggled at the description, which set Madison off into a fit of laughter.

Beliel flexed his hips and pulled out of her.

Madison's laughter died on a moan. She'd just come three times, and his withdrawal still felt good and had her wanting to go another round.

Micah flipped her off Nix and onto her back between them. He leaned up on his elbow and peered down at her. "You okay, kitten? Was that a hysterical laugh or a good one?"

She reached up, palmed the back of his head, and pulled him down to her. "Very good," she said against his lips. "You'll fuck me like that again. Soon. That's not a request."

Both her guys chuckled at her demand. Before she could catch her breath, Micah's head was between her thighs reminding her how fucking skilled he was with his tongue too.

Madison stopped counting orgasms when she hit eight. Her demon King never ran out of stamina, but poor Nix had been fed angel dust three times. Not that he'd complained. She snuggled against her Sherlock, trailing her fingertip over the dragonhead tattooed on his shoulder. Micah cradled her ass against his pelvis, with his chest to her spine, and his finger created circles on her hip. Cuddled between her men...*this* was her happy place.

"I almost forgot, I have a wedding gift for you, baby." Nix slid his arm out from under her head and shifted off the bed.

Micah rolled to his back, taking her with him so that she half-reclined on him and half-reclined on the mattress.

"I didn't get y'all anything." She hadn't even though about it.

"You gave me you," Nix said, looking at her, his eyes darkening as Micah inserted his hand between her thighs once more.

"Micah," she whispered, a small protest that halted the moment he fit two fingers into her.

"Shh...I want you to come again after he gives you his gift. Let me play until then." Micah's lips moved against her shoulder as he spoke.

Nix retrieved something from the table beside the bed and then crawled toward them. With his face against her tummy, he kissed the area where she cradled their child. "You also gave me more than I ever hoped for with the baby."

He caught her knee and pulled her leg up and over, to anchor behind Micah's thighs. The new position opened her to Micah's touch, his fingers went deeper, and Nix watched as her hellish husband finger fucked her.

After a long moment, Nix lifted his gaze to her and opened the small jewel-sized box in his palm. Pandora's Box was nestled inside on a bed of red velvet. "You lost it in Hell when you killed Pandora. Zen said he could trap your power with the Box if he had it, but that didn't feel right to me. Since the day you were born, you've been a chess piece for different paranormal factions. No offense, Micah."

"None taken." The King of Hell's fingers went knuckle deep and he rubbed the heel of his palm against her clit.

Madison whimpered.

"Beautiful sound." Nix smiled, dimples blazing, but his gaze lowered for a moment to watch Micah's foreplay. He licked his lips and looked at her once more. "This is my gift to you, baby, so *no one* will *ever* govern you again."

She croaked out a weak "thank you", but Nix wasn't interested. Instead he gave Micah instructions, "I've got a front row seat to watching her go off, quit fucking around and make her come already."

Micah's chuckle tickled her ear, and sent shivers along her body. He clamped is hand around her throat and muttered, "Too cute, Phoenix thinks he commands me. Thanks to your Ark, I'll keep you on edge awhile just to annoy him."

And true to his threat, he brought her close more than once, only to back off and leave her frustrated. Begging got her nowhere, and even Nix seemed to enjoy her sexual frustration. The more excited they came by doling out sexual torture, the more she fed, but despite her succubus's gluttony, she wanted to come *so* bad.

"So goddamn sexy when you're right there on the verge of climaxing, baby," Nix said against her mouth.

"Do you want to come, Usha?" Micah's thick accent was heavy in her ear.

"Yes," she panted, rocking against his hand as Nix claimed her mouth in a long kiss.

When the kiss ended, Micah's smug voice infiltrated her lust. "Tell me who owns you, succubus?"

Beliel's vow that he'd own her succubus, jolted Madison. Usha was unfazed by the gloat, and responded immediately, "You do, Micah."

"And?" Confused, she panted as his thumb flick over her clit. "Who else owns you?"

"Nix. Micah and Nix. You both own me in the

bedroom."

She felt Micah's grin against her ear, but a second later she couldn't care less that he gloated because she came hard, and intentionally forced them to climax with her.

Her body absorbed the semen covering her, and she felt the nourishment in their ejaculation. Micah played games to feed her succubus, while demonstrating his love and teasing nature along with it.

Nix seemed to know the rules and played along.

When she could think again, she wiggled until she lay on her back between them. Micah peered down at her, while Nix nuzzled her belly with his face. She slid her hand into the short locks of Nix's hair, and wound Micah's longer strands around her fingers. She tugged just enough to get their attention. In response, Nix nipped her belly.

"Neither of you forget, *I* still *own* both of your climaxes."

Micah chuckled and gave her a fast, hard kiss.

Madison squealed into Micah's mouth as Nix buried his face between her thighs.

Her Kingly-husband braced her upper body with his. As she squirmed beneath him, he Eskimo kissed her and taunted, "I dare say Phoenix rose to that challenge."

Speak of the devil, he grunted against her pussy, wrapped his arms around her thighs, and anchored his hands on her belly to hold her motionless beneath him. Micah watched her closely, grinning when she began to make raspy noises.

Madison strained against them, as pleasure corkscrewed through her in a quick lashing type pattern she couldn't explain.

They win, they win, Usha sounded ragged in her head.

When she arched her head back into the mattress and her breath was dying in her lungs, Micah said, "There we go, Phoenix reminds you who *owns you* once again."

Madison shattered into a million pieces. When she finally oriented herself and opened her eyes, it was to Micah watching her. She was straddling him and had no recollection of getting into that position. Her eyes widened in surprise when he pushed into her swollen pussy. Just as she was getting her breath back, Nix slid into her ass and stole every ounce of air she possessed.

"Oh, my gawds," she whimpered in awe.

How can I keep going after that whopper of an orgasm?

You're succubus. That's how, Micah's words flirted through her head, proving she'd projected the thought to him. *You and I both can outlast Phoenix.*

She interpreted that to mean he'd fed Nix angel dust again. As Nix thrust into her bottom, she kissed Micah. Succubus and woman were unanimous. Micah and Nix were *her* gods in the bedroom. She'd submit to them for an eternity so long as they always made her feel this good.

Chapter 12

MADISON RAN HER fingertip along the rim of her glass. The iced tea was just the way she liked it...ice cold and too sweet, but oh, so yummy. Sweet iced tea was a Southern thing and while Nix loved her cooking, he wasn't a huge fan of her favorite sugary drink. She scanned the café, cataloguing all the patrons as humans in one quick scan.

Across the table from her Amos dived into his sundae and chattered about the new horror-flick they'd gone to see—*Zombie Apocalypse*—because he'd been "dying to see it".

"It was *soooo* cool when the zombie's head popped off and went spinning toward our faces." Amos dug his spoon in his ice cream, as she shivered at the memory of the gory 3D movie she'd been conned into watching.

Like we haven't already lived enough horror in our life, and he insists on watching more? She shook her head and peeked at Nix. Seated beside her, he sipped his coffee and ogled the door like a 007 agent. With her demon radar on high alert, she determined none approached. Not that any would offer her any headaches now that she claimed one of the five seats of royalty in Hell.

"I almost dodged sideways to miss the head." Nix set his mug on the table and winked at her son. "Very cool."

Madison rolled her eyes. Leave it to Nix to agree with her child. As if he sensed her mood, he settled his palm over hers that rested on her thigh and laced their fingers together. She gave him a small smile and entered the conversation, "Kinda gross if either of you ask me."

"Oh, Momma! You can't think it wasn't cool. It looked like it was coming *right at us.*"

"Yep...gross," she reiterated, chuckling inside at his exasperated expression.

"You're such a *gurl*," her eleven-year-old accused as if her gender was offensive. "Squeamish."

Well, that clarified everything. Madison chose not to engage. As his mother, he was obligated to think her uncool in every way imaginable.

Married a month to her guys, they hadn't had much in the way of peace, but her nights were rapturous. Micah and Nix took turns going off with Zen to hunt Elias. She wished they'd give the search a break, but when her husbands ganged up on her, she seldom stood a chance.

She'd also suffered the Catch-22 of being at the center of more than one knock-down-drag-out fight between Nix and Micah. Usha liked the excitement, and wanted to encourage the drama because she liked the angry sex afterward, but her practical side asserted they cut out the macho bullshit.

Just last night they'd come nose-to-nose with a disagreement. She still had no idea what caused that tiff. Both were tight-lipped, neither saying the reason for the spat. Usually their differences centered on what each felt was best for her, rather than who spent time with her. One-on-one time with them never posed a problem.

Unease prickled along Madison's skin like

sandpaper scraping over her flesh.

What's wrong? Zen's mental voice popped into her head.

Nothing. Just feel something, she replied back, his concern soothing her agitation. *A passing demon might've been the cause for prickling my senses.*

Panicking solved nothing, but Zen remained on high alert, determined to protect her.

Don't take chances with your lives, Madison. I'm coming.

Wait, she shot back. *Let me scan a little harder first.*

Another quick probe verified those present remained only human, so none of them could be the issue. Through the window, her gaze locked on a set of three men as they strode toward the establishment.

Not demons, something worse. Usha pushed just below the surface to survey the three men. Uptight fuckers with an agenda to snuff the life out of all paranormal creatures regardless if they were good or bad.

"Sherlocks," she said as one of them saluted her through the glass.

From the corner of her eye, she caught Nix's flinch. She couldn't imagine how difficult it was for him to see men he'd once aligned with now consider him their enemy.

Sherlocks, she told Zen. *We got this. Easy-peasy.*

Notify immediately if the situation deviates.

Madison sent Zen a mental eye roll at his command. Since learning she was pregnant, he was as determined as her guys to fight her battles for her.

"How'd you know they were Sherlocks?" Nix created circles on her hand with his thumb, but despite his random movement, she felt his tension.

"I can feel them." She broke eye contact with the lead Sherlock and faced Nix. "The one in the front...his aura is stark white and abrasive. His presence makes me feel like someone is dragging gravel or sandpaper across my skin." The aura of a paranormal reflected their power. A human's aura indicated emotions and choices made. "White doesn't represent goodness, Nix, but the iciness of his emotions. Given a chance, that one will gut us and enjoy it."

Silence descended as if the world was suddenly blanked to her senses. Weird. And a little unnerving. "That's Darren Shaw." At Nix's comment Amos glanced over his shoulder. "He sees the world in a black and white landscape, and he doesn't give a shit that Amos is only eleven. A monster is a monster, with no gray lines. The other two are brothers, Jack and John Bell."

The men entered as Nix spoke. As soon as the Sherlocks breached the door, they headed straight toward them full of cocky swagger and arrogant self-confidence.

Madison's demon crawled beneath her skin, eager to show them her monster. She watched them approach, ill-concealed weapons bulging beneath their clothing. The hunters stopped at their table. Darren Shaw's cool stare contradicted the warmth of his charming voice, "Nix." His glance flicked to her, before scuttling across Amos and returning to Nix. "Succubus...and offspring."

Amos continued to devour his sundae, seemingly giving his treat more attention than the Sherlocks, but Madison knew better. It was like a superpower. He paid attention and caught subtleties others missed, even when he appeared to have checked out of a conversation.

Nix gave Darren a hello nod, but remained silent. She could sense his power building. Even his aura grew choppy about the edges. Darren's however, remained bright white and flat, indicative of no emotion. The men with him held blue and purple auras, that'd grown static since contacting them. The Sherlocks would glory in defeating any one of the three of them.

Wonder what the Sherlock foundation would pay

them for one of us? Nix had once told her that the foundation paid top dollar to any hunter that took out high-ranking targets. Best she could tell, she and Amos were the highest, with Nix as a close second.

Touch my kid and they're dead. That's how I'll pay them, Usha intoned, her demon tone dark with conviction.

Got that right, Madison agreed.

"We've heard rumors, Nix." One of the Bell brothers—she identified him as Bell One—sidled away from Darren and moved closer to Amos.

She would've taken the action as a threat if she doubted her ability to diffuse them.

"Yep," the other Bell brother spoke up, stepping to the other side of Darren, surrounding their table. "Alarming rumors."

No, she telepathed to Amos when she felt his magic swirling and visibly witnessed a spark hit the spoon. Defending himself at this age wasn't something she was prepared for him to handle. He met her gaze briefly before yielding to her command and lowering his focus, continuing to eat his ice cream.

Patience wearing thin, Madison leaned against her seat and said, "Cut to the chase."

Darren met her gaze dead-on. "Rumors of Nix being in cahoots with the King of Hell, and shooting some of our friends. Almost killing them with golden bullets or some shit like that. Heard you met with Vela a few weeks back, and you refused a new type of exorcism."

"Rumors he's the descendent of Jesus Christ." Bell One flicked his thumb back and forth along the edge of his belt buckle.

A supernatural presence pinged her radar so suddenly it distracted her from the conversation, and she glanced about. Still nothing out of the ordinary.

Bell Two added, "Rumors you're carrying his child."

Hard to be rumors when all of it's true.

"I'm betting crossbreeding so-called Heavenly DNA with demonic whores is against the rulebook." Darren eyed Amos, disgust clouding the Sherlock's features right before he said, "He's abomination enough without adding another to this world."

"We've Demon Locked the building," Bell Two sounded and looked so smug, Madison would've laughed at his cockiness had she not spied an angel through the window across the street, verifying the heavy number of paranormal pings she'd just received. *Zen? Micah?* As she suspected, the telepathy bounced back, evidence a Demon Lock surrounded them. She surmised that'd been the silence that surrounded her moments ago. No matter, she still held an ace up her sleeve that even Nix had no knowledge of.

Nix eyed the three of them one at a time. "If every rumor is true, do you really believe you'll escape this hunt alive?"

"They've got supernatural help." She motioned toward the windows. "Angels." *And something else I can't identify.* Madison could feel the creature's power, strong, and crippling to all she turned it against. Usha coveted the magic enough she began to plot ways to claim the mojo. "There's at least two-dozen. I'm guessing that's why your friends are so brash."

She had to give Nix credit, he remained visibly relaxed, just peered out the glass to take note of the angels, while muttering about the Sherlocks surrounding them, "No longer friends of mine."

That he can remain aloof when we're outgunned is part of what made him an excellent hunter. Her succubus gloated with pride.

"What happened to you, Nix?" Bell Two removed his revolver from his waistband, but held it near his belly she presumed so none of the other patrons could see it and alarm the authorities. "Sterillium-laced bullets just for you, sweetheart. Courtesy of the angels."

"Don't count your chickens too soon, hunter." She'd died thanks to Sterillium seeds and angels, and Nix had brought her back. He'd almost drained his power to save her, which would've killed him. She'd swallowed those seeds willingly to save her son, but she'd be damned before she'd sacrifice herself again.

Her succubus laughed, a sultry sound of amusement and sex rolled into one. *We are so damned with our willingness to crucify humans.*

Claiming her seat of power in Hell lent her a dose of arrogance, as well. Because Hell packed her hits of magic with a stronger punch, she calmly considered her plan of attack.

Nix's fingers curled into his palm on the table, fisting until his knuckles turned white. "There are humans present."

"Like you care," Darren scoffed.

"I do care." Nix's hand glowed golden.

Madison suspected he readied to launch his deadly gold-bullets she'd witnessed him use a couple of months ago.

"Once upon a time, you fucking cared too."

"You were one of the best Sherlocks I knew." Darren sucked on his teeth, and the first uneven line in his aura appeared. "I emulated you, Nix, wanted to be like you."

"Your mistake, putting me on a pedestal."

"I doubted the goddamn rumors because there was no way my hero could be a sellout to his own race." Darren blew out a breath, his jaw hardening. "Then I talked to Gage last month."

Madison felt Nix's recoil more than she saw it.

"Even after hearing the truth from Gage I don't want to do this, but it's my job. You understand." His aura flat lined once again, evidencing the supreme control he held over his emotions. "The angels came to us, offered to protect the humans if we delivered your cunt-whore and her diabolical son to them."

"What of Nix?" she asked, curious what their plans for him were.

Darren shrugged. "They don't have a beef with him."

"Sherlocks do," Madison countered.

The hunter's aura spiked just a little, but enough she caught his agitation. "His demons will be cast out. For good this time."

"Fools. You're walking blind without a clue as to what you're dealing with." These hunters couldn't seriously be this ignorant.

Darren said nothing, but the tight creases at the corners of his eyes indicated she'd hit a nerve. In that moment, Bell One made the worst mistake of his life and whipped out his knife, pressing the tip to Amos's neck.

He'll be the first one I hurt. Madison wasn't sure which one of them said it, her or her demon, not that it mattered since they were unified.

Time slowed down, her focus honed on the weapon, and her son's pulse beating against the blade. One, two, three...power rushed her nervous system, and she reacted, pummeling the room with a blast of magic.

Madison vaulted to her feet. No one moved, not even a blink. She glanced around the café. Everyone was frozen in place like blocks of ice, without the ice. Even the clock behind the cashier no longer ticked off the seconds.

I froze time. Holy Hell! Must be a new power of mine. They kept manifesting, surprising her with each new one that surfaced. This one would've come in handy when the angels had held Amos hostage while forcing her to eat the Sterillium seeds to save his life.

Unsure how long it'd last, Madison strode to Bell One and yanked the blade out of the Sherlock's hand. She buried the knife to the hilt in his thigh. Striding to the door, she pushed it open. The angel across the street glared at her, as well as the unknown creature's power she coveted, but neither made any move toward the coffee bar. After a quick survey of the land, she spied the Demon Lock, but instead of tossing a fireball at the line in an attempt to eradicate it, she turned her head to the side and said, "Kur."

Her dragon materialized before her eyes, leaning

against the wall next to the door. "I see them," he said before she could ask about the visibility of the angels.

The dragon had to be why the holy-fuckers weren't approaching. Dragons were toxic to demons and angels, so they'd be cautious before inciting a commotion. Since her death at the hands of the Esdras angels, she went nowhere without at least one of her dragons, usually Kur. A safeguard for the baby she carried.

She quickly detailed what happened inside the establishment, and he glanced over her shoulder to verify the frozen status of the occupants. "Nifty trick. Would've been handy when the Esdras came for you."

That's what I said, Usha agreed.

"The one with the multi-colored hair...what is she?" Madison could sense she wasn't an angel, but otherwise couldn't identify the type of paranormal.

"Baltic." Kur's sapphire gaze held hers. "She's like Zennyo Ryuo, one of a kind."

"Her power is neutralizing other powers, right?"

The dragon nodded. "How could you tell?"

"I can sense it." Either that or the Baltic projected the details of her magic somehow, which would signify she wanted Madison to know her power. She stared at the Baltic, her waist-length hair fascinating and beautiful in its unique rows of colors.

I want her.

Well, she wanted the Baltic's power, to be more precise. She'd take the Baltic's magic after she captured the creature.

Once all threats are neutralized.

One step at a time. She could be patient. By the end of the day, she'd own the Baltic's mojo.

"She's one of the Cursed Souls like us dragons."

That got her attention. The Scrolls of Cursed Souls were divvied up into five small pieces of scrollwork that gave the wearer control over that particular faction. When the Scroll was placed on a person's body, the scrap melded to the skin and looked like a tattoo. Zen had possessed the dragon's Scroll and given Madison charge over them before she'd entered Hell to save Nix from Micah. The theory had been once she commanded the dragon army she'd hold an advantage over Micah. Partially true, things still hadn't turned out how any of them planned.

It seemed like ages ago, but it'd only been a few months. "I want her Scroll."

Madison didn't realize she'd spoken the thought aloud until Kur said, "Your wish is my command, my *Noaal.*"

It frustrated her that he insisted on calling her his queen, but she chose to ignore the title.

"The angel beside the Baltic owns her. That tattoo on his wrist is the Baltic's Scroll. The angel will have to be dealt with before you can claim the rainbow-haired devil for your own."

"Whatever you gotta do, Kur, make it happen. Should I kill the angel now or can you take him to Hell too?" She could suck his power if she got close enough, but it'd be easier if the dragons could scurry them both to Hell since the domain would solidify Madison's control over them, while eliminating their magic.

"I can get them to Hell, you don't worry about that." His tone held a flirty quality. "You'll inherit the angel's powers if you kill him. Are you sure you want them? Or do you want my dragons to take care of him?"

Unable to get a read on the angel's potential, she met the dragon's gaze once more. "What *is* his mojo exactly?"

"They're Scythe angels. They infest humans or demons with disease that always leads to death. A slow death." Kur nodded behind her. "They're starting to move in minute increments."

Facing the room, she noticed the slight shift in the people, along with a slow tick on the clock confirming time reengaged. Without wasting a second more, she slammed power through the enclosed area. Everyone and everything immobilized again.

She grinned her head off. *Gawd, that is amazing.*

No time to enjoy her newfound power, she shifted her concentration back to the Scythe angels. Demons were already her bitches, and humans offered no competition as was evidenced by the Sherlocks inside, so...."The Scythe's power is useless to me, so just get him to Hell."

Useless unless you want to kill a demon slowly, or even turn it on another angel. There was always that option, Madison agreed with her demon. Could come in handy. She'd consider stealing his mojo after the current predicament was settled.

"Get me Micah and Zen *after* you quarantine the Scythe and Baltic." Zen would no doubt argue against her necessity for the Baltic's magic.

If I have two of the Scrolls, that leaves me with only three more to locate...and own.

She ignored how power-hungry that sounded. "They should enter straight into the café so the angels can't see them. Tell Micah to block his presence. I can't telepath them with the Demon Lock, but I don't want it broken because I want the angels to think they have the advantage."

Chapter 13

ZEN TELEPORTED INTO the café seconds after receiving Kur's report. A quick glance about confirmed the dragon's account. Time had obviously been frozen. Madison leaned against a table, a satisfied grin demonstrating her pleasure at the display of her newest power. On either side of her, Sherlocks appeared as wax figures.

Her mojo escalated, often surprising him with how quickly she learned to micromanage them. This was a new one. Unexpected, but a convenient one to possess.

Micah portaled into the café, his mode of transportation a fraction of a second slower than Zen's. Madison's gaze welcomed her spouse, despite his murderous expression.

"You do this?" Zen nodded at the motionless occupants.

"Yup." Her eyes glittered with her demon, bright pink, with a hint of Pandora power encircling them, and her pupils burnt orange. She had every right to be proud of her conquest.

"How long does it last?" The fallen angel moved

through the crowd considering the scene.

"About five minutes, then I have to redo it."

Micah halted beside the Ark of Heaven. "Release Phoenix from the spell."

"I don't know how without releasing everyone," she admitted, tugging at her bottom lip with her teeth.

The chime above the door tinkled, a loud oddity in the near silence of the room. Kur strode inside. Despite the dragon's swagger and confidence, Zen was thankful the dragon took her safety seriously.

"You secure my new acquisition?" There went that demon sparkle in her eyes again.

Knowing that look boded ill, Zen bristled. "What acquisition?"

"Secured in Hell awaiting you, my *Noaal.*" The dragon pinned hair behind his ear. "We've deterred the Scythe angels from engaging."

Scythe angels? Zen flicked his focus to Micah who went rigid with the news.

"How'd you deter them?" The King's fiery gaze skimmed the terrain outside the windows.

Scythe angels weren't easily deterred, but then they held no need to touch someone to harm them.

"Iced them all into submission."

Micah smirked at Kur's reply.

Zen gave them credit for creativity. "What is secured in Hell?"

"I'm in possession of a Baltic."

The sheer eagerness of Madison's tone kicked Zen into precautionary mode. Legend held that a Baltic could neutralize all powers, and that only one of the species remained. Reality was only one Baltic had ever been crafted. She nulled magic, but not *all* magic. "Give me one reason why you should own the power of a Baltic."

"Give me one reason why I shouldn't," she countered, holding his gaze. The unsure woman he'd first met had been obliterated over the years, until confidence reeked from her in this moment as she challenged him.

"I can give you one, Zennyo Ryuo." Micah gripped the chin of one of the Sherlocks. "I recognize this one." Sherlocks are the least of her worries, they're easily defeated now that she's Hell-strong. Owning Baltic power protects her from her supernatural enemies, my angel brethren, as well as any other stupid motherfucker that'd make a go at her, which also protects our children."

Agitated, Zen flicked a glance in Micah's direction before returning his focus to Madison. His sole priority was to protect his family. His family consisted only of Madison, Amos, and the unborn offspring. Micah factored as only a pesky necessity to endure and play nice with because he offered safety to Zen's adopted kin.

Zen ignored the fallen archangel and said, "One reason, Madison, and don't tell me because you want it."

A week ago, she'd wanted the Durango's magic they'd discovered contaminating a neighborhood in Montana, terraforming the locale for her unborn child. He'd talked her out of consuming all of it by reminding her not all power was worth stealing and if she took the Durango's, the next time she was agitated she'd stink up the house like a skunk. None of them wanted that. Before that, she'd almost swigged a Salno dry, and all they were good for was killing nature, which was the antithesis of her Lynx magic, which created life. Taz for instance, was a perfect example of her life-giving abilities. As well as her ability to sow food and ripen it to harvest in a matter of hours.

He knew her Lynx drove her quest for more power, because it was her demon's nature to covet strength. Her demon struggled with her humanity, and he chose to serve as her moral compass. Yet, he couldn't dispute Micah's accuracy, the more dominance she could toss around, the less other paranormals would threaten her or instigate attempts at genocide.

Despite her upbringing and Micah's original design

for her, Madison was the strongest person he knew. Hardheaded, with a determination to map her own future without settling for the designs originally charted for her. Didn't matter she couldn't avoid her fate as a demon. That was genetics. Didn't matter that she'd accepted her role as the Queen of Hell. He'd realized before she had that some fates couldn't be denied. What mattered was how she utilized her destiny.

Madison, he began to prompt her with the question once more, but she cut off his mental prod.

"I've not yet decided if I'll take her soul." She gave him an offhand shrug, but her indecision rolled over his skin like suffocating oil. "The Baltic seemed so sad standing beside the Scythe angel that bears her Scroll. I refused Micah's slavedom"—the hellish King grunted at her description of his plans for her life—"how can I enslave the Baltic?"

Micah captured a fist full of her hair and demanded all of her attention. "Take it. You're the Queen of Hell. It's yours by right. Wield it just once and few immortals will have the balls to cross your path."

"Micah, I know you mean well, but is it *morally* right to take it just because I can?"

Her husband scowled. "A moral Queen of Hell. *Blasphemy.*"

Zen heard her mental apology, but only because he was in her head, snatching the snippets she couldn't hide from him. He was pleased when the words remained unuttered on her tongue.

"*Li.*" No. She tangled her fingers in Micah's hair and gave a smart tug. "Blasphemy is a Queen that'll allow the Kings to guide her conduct, or dictate her moral code. None of you would respect me if I caved to your wishes."

Baltic was born from the tears of slain souls, Zen confessed mentally into the silence, interrupting the couple's staring. *Sadness is an inherent part of her DNA.*

"Not just any slain souls, though, right?" Quick to

134

read between the lines, she released Micah and faced Zen once more.

The King of Hell scowled as Zen shook his head, and confirmed her statement. *Innocent Atlantean souls slain in the conflict against warring paranormal factions. Before I caged her with the Scroll, she wandered between innocents in an attempt to save them, but often failed.*

Madison sighed and rubbed her forehead with her fingertips.

"The timespell is wearing off. We can continue this idiotic discussion another time." Micah strode to the Sherlock beside Amos. He yanked the blade out of the hunter's thigh and licked the blood off the steel. "I'll secure the Sherlocks—"

"Don't kill them."

Frustration tightened Micah's features at Madison's command. "Death is too tame for what they deserve." He held up his hand to halt whatever she would've said. "They're Phoenix's people, so I'm leaving their fate in his gentle hands."

That reply unsettled Zen more than the idea of Micah seeking revenge. He had seen what the Ark of Heaven was capable of when he'd Fallen to Hell's designs before. Anyone could make the argument that Hell brought the worst out in people, but a man of Phoenix's caliber with his special genetics should've withstood the lull longer. And the heir of Christ had enjoyed the chaos he'd spawned.

"Immortal." Micah looked at Zen. "Transport Amos and Madison to safety, while Phoenix and I clean up here." The Fallen's gaze hardened when he spied his Scythe siblings through the windowpanes, all encased in blocks of dragon ice that sported flames around the edges.

"Screw safety, Micah, I want—"

"I'm *not* arguing with you over this." Micah's fingers tightened on the blade, his voice icy cold when he cut Madison off. "You're pregnant. Get your ass to safety."

Madison sent him a mutinous glare.

"He's right." Zen teleported Amos to his bedroom and when he returned for Madison, she remained in an eye-battle with her husband. "I'm not taking his side." He gripped her arm, and squeezed just enough to draw her focus to him. "I know you can take the hunters with ease, and I know it chafes your pride to walk away, but it's not running. It's practical. Wise." Palming her belly he rubbed back and forth. "They're more important than your pride."

"*They?*"

Leave it to her to pick up on that one word out of all he'd said. *Surprise*, he said into her mind as he teleported them home.

By the time they arrived safely inside her bedroom, she was mentally throwing up shields to lock him out of her head and thinking the most random thoughts. He understood her need for privacy, but there'd been little privacy between them during their friendship.

Kur arrived moments later, and extended his hand to Madison.

"Shut me out, but we still must discuss the Baltic dilemma." Zen would not be dissuaded.

The sister of his heart slid her palm into Kur's upturned hand and met Zen's gaze. "Sorry, but some things I have to decide on my own."

Kur transported her through a dragon doorway a second later.

Realizing she'd discombobulated him with her thoughts with the intention to flee, he would've cursed a blue streak, but that wasn't his style. Instead, he settled in and waited for her to return, praying she made the right choice. He would've felt better about that outcome had Madison held all the facts about the Baltic.

Chapter 14

MADISON AND KUR entered Hell straight into one of the cages personalized to Madison's power. The Baltic stood in the center of the room, hands at her sides, staring straight ahead without any expression, reminding her so much of Zen.

"Thanks, Kur. I'd like to be alone now."

The dragon studied the Baltic a long moment. He tugged his long fingers through his midnight-black hair, detaining the locks at the back of his neck. "Don't underestimate her, Madison. She's considered hell spawn or Zennyo Ryuo wouldn't have trapped her with the Scroll."

"Not planning on it." She understood his concern. But, as Queen of Hell that meant *her* power nulled the Baltic's while in Hell until Madison chose to release her. His worry for her was cute though, even if it was only because she was his Queen and bequeathed his loyalty thanks to the Scroll of Lost Souls.

His dark-blue gaze shifted back to Madison. "I'll be on alert and around the corner if you need me."

Nodding, she watched as he walked away instead of

creating a doorway. If she were a betting woman, she'd bet he remained within hearing distance.

She studied the Baltic, taking in her petite frame. With the multi-colored hair she looked like any other teenager. Her age was in her mature presence, not her appearance.

Madison stepped into the room and circled the creature, running her fingers along the wall. Souls screamed with each step. Faces appeared in the macabre tableau of the shifting walls and began to chant, "Kill...kill...kill...kill."

"*Joqalya,*" *Silence*, Madison commanded, and the damned souls submitted to her bidding. Her captive cast Madison a guarded glance. "You have a name, Baltic?"

Eyes remaining straight ahead, she shook her head, her hair shimmering like tinsel. "No name, only my designation."

"Like Zennyo Ryuo."

The Baltic's gaze shot to Madison. She couldn't be sure, but Madison thought fury might've flashed across the woman's face. "You know them?"

"Only one remains. He's my brother."

The Baltic's multi-hued eyebrows drew together in a tight frown.

Madison thought she understood the confusion, so she explained. "He's my adopted brother. He goes by Zen now. Would you like a name?"

Turning her head, the Baltic gazed straight ahead like before and shrugged her shoulders as an answer to Madison's question.

The Queen of Hell prowled around the diminutive female. More than usual, she felt like a giant next to the much shorter woman who topped out at five-foot max. She halted in front of the Baltic. "You let your presence be known to me before the angels attacked."

No emotion, not even a blink, much less a solitary move indicated she heard Madison.

"I have a theory. Care to hear it?" Again, nothing, the Baltic just stared through Madison so she continued to theorize aloud. "The angels never planned to attack. Nope, they wanted me to *think* they were going to attack. The Demon Lock was a nice touch, added credence to their mock strategy."

A slight crease fanned outward from the corners of the Baltic's eyes, before her black eyes shifted off Madison's throat and met her gaze.

"Surprised I figured it out?"

"Yes."

"Do you care at all about the Sherlocks that were used as scapegoats in the Scythe's plan?" Madison felt no sympathy for them even though they were in Micah and Nix's not-so-gentle hands. They'd turned a weapon on her son. Of course she held no sympathy.

"I hold no voice among the Scythe."

"I know. You're their weapon."

More silence from the Baltic, but she folded her arms across her middle as if she hugged herself.

"I possess the angel bearing your Scroll." A flash of something flickered in the Baltic's eyes. Wonder, maybe? Madison wasn't sure. "My dragons overpowered him and took him for me. He is quarantined, as well."

"How do you have dragons? The last I understood they were imprisoned in a chamber below Hell"—she glance around as if to say *this* Hell—"after the Scrolls were crafted."

Madison stepped into the Baltic's personal space. The tiny creature craned her head back to maintain eye contact. "I wear their Scroll. The Zennyo Ryuo that created the Scrolls is my brother. He gave me control over them."

The Baltic's eyes widened a fraction of a second before they narrowed and her mouth tightened. "What makes you special?"

"I don't understand what you mean."

"He trusts a Queen of Hell but trapped me, and I never willingly harmed anyone." The other woman's bitterness was evident in her voice if not her features.

"Your magic makes you dangerous to him, to all creatures." Madison understood why Zen bound her with the Scroll, but understanding and agreeing were altogether different things. Others tried to null her because of the danger she and her offspring presented, so Madison could empathize with the other paranormal. "You would do the same to anyone that endangers you."

"You don't see me nullifying your magic."

"This is my domain. Your magic is useless here unless I grant you access to it. I'm confident you would do anything to guarantee your safety." The Baltic turned mute once more, and went back to staring through her. "What I think, Baltic, is that your Scythe owner wants me to drain your magic, because if I do your power will forever null mine. Correct?"

A startled glance from the petite woman. "Yes."

Bitterness burned through Madison. She'd wanted to drain the Baltic's magic because she craved the clout to cancel out the power of others, but then she'd smartened up and realized all of the parties involved had been captured with no effort. Without a fight. No angel would ever go down that easily.

Mistake number one, you morons, Usha drawled. "Did your Scythe owner explain if I ingested all your power you would die?" The creature's sudden paleness was all the answer Madison needed. "I didn't think so. I'll make you a deal. Your Scythe owner will die today. His Scroll will come to me because I'm the most powerful in this domain." Madison indicated the cavern with a wave of her hand.

"Then you will become my new master."

Not a question, but she appeared to be so at ease with her future slavery that Madison grew uneasy. She wouldn't wish to be a slave to anyone, yet to place the Scroll on her body would give her mastery over the Baltic. "You'll be given limited freedom." Why she promised that, she was unsure. "The world is different, and I can't allow you to roam freely with your magic unchecked." Damn sure not unchecked and at her disposal so it could be used against Madison or her family. She required some security that the Baltic wouldn't turn her magic on them. "I offer you a blood covenant, possibly a friendship, and maybe even a family if all pans out."

"I'm listening."

Madison rubbed her slightly rounded belly. "You know I'm pregnant?"

The woman inclined her multi-hued head.

"Were you told my offspring is half Lynx-succubus and half Ark of Heaven?"

Rainbow eyelashes blinked over black eyes. "No wonder they want you dead. You and your child are an abomination in the eyes of Heaven."

"So I'm told." She thought she felt a flutter of movement from her infant.

Probably a protest against being called an abomination, Usha drawled, grunting her own displeasure over the slur.

"What are the terms of the blood covenant you offer?"

Madison was pleased the Baltic wasn't outright declining. "I'll need a nanny, one that can nullify the baby's magic until we can teach him or her to use it without the need to dominate all of mankind and the differing factions."

"What of your son?"

She shook her head. "Amos doesn't worry me the way this one does. As part of our alliance your magic is powerless against me. You have my protection, and you will wear my sigil, that makes you *mine.*" Her demon shivered in excitement over the prospect. "You'll acknowledge me as your mistress, owner of your soul. I won't require usage of your abilities unless my life or my family's life is in danger. In return you are granted unlimited freedom."

"Agreed."

"Don't you wish to think about it?"

"No. You offer me more than the Scythe ever have."

She's either reckless or desperate, her Lynx purred in her head. Madison agreed. "I will destroy your Scroll so it can never be used against you." The idea of returning it to the Baltic the way Nix had returned Pandora's Box unsettled her, so she went with her gut. She'd destroy it instead. "You answer to me and me alone. But...if you ever use your magic against any of my family or adopted family, with or without my knowledge, you will immediately be transported to Hell and tortured for all of eternity."

"I agree to your terms."

"Do you understand the ramifications of a covenant with Hell's royalty?"

"With clarity."

"You don't seek revenge against Zennyo Ryuo for enslaving you?"

"I hate him, but I've existed too long being utilized as a tool for revenge. I want no further part of it. I just want to live for once."

Madison couldn't decide if the Baltic was legit or not. "As part of the covenant, you're forbidden to lie to me."

"Deal." Before Madison could elucidate that the pact must be sealed with blood, the Baltic lifted her palm, and said, "Cut me and let us solemnize the agreement."

She felt her demon in her eyes and static prickled her fingertips.

The Baltic went to her knees, her gaze lowered. "My Queen, to a new era where I hope my service is only needed as protection for your family."

"Agreed." With her demon on the surface, Madison palmed the hilt of her dragon blade and slid it from its leather holster. She nicked her finger and held it to the Baltic. Without hesitation, the creature licked Madison's blood from the wound and elevated her hand higher. Madison dragged the tip of the knife along the Baltic's palm, smeared the life force over the edge and lifted the blade to her tongue.

In this moment she was the Queen of Hell making a

blood covenant rather than a succubus enthralling her victim. The outcome remained much the same since the Baltic would never be able to disobey her.

Madison secured the weapon back in its holster. "Now that the covenant is sealed, I ask you again, do you seek revenge against Zennyo Ryuo?"

"As I said, I hate him, but I'm done with revenge." The Baltic rose to her feet and met Madison's stare. "From this day forward, I forgive Zennyo Ryuo his transgressions against me."

Since the covenant wouldn't allow the other woman to prevaricate, Madison believed her. "Pick a name. From this moment forward, it's what you'll be known as. An individual rather than a designation."

Maybe it was hope that flared in the Baltic's eyes, but Madison couldn't be certain. Either way, the rainbow-haired creature said without a second thought, "Ginnie."

Very few paranormal creatures chose a last name, so she wasn't surprised 'Ginnie' offered no surname.

"Nice to meet you, Ginnie." It felt good to give someone liberty rather than the lifetime of bondage she'd known. "I look forward to our future together."

An hour later when she returned to Earth with Kur, the Scythe owner was departed, his soul trapped in Hell in a holding cell, and Madison had destroyed the filmy parchment that would provide another ownership over the Baltic. She located Zen in the library pacing. He stopped his stride the moment he spotted her and Ginnie.

"I didn't take her magic."

"Obviously," he said, but relief poured from his demeanor, which was unusual for his normally stoic state. "Thank goodness." He strode straight to her and embraced her in a rare show of emotion. "I worried the temptation would be too great."

"I figured out their plan."

"How?"

She sent the memories to him telepathically instead of giving him the verbal rendition.

"Smarter than the average cow," he said against her hair.

"Bear," she corrected with a chuckle. "Never call a woman a cow."

"Noted." He pulled back, clasping her shoulders in his palms. "I tried to tell you the effect the Baltic would have on your magic, but you left before I could explain."

"I realized."

"You're clever to comprehend you could control her another way. I would prefer to have possession of her Scroll, but this is your victory fair and round."

"Fair and square." She smiled. "There's no hope for you."

"My errors amuse you."

True. "She is no longer known as 'the Baltic'. Her new name is Ginnie, and she'll be the baby's nanny when it arrives."

He blinked at her, tossed a cautious glance at Ginnie, before telepathing, *Nanny?*

The babies are too powerful to act out the same ways Amos and I did.

His impassive expression gave away nothing. *Ginnie will nullify their magic?*

Until we can teach the babies to use their magic wisely, without greed, and for the safety of mankind, yes, Ginnie'll null their magic.

Wise move, he said. *I didn't think of it.*

"I gave Ginnie the room next to yours for now. She's agreed to give you a second chance."

"Welcome, Ginnie," Zen roped his arm around Madison's shoulders. "You'll love her cooking and be thankful you can't gain weight at the same time."

Madison grinned at him.

Zen popping off jokes wasn't a normal activity...at

least not in the presence of others.

"I can't remember the last time I ate something other than manna," Ginnie said, not able to appreciate the rarity of Zen's mood. "I look forward to tasting your fare."

Madison laced her fingers with his that draped from her shoulder. "Speaking of cooking, I should check on the pot roast I put in the crockpot this morning. We'll show you to your room, where you can shower, relax, watch TV, or even wander the house from there. However you spend your time is up to you. I'll have Amos come meet you and show you the way to dinner in a bit."

Ginnie nodded, and they led her down the hall to her bedroom.

"Don't get lost if you decide to roam," Zen told her as she hovered in the bedroom's doorway.

A smile quirked Madison's lips. "Let us know if you need anything."

That Zen chose now to tease instead of berating her for handling matters on her own, reminded her...

I love you, Zen. She hugged him to her side, as they left Ginnie in her room and headed to the kitchen.

I'm a loveable kind of crystal genie.

She laughed, surprised he referred to himself as Nix's derogatory nickname for him. *What's gotten into you cracking jokes like this?*

I'm happy you exceeded my expectations once again and survived a plan that should've been a success on the Scythe's part. It's how I would've come at you.

I have an excellent teacher. She gave him a pretend knuckle-blow to his chin. *Although eliminating my magic would've solved all our problems, so I'm a little surprised you wouldn't have preferred that outcome.*

Ripping magic from someone is like a death sentence, Madison. You would've never been the same again.

Madison pondered that a moment and changed the

subject. *You don't have to say it, I know you love* me *and not just my superior intelligence.*

Zen kissed her temple. *I do love you, but I see no need in saying the words when my actions prove my emotions for you.*

Ever practical, this was the man she knew. The scent of roasting meat wafted to her when they entered the kitchen. "Thank you for having faith in me."

He breathed deep. "Mmm...that smells good. You know," he said as he peeked into the crockpot with her. "It has suddenly come to me that my supporting you is proof a woman can win the faith of a man through his stomach."

Madison laughed, deciding Zen was trouble when in a teasing mood. Neither did she explain the true meaning of the saying. He was a hopeless cause.

Chapter 15

Three months later
Madison's former residence, Alabama

SINCE MADISON HAD wed her men, life had grown quiet. Maybe too peaceful. Any moment now, she kept expecting the bottom to fall out. The Birminghams' were on the road. Their relationship with Nix remained a little stilted, but she held hope it'd improve once the babies were born.

She'd texted Georgie a couple of times, and so far her replies back were slow, but at least she answered. Zoe was her best connection to the Birminghams at the moment.

"So..." Zoe said in a singsong voice. "You're really making this work with Nix and...Mic—King of Hell?"

"Yes." Madison kept her tone devoid of censure, but she was surprised the other woman had strayed into Micah territory. They normally talked about everything but her hellish husband. "You can call him Micah."

"I'd rather not get that familiar with him if it's all the same." A long pause emerged before Zoe finally continued. "Get him to detail how he broke Nix." The bitterness in her voice couldn't be dismissed.

"I know how it went down." Nix had related enough that Madison thought she understood the bigger picture. After Micah had his demon slice Zoe's throat and break Gage's neck, Nix had refused the King's offer. He'd remained steadfast in his decision until he thought Madison had been murdered. Everything had changed then. He'd made a pact with a devil to save her, only to discover afterward that he'd been tricked and Madison was still very much alive. His cousin, Gage, and his cousin's girlfriend, Zoe, however, had been very dead. In the end he'd accepted his heritage, and been walked through how to revive Zoe and Gage.

"Do you?" Disbelief tinged Zoe's voice. "Really? I don't think you can comprehend the vileness of it without all the gritty details."

Madison knew enough. The gritty details weren't necessary. Micah was a King of Hell. His ultimate gig was to wrench righteous souls from God's grasp. He'd also been on a mission, determined to win anyway he could.

"I'm not saying his actions were right, Zoe. I wish he'd taken a different approach, but I'm not going to stop loving him because of his bad choices."

How could she blame him while demanding mercy from others?

"I don't understand how you can be so forgiving." Horns blared in the background. Fitting with the mood Zoe was in. The noise also confirmed what Madison suspected...Zoe talked to her outside rather than in the presence of the Birminghams.

Clandestine conversations...what'd that imply about Nix's family?

"Nix sank an entire neighborhood killing men, women, and children. Innocents. Thousands dead because he sought revenge for my death." He'd been determined to amp up his power enough he could square off against Zen and get retribution for believing her immortal friend had killed her. "He would've murdered thousands more with the tsunami if Zen and I hadn't stopped him with Pandora power. You forgave him for his sins." Zoe sighed and Madison went on. "Why should I forgive Nix, but not Micah?"

"You can forgive him, I don't know that *I* can."

Fair enough. Madison couldn't say that she blamed her. Even though Elias had almost succeeded in killing her, she wasn't the one holding the grudge the way Micah and Zen were. But she figured all Zoe saw when she looked at Micah was the memory of her dramatic, early demise.

A bump against the dresser drew Madison's attention. In the darkened room, she saw nothing to cause the noise. "I get it, and I don't expect you to like him. That's not part of the pact he made y'all."

Did the lamp just wobble?

The tiny blip on her internal radar pinged. A supernatural creature she couldn't see neared. Kur could cloak himself...but she sensed him stronger when he disguised himself. Maybe he'd learned how to mute his presence.

"Zoe, I gotta run." She peered straight into the shadows where she thought she felt the presence. "Call me soon?"

She agreed, and they disconnected the call. Madison set her cell on the table and concentrated on the intruder. She got nothing. Not even a blip on her supernatural radar.

"Kur? Are you there?"

Silence.

Too much silence, her demon noted, going tense and readying for a battle.

Yeah. She couldn't even hear Amos down the hall or any other sounds of movement in the house. With the large contingent of folks present, she should hear *something*.

She ran her palm along her belly. There was more

than just Amos to protect now. A nudge of her mental mojo and the overhead lights flooded the room, chasing away the shadows the lamp created. Madison surveyed the room in a slow rotation. Nothing. Not even the slight depression of air that normally indicated another's presence.

Micah? When she received no response to her telepathy, she sent out another mental call. *Zen?*

Again nothing. She swung about and headed for the door. A few feet away something smashed into the back of her head, knocking her to her knees. Blackness coiled her vision, narrowing to pinpoints of light. Slamming her palms on the floor, she struggled against the encroaching darkness.

I won't pass out! Not now when an adversary attacked and two of her protectors were unreachable.

Her Lynx jacked her nervous system and thrust to the forefront, eliminating the intruding blackout. Still no visible magic coalesced into view.

All stealth evaporated as solid footsteps announced her antagonizer's advance. Madison tensed, readying her magic, while pretending defeat and waiting for her attacker to present oneself.

"I gave you the prophecy so you could avoid the outcome, you stupid bitch." A female voice snarled. "Not so you'd follow the divination."

Black footwear came into view, and Madison followed the attire up. A solid costume of black shrouded the female. No, not clothing...feathers. She tilted her head back to get a good gander of the creature's face.

Crow.

It'd been five years since she last saw the woman. So much of what the woman prophesized had come true.

"Nix, if you continue to squander and push aside what you desire most, you'll fall to a partnership of your own making. A pact with a devil in a hell you cannot fathom. The anguish of lost regrets will force you to submit to his satisfaction, become the monster

he desires, the tool for his entrance into a Kingdom not of his making. There's hope. Allies will come to your aid, and a new Phoenix, battle hardened by heinous exploits and shame, may rise from the ashes."

Every bit of that premonition had come true.

She'd told Madison she was strong enough to crush a King...and in a sense she had. Micah's original goals were voided. His aspirations no longer involved seizing Heaven from his father's hands. She'd been "forged in fire" when she became the Queen of Hell, and she'd exited Hell supernaturally strong. She'd even managed to "defeat a second King". In a sense she had. Elias no longer held the respect of his brothers thanks to his untrustworthy behavior.

Her fingertips tickled with electricity, but she held the power just beneath the surface. Madison notched her voice low, forcing it to sound breathy, and hoping the woman would think she'd been weakened by the blow to her head. "What outcome would you have had me avoid?"

A blur of movement and Crow struck her jaw. Madison chugged the feathered creature's magic for a minuscule moment, then the other woman's touch was gone, and Madison landed flat on her back.

Shit, that hurt!

Taking her down will be glorious. On that she and her succubus agreed. One touch at a time and she'd slowly drain the crow.

A kick to her hip and another to her shoulder, and each time the crow touched her Madison chugged more of her power. Another blow to her jaw...Madison tasted blood on her tongue and groaned at the pain that burst through her skull.

Going into defensive mode, she rolled away from the incessant kicks, but before she could evade the violence, the woman was on her, wrenching Madison up on her knees by the hair. The feathered woman tugged her head back until their gazes connected.

Black hair hung around Crow's face. Her eyes were

so black there was no visible beginning and end to her pupils.

"I gave you a prophecy so you would defeat the Kings by killing them." Hatred curled Crow's upper lip. "Instead you *became* the fucking Queen of Hell."

Madison reached back and touched the hand snarled in the strands of her hair. She swigged the bitch's power faster than a frat boy funneling beer. Crow's terror-laced scream caused Madison to wince, and her ears to ring. Crow reacted quicker than she preferred and shoved Madison away.

Madison rose to her feet, hopefully sending the message to her nemesis that she felt not an ounce of fear.

Crow tossed her hair over her shoulder and wobbled, a little unsteady on her feet with her magic depleted. "You're stronger than the last time we met."

"I'm the Queen of Hell. What'd you expect? Cinderella?" That's what Elias saw when he looked at her, so she wouldn't be surprised if Crow stupidly thought the same thing.

"After your failure to kill the Kings, I helped the Esdras angels take you down." Her black gaze narrowed on Madison. "My one mission was to kill you. Because you refused to *stay dead*"—she screamed the last two words, detailing her frustration—"Mauriel and Nexiel are after me because the locks are breaking."

No idea who those two were or what locks Crow referred to, Madison thumbed the leather ties on the sheaths holding her knives. Crow's gaze remained fastened on Madison's face, but she searched the feathered creatures eyes for small details.

"When I kill you today, those locks will be dead bolted once again and the world saved."

"Don't count your chickens before they hatch."

"What?"

Making no effort to explain, Madison palmed both of her blades. With a little bit of luck, the crow would be as allergic to the dragon scales as the angels. She planned for the opposite outcome though. The one Nix had given her for her thirtieth birthday had been modified. Her sigil was etched into the blade, along with an incantation, and it had been blessed by three of the Kings of Hell. That would neutralize her long enough Madison could enthrall her or kill her by ingesting all of her power.

"Knives...amateurish and ineffective."

She shrugged as Lynx mocked, *Pretend this is all the weaponry I have. It'll be your funeral, you feather-brained bitch.*

Not that her skill would intimidate the crow, but she rolled both weapons along her knuckles and hoped the winged creature took it as a taunt.

The feathered woman shifted into her bird state and dive-bombed Madison.

Holding her position, she flung her Nix-blade, and it sailed through the body of the bird. Only Crow shifted from bird, to fog, and into that of a woman at the exact moment the knife would've stabbed her, thwarting any damage it would've wrecked. Madison was on her before she completed the shift. The dragon blade caught her neck, nicking her flesh.

She went for the creature's blood so she could enslave her succubus-style, but Crow must've realized her intent because she morphed into a fowl again. Freed from Madison's hold, the crow dive-bombed once more.

Madison knocked the bird aside just before Crow would've gouged her eyes out with her beak.

The crow made another go at her, but this time Madison nailed her with electricity. Feathers rained the air as the black bird hit the floor with a thud. Before the quills cleared from the air and Madison could nail her again, Crow morphed back into humanity.

Madison executed a three-sixty spin kick and struck her opponent in the jaw. Crow slammed into the bookshelf lining the wall. Not missing a beat, she body slammed herself into the feathered creature, driving the dragon blade into her gut.

A freakish cawing sound emerged from the bird as tomes rained down around them.

Clasping the bird's throat, Madison chugged the feathered woman's mojo as blood spilled across the hand holding the blade. She twisted the hilt, pulled out, and rammed it in again. Crow cried out, and smoke spiraled upward from the wound as Madison twisted once more.

Unsurprised when Crow made a half-hearted attempt at dislodging Madison off her, she withdrew the blade and jabbed it into Crow again, while digging her fingers into the woman's throat and sucking her mojo slow for maximum terror.

As she drained Crow's power, Madison stared into her black eyes until they grew cloudy, graying at the edges. She slowed the ingestion further, but whatever magic the woman erected to silence the house dropped, and the sounds of the household boomed.

She removed the knife-edge from Crow's gut, and the woman whimpered. Maintaining her hold on the creature's throat, Madison took a couple of steps back. "How does it feel to know I defeated you?"

She felt Micah and Zen enter the room. A moment later Nix burst through the door, rattling it as it crashed against the wall.

Over her shoulder, she peeked at her guys and smiled. Nix looked harried, fire reflected in Micah's eyes, and as always Zen appeared cooler than ice.

"I got this one." She winked at them. "She's talking out of her head though, something about locks and deadbolts and a Mauriel and Nexiel. I assume they're angels?"

Micah nodded as he came to stand beside Madison. He acknowledged Crow with a scowl. "Power off the feed."

"She's *mine*." If Micah tried to steal her conquest, she'd fight him for her.

His hellfire and brimstone colored eyes deadlocked

on her. "I'm not challenging you for her, kitten."

Suddenly Nix was in her space cupping her face and dislodging her hold on Crow, irritating her Lynx. "You okay, baby?"

Was a whole fucking lot better before you took away my meal, Usha pouted.

"Peachy." Aside from where her teeth had cut the inside of her mouth when Crow struck her, she thought she'd done a damn fine job of holding her own against the quilled creature. With her adrenaline in overdrive and her need to feed almost overpowering her, she'd been unable to think rationally. Now that Nix had stopped her consumption of Crow-food, logic returned in gradual increments.

"The baby?" His palm touched her belly.

"Fine. I'd have already told you if the wee one was injured." Zen pondered the female, his finger running along her chin. "She is the Crow you spoke of?"

"Yes," Nix answered Zen's question as he turned to face Madison's newest acquisition, but maintained his hold on her upper-arm.

"What am I missing?" Micah peered at her, as she held up her hand that was coated in Crow's blood.

Nix quickly explained, and her husband laughed. "She's nothing more than a low-level oracle angel. Father used them at one time to determine his next step in Creation."

Crow's blood smells divine.

Yes, it does, Usha agreed. *Ingest it, and we'll own her.*

Owning her sounded like a divine idea. She could control her, make her do her bidding, and—

Micah caught her wrist. Their gazes locked, and she would've argued but he cut her off with, "You don't want to own an angel that way." The thumb of his other hand swiped at the corner of her mouth. He showed her the blood he'd smeared away. After a sniff, he licked it off. "Your blood, not hers. You know I love the way you taste."

He'd told her once that succubi blood was an aphrodisiac.

"You want to own her, kitten?"

"She's already mine. I defeated her and took almost all of her magic. She. Is. Mine."

Her hellish husband grinned, the fire in his eyes amping up with her declaration. "I like how possessive your demon is." He held his arm toward Crow and his *Scepter of Spirits* ejected from his palm, piercing Crow's chest. The woman cried out, slumping against the sizzling sword. "I reap Cawel's soul for the Queen of Hell's authority."

In that moment, Madison decided she'd thank him later, in detail, for that. She grabbed him by his hair and planted a kiss on him. Their teeth knocked together, and her tongue was in his mouth before his grunt completed its sound. She rubbed against him until someone cleared their throat.

Nix?

She reached to draw him into their web, but Micah set her away from him. She attempted to draw him back for another round, and when he pulled his head away to resist she yanked on his hair.

Micah chuckled. "In a moment, kitten. Zennyo Ryuo and Cawel don't wish to listen to you purr."

"They can leave."

The sword exited Cawel's chest cavity, and the oracle angel slumped to the floor. The feathered creature's breathing grew erratic. "Bastard," she slurred the word as she shot a black glare at Micah.

"Madison."

She glanced at Zen when he said her name.

He held out his hand and she peered at it, toying with the idea of rejecting his offer to take his hand.

Her demon wanted to play and was in no mood to deny herself. She glanced at Micah. The fire in his eyes said he'd fuck her until she couldn't move. A peek at Nix implied the same, but his held a touch less eagerness. She glared at the fallen woman, her feathers a mess around her, littering the floor.

Sighing, Madison slid her hand into Zen's palm, and he teleported her across the room away from her men. "You need to learn to focus and contain your demon. And you"—Zen leveled Micah with a glare—"should help her."

Micah shrugged. "Tell me how you know Cawel."

Nix pinched the bridge of his nose. "Zen's right. If you're not helping her contain her Lynx, then she'll struggle for control maybe eventually losing focus long enough to do some real fucking damage. That doesn't help her, Micah. Sorry, baby, for not jacking your jaws for going Hulk on her ass."

She made a face. "I'm fine." *I was fine until I ingested Crow's seraph.*

Not true. Usha sighed. *You lost it the moment I took over to take the bitch down.*

They'd needed to lose it to defeat her.

Her hellish husband's jaw hardened. "Cawel," he reminded. Apparently the other argument would be saved for a later date. Not that he cared if she went postal. It's what he'd originally wanted.

Nix explained quickly how Crow fit into their lives. Her husband's features remained bland as Zen released her hand and lashed his arm around her shoulders.

Micah peered at Cawel after her Sherlock completed the history lesson.

Madison brought all of them up to speed on what the oracle woman admitted about the Esdras angels and their attempt on her life.

Her King of Hell's talons emerged, and he ran the tips along the underside of Crow's jaw, until he hit her chin and tipped her head back to meet his eyes. "You aided our Esdras siblings? Came to finish the job they failed?"

Mutiny flashed through Crow's gaze. "Our siblings succeeded. If not for the Ark of Heaven, she'd be where she belongs. Dead."

Madison couldn't see his face, but by the sudden

tenseness in his shoulders, she could picture his face hard with rage. Black blood oozed from where his claw indented her skin. "Have you lost your fucking mind, sister? I will—"

"You will do *nothing* to her."

Micah's gaze whipped around. Madison laced her fingers with Zen's hand that draped off the side of her shoulder. One small touch by this brother-like-man and her focus went clear. Proof he neutralized Pandora magic with his mojo.

"She's mine." Owning souls wasn't her main agenda, but her Lynx had made a claim on the angel, and she wouldn't relinquish her jurisdiction. "You won't do anything I don't consent to first."

A stiff nod from her husband mollified her demon.

Nix fingered his spiky locks. "Micah, who are Mauriel and Nexiel that she mentioned?"

"Angel justice system. They haul misbehaving angels before their peers to determine their guilt. If found guilty, they dole out a fitting punishment." Micah pondered Cawel. "I've not known them to issue commands and punish when things went sideways."

"Things are obviously changing in Heaven."

Micah met Zen's gaze. Beliel gave an abbreviated nod and said, "I've confirmed what Jesus said. The Esdras weren't commanded to slaughter Madison. They worked alone."

Madison didn't know what to think. All these different angels and rules was giving her a headache. "What locks is she talking about breaking?"

All eyes focused on Crow. "I don't know."

Micah used a claw to slash her cheek to the bone. Black bones. Weird. "That'll leave a scar. Answer with the truth."

Fuck, he makes me horny when he's a hardass, Usha purred in her head.

He makes us horny just looking at him, Madison countered.

Valid point.

"I don't know!" Crow screamed, her body shaking

158

with her intensity, causing her feathers to create a weird buzzing motion. A few of them flitted about as if to highlight her declaration.

"You're an oracle, divine it."

Before Crow could respond to Micah's command, Nix placed his palm on her forehead. His gold magic engulfed her, and Crow squawked. A moment later he lowered his hand and stepped away. "She's telling the truth. I jacked her power to see if she lied. Even using her magic, I cannot determine what locks are breaking or why the justice system would want Mads dead."

Ooo...hardass number two, her Lynx cooed.

Stop it, you're making my panties uncomfortably wet.

Not my fault. Blame our men.

"I knew I liked that power of yours for a reason, Phoenix." Micah gave him a sardonic grin. "Kitten, let's deposit her in Hell for your future amusement."

"I'm coming with," Nix said.

"I'll watch out for Amos, update the dragons, and remind Petra we're still on high alert. Take care of her while you're there." Zen tilted his head toward Madison. "Her Lynx is unsettled and chafing my skin."

Micah smirked. "You think I can't see her Lynx?"

"Exactly," Nix agreed. "Her eyes are neon."

Chapter 16

A FEW DAYS later, Madison ventured back to Crow's cell.

The feathered creature paced her small area with hands clamped over her ears as if she attempted to block out the agonies of Hell. Once not too long ago it'd bothered Madison too. Now it served as white noise she rarely noticed. Cawel's black plumage quivered with each stride of her agitation, and she muttered beneath her breath, like a crazy woman.

Madison studied the oracle angel for several minutes as the other woman prayed to her relations detailing her defeat, giving her location, and requesting an immediate evacuation. None of the litanies exited the room, instead they crashed against the magical chamber and evaporated into mist. Not being of this realm, Madison wasn't surprised Cawel was unaware of the magical shield.

After several minutes, the angelic female realized Madison watched her. Cawel came to an abrupt halt and crossed her arms over her chest in a defensive stance. "My siblings will free me from this hellhole."

Preferring to let the other woman believe what she

wanted, Madison shrugged. There'd be no rescue because none of her siblings could venture into Hell without permission being granted. Even then, they'd never locate her because she was locked up tight with her magic hidden.

"You're an ignorant bitch who—"

Madison wiggled a finger, and Cawel crashed to her knees with a scream. The skin-stitched floor concaved like silly putty, before snapping back into place. It screeched right along with the damned oracle.

"Your momma really should've taught you some manners, Cawel." As the crow's feathers burst into flames and her skin melted from her bones, Madison sauntered into the room, drawing closer to her nemesis. "As your host I deserve more respect than middle school name-calling."

On her hands and knees, the black-feathered angel panted as the flames died out. "You're a fool."

The hellish magic crushed every bone in Cawel's body. "The magic is set. Each slur gifts you with torture. *You* are the fool if you continue along this road."

The crow supined on her back, glaring at Madison, but her fortitude remained intact. "You're wrong if you think I'll break."

Madison knelt beside her new acquisition. "That's not my goal. To break you means your suffering ends."

Cawel looked away. It satisfied the Queen of Hell to see the glimmer of a tear at the corner of the crow's eye.

"Did you even want to know why your brethren want me dead?"

"I follow orders, not ask questions." The parched creature glared at her. "Before your birth, I prophesized your rise in Hell. Micah cloaked you well. My first bead on you was the night I visited you."

"Did you see that my rise would damn you?"

Cawel shook her head. "I gave you the false prophecy to thwart my original vision."

"My son's a prophet too. Did you know that?"

Again Cawel shook her head.

"His accuracy is almost one-hundred percent. Even with your false divination, he never predicted I'd escape my fate." They'd only dodged it for a handful of years, and Madison's ultimate suspicion had been that she'd die before she became the Queen of Hell. Only recently had she come to realize fate couldn't be denied any more than her DNA could be. Madison rose to her feet and peered at the crow that'd once given her hope. "I pity you. You were doomed to fail from the moment you located me, and you didn't even know it. Welcome to your new home." She indicated the tight quarters. "I do hope you enjoy your accommodations. Recreation is part of your all-inclusive package."

"You're twisted in the head. I know 'recreation' is code for torture."

Noting the other woman's crispy feathers had begun to rejuvenate, Madison simply inclined her head, neither affirming nor denying the accusation.

As the Queen of Hell neared the door, Cawel said, "Why don't you just kill me?"

Madison paused in the doorway, turning slightly to peer at her antagonist. "That would be a mercy killing, and I don't pity you that much. Also, clemency is never granted in Hell. Just ask around. Besides, I'm curious how long you'll hold out before you're proclaiming allegiance to your new Queen."

The image of the crow on her knees petitioning Madison's favor drew a smile from her.

"Never," Cawel vowed.

"Time will tell."

Cawel's shrieks joined the rest of the damned as Madison walked away. Justice meted out to one that had wronged her. All was good in Madison's world.

Chapter 17

One week later
Birmingham, Alabama

"**YOU'RE A CHEATER**, Micah Dominus!" Madison flattened her cards between her breasts and glared at him. She wasn't imagining things. He *had* tried to wiggle into her mind to take a peek at her cards.

Micah presented offense. Madison wasn't buying it.

"Phoenix can tap into another's powers and use them. Why do you automatically assume it's me?" If she didn't know better, she'd be convinced of his innocence. But come *on*! The man was kinda like the original sin...he Fell first and brought his brothers with him. He might look like an angel, but since his exit from Heaven, he'd perfected duplicity and knew how to trick innocents into damning themselves.

"I'd have to be touching you to do that." Tone dry, Nix made a face at Micah. Both of Nix's hands rested on the table.

"You're lying." Which was remarkable since he

163

couldn't fib to her without physical discomfort.

"Didn't lie, kitten. I told the truth." He casually moved one card between two others. "Phoenix *can* tap into another person's powers and channel them. Now..." He elevated his gaze and met hers dead on. "If I said, I wasn't cheating"—he winced—"that'd be lying."

"Stop trying to dig into my mind and peek at my cards." *Or you won't be getting inside me anywhere else, either,* she added telepathically so Amos wouldn't hear her.

Micah mouthed "ouch" and cringed again. *The punishment doesn't fit the crime, kitten.*

It's stern enough you won't contemplate cheating next time.

Her husband laughed. "I knew you'd make a good Queen."

Amos threw in a red-wrapped miniature Reese's Cup. With candy on the line, her child took the game way too seriously. "I raise you another red." He couldn't sit still, and his excitement guaranteed he held a good hand.

Madison, do not play that hand, Zen's telepathy filtered into her head. *You'll lose.*

That meant either Amos or Nix possessed the better cards because he couldn't weed into Micah's thoughts. *That's cheating, Zen.*

She glanced at him in time to catch his aloof shrug.

"I fold." Madison set her cards facedown on the table.

Micah studied her and Zen for a long moment. In the end, whatever he decided, he cocked his head to the side and sent her a knowing grin.

He knows, her Lynx said.

Of course he knows. He's not been a corrupting King of Hell without skills.

He'll make us pay later for cheating. That idea excited her demon.

Especially now that I called him on his duplicity. But she wasn't worried about the punishment fitting the crime or being too hard for that matter.

They played out the remainder of the hand. Nix won, surprising her, she'd thought for sure Amos would be the victor. Her son sulked, like always, a poor loser. Micah punched their son's shoulder. "A prince should never brood."

Nix leaned toward her and claimed a winning kiss. When his lips left hers, their eyes met briefly before his hand on her nape tugged her close and he whispered against her ear, "I realize your crystal genie helped you out."

"Not guilty, and you can't make me confess."

"We'll see." He nipped her ear, and goose bumps spread across her body.

Amos dealt the next hand as 'breaking news' interrupted the show on television. Not that anyone watched the broadcast.

"This just in," the reporter said. Her chin length, brown hair bobbed with each move, and her eyebrows hitched up and down as she spoke. "A large fissure has opened in the Antarctic today, and a green vapor is exiting."

Micah portaled to his feet nearer the television set, as if he could access more detail by a closer proximity. The journalist continued the account.

"Two locals are dead after coming into contact with the vapors. Scientists are baffled by the emission. The gas appears to eat through everything like an acid. Dr. Edward Cochrane was critically injured after his HAZMAT suit was destroyed in an attempt to acquire samples. It is undetermined if the suit was defective, or if the gas caused the damage. Dr. Cochrane is being treated in St. Joseph's Hospital. At this time, there is no word on his condition. Dr. Jan Starr speculates—"

It all meant something. Volcanoes erupting, earthquakes going off daily, and the purple ring around the moon...none of it could bode anything good.

"Who is coming?"

She focused on Micah. "Huh?"

"You said 'he's coming'." She hadn't realized she'd said anything, or thought anything for that matter. "You didn't, you projected the thought. Who is coming?"

"I don't know." And she didn't, but by his reaction, he knew what this event indicated. "What does it mean, Micah?"

"Madison—"

"Please. Just tell me."

"There's a rift in Hakara."

She felt the color drain from her face. *That's where they told me I was.*

"Why do you know that name?" Her husband strolled straight to her and pulled her from her chair. "*How* do you know that name?"

"Am I missing something here?" By the sound of rustling clothing, she suspected Nix stood.

Over Micah's shoulder, Madison watched a female appear in their home, materializing as if she'd been invisible. Kinda the way Zen and Kur could camouflage themselves. Only Madison could see the edges of Zen's disguise. And she could sense Kur. This creature had been undetectable.

"I believe it's where she went"—Micah portaled to Amos, and their son was gone before the next breath...Hell was her best guess since it was the safest place for him—"when she died."

By the time the newcomer finished speaking, Micah invaded the other woman's personal space with the *Scepter of Spirits* indenting her flesh directly over her heart. The woman's flaming wings were dissimilar from the Kings' wings. And what a sight to behold.

In awe, Madison stared at the woman. Not a stitch of clothing covered her body. Pale gray skin, like ash, almost sickly hued, and crackled veins like ceramic pottery that'd been left in the kiln too long spread along her frame. In between those cracks in her skin, flames emerged from the broken flesh. It was as if she burned from within and the flames couldn't be contained.

"We've not come to harm your woman, Fallen." The new voice came from her exposed left side. A male. Everything about him was stark white. His wings were white and fluffy like snow, his skin a pure alabaster, but his eyes...dear God his eyes were the most amazing shade of ice blue, almost devoid of color. Even his lashes were white, the tips sparkling in the same hue as his eyes, as if dipped in glitter. Coupled with the colorless clothing it made for a stark appearance.

Zen teleported a bubble around the male.

He smirked at Zen but made no obvious move to destroy the magical rainbow cage.

Micah swiveled his head just enough he could peer at the newest guests. "Pardon me if I don't trust you, reaper."

Reaper? If they were reapers, then why were they showing themselves? Weren't they supposed to be undetectable until they claimed a soul to guide to their final realm? Not like she'd seen them when she died. Nope. She'd made her way alone to a place she tried not to think about often.

"We did not come to claim her or anyone from your family." A third voice announced from her right side. Nix stepped between her and him. This one possessed wings of midnight, his eyes soulless black. He was the exact opposite of the white guest, except hieroglyphic white tattoos lined the right side of his face. He reminded her of a biker with his ripped jeans, black t-shirt and leather vest.

"My wife died a few months ago. You arrive in my home unwelcome, getting beyond the barriers that should've kept you out."

"Nothing bars our entry." The female was their obvious spokesperson.

"You're not winning my trust." As if to prove his suspicion, Micah's sword pricked the female's skin, and fiery blood oozed down her exposed flesh like lava. When it dripped against the floor, Madison almost expected to see holes where the blood dripped. Instead it rested in a small pool, maintaining the lava-like appearance.

Weird. Just...weird.

"I don't need your trust or permission to enter anywhere," the fiery reaper said. "My *Scepter* will forever bar your entry to everywhere."

"Kill her." The white male trapped in Zen's bubble sounded bored. If he chose that moment to inspect his fingernails, Madison wouldn't have been surprised. Rather, his bland expression remained fixated on Micah and the female he threatened. He could give Zen a run for the most deadpan countenance. "Father will reanimate her."

"Not if I *reap her* to my realm." Micah sounded angry enough to do exactly that.

"I cannot be reaped like Domiel and our other siblings." The woman was ballsy inciting Micah.

When Domiel killed Madison, Micah took his soul, along with the others who'd assisted him, to Hell for punishment. The *Scepter of Spirits* allowed Micah to reap souls for Kingdoms. Before his Fall that'd been for God's Kingdom. She wasn't sure the *Scepter* had been intended for usage this way, but nothing had been done to alter the magic in the blade.

"You want to bet your soul on that theory, Pyrel?" Her husband sounded almost eager to show it could be done.

But...she now had a name. Pyrel. Fitting since a 'pyre' was where a deceased's body was burned in certain funeral rites. And this one looked to be burning from the inside out.

Neither sibling gave an inch, but continued to glare at one another. But the tiny twitch to Pyrel's wings left Madison wondering if maybe, *just maybe*, the reaper wasn't a little bit unsure about her future if Micah used the *Scepter* on her.

Madison stepped away from Nix. He made a grab for her, but she managed to sidestep him. Either way, he dogged her and had her back. When she halted and placed a hand on Micah's shoulder, Nix couldn't have been more than a foot length from her spine. Close enough she felt his body heat...and his displeasure with her.

When will they learn, we'll never do what they anticipate or expect?

Her demon could say that again.

Micah cast her a brief glance, his jaw hardened but he returned his focus to the female reaper. "Now's not the time to distract me, Madison."

"All this bluster is counterproductive." Proof too much power went to everyone's head, regardless of mortality or immortality.

"Madison's right." Zen prowled closer to her as if he couldn't teleport in a nanosecond.

"You want my trust, tell me your angelic names." Their names held power and could be used against them.

Eyebrows drawn together, Micah cast her a hard peek, but the tenseness in his shoulders eased a fraction.

"Pyrel," the female Micah threatened confirmed the name he'd just used.

"Sarel," said the dark angel. "I vow in Father's name I have no aim for your woman or family."

"None in this homestead." The white angel bowed slightly. "Jasiel."

All these −el names for angels. How did they come up with so many that ended like that?

Jasiel wasn't finished. He shoved his hands into his pant pockets. Hm...she hadn't been able to see any through all his stark whiteness. "If what we suspect is corroborated, drama is coming that only a select few can prevent."

"You asking for our help?" He shifted the angle of his *Scepter,* and the blade sizzled as he placed the tip beneath Pyrel's chin.

By all appearances Zen and Nix held no aspirations

of diffusing the tension and Micah readied to start taking heads, so that left it up to her to play peacemaker. "Lower your *Scepter*, Micah."

"*Li.*" *No.* Not a glance in her direction. "Get to the point of your meeting. Fast."

Jasiel exploded out of Zen's rainbow cage. Her immortal adopted brother proved he could teleport on a dime and was between her and Jasiel before she could finish processing the reaper's freedom.

Wings lowered and disappeared, as Jasiel took on a very human-like persona. His eyes darkened to a deep blue, and his flesh took on a more normal hue. His white hair remained, as did the snowy clothing. "Madison went to Hakara when she died."

"Her resurrection is responsible for the breaking of the locks." Sarel altered into a human state as well, his tattoos vanishing and his skin becoming one cohesive skein of mahogany.

If the locks break, he *will come for us,* her succubus reminded. Excitement spiked before she killed it altogether.

Micah lowered his *Scepter* and scrutinized Jasiel and Sarel for a long silent moment. She could almost hear the gears turning with contemplation in his head.

"I brought her back. That makes me responsible, not Madison." Nix slid his hand into hers. Probably for comfort, but she wasn't feeling the angst she maybe would've a month ago.

"Wait." Micah slashed his hand through the air. "What the fuck are you talking about? Madison's soul was Hell bound. She's Hell-made, so that's where she belongs. *Went.* Hakara is for the monsters Father created or the ones He found lacking in some way."

"Her soul entered Hakara, not Hell, Micah." The seriousness on Pyrel's features seemed a little grave since they didn't have a dog in this fight. "The three of us came for her, but none were able to get near her soul to guide her to Hell."

"We suspect Domiel bespelled her so we couldn't walk her soul into the afterlife." Jasiel never blinked, just stared.

"It's why she went to Hakara and not Hell," Sarel supplied the final piece of information.

Micah slammed his fingers through his hair. Zen just watched Madison, his expression void as always.

She could feel Nix contemplating her, too, but she didn't glance his way, just squeezed his hand. "Got something to add to that, baby? Like do you remember this place Hakara?"

The final question got Micah's attention. His head twisted, and his gaze honed on hers.

"I remember everything." Clearly. Much too clearly. When she'd woken up in Micah's arms, she'd been confused because moments earlier she'd been in Hakara conversing with *him*.

Anguish slashed across Micah's features. "That is not what should've happened to you." Fine lines spread out from the corners of his eyes. On a man that was devoid of age, it was a telling expression. He blamed Domiel for her trip into Hakara. The angel would pay even more with this new revelation. "Allow me to see everything, kitten?"

He showed her his hands, as if they would do the seeing.

"Can you handle it?" At the moment, she feared one wrong truth would send him on a rampage. "Promise you won't hurt Domiel and the other angels more."

A flicker of fire blazed in his blue gaze, and his jaw hardened. "Yes. I *can* handle it. Stow your morals. They murdered you in cold blood. No promises. I will vow to consider your request before I institute more torture."

That was the best promise she'd get. "Deal. You can have my memories."

"Broadcast them to me like the movie reels you made me watch in Hell," Nix said beside her. "I want to know what she endured, too."

Madison glanced at Zen. "And you?"

"Already in your head. I'll watch. Can't figure out

how you managed to hide it from me, though."

She shrugged. "I didn't want to dwell on it." She never thought about her time there. When she began to stray into turbulent thoughts of those long minutes in Hakara, she altered the course of her reflections. There'd be no escaping them now.

Chapter 18

ANGER BLED THROUGH Micah. He wanted revenge against those who'd harmed his woman. Revenge for sending her to the wasteland of monsters—*Piljhak*. All manners of evil resided in Hakara. It'd been reserved for the worst of the worst when there'd been no Hell, before his Fall, and he gave home to another set of outcasts. He'd fought alongside Zen purging the world of the most vicious of the motley crew. To know his woman had walked among them when he'd thought her soul had been safeguarded in Hell...that knowledge fucked with his reasoning.

I'll hold it together. Only for Madison would he ever restrain *his* monster.

He cupped her cheeks with his palms and kissed her forehead. The word sorry lingered on his tongue, but he wouldn't utter it. He despised that word because it implied weakness. But he couldn't deny guilt stalked him. Without his interference in her life, this atrocity would've never happened to her. The truth stung, wounded his psyche in ways nothing ever had.

173

"You ready?" he whispered against her forehead. At her nod, he glanced in Phoenix's direction. "You?"

"Waiting on you."

Micah wrapped one arm around her shoulders and pulled her snug against his chest. Resting his lips against her forehead, he lifted his other arm and cupped the back of Phoenix's head. "Brace yourself, kitten." A mind-merge was much different than reading her thoughts. He would have to dig through her mind, and marry her memories with his so he could relive every moment as if they were his own. Many found the experience not just unpleasant, but dizzying, too.

He pushed his magic into her and got lost in her warmth and love for a moment. The baby was there. Correction...babies. Plural. Two. Twins like him and Elias.

Fuck!

Interesting twist, Madison already knew there were two.

The Ark of Heaven was a lucky bastard.

He blocked that announcement from Phoenix at the last second, but allowed him to feel their presence. Shifting his hand from her shoulder and into her hair, he wrapped the soft locks around his fingers, and tilted her head back. Dragging his lips down her nose in a gentle glide, he felt the caress on his own flesh as if he was being touched instead of him stroking her, indicating they'd merged.

Stopping with his lips hovering over hers, he inhaled her breath and stared into her eyes. "Goddamn, it feels amazing being inside you like this, Madison." She vibrated against him, and he knew she felt what he felt. That's the way mind-melding worked. "Can you feel her, Phoenix?"

"Can we do this when we're making love to her?"

Micah chuckled. They could, they damn sure could. "Go flush against her backside, Phoenix. She might require our support. This can get intense." He waited until the other man shifted to align his chest with

Madison's spine. He tightened his grip on the back of Phoenix's neck, so he could telepath the memories. Micah remained where he stood, breathing every nuance of her into him. "Start with the beginning, and I'll take it from there, kitten. If at any time it becomes too much, say my name—*Beliel*. Use Beliel. Okay?" If she said Micah, he'd just think she was saying his name. The utterance of his angelic name would snag his attention.

Okay. Telepathy instead of the spoken word.

He gave her no forewarning, just dive-bombed the memory with his mojo. A slight gasp emerged from her as he threaded himself into her psyche, but the inhalation sounded like pleasure rather than discomfort.

Micah focused as he latched onto the memory...

The Sterillium poisoning felt like crushed glass flowing through her veins. No, that description failed to justify the depth of her anguish. Madison wanted to die. Anything to eradicate the pain. Her lungs burned, locked up...

"Madison, either move forward in the memory, or grant me control to fast-forward." This rancid agony was more than Micah could tolerate. Not because of the actual pain he felt or the grunt he'd heard from Phoenix, but knowing she'd suffered like that left him wanting to torture his brothers harder.

"Control it," she whispered.

Thank you, he telepathed and mentally rubbed against her soul to soothe himself more so than her because she seemed to be handling the recollection better than him. She'd lived it, so of course she would.

He shuttled the memory along in rapid succession, until the moment right before her death...

Blackness closed in on her, only a pinpoint of Micah filtered into her view. His anguish over her demise surprised her. Only someone who truly loved her and not what she could bring to the table would react that way. Not that his sorrow mattered when death became her newest lover.

She welcomed the final breath, anything to end the suffering. The pain receded as an inky void consumed her, a thick darkness with an oily texture and rancid smell. A deadened silence descended, the type that boomeranged around in one's head when they went too deep in a pool of water. Her temples throbbed, and she winced at the thick, subterranean resonance.

A sudden murky light pierced the pitch-black veil of obscurity. Not the white light everyone talked about in near-death experiences. This one reminded her of the shadows flames put off, flickering against an icy abyss of...evil and hatred, a vileness that presided in the approaching landscape.

One moment she converged upon the domain and in the next, she became very aware of her surroundings and her corporeal body. She glanced down, touched her arms, stomach, hips, and thighs. As real here as when I lived. *That alien concept confused her.* Shouldn't she be a specter?

Something clung to her leg. Alarmed by the sudden ankle-hugger, she lifted her foot to kick off whatever bugger had attached to her since her arrival. Madison froze with her knee bent and her foot elevated off the black, oily flooring. Oddly, there was zero shine on the surface.

In the place of a monster, a female child adhered herself to Madison's leg. Terror radiated from the youngster, she sniffled, but no wailing ensued. The little one vibrated like every pet she'd brought into the vet's office.

Madison ruffled the wee one's blonde hair, and the baby peered up at her. Blue eyes and dimples, she stuck her two middle fingers in her mouth and began to suckle. She could've been my lovechild with Nix in another life. *What deity lacked such indifference to cast innocence into this abyss? There should be stiff standards for damnation.*

Compelled to protect, Madison bent and swooped the child into her embrace, and snuggled her against her shoulder. The baby nuzzled Madison's neck with her face, the sucking noises against her fingers loud in Madison's ear. Only after the infant finished rooting into a comfortable position did Madison consider the possibility that it could shift into a monster and attack, but the familiarity she felt with the child was overwhelming. She couldn't explain her perceptions or the notions she held toward the baby, but she chose to trust her gut instinct.

A keening scrape like claws against slate—but worse—drew her attention off the girl. The bleak terrain possessed a greasy-like consistency, but her footing felt sure instead of slippery. Dark structures were in ruins around them, reminding her of the skeletal remains of Mayan temples...or the remnants of a bombed city.

From the shadows two creatures approached her, a male with horns above his head and two more flowing down either side of his face. She'd seen Satan depicted in the same manner in artwork. This one claimed a forked tail, too, and an at least eight foot tall frame that the stoutest linebacker would envy. His wingspan reached over his head another four feet, creating an imposing figure. Dissimilar to the wings of Kings or angels, his were red, with the look of a rubbery type material. He clutched a scimitar with etchings that glowed as if lava was trapped within the weapon.

The other was a female, half dressed, with only the important parts covered...nipples and vagina. Three horns on the right side of her head, with the center one hacked off closer to her scalp. Two larger horns protruded from the left side of her scalp, all five reminding her of fingers projecting from her scalp. Scales covered her left cheek, left arm, and down the left outer-side of her leg. On her right hand, her index *finger was coated in the same brown-colored scales, the shade of bark on pine trees. In her left hand, she held a staff that twined around itself and merged into a conglomeration of four snakes.*

Other creatures loitered in the shadows, welcoming her with their icy disdain.

Madison held her footing. Regardless that she entered their domain, she wouldn't be intimidated. I am born to be the Queen of Hell. *That had to mean something.* And she was a Lynx succubus. *Those two statuses mattered at a time like this.*

The huge male spoke, softer than Madison would've imagined, but despite his quiet voice the baby-soul burrowed closer and sucked harder on her fingers. "I smell angel on you."

The multi-horned creature leaned forward and sniffed her, as if to verify the truth of her friend's statement.

The female that approached with him, added her own two cents. "I smell something else, something more pure than an angel."

"You reek of the Ark of Heaven." *Madison turned her head to peer at the new speaker. He was the most humanoid of the three. Tall like the Kings of Hell and athletically muscular. Long, sin-black hair that shined even in this shadowy terrain.* "That is the purity you smell."

He swaggered closer. Leather-looking pants hung low on his hips, and his polished boots made zero noise as he approached. Deadly. "She's known an angel and the Ark of Heaven intimately. They've marked her in ways only intimacy can."

Impressive. Not just insightful, but she'd bet treacherous too.

His perfect facial features could've been ripped straight from any high-end magazine. He was so good-looking she felt the need to weep. Dear Gawd, I finally met a man that is more handsome than Micah. *He reminded her of how Hollywood would've portrayed a Goth vampire on the big screen.* He is no

178

bloodsucker. *Regardless of his companions' oddness or sizes, she sensed he posed the bigger threat.*

Two feet from her, he stopped and wings unfurled, one as blue-black as his hair and the other like red velvet. She suspected he wrapped them around his lovers when he fucked them. Most likely to trap them beneath him, damn sure not to show he cared. Because his type would care about no one but himself, a kindred spirit to her mother and Elias.

He oozed sex appeal like...like she could if she channeled her Lynx. Incubus. But not the average one that Micah employed. This one was more of everything...darker, unsafe, sexier, and most of all lethal.

Accented voice, his lilt flowed over her like rich wine, flavorful, intoxicating, and promised sinful delights. "I am Aramayis. I govern this realm. You may swear fealty to me now."

She would swear fealty to no one. Not Hell like Micah wanted and damn sure not this unknown creature. "You're an incubus."

"You are a succubus." *He trailed his fingers along her cheek, and Madison made no effort to stop his forwardness.* "Although, not very powerful. Pity. You will need power to survive our world." *He circled her.* "Maybe you can persuade me to protect you."

As if I'd stoop that low!

"You have fantastic lines, great breasts"—*he met her eyes briefly as he continued to prowl about her*—"hips a man can grip to anchor himself between your thighs." *He stopped behind her, his breath puffing against the back of her ear, much too close for her peace of mind. She also recognized it as a tactical move to dominate her.* "And a fantastic ass." *His fingers slid through her hair and down her spine*

She turned to face him just as his hand would've landed on her ass.

He smiled, devastating her for a heartbeat with his beauty. I want to fuck him. I need to—the asshole is mind-fucking me with his mojo.

The stretch of his power scared her a little. She couldn't enthrall without touch. That he could alarmed her.

Madison laughed. "You're good. I almost wanted to screw you for a moment."

A smug tilt hit one corner of his lips. Classy. Real classy. He bragged without saying a word. That took talent, not to mention big-fucking balls.

"That is why I govern this realm." *Aramayis swept his hand to indicate the cavern at large.*

He is much too arrogant.

Agreed, *said her inner demon.* Time to bring him down a notch...or ten. *Usha giggled like she'd enjoy his fall from the pedestal he'd placed himself upon.*

Madison lifted her hand and sifted her fingers through his hair. Cool tresses heated her fingertips. Everything about him must be designed to emit pheromones because she could feel them leeching into her flesh through his hair. Humanity would never be able to withstand his alluring vibe.

"Can you tone down your incubus elixir?"

"If I want." *He watched her, his gaze calculated, and his mouth turned into an eternal smirk.* "I rarely want." *Double innuendo there, she bet.*

"I'm Lynx." *His smile fell as his unnamed companions put some distance between them. At least they recognized her deadliness.* "I also own the power of Pandora."

"Pandora that fell the Zennyo Ryuo race?"

Madison nodded at the female's question.

In response, she slinked even deeper into the shadows.

Quickly, Madison turned toward the female, and the other woman froze as if she couldn't shift out of Madison's sight. "Your name." *It wasn't a request, but a demand.*

For a moment she thought the woman would deny giving it, but then she gave a reverent curtsy. "Indra," *she said before hurrying out of sight.*

"*That explains why she's the first soul to arrive since the dawn of mankind.*" The hulking creature bowed to one knee. "*Khoal is my name.*"

"*Indeed.*" Aramayis maintained his footing, his focus never leaving her face. "*We are all abominations.*"

"*Unjustly deemed too dangerous to populate Earth,*" the hulk intoned in his soft voice.

"*Not all of us were unjustly judged.*" Aramayis licked his full lips. "*I was not. I had fun while my reign lasted.*" He took another step closer to Madison, assaulting her personal space. "*What say you, Lynx, want to—*"

A sudden yank against her backbone and she stumbled backward, her arms cartwheeling to maintain her balance. Agony ripped up her back as if whatever pulled her snapped her spine. Madison cried out, bowing at the pain.

Aramayis zoomed to her and clutched her face between his palms. "*You are the prophecy.*"

What was he talking about?

He must've read her confusion because he said, "*You will release us from our prison.*"

They were domiciled here for a reason, and she wouldn't set them loose on humanity. Not as long as she had a choice.

The baby soul began to wail as if she too felt the stinging. "*I won't....*" She shook her head as another tug almost wrenched her out of Aramayis's grasp, but his grip tightened, and he clung to her.

"*You will,*" he insisted, his stare potent, bright with excitement.

His lips met hers in a non-sexual kiss. In that brief moment that he poured his elixir into her, the agonizing pull receded and pleasure invaded. Instinct propelled her to touch his face, and she doused him with her magic.

Aramayis groaned and nipped her bottom lip. "*Never tasted a succubus before.*"

"Won't start with me." Left in his presence too long, she sensed she'd break that vow.

He grinned and traced his thumb along her bottom lip, his mouth remained a fraction from hers. "I will find you, when the doors to Hakara fall, to claim a real kiss."

Unleashing him on anyone constituted an unforgiveable sin in her opinion. If the doors fell and these denizens embarked on humanity—

Another yank. Madison clutched her belly as heat furled through her entire body. Searing pain razored through her veins, and the child screeched.

She wrapped the girl in her arms, held on tight, and focused on channeling calm magic into her. It soothed the infant, and for a moment peace settled into Madison. Serenity cleared her mind, and words tumbled from her lips before she could process them. "I am the Alpha and Omega, the beginning and the end of Lynx...the mother of all abominations."

"No. We are crafted from the same Pyxis. I am the Alpha, you are the Omega—the beginning and the end. I am the father of all abominations—and your one true husband." Aramayis grinned, and chills scattered along Madison's flesh. "Until we meet again, my bride."

Her vision went cloudy as the pain burst through her chest like a detonation. No longer able to focus on soothing the infant, the baby shrieked before going eerily silent. She tried to peer at the child, but blackness embraced her. In stages she woke up. A fog billowed in her head. Pinpricks stung her skin. Her heart pounded.

Micah's scent was strong. His warm chest her foundation.

"Li," she mumbled and attempted—

Micah terminated the mind-meld so suddenly Madison gasped when he released her and drooped against Phoenix's hold. Unsure how to react, Micah stared at his woman. Complicated just became their new best friend. When she finally looked at him, her eyes blazed pink with the Pandora yellow rimming them.

"If you're thinking how this can benefit Hell—"

"I'm not." Not much rendered him speechless, but this...this left him dumbfounded. Aramayis wanted Micah's woman, had every right to her. They were connected cosmically through Pyxis DNA. As the first, and sole, living Lynx succubus, with Pandora power an integral part of her genetics, and Aramayis being the first and sole Lynx incubus, they each were powerful enough to split the world in half given the chance. Aramayis had given it the good ole college try before his incarceration. Micah worried the incubus's release would divide Madison's loyalties.

"You're realizing how big a monster I am, then?"

A smile twitched at the corner of his mouth. He lifted his hand from her shoulders and cupped her face, running his thumb along her cheekbone. "I've always known you are a monster, kitten. I admire your claws. I crafted you from the Pyxis, and it spawns nothing but monsters. I prefer you a little dark." Not that there was much about Madison that ran to the dark side of things.

"Then tell me what you're thinking, Micah. Your quietness is making me nervous."

"I'm thinking Aramayis wants you. You're connected to him, and he'll be next to irresistible to you. I will *not* share you with him. You're mine—"

"Ours," Phoenix modified.

Micah angled his head in agreement. "*We* won't share you."

"I don't want him."

"You will." He raked his hand through his hair, while maintaining a one-handed hold on her. The Ark of Heaven hadn't released her yet either. "Elias, Zennyo Ryuo, and I caged ninety percent of those in Hakara. Aramayis was one of them. He'll want us all dead."

"Who doesn't want Elias dead?" Zennyo Ryuo pointed out.

Yeah, his twin had a long line of enemies. Even he wanted his brother's head on a spike. Micah would prefer to torture him long and hard first as payback for harming Madison, but he doubted that'd be a likelihood. Chances were, the next opening he had to knock off his sibling would come with mere seconds of an opportunity to end his life.

"I'm okay." Madison took a deep breath and extracted herself from Phoenix's arms. She sent the three reapers a cagey glance. "What makes y'all certain these so-called monsters will come out of Hakara?"

So-called? They *were* monsters, nothing alleged about it. Almost all of them deserved their imprisonment. The world wouldn't exist if they hadn't been locked up. Something of his thoughts must've filtered to Madison because her telepathy was clear: *Maybe your father unjustly put them there the same way He unjustly damned you.*

She had a point, but before he could respond, Jasiel peered at Madison and said, "Once a soul is delivered to the realm, it cannot be removed without consequences. In Madison it split one into two." Micah translated that to mean Madison's resurrection was so traumatic it split the baby into two, resulting in twins. "Your extraction broke the locks to their domain. It is a locale worse than Hell, with abominations that have no rules. They'll rise. You can be certain of that."

"The dead should remain dead," Sarel appeared bored, but he sized Phoenix up as if he contemplated taking him on. His sibling would have a rude awakening if he tried.

Micah stepped forward and got in Sarel's space. "They're under my protection. Prepare for the *consequences* if you make a go at anyone under my protection."

From the corner of his eye, he spied Pyrel going up in smoke. Before he could warn Madison, his sister wrapped her smoky body around his woman. A moment later pastel orbs pockmarked the smoke and reformed across the room. Zennyo Ryuo came out of the teleport with Madison in his arms, coughing from smoke inhalation.

Pyrel came out of her style of teleport and glared at the immortal.

"I'm faster," Zennyo Ryuo stated the fact without an ounce of mockery.

"And I'm a hell of a lot more ruthless." Micah buried his *Scepter* between her shoulder blades, the point coming out of the other side between her breasts.

She threw her head back hard enough it hit his chest, and she screeched.

"Missed your soul by a quarter of an inch, sister, and I officially claim you for Hell's dominion."

The imprint of her soul branded along his senses, a clear indication he now owned her. She served him and would be compelled to perform his requests only.

"You'll release her or I'll take the Ark of Heaven as recompense." Sarel held Phoenix in a loose headlock.

Micah met the Ark's gaze. Phoenix offered him a brief smile, his silent way of stating he'd already tapped into the reaper's magic without him knowing. The irony of it all, Sarel would have his powers hijacked by someone he considered the lesser paranormal.

"We came in peace, not to instigate war," his alabaster brother, Jasiel, remarked, but the creases about his eyes said despite his claim they'd prepared for battle.

A second later, Zennyo Ryuo teleported Madison to Jasiel. As her eyes ignited pink, she touched the bleached reaper's arm, and Jasiel dropped before any of the reapers could've predicted Madison's threat. The immortal pulled his kitten away from the comatose angel before she could consume all of his spirit. Panting, she licked her lips, and dragged the back of her hand over her mouth.

Pyrel whimpered in his arms. "We came to aid—"

"Silence," Micah hissed in her ear. "You came after my woman in your smoke form. That constitutes an aggressive action. I already own your soul."

Her breath hitched.

"The only question remaining is do I twist the *Scepter* and kill you now or allow you to redeem yourself?"

"Your Ark will be dead before she is, Micah." Sarel placed a palm against the side of Phoenix's head and added enough pressure to angle the Ark's head sharply.

"You're already fucked, Sarel." Just to taunt his sibling, the King of Hell sawed his *Scepter* in and out of Pyrel. She rewarded him with screams of agony.

The sound drew Madison's hungry gaze off the reaper she'd just decimated.

"Cease! I'll snap his neck," Sarel warned.

"He's immortal," Madison said, her jaw hardening as her Lynx eyes brightened when they landed on Sarel. Not knowing her, the angel possessed no idea what that look implied. Micah could translate for him—she'd kick his ass before she allowed him to harm the Ark. "Micah gave him immortality, so only *he* can kill Nix. Micah, I want to taste them all."

Madison's request was delivered in an indifferent manner, but he could see the seriousness on her face.

"No," he thought Zennyo Ryuo said. In response her eyes narrowed.

"Abomination," Pyrel whispered. "She belongs in Hakara."

Ignoring his sibling, Micah spoke to Madison. "No." The last thing they needed was for Madison to start feeding on hosts with unknown side effects. Her gaze whipped about, and the Pandora yellow ring around her Lynx pink intensified. She'd challenge him if he failed to convince her against the consumption. "Kitten, think of the babies."

"Babies?" Of course Phoenix would hone in on the plurality of that word. The Ark obviously used the

186

reaper's magic against him because the angel collapsed an instant later. A moment after that he was in Madison's space.

"How'd he...manage"—Pyrel coughed up lava-like blood—"that?"

"You've got other things to worry about, sister."

"As do you, Micah." Her breathing was labored, but he paid her little attention as he watched Phoenix palm the baby bump on Madison's belly. "When the walls fall between Earth and Hakara, there is nothing standing in the way of rivers of blood."

"That's a bit dramatic."

"It's not." Zennyo Ryuo trapped the two fallen reapers in orbs of his magic. "Most of the Hakarians we imprisoned before they knew what we planned. Only a few gave us trouble. Once out, if all of them incited chaos at once, humanity would collapse before your angelic brethren could plan retaliation."

If his siblings cared enough to save mankind. The only reason Micah gave a damn about humanity was to thwart his father. Then he recalled Jesus's words. "Zennyo Ryuo, I'm speculating here, but I'm guessing since you've been given responsibility over humanity, saving them would be your problem, not the angels'." He exhaled. "We should have the dragons ice Jasiel and Sarel in angel locks long enough to determine our next step."

"That'll cause an imbalance." Pyrel angled her head to cut her eyes in his direction. "We must be able to reap."

"*You* will have to suffice." For the moment, he'd keep the other two as collateral. Micah wrenched the *Scepter* from her body and watched her crumple to the floor. On her hands and knees her lava-like blood flowed, creating a glowing puddle. He placed his palm against the wound on her back. "*Eyc tauq.*" Icy heal.

Pyrel screamed and collapsed face-first on the hardwood. Being an angel of fire, had he healed her by searing her skin, she'd have suffered nothing. Healing her with an icy burn was as good as dousing her flames with ice water.

"Enough, Micah." The immortal sounded as prudish as ever.

Micah elevated an eyebrow at the male. They were allies once more only because of their relationships with Madison. But if the uptight fuck thought his love for her tamed him, the immortal would learn the error of his belief. "Zennyo Ryuo, the other two must be in an Angel Lock prior to reviving."

"There's no need to torture her further. You own her."

Micah grinned. He'd owned her the moment he impaled her on his *Scepter*. "You've never seen torture if you believe this constitutes it. This is a lesson to dissuade her from becoming brave enough to make another play for Madison."

"It's not right."

He held Zennyo Ryuo's haughty stare. "It's the *only* way to maintain respect in my world."

The immortal's jaw hardened, but he touched both of the defeated angels and teleported from the room with them.

His kitten knelt beside his sister, her gaze traveling over his sibling. What went through her head?

At her back, Phoenix stood, watching her, too. The creases at his eyes suggested he waited to halt Madison from feeding.

Micah crouched at Pyrel's side. "Roll over so I can complete the repair."

"*Li*," *No*, she gasped, attempting to inch away from him. "I can self-heal."

"Not from the *Scepter* you cannot."

His wife ran her fingertip along his sibling's puckered flesh and down her spine. Micah caught her hand, and she took a long moment before she elevated her gaze to him. Lynx fizzled in her eyes. Holding her hand, he stared at her as he used a smidge of magic and flipped Pyrel to her back. "No taste-testing, kitten."

A sweet grin spread across her features. "I'm not."

But she'd planned to. He could read that truth all over her face. "How'd Jasiel taste?"

"Not as good as you and Nix."

Micah grinned. "Good to know."

"There's a way to halt, possibly stop the breaking of the locks." Pyrel placed her hands over the seeping wound on her chest.

"Not an option, sister."

Phoenix placed his hand on Madison's shoulder. "Why isn't it an option, Micah? What are we missing?"

Before he could respond to the Ark, his sister spoke. "You would damn the world for her?"

Her question angered him. Of course he would damn the world for Madison. He shoved Pyrel's hands aside, hovered his palm over the wound in her chest, and thrust his healing magic into her.

She bowed beneath his touch and went limp the moment the wound was healed. "I would cut out my soul for her, Pyrel. I'd damn the world, the universe, and any other solar system that threatened her life."

"The same." Phoenix knelt and caught Micah's gaze. "What am I missing, Micah?"

"For the locks to stop breaking, Madison would have to return to Hakara."

A single nod from the Ark of Heaven verified they were united. "We're agreed. That's not an option."

Chapter 19

LIVING WITH MADS could be likened to riding a rollercoaster without brakes. Boredom would never become a problem. With another threat looming on the horizon, worry twisted Nix's stomach for not just his woman, but also his unborn children and the survival of the world.

Mads continued to watch Pyrel as if she'd make a go any moment to taste her angelic elixir. Getting her appetite under control was more difficult than any of them suspected. That spawned further worry. He and the King gave her access to their messian and seraph throughout the day, whenever she craved food. That she carried twins instead of a single birth could account for some of her hunger, but not her irrational need to feast on anything with power. But she seemed more fixated on comparing the taste of magics than experiencing actual hunger.

"Your reapers are iced." Kur strode into the room with all the swagger of an immortal that knew his security among his fellow residents. His gaze zeroed in on Mads. "Any of them hurt you, sweetheart?"

That the dragon had grown comfortable enough

with Mads over the last couple of months to use endearments chafed Nix's nerves raw. Micah's jaw hardened, indicating he felt the same.

"Madison is self-sufficient." Micah's hot glare contradicted his cool tone. "She dropped Jasiel into his catatonic state."

Kur grinned and halted in front of her. He executed a playful cuff beneath her chin. "That's my girl."

"One day, dragon, one fucking day...." Micah's fragmentary promise caused Kur to smirk at the threat. When that day came, Nix planned to aid him, *if* they ever followed through with their desires.

"We can't send Mads back to Hakara, so what do we do?" Nix pulled her against him, placing his palm on her rounding tummy. *My daughters.* He couldn't figure out what he'd done right to deserve such a blessing. "We need a plan before the catastrophes blindside us."

"They'll blindside you, Ark of Heaven." Pyrel pushed to her feet in jagged shoves as Zen teleported into the room. The reaper coughed up smoke, and a fine bead of lava-colored blood rolled from the corner of her mouth and down her chin. Nix hoped she still hurt from Micah's *Scepter* for the simple reason she'd threatened his woman. "None of you understand the horrors trapped there."

"Micah and I understand better than you, reaper." Zen crossed his arms over his chest. "We fought them to put them there."

"We'll require Elias's help."

Nix's arm around Mads's shoulder tightened at her out-there statement.

"No." Nix's knee-jerk reaction was to agree with her, but only so they could finally locate the bastard and then kill him for hurting her.

"Fuck no."

Sometimes he adored Micah's elegant way of putting things.

"*Woyr li,*" he repeated in Xapil, a clear indication

she'd rattled the King when he switched between dialects.

"Why would we trust him, Madison?" Zen leaned against the arm of a chair, hands gripping the furniture, his fingertips white, in direct contrast to his stoic expression.

She met her crystal genie's stare with a slight jutting of her chin. "The Hakarians endanger Hell's power and—"

"We've limited Elias's power in Hell, kitten. Soon he won't have a reason to want to protect our domain."

Interesting news to all of them, and Nix wondered why Micah hadn't shared the information with at least him and Mads.

"You know I don't agree with that decision."

Apparently he *had* shared the news with Mads. When had he missed out on the tell-all conversation?

You're not vital to Hell, so you wouldn't be informed, Zen slithered into his mind. A hard, uncomfortable shudder racked Nix's frame, and he shot the immortal a sharp glance. He despised the man getting into his head, but the astute words had him giving a slight nod of his head by way of acknowledgement.

What Nix struggled to comprehend was *why* she'd side with the monster that would've killed her if not for her accepting her power as the Queen of Hell. At that point, her choice had only been to accede to her fate or die.

"Tough love, Madison. He deserves the rebuke." When she opened her mouth to argue, the demon King talked over her. "I won't engage this particular argument further."

"I'm the Queen. The insult was to *me*. I should be given some consult in that decision!"

Before Nix could thwart their feud, Zen interfered. "You waste time on disputes that have no bearing on the problem at hand." The immortal fingered hair off his forehead. "Elias is a minor problem compared to the residents of Hakara."

"Debatable. They're more of an emergency. Elias can wait." Micah shot a pointed glance in Pyrel's direction. "Knowing the location of Hakara's locks would be helpful. We could add our own locks before the others break."

"I've no idea where they're located, but I remind you this is apocalyptic in nature." Pyrel's assistance surprised Nix, but since they'd come under false pretenses his limited trust kicked into high gear, and he contemplated her motives.

"Does she speak true, Micah?" Zen asked.

"Yeah." The King considered his sibling, forehead creased with a frown.

"One of the four Horsemen would've been notified of the imminent threat," Zen added to Beliel's limited reply.

"They cannot interfere with end times. It's forbidden." Micah ran his palm down his face.

"How's that a problem?" Kur held up his hand when the King looked ready to rip into him. "Find one of these Horsemen, use your *Scepter* on him and claim them for your domain. Loyalties transition then, right?"

Seemed reasonable. Nix peered at Micah to gauge his response, but the Fallen shook his head. "Doesn't work that way with them. They're immune to the power of the *Scepter*."

"All the same," Zen pushed away from the chair, "I know how to locate War. It won't hurt to ask."

"Want me to join you?" Micah asked, but his stare remained on his sibling.

"No." Zenny smirked. "After your last encounter with him, you're likely to incite complications rather than provide aid. I'd recommend keeping Amos housed in Hell until this issue is resolved."

Pyrel laughed, and it sounded more demonic than some demons. "Just one of Hakara's residents escapes and it'll never be safe for Amos to exit Hell."

"Can I ice her mouth?" Kur nodded at the reaper.

While the question had been delivered in a neutral tone, as if he discussed the best way to grow crops, his sapphire eyes flickered with something unholy. Although Nix hadn't witnessed the totality of the dragon's powers, the male had demonstrated his lethality more than once.

The door opened, and the Hellhounds and Taz burst into the room. Taz beelined for Mads and launched into the air ten feet away from her. As the creature knocked Nix's arm off her shoulder and curled around her neck, the canines came to a sliding halt at her feet.

Protective beast. Taz held zero respect for Nix's place in Mads's life. Nix ran his finger over the mini-dragon's head. The creature executed a mock growl.

"I'm okay." Mads ran her fingertips over his snout. At her touch, that growl turned into a light purr, but the way the mini-dragon peered about was a clear warning for all to stay back. She knelt and scratched both pups behind their ears. Devlin whined, and FiFi woofed. "Micah, Nix, and Zen would never let anything happen to me. Y'all worried for nothing."

"I'm insulted." Micah rolled his eyes in mock insult. "I didn't see one of you in here kicking ass...or biting ankles."

FiFi bared her teeth in reply as Petra strolled into the room, her sultry presence preceding her seconds before her arrival.

"Not sure what went on, but these three went ballistic wanting into this room. Taz was pulling on my hair." Petra rubbed her scalp and glared at the dragon. "That hurts. And Devlin kept nipping at my heels to make me run faster."

Nix chuckled. If the Hellhound had nipped hard enough to break skin, she'd have died from toxins in his saliva. Devilish to scare her like that, but the threat seemed effective. What Nix wouldn't have given to see that sequence play out.

"I'm not amused, Phoenix." Petra tossed him a hostile glare.

"Catch Petra up to speed on what's going on while I

put some feelers out for War," Zen commanded, taking charge like always.

"War?" Petra paled as Zen teleported in a swirl of pastel rainbow orbs.

"Let me guess, he hates you as much as me." Kur bumped into Petra making her stumble to catch her balance. "My bad."

Micah blasted the dragon with enough power to put him on his ass. A bellow of smoke puffed from Kur's nostrils.

"Mind your manners," the King of Hell glared at the huffing and puffing dragon. "She's my daughter." Demeanor collected and in total contradiction to his aggression toward Kur, Micah turned to his demon-child and explained the circumstances.

Mads's stepdaughter retrieved a lollipop from the pocket of her jeans and removed the wrapper. "So, basically, Phoenix is to blame for this fuck-up since he brought Madison back to life."

"If he hadn't revived her, I'd have found a way. Even if I had to break the locks on one of those goddamn doors myself."

Recalling their time in Hell when they'd both believed Mads died at Zen's hand, Nix knew Micah spoke nothing but the cold hard truth. The King held zero qualms about burning the world to cinders to ensure her safety.

Nix would stand by his side and assist him regardless of the outcome. *Anything for Mads* might've been his motto in Hell, but he hadn't altered from that proverb since breaking the chains of his Fall. "I should call my family. Let them know what's going on. Have them put a call in to a few Sherlocks. That way if the doors collapse the fallout will be less."

"I'll send four of my best demons to guard the Birminghams." Sometimes Micah managed to surprise Nix. This counted as one of those moments.

"Thanks, but you know they'll shun the protection." His family's stubbornness could eclipse his own at times.

Madison looked at him, her fingers roaming over the mini-dragons snout. "The way I see it, they can like it or lump it, either way they're getting our protection."

God, she was sexy. And she'd protect what she thought of as hers regardless what they wanted. He loved that about her. As Cael—the other dragon—entered the room, she palmed her belly and caressed the slight bump.

He'd bet his bank account that indicated she was hungry. No surprise, she always seemed hungry for food, seraph, messian, or sex.

Micah held his hand out in her direction, a silent offering to dine on his seraph. Mads accepted his offer, curling into his side, she encircled his waist with her arms, supporting herself. The King curled his other arm around her low back, hauling her against his larger frame. Ingesting his power always affected her libido, so she'd require his assistance to remain upright. If she consumed his mojo too long, she'd climax just from his magic.

"The reapers are beginning to wake." Cael stared at Mads. "Want me to fuck-em-up, sexy Q?"

"No." Micah's voice hardened. Mads feeding from him had the same effect on his arousal. "That's my job. Get Ginnie so we can defuse their magic. I'll deal with them later after they're neutralized and Madison's fed. Phoenix, I'm going to take her to the bedroom. When she's done"—double meaning there— "I'm going to Hell to put mine and Madison's demons on your family and then send some out to scout the hotspots with the most paranormal activity." Made sense that those would be near the doorways to Hakara. There was no guarantee Zen could convince War to assist them, so the plan seemed like a solid idea. "Even when Phoenix is watching over her, I want you both on her." He leveled his gaze on the two dragons.

"Is it your intention to offend me?" Kur crossed his arms, having risen moments before. "She's my queen. I'd defend her against *you* if need be."

"The same." Cael tossed his long, honey-colored hair over his shoulder. Nix couldn't decide which of the two irritated him more. "Loyal to Madison and Madison alone. Don't take commands from you either."

Not rising to either dragon's baiting, Micah smirked and lifted Mads into his arms. "Let's finish feeding you, kitten." The King of Hell went through a portal with their woman.

Knowing Mads's feeding would end in her climax, Nix itched to join them. But securing his family's safety was paramount to his sexual inclinations. There'd be time for loving later.

Chapter 20

ZEN LEANED AGAINST a pillar in the local mall as customers weaved around one another to get to various retailers. Evening fell across the land in an unnatural conglomeration of purple streaking the horizon. The clouds billowed like fiery brimstone against the mauve skyline. The view could easily pass for a special effects scene from any doomsday movie. He suspected Hakara's rise was to blame.

Customers stopped to stare through the windows at the eerie manifestation. Every television in the food court and the sports store across from him reported the odd phenomenon. Scientists were baffled. No surprise when there was nothing natural about the occurrence.

Over four hours ago he left a message for War with a mutual acquaintance to meet here at his earliest convenience. Zen began to suspect the Horseman would be a no-show. All Horsemen were unpredictable so even if he did put in an appearance, Zen held no real hope the warmonger would aid them. Halting an apocalypse went against the rules. Rules that could cause them great suffering.

198

"Zennyo Ryuo." The sound of the Horseman's voice came from his side. Zen had had only a second to feel his approach before he spoke. Out of the four, the Red Horseman—War as he was known among the angels—was the most treacherous. "Thank you for meeting me, War."

"What do you want?"

He respected the way the other male always got to the point. "Aid."

"You're wasting my time."

"It's not like you had anything better to do." These four brothers lived among humans, surveyed the goings on, but never reacted unless they witnessed one of the signs that heralded end times. "I'm not asking you to assist. I require only the location of the Hakara locks."

"There are other angels that could provide you with that information." War shifted enough that Zen caught a glimpse of him from the corner of his eye.

"How many angels do you think will assist me without wanting to throw the Queen of Hell back within Hakara? The reapers came to take her, not to assist." Many might want to put him there too since his recent Fall, or maybe not since Jesus saddled him with protecting humanity from apocalypse.

Unnerving silence from War lasted so long Zen thought the other man might've departed. When he spoke, Zen executed a mental sigh of relief. "Why such loyalty to the Fallen's wife?"

"She's worth fighting for."

"And Falling for, apparently."

Zen inclined his head, but remained silent.

That War wasn't outright denying assistance surprised him. "What good is knowing the whereabouts of the locks?"

"We have a plan to ensure the locks hold." No point in giving War all the details.

"We?"

Zen turned his head to peer at War. The other male

looked like a thug or biker, a fitting motif considering his role to play in end times.

"Does the 'we' matter when our sole, united intention is to halt Armageddon?"

War smirked. "Armageddon is not at hand, even if Hakarians join humanity. The reapers provoked drama and hate, nothing more."

Good to know, but not what they'd been led to believe. "The reapers believe the locks breaking would kick start the end times."

"No signs point in that direction." War shrugged.

War would be the first Horseman to receive notification of end times.

He considered the other man a moment. As long as Zen had known the Horseman, prevaricating had been beyond his realm of comprehension, so Zen knew the warmonger spoke the truth. Maybe the reapers' agenda wasn't as nonviolent as they claimed and they really only wanted Madison back in Hakara. They wouldn't be the first angels to come for her with nefarious intentions. And only Sarel and Jasiel had vowed they came in peace. Pyrel never made the same assertion. "Either way, too many lives will be lost if the monsters exit Hakara. Are you prepared for their blood to be on your hands?"

War stared straight ahead, but an amused chuff came from him. "I incite wars. Slain blood is always on my hands. Lost lives are not my concern." The Red Horseman's moral code *was* different than most angels.

"You have no reason not to assist us."

"I have no reason *to* assist you."

Valid point even if its truth irritated Zen.

"If I do this, you'll owe me a future favor."

That was a dangerous arrangement to make with any angel, but especially one of the Horsemen.

"I retain the right to refuse." There must be options to this deal if he would give it serious consideration.

"Two refusals." War held up two fingers as he scanned the crowd. "After the second, you must perform the third task requested."

Zen preferred to be indebted to Micah rather than War. The King of Hell was a little more predictable. He would do anything to protect his relatives, but the things War could ask might circumvent Zen's loyalty to his adopted family. "Whatever you ask cannot directly or indirectly harm my new family."

"If I asked you to do something that caused the first step toward Armageddon—"

"I'd tell you to go fuck yourself until the end of time." Zen would damn his soul again before he'd harm his family.

War grinned. "Eloquently put. I agree to your terms."

Chapter 21

MADISON STARED AT herself in her bathroom mirror. Palming her belly, she stroked the slight swell, mentally reminding her daughters how much she loved them. That she'd protect them at all costs. As if to say they loved her back or maybe trusted her to keep them safe, a bubble of warmth spread from her stomach upward to settle at the center of her chest.

Reliving the memories of her short time in Hakara unsettled her in ways she couldn't comprehend. Torn between securing the locks and greeting monsters that she felt an unnatural affinity with, she blew out a breath as she set her demon free. Her eyes blazed pink, Pandora yellow circling her irises. Thanks to Micah, she feared her demon less each day.

Aramayis. Her fear of him was sensible. That he could force her to desire him terrified her more than she wanted to admit.

She squinched her eyes to ward off his memories, but that only brought to mind a clear vision of him. Madison felt certain he'd exit the realm before any of the others. His ego wouldn't allow for another to be the primary defector. The certainty she'd be his first objective overrode all other thoughts. That he seeded worry in Micah supplied her with all the resumé she required on the incubus to make an informed opinion. If he succeeded in claiming her like he'd warned in Hakara, the outcome would result in severe ramifications for Hell.

I hope he comes alone. He'd be easier to deal with by himself. With other Hakarians in tow, she feared defeat would be inevitable.

Pastel orbs formed in the mirror's reflection mere seconds before Zen teleported into the room. "What disturbs you, my sister?"

"Everything." Safety for her children, her husbands, Hell, and even humanity plagued her. Shrugging her anxiety aside, she pivoted to face him. "Did you meet with War?"

He glanced over her shoulder for a brief second. Madison knew his telltale signs of avoidance and recognized the lack of eye contact as one of those signals.

"He gave me the location."

"At what price?" She cupped his chin when he would've looked away once more. "*At what price,* brother?"

"A future favor." Zen's silver gaze held hers without blinking. His expression gave nothing away, but she knew him well enough to read between the lines and connect the dots.

"This favor worries you?"

The back of his hand bumped against hers, and she hooked their pinkies together. Zen leaned his forehead against hers. A classic sign he sought comfort. "An inconsequential price to pay for protecting my family."

"But War isn't someone you owe a favor to lightly." It wasn't a question, but a statement, and he must've taken it as such because he offered no reply. Instead they just stared at one another.

That he was called to protect her once again angered her. That he'd felt forced to promise the

Horseman something because of his need to protect her frustrated her even more. She'd placed her family in danger one too many times for her peace of mind.

And the hits keep coming. Would they ever find peace?

Being a one-of-a-kind Lynx succubus held benefits, engineered respect from the weaker immortals. She also could easily protect her family against many would-be enemies. But those same one-of-a-kind attributes incited hate among others, which generated uncalled for attacks to attempt annihilation of her and her offspring.

Once this newest drama ends, gaining further power will be my main goal. That was a promise her and her demon alike could uphold. Like Zen said, it was an inconsequential price to pay to protect her family.

"The reapers were taken from Micah," she said, catching him up-to-date.

"Pyrel too?"

"Yes." While Zen met with War, Micah had requested Ginnie to invalidate the reapers' magic. The Baltic had performed as requested and a few minutes later the reapers vanished. It'd been an anticlimactic turn of events.

Zen inclined his head, indicating he read her mind and the sequence of events during his absence. "It was to be expected. Only Micah's arrogance that he can do anything he desires had him believing he could claim them for his Kingdom. His father most likely harvested them."

Micah said the same, but he left out the arrogance part.

Zen grinned. *Of course he did.*

Madison journeyed to Hell to update Amos on what

transpired. She discovered him playing basketball with a group of the youngling-demons. Of all the ways he could pass time in Hell, he surprised her by finding companionship in a human way with non-human children. Regardless of his princely status, from the way they ribbed him for missing shots none of them cared about her son's hellish rank. He laughed with them, egging them on with all the bluster of his father.

Amos spied her and would've joined her, but she waved him away.

Finish your game. I can wait, she telepathed.

While he goofed off with the other youngsters, she strolled through Hell until she found the cavern Elias had employed to torture her. Littering the floor were the devices he'd used on her...the bone jaw-clamps that pierced her skin and strung her up so he could use the whip of rusty nails on her, peeling away her flesh like one would skin a potato. It was as if both devices were forgotten and left to rot after her suffering ended.

Madison turned away from the sight of the gadgets. The torment hadn't ended when Elias had been stopped. Every little detail of that anguish could be brought forth with ease. She squirreled the memories away because the smallest recollection of believing she'd murdered Nix and Amos still caused her immense distress. Her physical pain had been minimal compared to her mental angst, which had almost broken her.

The look-alike Nix had been gagged, so he couldn't scream as she'd been compelled to saw the rusty knife across his flesh, the blade lurching because of its dullness as she dragged it across his neck. Then she'd been forced to turn the weapon on her son, the warm blood of the Amos-double had coated her hands, causing her to wish for her own death.

Tears blurred her vision as she shook her head, forcing the remembrance aside. She spied the point of something reddish-brown across the room on the floor and walked toward it. Once she neared, she realized it was the blade Elias had forced her to use on the Amos and Nix doppelgangers.

"Reliving the dark memories aren't healthy, Madison." Hielel intruded on her gloomy interlude. "They serve no purpose."

"Not true." She looked at the ever-changing appearance of the fallen archangel known to the world as Lucifer. "The memories remind me that even the most reliable are *not* trustworthy."

"I believe you know that to be untrue."

Madison offered him an indecisive shrug. Most of her motley crew she trusted implicitly, but Elias's betrayal taught her to second guess even that belief.

"If you wanted revenge, you could lead Beliel straight to Eliel, but you don't."

"No," she agreed, rolling with the topic shift. "Revenge isn't on my agenda regardless of what Micah wants." She could track all the Kings at any given moment, including Elias. Choosing to withhold that information from her husbands wasn't something she elected to do lightly. Despite her hatred toward Elias, he was Micah's twin, and she wanted no part in Elias's demise. "Three wrongs don't make a right."

He elevated blond eyebrows that shifted into the color red.

The first wrong came when Elias tortured her to force Madison to become the Queen of Hell. The second wrong was when the Kings reduced Elias's clout in Hell, a Kingdom he'd helped create. No way would she spread further wrongs by leading an avenging brother to his twin. But there was little point in elucidating her meaning when Hielel could figure out her comment on his own, so she navigated them back on topic. "Why haven't you told Micah I can locate Elias?"

"It's not my secret to tell."

"Uh huh." She wasn't buying that.

"You have your reasons."

"I thought Kings were always honest with one another?"

"We are." Hielel shifted into one persona and held the form. "If Beliel asked me outright, I'd tell him the truth."

The former archangel was gorgeous. Glossy blue-black hair framed his drop-dead, model-perfect features. He must've caught her surprise because he smiled.

"I can't speak for Beliel or Raguel, but my verdict against Eliel has sound reasoning behind it," he said. "Eliel deserves his punishment. Forgiveness can be granted, and his status returned. Like Beliel, Eliel walked a dangerous path of bitterness, neither of them realizing Father granted us freewill and freedom to purchase our own future. They resented that He gave us what we wanted."

She'd thought for a long while that He allowed their Fall because it served His purpose.

"You gave Beliel the peace he sought."

"Me."

He inclined his head. "Now it's Eliel's turn to find that peace, and he cannot do it with us at his side. He requires a different kind of Fall before he can discover happiness." Lucifer's bright green eyes creased at the corners with sadness. "Beliel and Eliel loved Father most. They cannot see that He loves us still."

Ruminating over all that Hielel said, Madison knelt and retrieved the blade. She stood and turned to face him. "We will defeat this new problem." Peering into his emerald eyes, she realized all of his chatter had been uttered to direct her path. And she knew exactly what direction she'd take regardless of her husbands' opinions. "Elias *will* help us."

"What the Queen wants the Queen gets."

Madison strode to Lucifer and hugged him. "Thanks."

"For what?"

She pulled away and made a circling motion around her face. "Trusting me enough to reveal the real you." He held her stare until she confessed, "And for reminding me that even those who've wronged us deserve second chances to demonstrate the truth of their devotion."

With Amos's hair damp and sweat creating a pungent aroma, he was all grins when he located Madison a little over an hour later.

"Who won?" she asked, setting aside her e-reader.

"They did." Amos laughed. "I think they cheated."

"That's a pretty safe bet." Even with their duplicity, they would've beaten Amos at that particular sport. Amos excelled at many things, but basketball wasn't one of them.

"I know why you're here," he said, slumping into a chair near her. "He's dangerous."

Amos can say that again, Usha chimed in.

"How much do you know?"

"Enough to scare me. You're good at blocking details from me when you don't want me to know them."

Thank Hell for small favors.

"I know you died for me when those angels came."

Madison grimaced. She'd tried to hide that from him.

"I know Daddy-Nix brought you back. I know the one stalking you now is really, *really* dangerous and he comes from the other side when you were dead." He palmed his face and wiped his sweaty hand on his pants afterward. "He makes Daddy nervous."

And they both new Micah worried only when warranted. "Any visions on how I should proceed?"

He shook his head. "Not yet. It's like I know there's something coming, and a prophecy inches close, but I can't *see* it. When I try to force it, what I *can* see fogs over and I get a bad headache."

She never wanted him to suffer on her behalf. "Stop pushing it. It'll eventually come."

"Yeah. I guess."

"Go get a shower, and we'll head home to eat dinner afterward."

"You care if I stay here? Me and the boys scheduled a rematch for later."

The grin eating up his face infected her and she smiled. "Have fun, angel. Let one of your uncles know if you need something."

Chapter 22

THE NEXT DAY, Madison dove into cooking as a way of warding off worry of the unknown. So far none of the creatures had managed to squeeze through the breaking locks of Hakara, and she wanted to settle this problem sooner rather than later because a monster could escape at any time. The death of any human that followed would be on her conscience. Thankful for small favors, they lucked out with the locks eroding slowly rather than breaking outright.

Micah dismissed seeking Elias's help, but thanks to her conversation with Hielel she knew—

A tingle started at the base of Madison's spine, startling her as it worked upward to the nape of her neck. She spun around in time to witness Aramayis utilizing his incubus skills to incapacitate her protectors. The colors coming off his magic were blood red and interlaced with a hot-pink lattice design. An odd conglomeration that should clash, but instead the design was beautiful and alluring.

To be captured in his web is nothing more than a pretty lie.

Cael gasped and hit the floor where he stood in

front of the refrigerator with the door wide open. Kur groaned, and tilted forward, his forehead making a soft thumping sound against the windowpane. The dragon remained motionless with his arms crossed over his chest. Nix went to rise, but a blood-red glob punched him in the heart. Her husband shot an alarmed glance in her direction before collapsing back into his chair and slumping over the table in silent surrender.

Madison let her demon free in a burst of magic that hit so strong her heart beat painfully against her rib cage.

That's some serious mojo. More than she could throw off. Touch was vital to her magic.

Aramayis elevated his arms out and smirked. Madison's free hand fisted, wanting to smack the gloat off his face. The bowl in her other hand cracked from her grip. He'd decimated her crew without a fight.

"Told you I would come for you. To claim a real kiss. One you will never forget."

Without looking, Madison set aside the bowl she'd been mixing cake batter in. They stared at one another. His sexual appeal was as hypnotic on Earth as in Hakara. A bubble approached her like a storm cloud, and she threw out her hand to ward off the encroachment of his magic.

He grinned when his enchantment continued to advance.

"Back. Off." Intolerant to manipulation, she wouldn't allow his violation.

"I would never harm you, my bride." The sultry tone of his voice tangled around her eardrums and morphed into her bloodstream like heroine. It served as a hallucinogenic, and she began to envision them twined together in explicit detail.

Mind fucking me like in Hakara.

Won't stand for it, her succubus chimed in.

"Not your fucking bride." Madison shook her head, but failed to clear his mind-altering affect. Trembling all over, she locked her knees to maintain her footing. "Have...two hus-husbands already." Tongue feeling two sizes too big, she struggled to eject the final word.

Treacherous, Lynx gauged him with caution. It took talent to make her demon leery.

Amos warned he was very dangerous. Too new at finagling her powers, she had no idea how to combat his brand of magic, especially when she could only control others through the ingestion of their blood. She shot a bead to freeze time, but it was ineffective. Or he was immune.

"*Had*," he said, which confused her.

Had what?

"I can rectify that issue."

He made no sense whatsoever.

Madison leaned against the counter, inhaling and exhaling in long deep breaths. "Dial it back."

"I do not comprehend."

Great. He was old school and didn't understand new slang. "Withdraw your magic."

"I prefer you like this. Flush with arousal, your eyes over bright." Until he spoke, she didn't realize he'd approached her. "Do you really want me to extract my elixir?"

"Yes." *Do we?* Usha asked, growing indecisive as she surveyed the incubus with new insight. What he's doing feels so...

Divine, Madison finished the sentence for her.

Yes! Imagine how good his magic would taste if we ingested it.

Madison groaned as the sudden all-consuming need to taste-test slugged her like a bad case of hives. Seriously, this junkie reaction to sampling powers got old. Refusing to look at him for fear she'd cave to her desires, she turned her head aside and gripped the countertop.

Drink him down. Usha prowled just beneath her skin causing goose bumps to spew along her flesh. For the first time since encountering her ability to consume powers, she feared what his would do to her if she partook.

"I do not believe you wish for me to tone it down." He touched her face and trailed his fingertips along her cheek. Madison jerked at the contact, and his smugness grew. "I want to watch you go up in flames." She held zero doubt what type of flames he wanted. She wouldn't grant him the privilege. Not ever.

Blue fire erupted along her body as she knocked his hand aside. She slammed both of her palms on his chest, and flooded his system with hellish flames. It sufficed enough to send him reeling backward.

Smoke spiraled from where her palms burned his skin in the shape of her handprints. He fingered the blisters, eyes wide with...she couldn't be certain, but she thought it looked like admiration. "I adore a woman into kinky foreplay."

"In. Your. Dreams."

A lecherous grin curled his lips. "I make dreams come true, bride."

Madison sidled sideways so he couldn't trap her against the counter again. He followed her step for step. As one unit they stopped and stared. He played games with her, stalking her like prey. "What do you want, Aramayis?"

"Many things." He abandoned his post and strode about the room, peering at Cael a long moment before drawing closer to Nix. Madison would've scrambled across the room had she thought she could reach him before the incubus. "You granted me number one at the top of my list. Freedom from Hakara." He nodded at Nix. "One of your soon-to-be former husbands?"

"You just damned yourself." Pandora magic crackled along her fingertips. The incubus glanced at her hands before slowly lifting his gaze to her face.

"Such firepower. Do you know how to regulate it?"

"Why wouldn't I?"

Black eyebrows elevated. "Indeed. Why would you not?" Watching her, he trailed his finger along Nix's neck.

Jealousy slammed through her.

He touches what's mine, her Lynx screamed.

Madison took a step toward him.

"Ah-ah." Magic sizzled on his fingertips. "I will claim him as mine if you attempt to come between us."

Micah appeared behind him as Madison said, "You'll regret that threat."

Aramayis grinned.

Micah placed his hand on Nix's shoulder and portaled them both across the room to Madison's side. "He's as much mine as he is hers, incubus."

"Micah." The incubus's eyebrows elevated, detailing his surprise. "Your other husband, bride?"

Madison nodded. "My first."

"An archangel and the Ark of Heaven. Interesting combination."

"I have a new title now." Micah settled Nix on the floor and whopped him with magic.

Rainbow orbs appeared behind Aramayis, and a second later Zen tapped him on the back of the head with a shot of magic strong enough the incubus cried out, eyes widening a long second before he hit the floor like a bag of useless garbage.

"I cannot wake Phoenix. He needs a succubus's magic to lure him away from the incubus."

"The dragons will require her as well." Zen peered at the fallen incubus. "Can you lock him in a cage in Hell?"

"Will it hold him?" Madison channeled her mojo into Nix until he began to rouse. "My time-freezing was ineffective against him."

"It should cage him since it's our domain. If I need to I can get Lucifer and Raguel to add their magic."

"We need Elias's aid."

Micah glared at her. "Not another fucking word about that."

"She may be on to something." Nix groaned and clutched his head between his hands.

"I don't trust him with her welfare." Micah glowered at Nix. "Do you Phoenix?"

"Fuck no, but she's the Queen of Hell now. His loyalties lie with Hell. Aramayis and all of Hakara disrupt Hell's control. Endangers mankind." Nix caught her wrist and met her gaze, his eyes drowsy. "Baby, that feels fucking good."

She smiled at him as she dialed back her magic.

"Fuck mankind." Anger jazzed Micah's aura in spikes of blue. "You're either with me, Phoenix, or against me."

"Go fuck yourself, King of Hell. Just because I share Mads with you doesn't always mean I'm on *your* side."

A groan from Aramayis drew everyone's focus in his direction. Before Zen could react with another knockout-blow of magic, the incubus was on his feet with a wall-cloud of power separating them from him. "Well played, bride."

A red and fuchsia mist swirled around the incubus's feet, rising upward to rotate around his body. He vanished.

"Goddamnit!" Micah bellowed. "Can something please go right?"

The hellhounds skidded into the kitchen with a bevy of ferocious growls. Taz joined them cawing like a demented demon or one in grave pain.

Next time it'd be harder to take the incubus by surprise.

I know how to stop him, her son told her telepathically, his excitement evident in his mental voice. *But Daddy won't like it.*

Chapter 23

PETRA WATCHED THE Sherlocks. Fantasies of fucking them and feeding from them cartwheeled through her head. She'd ingest their spirit until she was stuffed and they were corpses. One little bead of her succubus magic and they'd follow her home without a word of encouragement. It'd be so easy to claim them. Good times...until she had to deal with Mommy Dearest.

If Madison knew she stalked these two or that she nourished daydreams of them as often as she did, her stepmother would be pissed off. Madison could be scary when she put her heart into it, and she'd make Petra regret fancying any mortal.

Daddy and Amos love me, so I'm confident they would diffuse any real threat Madison instigated.

With an exasperated sigh, Petra blew wispy stands of hair off her face.

I kid no one, least of all myself.

Daddy might be one of the formidable Kings of Hell, but he sucked at controlling his kitten, aka his wife and Petra's wicked stepmother. Yeah, okay, labeling Madison that way was unfair, but so-fucking-what. Thanks to the wicked Queen's fun-sucking ways, Petra's mood ran dark and deep tonight. *She fueled my resentment when she told me I couldn't have the guy at the movie theater.* The selfish bitch had two guys at home to see to her needs. Petra had to hunt for tasty nourishment. Not all humans tasted the same. Demon nourishment lacked the protein required to stave off midnight cravings.

Tomorrow Petra knew she'd feel differently. It wasn't the first time Madison had killed all of Petra's fun, and despite her agitation tonight, she'd still give her life for Mommy Dearest, and she'd even follow Madison into Heaven if necessary.

An involuntary shudder rolled along Petra's spine at that gruesome idea, mostly because she wouldn't put it past Madison to attempt a revolution if prodded. If Amos's safety were at stake, Madison would rip those heavenly pilings from their very foundation. Bluntly put...Petra would place her bets on Madison's victory.

To say Madison could be intimidating just didn't cut it. A bear growling in a human's face was intimidating. There'd been a time or two where all Madison had done was cut her eyes at Petra, and she'd been quaking in her shoes, eager to do Madison's bidding all over again.

Petra heaved another sigh and focused on the Sherlocks once more. Sulking some more, she sighed longingly at her obsessions. She craved ingesting them so bad, hungered for them so much she'd begun to fixate on them.

Is this what insanity tastes like, I wonder? Or boredom feels like?

Obsession without claiming was the first sign a succubus's reasoning slipped. She needed them beneath her, above her, but mostly just inside her while she gulped down their essence. To resist her urges went against her species. A succubus was supposed to feed off humanity's sexuality. And boy could she feast on these two. Before Madison she'd fed on humans often, but since joining her team, she'd dined mostly on just demons or—

Hello, handsome!

Petra sat a little straighter when the newcomer swaggered into the café. Pitch-black, waist-length hair, eyes black as sin, a nice big bulge in his crotch that she could work with *all night long*, coupled with all the strut of a man confident of his sex appeal. A tight, black shirt encased his six-pack abs and well-proportioned, muscle-bulging arms. Black leather pants hugged his fine ass. This one would know how to fuck. Hard. With balls-to-the-wall flair.

Too late she realized he'd honed in on her and walked straight for her.

"Do you mind if I join you?" He pulled out the chair across from her and sat, as gooseflesh prickled along her skin.

His rudeness would've surprised her had he been mortal. "You're not human."

"Neither are you." He tugged his shirt off, over his head, and tossed the garment over his shoulder. Twin handprints scarred his chest.

Frowning at his disrobing, Petra surveyed the room. A funny, glazed miasma entered the eyes of the coffee shop's patrons.

"I am Aramayis." Her focus shot to his face, and her heartbeat accelerated. "I see my reputation precedes me. Good. Lessens any prerequisite to explain my requirements." Aramayis leaned forward a little. Like a scroll being unrolled, wings expanded from either side of him, one black, and one velvety red.

Petra gulped. Her interest in him died with the divulgement of his identity. Or at least *mostly* died.

"I require sustenance. It has been a while since I enjoyed a real meal, and you are on my menu... Petralegija, daughter of one of my vilest enemies."

She leapt to her feet with all intent of getting the hell out of dodge. "Thanks for the offer, but no thanks."

He leaned against the back of his seat, stretched his legs out in front of him, and crossed his ankles. "It is amusing that you believe you have a choice."

A warm, invisible bubble punched her in the gut. Petra stumbled from the impact of his enthrallment. She clutched the table for support. A mocking grin tilted one corner of his fucking sexy mouth. Why'd his dominance turn her on when *no one* had ever dominated her?

Aramayis crooked his index finger at her in a come here motion. Every ounce of her succubus clout went into usurping his incubus magic. She'd enthralled others, but never had the same magic used against her. In the end, she wasted a minute fighting his sway when she should've been telepathing for backup. Unable to disobey him, anger churned in her gut as she sauntered toward him.

Fingers curled into her palms, her nails digging into her skin. Petra halted beside him and glowered. She threw a punch.

He caught her fist in his hand and sat up. "I like a woman with spirit." Aramayis released his grip and commanded, "Strip."

Once again, no matter how hard she strained, she couldn't defy him, so she yanked off her clothes while shooting eye-daggers at him. She balled up her jeans and flung them in his face. He chuckled as he knocked them aside.

"If someone walks in—"

"My magic invades the perimeter." If true, he exceeded the limits of the power she'd predicted he possessed. "Anyone that comes within five meters of the door will become enthralled. That includes any aid on your behalf."

She bit her bottom lip when his hand slid between her thighs. He grinned when he discovered her wet. No way he could be more surprised than her that she still found him fuckable. A human might've been embarrassed by their body's reaction, but not Petra.

She'd been born to fuck and she'd fuck him until his eyes crossed.

"You know how this goes, love. If you are *good*"— she had no doubt what type of 'good' he meant—"I will give you the mortals you want as a gift from me." As he finger-fucked her, he used his other hand to release the enclosure on his pants. His huge cock bobbed free of the restraints, hard, long, and thick. Petra licked her lips, and he chuckled. "Fuck me, Petralegija."

Too eager to test-drive his Thor-sized equipment, Petra didn't even attempt to gainsay his command this go-round. She straddled his thighs, caught the base of his dick, and met his black eyes as she nursed just the head of his erection at the entrance to her pussy. As she wrapped her fingers in his hair, she tugged hard on the strands and slid down his shaft, gasping at his size.

Incubus, you were just what I required, she decided as she fucked him.

Aramayis curled his fingers around her neck, as his wings embraced her. "Make me come in under five minutes and I will invite your humans to join us. If you fail, I am keeping you as a pet."

Petra increased her efforts, contracting around his erection as she moved on him. Aramayis's smug grin challenged her to try harder, so she thrust her elixir into him—and she never shared her mojo with anyone.

"Your attempt delights me," he said, but with his unaccounted for stamina she predicted she wouldn't succeed in his stated time to receive her Sherlock-reward.

She dragged her nails down his chest, creating track marks on his flesh. Fine beads of blue blood welled to the surface. In response his wings drew tighter around her. Petra licked the blood from the gouges she'd created, and his groan pleased her, giving her a false sense of hope.

In the end, she *still* failed.

A normal incubus would've gloated. He had every right to rejoice in his victory, but she suspected he foretold her defeat from the onset.

Aramayis rose with her in his arms, and withdrew from her body as he placed her on her feet. He spun her around and shoved her face-first over the table. The coolness of the surface against her front contrasted with the heat of him at her back. One of his hands clamped on her nape, pinning her to the furniture, while his other hand curled around her waist and his fingers discovered her clit.

"Feed me orgasms, succubus."

He thrust deep, and hard, demonstrating his aptitude for fucking with balls-to-the-wall flair. Before he finished, Petra had cheered him on with a dozen screaming orgasms. After he filled her with his own climax, he indifferently buttoned his pants before crooking his finger at the Sherlocks she coveted…and fed *them* to her.

An hour later the decimated body of a Sherlock was dumped on their lawn. The note attached to the former hunter set Micah off...

*Petralegija is the perfect candy
for an incubus. Who knew
mixing angel with succubus
would create the perfect
incubus-treat. Thanks for
introducing me to my new
favorite indulgence. If you*

Royal Partnerships

want your daughter back, you will hand over my bride.

Your loyal enemy,
Aramayis

Chapter 24

MADISON RECLINED ON a lawn chair and peered at the evening sky four days later. Stars pockmarked the black terrain like shimmering crystals. She hoped no matter how long she lived, this view would never lose its splendor.

Micah had forbidden her to go through with Amos's vision even though Aramayis made it clear he held Petra hostage. She'd shrugged as if she agreed with him. In return, he'd given her an untrustworthy stare, and told her he 'meant it'. Madison had smiled serenely, crossed her fingers, and told him truthfully, "Your wishes always matter to me." Then she'd plotted telepathically with Zen. More than her safety was at stake, but now Petra's life was on the line. Her stepdaughter remained missing and no matter how much demon-power Micah put on locating her, not even a trace of Petra's magic was unearthed. His frustration had reached its limits. Demons who came back empty handed or with no news at all of Petra's whereabouts cowered in fear, some suffering death, dismemberment, and even torture by her demon King's hand.

Failure is a new concept for Micah. Usha had that right.

Yeah, Micah's wishes mattered to her, but not when her son gave her a detailed play-by-play of how they could annihilate a foe. What was the point in Amos's prophecies if they didn't use them for their benefit when he had one? If she could stop Aramayis, he'd be another headache scratched off their list, and they could devote the rest of their attention to shutting the door to Hakara. *And* Petra would be free from Aramayis's diabolical clutches.

Silly man. She knew Micah wanted to protect her, and on a normal day, she'd let him. But not even on a good day would she allow her King of Hell to command her actions...or inactions for that matter.

Stubborn ass better be glad I love him.

Old habits die hard, Usha reminded her. *He only wants to protect us. We'll have to defuse his fury later.*

Yeah, and she guessed she couldn't expect him to change overnight. Good thing they formulated a plan without necessitating his aid. Zen and Nix had been onboard, and helped her plot.

Strategy committed to memory, all they waited for now was Aramayis to show his sexy self. And he would. She had no doubt he'd present himself soon. With Petra in his clutches, the incubus would probably demonstrate even more conceit and erroneously believe he could disable them all with ease. His arrogance aided them, and hindered him. Madison counted on that outcome.

The crickets chirped on the evening air, and a warm breeze fluttered her hair. The scent of honeysuckle gave off a pleasant aroma. She closed her eyes as she fingered Pandora's Box through her jeans' pocket. No bigger than the tip of her pinkie, it was easily hidden. A wedding gift from Nix, and she couldn't decide on the perfect hiding spot. Thanks to her Sherlock no one would ever control her again.

"Fancy meeting you all alone and out in the wide

open." She opened her eyes in time to catch the incubus emerge from the shadows, his gaze assessing the area like a CIA agent on a national security mission. "Is this a trap?"

"You wouldn't believe me if I said no." She nodded at his chest. "I see you located some clothing." The black shirt fit the tone of his dark intentions.

"The evidence of your handprints caused a stir among the Hakarians. They doubt my ability to manage you."

She grinned at that information.

"Do not gloat, bride." He snagged her ankles, lifted them, and sat on the end of her chair.

"I have big plans for *our* Hakarians."

"They are mine, and I do not share what is mine." Aramayis settled her feet in his lap.

"You've got something of mine."

He glanced up from her foot with a question in his eyes.

"Petra," she clarified. "I want her back."

"Aramayis lesson number one...take better care of your property or someone else will snag it from you. Unattended pets have a way of going missing."

The smug bastard had a few lessons of his own to learn. "Either return her, Aramayis, or I'll take your Hakarians from you."

"You are weak, not worthy of their loyalty yet." Madison didn't give two-shits about their loyalty, but she held her tongue and he went on. "I cannot decide if your feebleness disgusts me or offers me a beneficial opportunity."

"I'm newly made."

"Inconceivable possibility. You are Lynx."

Of course he would assume just because of her genetics she'd be mature. "I'm thirty years old. I only accepted my demon—"

"What is a demon?"

"I accepted my Lynx only recently. In the last couple of month or so."

Aramayis stared at her so long she grew antsy beneath his gaze. "You jest?"

Madison shook her head. A slight twinge of Zen's magic tickled her skin. She hoped his obvious presence distracted the incubus enough he didn't notice Nix's company.

He removed her sandals and put his thumbs into her insoles. First one foot, and then the other. Not one to pass up a good foot massage, she permitted his forwardness for the time being. She rewarded his efforts with a soft groan of delight, and he smiled at her.

"Where'd you learn that, incubus?"

"Bride, everything I do is designed to elicit arousal." He sent a bead of pheromones into the bottom of her foot, and she yanked her foot out of his grasp.

Sitting straight up, she pummeled him with a Hellish fireball, knocking him off the lawn chair to the ground. She rose to her feet, braced them apart to maintain firm footing, and loomed over him. His black eyes met hers, and for a scant moment she thought he was mystified, but then he covered it up with one of his sexual innuendos. "I look forward to discovering if your violent tendencies roll over into the bedroom."

"Here's a Madison life lesson for *you*, incubus. Kidnapping my stepdaughter is a poor way to start this relationship." She motioned between them with a flick of her fingers. "If you want me, you gotta convince me you're worth the trade-off. Convince me you're a better catch than what I've already got, because right now all I'm seeing from you is tyranny."

Aramayis pushed to his feet and slapped dirt off his leather pants. "With me the world will bend their knees to you."

"I've already got that with my two guys." *If* she wanted the human occupants on their knees, it would take little effort. "I'm also the Queen of my own domain with all residents eager to do my will." That she shared that domain with four other Kings wasn't a notable detail. "If all I wanted was power, I could

226

attain that *without you*. So explain to me again why I'd leave my guys for a son of a bitch like you."

"We are Lynx. Made for one another."

"Try again."

"You want me."

"Delusional on top of conceited. Try harder."

Frustration bled off him in the jagged lines of his aura. "What do you want?"

"I'm not doing the work for you, incubus. You want me, you gotta make the effort to figure it out."

"Do all women of your time require this excessive attention?"

She laughed, a sound wholly without mirth. "Madison life lesson number two...I'm a succubus, genius, I have the same needs as you. You want to be coveted, and I demand the same. Will tolerate nothing less. That's a classic succubus requirement."

"You challenge me, defy me. I find myself peculiarly fond of that." A glimmer of mauve appeared in his pupils. "Which one is the father of the infant in your womb?"

That question came from nowhere, and she stuttered over her reply. She wasn't aware he was even cognizant of her unborn. With hesitation flavoring her voice, she asked, "Why?"

"So I will know which one of your husbands will give me the most trouble when you are mine."

She snorted. "Your conceit makes *you* weak."

Two steps put him in her personal space, towering over her. Even though she could sense his strength, knew he could outgun her, she'd bluff her way through the confrontation. She craned her head back and met his gaze. A quick shift and he grasped her neck with his hand, his fingers digging into her skin. "You will learn your place, bride, on your knees, pleasing me for morsels of my affection."

His seriousness was so vibrant on his strained features, she almost laughed. To deflect her humor, she allowed a smirk to twist her lips. "Madison life lesson number three...never count your chickens before they hatch."

"Explain." Frown lines gouged across his forehead, while his thumb executed a circular pattern on her skin.

Madison could feel his magic penetrating her pores, but so far she'd managed to channel it back out of her body and avoid his enthrallment. She figured her ability to circumvent his mojo came with an immediate expiration date.

"I have the power to trap you in one of two boxes." With a wisp of her fingers across her jeans' pocket, she petted Pandora's Box nestled there.

"Now who is conceited?" He blew into her face. The scent intoxicated her, and her knees buckled. Her head spun, but he held her steady, with his hand on her neck and an arm wrapping around her waist. Clasped to his chest, she felt every inhalation against her nipples. She dug her fingers into her thighs to keep from grasping him to her and grinding against him. He offered her a gloating beam. "You cannot resist me, bride. I am your superior. Your one true husband." Aramayis's voice dropped to a husky timbre, as if he grew aroused, "In time I will teach you the tricks of the succubus trade, but for now even with your Zennyo Ryuo stalking the shadows, I surpass your potential. If you desire his continued safety, call him off, Madison."

Panting through the arousal coursing through her, she forced her ultimatum out, "Return Petra and help me close the doors to Hakara, and I won't put you in my box."

"I shall enjoy breaking you the same way I broke Petralegija. I do hope you afford me with more of a challenge than she did." Aramayis lowered his head, grazed his lips across hers. Governed by his sway, Madison was powerless to halt his advances.

The incubus slumped, his body dragging down along hers as he collapsed to his knees before her in the grass. He gagged against her belly, hard choking sounds.

His incubus spell dropped with him, and Madison sighed in relief. Behind Aramayis stood Nix with his hand on the male-Lynx's arm. The tight line of Nix's lips testified to his outrage.

Making eye contact with Nix, she nodded at him as she wiped her mouth with the back of her hand. Her conquered enemy continued to hack against her stomach. "Amos, will you transport us now?"

"What have you done to me?" Aramayis coughed, spewing red and pink fumes from his mouth, his hands gripping her hips for support.

Amos opened a portal to Hell. With a hand beneath the incubus's arm, Nix hauled Aramayis to his feet and away from Madison. Her husband shoved Aramayis through the doorway and dragged him down a narrow hallway before tossing him into the cell specially crafted for the Hakarian.

"I stole your power and used it against you." Nix shoved the incubus to the floor, and he continued to retch up a mixture of red and pink mucus. "You ever touch my wife again and I'll decimate you with your own magic."

"Our powers"—*cough, gag, cough, cough, dry heaves, gag, cough*—"are toxic to us, bride."

"She's *my* bride." Nix zapped him again, and Madison shook her head at Nix's jealous wallop.

"The irony since I didn't much like the way I felt with your magic turned on me, either." Madison rested her palms on her hips. "What you mean, incubus, is that *your* power is toxic to *you*. Pardon my lack of empathy since you suffered no moral dilemma using it on me or Petra."

He looked up at her, his long hair creating a puddle of black strands on the floor. "You have not defeated me."

"Look around you, Aramayis. Your location corroborates that we have defeated you. I told you your conceit made you weak." She indicated his cell with a hand gesture. "I'll allow you to familiarize yourself with your new accommodations. It's a step up from what you're accustomed to. Less gloom. If you require something, keep it to yourself because this isn't the Ritz Carlton."

"When I get free, I am going to fuck you until you are—"

Nix punched the incubus with another burst of his stolen magic, which put Aramayis on the floor writhing in pain. With one hand clutching his head, and the other grasping his stomach he moaned, rocking from side-to-side. The skin-stitched floor pitched beneath him, souls screaming at the agony he caused them.

"Happy sulking." Madison wiggled her fingers in a faux wave and walked out of the room, leaving him to stew in his defeat.

But she came face-to-face with a new adversary. Micah. The hellfire glow of his pupils attested to the depth of his anger.

"Micah—"

"Not a goddamn word!" He sent a glower in Nix's direction. "You motherfucking bastard! I expected you of all people to talk her out of this idiocy. Instead you put our woman in harm's way."

"She was never in any danger." Nix folded his arms across his chest. "The choice was hers to make, not yours."

"Don't take your anger out on Nix. This isn't his fault. I would've done it without him if he hadn't agreed."

Micah scowled at her, gripped her arm, and towed her toward their chamber. "I'm aware you skirted the line of truth with me. There was no other way you could've agreed to my terms—"

"Demands."

"—without toeing the line of veracity." Once inside their bedroom he stalked across the bedchamber, rammed his fingers through his hair, and leveled his glare on her. Nix stood at her back, the warmth of his body heating her backside, providing her with support.

"The only thing that keeps me from turning you over my knee and blistering your backside is that Petra arrived in Hell the moment you defeated the incubus." As if she'd *let* him abuse her like that, but she understood his fury and had expected it. "Scream and yell, throw a tantrum if it makes you feel better, Micah."

"You could've been injured!" At his outburst, the wall tableau behind him recoiled in expressions of fear.

"Bullshit. I could've been enthralled like Petra, subjected to the same *injury* she endured. Real injury wasn't on Aramaysis's mind."

In response to that, Nix gathered a handful of hair in his hand and jerked her backward into his chest. He tugged further until her neck muscles ached with strain, and he could slam his mouth down on hers. His tongue breached her lips, and he smooched her until she rocked her bottom against his crotch. "If the incubus ever touches you like that again, I'll kill him."

"I couldn't help myself when he tried to kiss me. I wanted to push him away, but I couldn't. The out-of-control feeling was awful, but, Nix, I *want* to know how to *do* that without touching someone."

Nix's finger circled a nipple through her shirt. "Who you planning on enthralling, baby?"

"Don't know, but the firepower was impressive. I want it."

Her Sherlock kissed her again.

"She doesn't deserve to come." Micah ripped her shirt off, announcing his angry participation. While Nix continued to kiss her, her King shredded her jeans and panties.

"Then deny me," she dared Micah when Nix released her mouth and hair. "But don't be mad at me—us—for taking the initiative to eliminate one of our enemies and save Petra."

The angry sex that followed...*whew!* She *liked* angry sex a lot.

Chapter 25

Two days later
New York, New York

"**HAPPY FUCKING BIRTHDAY** to me. My peaceful night just went to shit." Madison's brother-in-law peered about, his expression bland and in contrast to his words.

"It's not your birthday." Madison studied him.

Elias's jaw clenched just enough she noticed the tension. "How'd you find me, princess?"

"Good to see you too." She grinned when he shot her a fiery glare. Almost certain Zen had followed Petra's portal with a teleport of his own, she hoped he gave her enough time to say what she came to say before interfering. Sneaking out without her husbands noticing had been tricky, especially after her shenanigans with Aramayis, and she didn't want to lose this rare opportunity to speak with Elias without interference. "You're going to find this interesting or disturbing, but I know where all you Kings are at any given moment."

His blank stare gave away nothing as he hit the

cigarette clenched between his fingers, the tip glowing bright orange as he inhaled.

"So which is it? Disturbing or interesting?"

"Undecided." Elias exhaled a stream of gray smoke. "What do you want?"

Peace, just fucking peace. She tucked her hands in her back pockets and scanned the area. "Whoever you're hunting, you're not exactly all that incognito."

He shrugged. "Can't stop me anyway. I'm collecting his soul. I repeat...what do you want, princess?"

"Haven't you heard? I upgraded to Queen."

A faint upturn to the right side of his mouth. She'd have missed the tilt if she hadn't been studying him. "Didn't need to hear, I felt the transition. Where's your watchdog?"

"Zen?" At his nod, she went on. "Not sure." Somewhere nearby, that she could guarantee. "If he makes an abrupt arrival, you might want to run."

"I run from no one." His dry tone implied she was an idiot if she thought otherwise.

"You *ran* from Micah in Hell." No need to resist that prod when it felt good to needle him.

The corners of his eyes crinkled as they narrowed on her. "Micah was furious. He'd have crucified me first and regretted it later."

She executed a one-shoulder shrug and glanced around the darkened city street. "Still ran. You should've thought of his reaction before you tortured me. Killed me."

"You look pretty fucking good for a corpse." Another drag on his cigarette. "I gave Micah his wet dream. You." She looked at Elias in time to catch the distasteful curl on his upper lip. "His very own Queen. Whatever it took to make you Fall. We agreed on that. *He* reneged on our deal. Not me."

"Killing me was part of your deal." She doubted that.

His smile might've appeared warm, but his eyes were cold. "He knew I would kill you if you refused your status as Queen. It's why he covenanted your life to his. He has always protected you from me. With the covenant displaced, I took advantage of the situation. Even as a child you were a hardheaded hell-raiser. I should've known you wouldn't fall into line easily. You surprised me when you overcame my angel dust." That'd been after she thought he forced her to kill Nix and wanted her to kill Amos. Usha had been just as distraught and devastated as Madison. Somehow she'd managed to break through his subjugation and claim her demon again. Madison couldn't even explain how she'd succeeded in overriding his power.

"A little too late." He would've still succeeded in killing her if Micah hadn't come to her rescue, but more importantly if she hadn't claimed her seat of power in the hellish domain. She should be furious with him for forcing her Fall, but she couldn't generate the sentiment.

"Same results and what Micah wanted. You both can thank me later."

Fuck him. She'd thank him never. "Don't hold your breath."

"Where's your Jesus-toy?"

Why he insisted on calling Nix that absurd nickname she'd never know. Not that she cared enough to ask. "Home." Nix would be frantic when he discovered she'd disappeared. That worry would probably turn into pissed off the moment he realized she'd eluded him on purpose. The same went for Micah. She could use some angry sex again.

"I knew you'd keep him." Elias made one final drag on his cigarette before flicking it to the ground and crushing it beneath his boot. "You always were an ignorant bitch."

Madison grabbed his wrist. He jerked back and out of her reach.

"I had enough time before you reacted to drain a quarter of your magic. Don't call me a bitch again, Elias." She wasn't the same woman she'd been before he tortured her. "Why shouldn't I keep Nix?"

"Micah is why." Eliel glared at her. "He gave up all his dreams for you, and you traded him in for the uptight, pristine Jesus-toy. Micah *is* the better man. Just like you not to appreciate the gift you've been given. Why I expect more I'll never know." He rubbed his forehead. "You showed such promise as a child. You've been one disappointment after another since then."

He had no idea she'd stayed with them both. That surprised her. She figured he'd tapped into that hell-brain they were all somehow linked to magically and know all that transpired, but apparently not.

"Why are you grinning?"

Madison hadn't realized she was until Elias pointed it out. "Because you don't know me as well as you think."

His gaze remained focused on the building across the street, but he snorted at her statement. "I know you well enough."

"I stayed with Nix *and* Micah."

His head jerked about, his attention razor sharp, his nostrils flared, and his mouth parted just a fraction.

"Don't know me as well as you thought." She smirked. "Score one for the princess bitch, eh?"

"Do they get to fuck you together or take turns?"

Fantastic. He reverted back to crass Elias in a heartbeat.

"I hope they at least get to watch while the other fucks you."

At least she'd had the opportunity to enjoy his surprise while it lasted.

He came away from the wall and surveyed their surroundings. When he completed his perusal, he eyed her warily. "If you're with Micah, why isn't he with you trying to gut me?"

No doubt Micah would be furious the moment he discovered her whereabouts. He'd been searching for Elias since her Fall. Allowing Micah to kill his brother would be counterproductive. An action she was certain her husband would regret with the passage of time. They were twins, had endured only God knew what together, and she in no way wanted to be the reason they hated one another. Besides, this couldn't possibly be their first argument.

No point in giving Elias that information though. That'd be like handing him more ammunition against her. "I need your help more than I need you dead."

"Give me one reason why I'd help you?"

"Amos. Micah. I'm Hell's Queen, and regardless that you hate me—"

"I don't hate you."

"You don't *like* me."

He shrugged. "You've given me no reason to like or respect you.

"I'm not seeking your approval. All that matters is that I'm your family, and you don't turn your back on family." She elevated her eyebrows and gave him a moment to deny they were valid reasons. She might not approve of his methods when it came to helping family, but she could put aside her personal opinions for the good of her hellish-husband, son, and unborn daughters. "I gave you four reasons you'd help. Would you like more?"

"Don't get cheeky. I'm not as predictable as you think. Micah'll be furious when he discovers you've duped him."

"He'll understand eventually." She hoped. "The doors to Hakara are crumbling. Soon the creatures within will run rampant on earth. Aramayis, the incubus y'all put there, is already free of Hakara." She saw no point in detailing the incubus came for her and, as a result of his failure, resided in Hell under her influence. "The reapers want me dead or returned to Hakara...either will do for them at the moment. I'm not partial to either outcome, but—"

"Hold up a second." He held up his hand. "Why would they want you in Hakara? It's been closed for a couple of millennium."

Madison caught him up to date with the short

version.

He whistled low. "Got to give Domiel credit for planning that coup. Well played." He'd been the head-Esdras angel in charge that forced her suicide through Sterillium seeds. "You only have *a* child. Not children, so I'm not following the last of it."

"I'm pregnant."

That stunned him long enough for a couple of blinks. He chuckled, shaking his head. "You're full of surprises tonight. Who's the father?"

"Nix. It's why your brother, Domiel, killed me. Apparently, they're a wee bit worried that the demon slash Ark of Heaven baby I'm having could open the doorway to Heaven and cause a lot of problems." She rolled her eyes. "Cowards."

"The Reapers work by a different set of laws, just like Mariel and Nexiel that sent Crow after you."

"Yeah, yeah, I know. Reapers guide you to the afterlife." She made a circular motion with her hand. "Mariel and Nexiel are the angelic justice system. Got a problem, they'll haul your ass in before the jury to determine your guilt. Since *I* can't enter Heaven, that's going to be problematic. Taking my unborn anywhere without me is an even bigger problem. I have no idea why they want Amos. And I damn sure have no desire to return to Hakara with or without my children."

"How do you know this stuff?"

Madison tapped her temple. "Plugged into the same database as you, remember?"

"Data is one thing. I know the two of them personally. What makes you think they're coming for the family?"

"We had a visit from Cawel. Micah was extremely upset to discover she was the crow that prophesized Nix's fall into Hell and my defeat of two Kings."

Brow furrowed, he said, "I think I missed something in the translation. You've not defeated two Kings."

"I kinda have." She sent him an apologetic grimace.

"Although at the time I thought she meant I'd kill you both." That was what Crow had wanted from her. "Instead, I altered Micah's new trinity plan, and because of me you're blocked from tapping into parts of Hell's powers. Call it whatever you like, but they're forms of defeat."

Elias's Kingly eyes glowed at her in the night, and he ran his fingers along his jaw.

"You're not playing your best game, Elias, if you're letting me push your buttons."

"You wish."

She grinned. "I'm just telling you what happened and how I interpret it. Crow—um...I mean Cawel told me higher creatures were watching my progress all those years ago. The angelic jury obviously."

"Obviously." His voice was so cool goose bumps broke out across her exposed flesh.

"Anyway, back on point. At her first visit five years ago, she pretty much told me Micah was evil and that I should run from him." Madison shook her head, unsure that she'd have accepted her fate and her love for Micah any sooner. She'd definitely run from Nix because of her suggestion. "Micah said she was an oracle angel."

"This was a couple of days ago? Two, maybe three?"

"How'd you know?"

"I felt a disturbance with Micah. Genuine anger has that effect on us both. I almost came to help before I remembered he wants me dead." His direct stare suggested Madison was the cause of their argument.

"That's on you, not me." She hadn't wanted to be tortured and almost killed...*again*. "We gotta trap the Hakarians for the good of Hell."

"If I do anything to help you with this, you'll owe me."

"No." She shook her head. "I'm keeping Micah off your ass. We're even. You're helping because we're family. Act like the cocky son of a bitch you are, but you don't fool me. I know you love Micah and Amos."

"Mention that 'love' word to me once more and I'll

be tempted to slit your goddamn throat."

She elevated her eyebrows in surprise at the vehemence in his voice.

"Micah's 'love' for you altered everything, came between us."

A sparkle to the right caught Madison's attention. "You should leave."

"I'm here for the mortal. His deal has expired."

"Zen will be here in under ten seconds." If it took that long, and they both knew how it was going to go if Zen caught sight of Elias. "The mortal's expired deal will wait another hour." She was surprised she felt nothing for the human's soul. And she had no doubt Elias planned nothing good for his errant victim.

Elias came away from the wall. "I'm not a goddamn pussy."

"No, just an arrogant, prideful fool." She faced Zen. "You followed me here earlier so why the showy entrance now, Zen?"

Her immortal friend peered at their locale. "It gave him a chance to escape."

"From you?" Eliel laughed and produced another cigarette. With a casual air, he lit it with fire from his fingertip and inhaled the nicotine.

"The dragons send word Micah will arrive," Zen told her while keeping his focus locked on Elias.

"Overprotective bastard." As much as she loved his protective tendencies, sometimes they aggravated her just as much. She glared at Zen as if he could be blamed for Micah's imminent arrival.

Her immortal friend held her stare, his expression blank, but his silver eyes said much. He was as sold on Elias's aid as Micah was.

"Trust me, Zen. We need Elias."

Her brother-in-law elevated a dark eyebrow, questioning her meaning behind that statement.

She refrained from elaborating. "I can't convince him to help if Micah's trying to kill him. Privacy is not overrated in this instance."

Eliel eyed her speculatively as if he waited for the punch line of a tasteless joke. He inhaled deeply of the nicotine and pointed the two fingers holding the cigarette at her. "You wish privacy with me?"

Understanding his disbelief, she shrugged.

"I can't wait to hear how I can assist you better than my twin." He touched her arm, and she glanced at his loose hold. "Just this once, your wish is my command, princess." He saluted Zen with his cigarette hand and yanked her through a portal.

They arrived in Hell a moment later, and she peered about. "I don't recognize this part of Hell."

"It's private. Mine. Accessible by only me."

That should alarm her, but not as much as she would've suspected. He crushed the cigarette beneath his foot. It was such a commonplace action in the cesspool of torture that the grin hit her lips before she thought to axe it.

Micah will have a bigger axe to grind with him after this.

Micah's being unreasonably stubborn. On that she agreed with her demon.

"Convince me to service you, princess."

The man was lecherous and made her skin crawl. Ignoring his sexual allusion, she met his stare head on.

Amusement crinkled the corners of his eyes. "You're already on board, so why waste time convincing you?"

"I wish to hear you beg." He buried a hand in his slack pocket, and she realized he didn't deny her proclamation. A wicked grin surfaced. "I'll enjoy taunting Micah with how pretty you beg."

"You're enjoying your spat with Micah."

He ran his thumb and finger along his eyebrows. "It's not the first quarrel we've endured."

She bet it broke up the monotony of immortality.

"This time you would've killed someone he loved." She didn't get the man and how he could be so casual about Micah's need for revenge.

"Micah has mistaken love for obsession." He made a

face, and she knew well how he felt about the *pathetic, human emotion.* In his eyes, she'd turned Micah weak, and he couldn't see how she'd strengthened his brother. "Now that he has what he wants, he'll become reasonable again. Realize I fulfilled my end of the bargain."

If he kept telling himself that, Micah'd put him in an early grave. "Your death brings about red diamonds, right?"

Chapter 26

ELIAS BLEW OUT a bored sigh and inclined his head. "Is this going somewhere?"

Seriously he had other shit to do, like expired souls to claim and others to torture. Fun shit that the uptight princess wouldn't receive an invite to.

He'd brought her here to his personal section of Hell to goad not just the immortal, but his sibling too. A gentle prod that Madison wasn't inaccessible if he wanted to butcher her curvy ass.

"You keep thinking the way you are, and I'll make a set of jewelry out of your remains."

"You'd love that." The bitch would thwart his relationship with Micah as much as possible. Not that he expected more from her. Except...she *had* shocked him when she confessed she remained with the Jesus-toy *and* Micah. That'd been unexpected. And truthfully, he was somewhat surprised his brother had agreed to the arrangement.

"No. I'm certain in the long haul of eternity Micah would ultimately regret killing you. I don't want that regret on his shoulders."

Unable to determine if he could trust her, he

considered her. She couldn't lie to his twin, and while the Kings couldn't fib to one another either, he wasn't sure where Madison resided on that rule.

He elected to alter the subject. "Back to your begging. I prefer beggars on their knees."

"In your wet dreams."

He elevated his eyebrows and executed a small headshake. "Don't flatter yourself. The only wet dreams you star in, princess, are ones where you're strung up and screaming your lungs out in agony. Like our last date." *Good fucking times right there.* "Start convincing or I'm out of here, and you can figure your own way out of your mess."

"I explained what's going on."

"I don't see how I fit into your dilemma."

"You want Amos safe." True, he adored that kid regardless of the stick up his mother's ass. "You want Hell safe."

"The doors to Hakara falling don't hinder Hell."

"Don't they?"

"Princess—"

"Shut up and listen, asshole."

A grin tugged at his lips.

"All of angeldom wants Amos and I dead. We both bring a lot of firepower to Hell, maybe enough to tilt the tide in your favor. And Nix isn't factored into that equation yet, and I know he'll side with me. If those monsters exit Hakara, they won't remain hidden, but they'll expose themselves to humankind. One thing I've learned, most humans *are* weak like you and Micah insist. They'll worship the Hakarian residents, which will take away residents of Hell. If I understand correctly, souls are the battery power to Hell. If the toxic abyss of Hakara starts stealing souls out from under *our* domain, then we've got serious problems."

As much as he hated to admit it, she had a point. "I'm protection detail?"

"Not so much. I've got too much protection. And I'm at the heart of the problem with Hakara's doors blowing off their supernatural hinges. Only my blood will close the doors."

Eliel laughed. "Surely you're not inviting me to bleed you." *That* is *my wet dream.*

"No." The selfish bitch never gave him what he desired most. "I'm looking into other ways to hold off their relocation to Earth without sacrificing myself. That's where you come in. None of those in my group will do what's gotta be done because they're too busy trying to protect me."

"If I dumped your pretentious ass back into Hakara would the doors close?"

"Yes." She noticeably held her breath. Smart girl to mistrust him when he was a hair's breadth away from doing just that since it would solve all their problems—including eliminating the royal pain in his ass—with one single action.

"But then Hell would be maimed by my loss."

Genius girl reminding him of her importance to their domain. Fuck him, he liked her tenacity, even if he disliked her most of the time.

"You've been Queen a total of two months. Don't overinflate your importance to a domain that's survived *without you* for more millennia than you can comprehend."

"Don't *you* go underestimating *my* importance. You're the one kicked out of the in-crowd in exchange for me."

Anger slammed through him. Because he'd given his twin *his* wet dream, his brothers had excommunicated him from a power hub he'd helped craft. When she wouldn't accept her status as Queen, he'd done what he'd promised thirty years ago. He'd offered her a drink from the *casket* under false pretenses, which should've guaranteed her death. Still unsure how she managed to survive when none before her had, he only knew his actions gave his brother what he wanted, while Elias lost everything important to him. To say things had not turned out as he'd planned was an extreme understatement.

Elias clutched Madison by the throat and shoved her against one of Hell's gyrating walls. She offered no struggle, just dished out a smug expression, taunting him with her lack of fear. He grabbed her hand and slapped her palm against his neck with a *whack*. "Your power is useless here, bitch. *Try* and chug my magic."

He felt a slight tingle along his skin, indicating she attempted to do as he requested. Her eyes widened when her succubus power failed to ignite.

Elias returned her smug grin as her conceit evaporated and alarm finally flared in her eyes. Oh, how he delighted in the way she wore her anxiety. It was her best accessory.

He tapped the tip of a claw against the pulse in her throat. "Don't forget I don't fucking like you, Madison. Nothing is stopping me from killing you right here, right now."

"Your devotion to Micah stops you." Her nervous swallow lessened her show of bravado.

Thanks to this bitch my brother wants me dead!

"My devotion to Micah has fucked me over, left me on the outskirts of *my* goddamn Kingdom!" He ran a navy-blue and a gold talon along her cheek, admiring the red welt left behind. Just a fraction harder and he'd leave gouges in her flesh. "Give me one reason why I shouldn't kill you or leave you holed up here, powerless and lost to my sibling."

"My disappearance would devastate Amos."

Motherfucking bitch tugging at my heartstrings like this. That kid was his sole weakness. But at the end of the day, he'd do anything to protect his family, and as much as he might dislike Madison she counted as family since becoming Queen.

Maybe some ground rules were in order. "If I do this, I want something from you."

"Open-ended favors are out of the question."

He wanted more from her than something so vague. "I want you to collect the soul I went for tonight and help me torture him until he breaks."

A sharp gasp jerked her entire body. She had no idea how important her decision was. *Time to grow a spine and act like royalty, bitch. Show me you've got the balls to be Hell's Queen and you'll have my true loyalty forever.*

"If your answer's still of the negative variety, then you're on your own. Good fucking luck. Maybe I'll join Hakara and build a new empire to compete against Hell."

"You wouldn't!"

Doubtful because he was too loyal to his siblings even if they were giving him the cold shoulder at the moment. Their cold war wouldn't last, it never did, but then he'd never seen Micah so furious or distraught either. "Now might be a good time to divulge I already know how to lock those doors without tossing your uptight ass through them."

"How?"

"My secret until I have your agreement."

"That's blackmail."

He shrugged.

She bit her bottom lip and stared at some unidentified object over his shoulder. "Maybe I can convince Nix and Zen that this is for the best and they won't be so mad—"

"Your Jesus-toy and Micah *must* be present throughout the soul's torment." He knew his brother wouldn't have any issue with her torturing souls. Micah'd probably encourage it in an alternate situation.

"You have a hidden agenda."

"I *always* have a hidden agenda."

"O-okay. I agree."

Elias grinned. "Think I'll go chat with Micah before I decide."

Her eyes rounded. "That's unadvisable. He will *kill* you the first chance he gets."

"You better hope he fails."

"But I agreed to your demands."

"Whining really isn't an attractive look on you,

Madison." Elias winked as angry fire smoldered in her eyes indicating she'd indeed Fallen. With a grin, he portaled from his domain, leaving her behind to stew over her entrapment. If Micah slaughtered him, she'd be trapped in his domain for an eternity.

Chaos greeted him. Okay, maybe not true chaos because Micah was too refined to lose his shit—except for when Madison died, and even then Beliel's reaction had stunned Elias. At present, Micah's fear and anger was obvious as he conversed with Zennyo Ryuo.

"Brother," Elias said mildly when Micah faced him. He caught the brief sizzle along Micah's fingertips, evidence Beliel wished to gut him like a dog with his *Scepter*. He smirked. "Control yourself, *zkihtak*, I have your girl."

Visible tightening of Micah's jaw. "Where is she?"

"Indisposed." They held one another's gaze, Elias somewhat mollified he'd managed to rankle his twin. He'd do anything for Micah. Turning aside his sister-in-law's aid wasn't an option, but neither had to know that. "I know how to lock the doors without sacrificing Madison."

More sparks at Micah's fingertips. Did his brother struggle to hold back his *Scepter*?

"I cannot lie to you, brother." Elias goaded him with that reminder and glanced at Zennyo Ryuo. The haughty bastard stared without blinking. With multiple run-ins with the immortal under his belt, he held no desire to fend him off again. If he continued to watch the Queen of Hell, then they were on the same side...even if neither of them believed his motives.

"Why would you offer your assistance?" Micah's tone implied he mistrusted Elias's motives.

He guessed a simple 'she asked for it' wouldn't suffice. "She's the Queen of Hell. Isn't that reason enough?"

"That she was destined to be the Queen should've stayed your former actions." Zennyo Ryuo still had that stick up his ass.

Elias glared at the male.

"You would've killed her if I hadn't intervened!" Beliel yelled.

"Something I have no regret for." As Elias watched, Micah's eyes flamed with Hell's fire and he rammed Elias against the brick wall behind him. The *Scepter* descended from Micah's hand and with a flick of his wrist, Beliel laid the edge against Elias's throat. Against anyone other than Micah, Eliel would have attacked. Their bond was unbreakable. Not for a moment did he believe Micah would really kill him. "I gift wrapped her for you."

A tug and the *Scepter* sliced open a section of his neck.

Fuck that hurts!

He recognized the gleam in his brother's eyes, coupled with the hard slash of his mouth...*He'd kill me without a second thought.*

The reality was sobering. They'd endured sibling rivalry and spats all of their existence. To know his twin desired his death confounded him.

My brother truly hates me.

"The only reason you're not dead is because I cannot locate Madison's signature."

Somehow he had to earn Micah's trust. Only then could he work on eradicating his hate. "How'd she survive the drink of the *Casket*?"

"By claiming her status and dining on my seraph. She almost died before she gave in." Beliel closed his eyes and shook his head. The pain that burned in his twin's eyes when he opened them caused Elias to pause. Could he have misread his brother's emotions toward Madison that much? Love was such a foreign concept—except for when it came to their twin bond— he couldn't fathom the sentiment. "Watching her suffer and knowing she would die...if I couldn't have saved her, I would've joined her and drank from the *Casket*."

Nothing but the truth because Micah couldn't lie to him. The lump in Elias's throat choked him, made it difficult to swallow. He'd forced Madison to claim her seat in Hell, but if his plan had backfired, he'd have been the reason his twin perished too. Could he have worn that guilt? *No.* No, he didn't think he could've endured such culpability. He'd watched his brother's agony when the angels killed her, so he should've gleaned a modicum of his feelings. Angry when she refused to claim her seat, he might've let his resentment guide his actions more than he should have. But he'd never uttered an apology before, and he wouldn't start now.

Elias cleared his throat. "Madison's blood closes the door to Hakara."

"So we're told."

"Is it a source you can trust?"

Micah tilted his head to the side in an offhand shrug. "As reliable as you."

Fair enough, his brother didn't trust him.

"Sacrifice Celeste instead of Madison." The sizzle of the *Scepter* evaporated, and Micah gave him some room, stepping out of his personal space. Elias remained against the wall. He ran his fingertips over the wound his brother inflicted. Black blood coated his fingertips, and he wiped it off on his pants. "They have the same lineage running through their veins."

Chapter 27

MICAH CONSIDERED HIS brother. He couldn't recall the last time Elias offered anything without asking for something in return. A cease-fire would benefit Eliel, yet he asked for nothing. Confused, he dove into conversation determined to wheedle out what his brother wanted. "It's doubtful Celeste will close the doors completely."

Elias shrugged. "They'll close enough. We can use our—"

"We?"

"Yes, *we*. I remain a King of Hell. Fucking deal with it, *zkihtak*. I'm willing to assist eliminating the threat only for the princess. Fuck the humans. Despite your erroneous assumptions, *that* should tell you where my loyalties reside." Elias dragged in a breath. "If *we* unite our power, we're stronger. We can create a portal from Hakara's inconvenient opening straight into Hell. Any escapee will be trapped in our domain under *our* control. A win-win scenario for us all."

Micah couldn't overlook the advantage of the proposal. Accepting aid from Eliel after his attempt to kill Madison chafed his pride though. Yet, she'd gone to Elias against Micah's wishes asking for help. That rankled almost as much.

Beliel crossed his arms over his chest. "Your prior actions speak louder than your hollow words. I cannot trust you around Madison."

Elias held his stare unblinking. "She's the Queen of Hell. It's all I ever wanted or expected from her."

"Bull-fucking-shit," Micah snarled. His talons extended from his fingers before he could suppress them.

"She provides Hell with stability and power. That means I'm honor bound to protect her." Elias pointed at Zennyo Ryuo. "You buy his sincerity when it comes to protecting her? The goddamn immortal that snacks on fuck-ups like Madison? That's what I call *bull-fucking-shit*. You know as good as I do he'll eventually suffer a change of heart, and when he does he'll gut her."

Micah forced his frame to relax and plugged his fingers through his hair in a casual manner, even though his nerves were strung tight. "I know you. You're scheming something. What the fuck is it this time? Don't you dare wrap Madison up in whatever it is."

"You wound me, brother." Eliel's eyes changed to the Kingly color shade. "*She's family!* I never turn my back on kin. I *vowed* to do *anything* to make her Fall. I upheld my end of that bargain. You. Did. Not."

Anger snapped through Micah like a forest flash fire. Everything sped up. The *Scepter of Spirits* sizzled into his palm without thought, and a heartbeat later the tip of the blade indented Elias's skin beneath his chin. Micah forced Elias's head back with the magical sword. He wanted his brother to fight back, needed a reason to gut him, but Eliel remained passive beneath Micah's threat.

"You went too far, Eliel." Micah'd said all this before. He wouldn't waste his breath and repeat himself again because Eliel would never understand.

"My trust is blown." *Never to return.*

"Be that as it may, brother, Madison trusts me. *She* asked for my aid. So go fuck yourself and your trust issues."

Desire to rip into Elias with his claws tore through him like a demon on steroids. Micah clenched his teeth and defied his base urge. If he could locate Madison, he'd carve up Elias without remorse.

Elias placed a fingertip against the *Scepter* and shoved it aside. "Hate me for giving you what you wanted. I don't fucking care. Your pussy-whipped issues aren't my concern."

Micah punched him in the dick.

Eliel keeled over clutching his crotch, gasping for air.

Any other time the violence would've soothed his wrath, but it proved ineffective in this instance. "If you even blink at her in a harmful manner, you'll suffer the consequences."

His twin choked on a laugh.

Micah's knuckles itched to coldcock him again. "Take me to my woman."

"I have a condition first."

Of course he does.

Micah delivered his knuckles into his twin's teeth. Elias shot backward and slammed into the concrete wall, indenting the brick. Mortar crumbled around him.

Zennyo Ryuo shook his head. "Violence is counterproductive."

Micah ignored the immortal. Having Elias in his presence and knowing the resolution he sought would have to wait until he freed Madison from Elias's cuckold ate at him. But...*why isn't Eliel fighting back?*

Elias laughed, licking blood from the corner of his mouth. "*Zkihtak,* you feel better?"

Only his demise would provide Micah with a sense of satisfaction. "You have a condition while claiming you wish to help because Madison is family. Which is it? Do you want something or do you wish to help my wife."

"What I want helps the princess." Micah's twin pushed to his feet, not in the least weary or injured. "I gain nothing from it."

"Spit. It. Out." Micah glanced at Zennyo Ryuo. The immortal's features remained impassive but his sharp gaze was zeroed in on Elias.

"Madison will deliver Celeste through the doorway."

For what purpose? Madison might happily toss her mother into Hakara, but then again she might not. In the best case scenario Madison remained unpredictable. Case in point...she sought Elias's assistance after Micah forbade it. *I also forbade her plot to take down Aramayis, so this shouldn't come as a surprise to me.*

Committing matricide was an altogether different request though. How she'd respond was anyone's guess. "Since she's my demon, nothing stops me from sacrificing Celeste myself."

"True." His brother took his time lighting a cigarette, and Micah's agitation swelled. "You could order Celeste to forfeit herself. She'd be compelled to comply. Except I'll keep Madison in my little slice of Hell indefinitely unless my terms are met."

Anger shuttled through Micah like a punch to the gut. "I grow weary of your games."

"No games. You give me your word you won't interfere with Madison dumping Celeste in Hakara or...pick the alternative." He shrugged. "Want to know the option I prefer you choose?"

There was no way he'd select the alternative. Elias knew that too, but fucked with him instead. "I cannot guarantee Madison will agree to sacrifice Celeste. It's her choice."

Gazes deadlocked, Elias reiterated, "Do you give your word as a King of Hell *not* to interfere?"

He glanced at Zennyo Ryuo. The immortal's expression remained blank, as if he'd checked out of the conversation, but his total focus on Elias gave away his concentration.

"Madison's wish is my command. Now bring me to my wife."

Fucking pussy, Elias's thoughts slithered into Micah's mind, but he said, "You cannot compel Celeste to cooperate. Her sacrifice is solely up to Madison."

Micah stared at his twin. How many more details were necessary? All Micah cared about was getting Madison back to safety. "I won't interfere. Madison has my permission to do whatever she wishes to Celeste *without my interference in any way whatsoever.* Satisfied?"

Eliel ran a finger along his jaw as if he needed to contemplate the inquiry. "Almost."

"Goddamn you and your motherfucking games!" Micah put his fist into the brick wall next to Elias's head.

"Drama, brother, it doesn't suit you."

"You're unnecessarily taunting Micah." The immortal zoomed into Elias's personal space. Despite their height differences, Zennyo Ryuo's power sizzled in the room with a quiet hum. "He makes a lot of deals that I'm not required to uphold. You will speak the remainder of your wants, or I promise nothing."

"Cool your jets, guard dog." Elias pat the immortal on the head. Zennyo Ryuo surprised Micah when he remained neutral, failing to rise to the bait. "I request a cease-fire until Celeste is sacrificed, Beliel."

"Deal. Return my fucking wife."

Chapter 28

ELIAS GRINNED AT Madison when he returned for her. Before she could ask what transpired between him and Micah, he whisked her through a portal into a room clogged with tension. She took stock of her men. She'd never seen Micah so angry, and he'd been pretty upset with her the other night over her reckless behavior—his words not hers—concerning Aramayis. Micah sent her a glare that promised she'd account for going against him. Something told her angry sex wasn't going to get it this time. Zen was sullen and quiet. Nix...well, he demonstrated why he was her rock, by walking straight to her and looping his arm around her shoulders. She snuggled against him, wrapping her arms around his waist and used his energy to give her strength.

Micah paced, sending his brother a murderous scowl every few steps, shocking her with his non-violent behavior. She would've expected him to attempt to ram his *Scepter of Souls* through Elias's heart by now.

He came close earlier.

255

Startled by Zen's sudden telepathy, she looked over at him.

What's wrong, Zen? she shot back mentally.

Her adopted brother shook his head. *You're about to find out.*

Just after Zen telepathed, Elias leaned against the arm of the sofa and captured her attention when he spoke. "We've agreed"—he motioned between himself and Micah—"if we thrust Celeste through the breach to Hakara it'll mostly close."

Madison flinched at her brother-in-law's strategy. Blindsided by that plan, she thought about the last time she saw her mother. Celeste had been aiding and abetting Elias in Madison's torture. *She watched stone-faced as Elias tortured me and then tried to kill me.* Celeste wouldn't receive the mother of the year award anytime soon.

Feeling anything but grounded, she cleared her throat, relieved when her voiced emerged strong. "Mostly doesn't work for me, Elias. One of the Hakara monsters could sneak out and harm a human."

"He endorses a spell that the five royals will craft. The magic will hook a portal between Hakara's opening and Hell. Once they escape, they'll be trapped and under our dominion," Micah clarified the strategy.

"Why not just create the portal without sacrificing my mother?"

Nix ran his palm up and down her back. A soothing gesture, and she loved him all the more because of the silent way he infused support.

"Once they realize Hell is simply a new cage, I'm sure they'll prefer to remain in the domain they control."

"I like the way you think, princess." Elias ran his fingers along his jaw. "If we siphoned their power and fed it into Hell's magical cauldron it'd give us more power. With your unique set of mojo, you could do that for us."

The fine creases at the corners of Zen's eyes exhibited his distress over the possibility.

Madison shrugged. "No promises."

"You agree to leave Celeste out of this?" Micah stared at his sibling like he couldn't figure out his brother's endgame.

Before Elias could respond, Madison said, "She'll just crawl out and re-enter Hell. It'll solve nothing to toss her into Hakara."

"Celeste must be sacrificed." Elias peered at his fingernails as he uttered those words in a cool, detached manner. He tilted his gaze to hers and his Kingly eyes stared at her. "And Madison *will* push her through the hole between worlds."

"I won't."

"You will." His confidence irritated her. "You need this to cleanse your soul. To prove to our demons you're a committed Queen. You're feeding your unborn children hate every day that Celeste's misdeeds go without retribution. Tarnishing their hellish legacy by not seeking revenge."

Nix's grip tightened just a fraction on her nape. "Micah punishes her. And those children are half mine, half Heavenly creatures."

Elias elevated his eyebrows. "Indeed." He made a repulsive expression. "Micah's punishment does *nothing* for Madison's sense of justice. Neither does it uplift her status in Hell. Micah has earned the demons' fear, but Madison still has a role to fill. You're half Jesus-toy, Phoenix, and that didn't stop your Fall. She's not just a demon, but a Lynx with the power of Pandora, she *must* demonstrate her method of justice or none of our demons will respect her."

Madison snorted, calling bullshit with the sound. "I'm not sacrificing Celeste."

"You're a goddamn demon. It's past fucking time you *act* like one. Even my brother cannot disagree with that." Eliel rose from his seat and closed the distance between them until Micah and Zen blocked his path. Elias smirked at them, and held her gaze between their wall of shoulders. "All demons have common traits. One of them is the need to seek revenge. You must do this or Celeste's actions will haunt you. Your bitterness will continue to feed your unborn and come between your relationship with your men. Failing to show dominance diminishes Micah's leadership in Hell."

All seemed like valid points on the surface, but even given her immense dislike of her mother, she held no desire for retaliation, couldn't bring herself to hate her parent, and sacrificing her was nonnegotiable. "What of your wrongful actions against me, Elias? How do I get over those? How should I demonstrate my 'need to seek revenge' against you?"

Micah gave his brother a considering look.

Elias grinned. "Do you want vengeance against me, princess?"

"Yes," she said without hesitation.

Zen shot her a surprised look. Nix pressed his lips to her temple, and took a deep breath as if her response surprised him too.

Micah laughed. "That's my bloodthirsty girl."

"Given half a chance, I'd make you suffer, as well," Zen said straight-faced.

"I'll settle for locking down Hakara. Saving humanity and Hell is more important than acquiring vengeance against you." Her brother-in-law gave her a slow toothy smile that failed to reach his eyes. Her best interpretation was that she disappointed him like always. "An eternity will provide me many opportunities for revenge." As for gaining the respect of demons...."Demons will respect me because I'm their Queen, and they're unsure how I'll retaliate for an offense. The unknown is sometimes scarier than the known. My actions or inactions reflect on all of our power, not just Micah's."

If a single demon believed she'd tolerate insubordination in any way, they'd quickly discover the error of their thinking. Demons required no leniency, and she'd give them none.

Nix massaged her nape with his fingers. She smiled

at him and hugged him tighter. Creases fanned from the corners of his eyes. Something about her words or the situation bothered him. Madison shrugged his unease aside. He'd have to deal with her new life. None of it could be altered. She'd made a choice in Hell to live, and accepted her role as Queen. The only other decision would've resulted in her death. At the time he'd supported her decision.

Too late for regrets, Nix.

"Micah has agreed with me that you'll sacrifice Celeste, so you'll do this." Elias strolled to the window that overlooked the backyard.

"We have our own deal." At her comment, Micah's head wrenched about, his blue eyes a haze of red, as he narrowed them on her. Nix's fingers clenched once more on the back of her neck. Zen gave a slow blink. "Celeste wasn't part of our deal, Elias."

What was your deal, Zen's telepathy filtered into her head.

The flash of anger that surfaced on Micah's features evaporated the moment Elias said, "She'll help me collect and torture a soul I bartered for."

Nix winced, and Zen pinched the bridge of his nose. Micah's taut frame relaxed.

"That deal doesn't worry you, Micah?" The strain in Nix's voice detailed his alarm.

Micah shrugged. "She's a demon, the Queen of Hell, this is who she is."

Nix looked at Zen. "Zen?"

Her immortal bestie peered at her a long moment before walking out of the room. No idea how to interpret that exodus, she figured she would get an earful later.

Her Sherlock grew more frustrated, pulling away from her and dragging his fingers through his short hair. "I know what effect that type of behavior has on a person. Micah, do you really want her to alter that much?"

"I do." Elias kept his gaze locked on her.

"No need to fret, Phoenix." A sheen of excitement glinted from her husband's eyes, as he too watched her, his expression one of delighted smugness. "She was designed for this lifestyle, you weren't."

Doling out torture would have little to no effect on her. Or that's what she told herself, even as she admitted if Elias wanted this from her, there'd be some effect to her. And she wanted this.

No, I need *this.* But that concept terrified her because it demonstrated how much she'd Fallen.

It'll be fun, her Lynx piped up. *Watching him bleed as I inflict pain, making him scream, and—*

Madison shut down her demon a second before Micah surprised her with a hard kiss. Tongue swiping across hers, his talons dug into her hips, and he jerked her against his erection as he rolled his pelvis against hers.

"Right where she belongs in Beliel's arms," Elias said, a clear taunt for Nix.

"Your demon was in your eyes," Micah whispered against her lips, explaining his sudden arousal. He skimmed his jaw along her cheek and pressed his lips against her ear. "Does the anticipation excite you, kitten?"

Yes, she responded telepathically. Even though she couldn't see him, she felt his grin against her ear.

Madison used her fingertip to write invisible demonic words on the floor-to-ceiling windowpanes that overlooked the city below. No idea where they came from, they surfaced in her mind faster than she could write them. A spell that would require her blood mixed with royal magic to create the doorway between worlds. The fix was easier than she'd anticipated, and proved the reapers borrowed trouble over the erosion of the locks. Or sought her ultimate demise like all the rest of angeldom.

Get in line, Usha drawled. *I'm not going down without a fight.*

To no avail she'd resisted her fate too. She didn't regret the time she'd wasted running from Micah because those had been learning years. The knowledge that had flowed into her since accepting her destiny was amazing. What she'd known before her Fall hadn't been one-percent of what she knew now. It felt like a database of information was at her disposal. It was refreshing. Liberating knowing she could protect her family simply because of her genetics.

Insidious reminders she could collect souls and create more demons to do her bidding infiltrated her thoughts. Each one would benefit Hell, generate more power, and seed their domain with a solid foundation. Temptations she rejected because she worried where the actions would take her. No matter how far she Fell, she never wanted to stop fighting for humanity.

She sensed Zen's arrival despite his lack of identification.

"You're bothered by my agreement with Elias?" She acknowledged his presence, keeping her back to him.

"I'm concerned." The reflection of him in the window drew closer. "Why do you write demonic spells on the windows?"

Surprised he could see them Madison swiped her palm across what she'd written before turning to face him. "I'm working on the doorway spell between Hakara and Hell."

"It's a spell all of you will have to execute for it to work. Why do you tweak it without them?" His silver eyes glowed for a brief moment, indicating he utilized his power for a fraction of a second.

"Why not, Zen?"

Tension palpable in the silence, she couldn't get a lock on his thoughts.

"Collecting and torturing a soul is dangerous business, my sister."

"So was becoming Queen of Hell. What's problematic about going with the flow?"

More of the same unblinking stare from him. "If you go rogue, Madison..."

She slammed against the window-wall behind her. Despite the pane's solidness, she felt it shimmy when it received the brunt of her weight. Recognizing Zen's new demonstration of power, she elevated her eyebrows at him. With a smirk, she rubbed her back against the glass. Before she realized her intentions, she palmed her dragon blade as she flung a ninja star. He leaned to the side, dodging the star with ease. Of course she missed.

"You can't kill me."

Only his creator could take him down. If God hadn't taken him down when he Fell to save her, she predicted He wasn't ready to call him home yet.

Madison palmed her other dagger and eased away from the window. "Is this *you* coming for me, Zen?"

His one-shoulder shrug sufficed as an answer. The pounding on the door, followed by Nix and Micah's yelling further answered her question. Zen had magically locked them out. That'd been why she saw his power flare for a brief second during their conversation.

She went for him. He blocked each jab and slash. Every kick and punch. She eyed him as they circled one another.

He toys with us, Usha remarked.

Of course he does, that was Zen's way when they sparred.

"Have I not taught you anything?" He smacked her across the cheek in a whip-like move she hadn't seen coming. It wasn't hard enough to hurt, but the blow stung all the same. "You tire yourself knowing I'm the superior fighter. It's like you sacrifice yourself to me. Too easy."

They went at it again. She tripped over a rug, stumbled backward, and came up dead-footed with her spine against the windowpanes. He moved into her space. Eye-to-eye they stared at one another, her panting the only racket in the room.

"So this is how it all ends?" she asked as he elevated a hand and braced it against the glass next to her head. "Maybe...."

The door practically throbbed from all the kicking, pounding, and magic thrown at it. "You're scaring my men."

"They should be terrified."

Madison settled her hand on his arm. "I trust you."

She chugged his magic harder than she ever had anyone's, and screamed as pain slashed through her head. Zen's eyes widened, silver bright, and he jerked away as his magic held strong, barring her husbands from the room.

Zen stumbled, his footing off, and he swayed a moment before going to a knee. Wincing as the pain receded, Madison circled him and secured her blade in its leather holster.

She threaded her fingers in his hair and pulled his head back. His shallow breathing surprised her, "Concede defeat?"

He delivered an off-kilter grin. "Excellent job."

The door gave way, and Nix fell into the room, lurching to catch his balance. Micah appeared beside her before Nix could right himself.

"It was an exercise." Madison indicated Zen on his knees. "Zen lost this round."

Zen confirmed her the champion. "Can you put me back?"

Madison combed his hair off his forehead and leaned down to kiss his brow. She injected her energy into him, returning his magic. Zen shot to his feet and hugged her. "I'm impressed, my sister. I didn't see that one coming."

"I don't get you, Zenny." Nix pulled her out of her immortal friend's arms and took his time patting her down for injuries, amusing Madison in the process.

Arms relaxed at his side, Zen pondered Nix for a

while before asking, "What's difficult to understand?" Micah was the one who answered. "If anyone will succeed in killing her, it'll be you. Why do you prepare her against you?"

Zen stared her demon-king husband straight in the eyes. "You know there are others who could kill her. At present they've decided against joining the fray. Your angelic siblings won't concede. I prepare her because she's my adopted family, my sister, and I'll die before I allow another to harm her. Even myself."

Chapter 29

IF NOT FOR his bought immortality, Nix suspected he'd have perished from a heart attack when he thought Zenny attempted to kill Mads. It'd been a plausible likelihood given his displeasure over her agreement with Elias to collect a soul he'd purchased and then torture the spirit until the former mortal caved to its owner's devious whims. Nix lived with the mindset that Mads's crystal genie was always one breath away from offing her. Now that she'd accepted her destiny, Zen was also the only one with any real clout who could take her out.

He splashed water on his face and looked at himself in the mirror. He wasn't sure what the hell he'd expected when Mads accepted her fate and became the Queen of Hell. Sure, he'd expected crazy shit and motherfuckers making a play for her life. Jumping feet first into helping the fucker who'd actually been determined to kill her, had never made his list of 'could happen'. The only way he'd seen Eliel in his future was helping Beliel kill the rat bastard.

More cold water doused his face, but it didn't help

265

clear his head.

He loved Mads without limits, but terrorizing souls could alter her deeply. In the end, she could become someone entirely different, darker...even more demonic.

Water dripped from his chin as he stared into his eyes. Could he love a darker Mads? What of his unborn children? How would her actions affect them?

A heavy sigh burst from his lips, and he closed his eyes. He had to face reality. At the heart of the problem, he worried more about himself embracing darkness than Mads taking a permanent stint down that road. Liberated in his dark ways, he'd loved the freedom, and he continued to struggle with his desires to return to the 'good times' he and Micah shared before Mads 'saved' him from Hell.

Arms went around his waist. His eyelids flipped upward, and he startled at the unexpectedness of Mads's hug.

Speak of the devil. He placed his forearms over hers, lacing the fingers of one of their hands together. The slight bulge of her belly pressed against his lower spine, and he softened. She was giving him a gift he'd never hoped for. Children to love as much as he loved their mother.

My personal devil. God, he adored her. There were no words for how much he loved her.

Their eyes caught in the mirror.

"What's wrong, Nix?" She rubbed her cheek against his shoulder, holding his gaze in the reflection.

Noting the pink in her eyes, he shook his head. "Why's your demon showing?"

"What. Is. Wrong?" A playful nip to his flesh functioned as a rebuke for dodging her question. The nails of her free hand scraped across his abdomen. "Even if I couldn't tell you're brooding, your aura is messed up. Talk to me...*baby.*"

A slight grin tugged at his lips at her using his endearment for her.

Secrets weren't allowed in their relationship. While

266

he agreed brutal honesty served their fucked-up relationship best, right now he wanted to guard them, protect her even from his sensitive and illogical emotions. At his silence she pinched his belly. Throwing caution to the wind, he gave her what she wanted. "I worry about losing you."

"I'm happy. Why would I leave you?" She nuzzled her cheek against his shoulder again.

"I'm worried about *losing you*, baby, not you going anywhere." She halted her rubbing that he liked way too much and pressed a kiss to his shoulder while meeting his eyes in the mirror's reflection. He stabilized his misgivings and went on. "You have no idea how addicting it is to torture a soul until it breaks."

It hadn't been all that long ago—less than six months—he'd been creating mayhem alongside Micah, damning souls, and eating up the exhilaration he felt while brutalizing the less fortunate. He still struggled with his personal demons. No one quite understood how tightly he tiptoed along the edge of backsliding.

He couldn't see her mouth, but the slight narrowing of her eyes hinted she smiled. Why the fuck would his anxiety amuse her? More to the point, why the fuck did the glint in her eyes affect him in the crotch like she jacked him off?

The husky tone of her voice produced a buzz along his skin. "Was it fun, Nix?"

"More than I care to admit."

The pink in her eyes ignited, drowning out the blue. "Why does that excite me?"

Probably the same reason it did him...being bad was easy, therapeutic in a way being good never had been for him. Since he had no answer to her question, he remained silent.

Her hand lowered, a slow, hard drag down across the front of his jeans until she rubbed only the heel of her palm against his crotch.

Nix groaned. The Mads he'd known six months ago hadn't acknowledged her sexual needs. The succubus in her executed advances with ease.

"Would you be my victim, Nix?"

"I think I've proven I'd do anything for you, Mads." The painful truth.

"Mmm..." She nipped his skin again. "Remember the night you and Micah kept me on edge for hours, refusing my pleasure, until I forced yours and took mine?"

He grinned. "Like it was yesterday."

Sexually tormenting her was his personal drug of choice. He closed his eyes, vividly recalling the way she'd writhed on the bed, begging for release, as they brought her close to climax over and over again, pulling back right before the crucial moment. She'd been desperate, had tried to force them to keep their heads between her legs or their fingers on her, but somehow Micah had neutralized her power each time. They'd gotten her so sensitive a light brush of his fingertips against her nipples had had her moaning and her muscles tensing.

Then when she'd had more than she could tolerate, her Lynx took over. She'd forced their orgasms with a blast of her power, which had triggered her release. Micah had been pleased by her dominance, fed Nix some of his special angel dust, and they'd taken turns making love to her through the remainder of the night.

He didn't understand why orgasm denial fed a succubus, but she'd been so jazzed afterward she hadn't required sustenance for three days. Nix couldn't feed her the way she required without growing sick or being unintentionally killed. Micah was the best source of food she had, but he got off on nourishing her other ways. Nix couldn't deny he'd enjoyed this way immensely.

"That's what I'd do to you. Deny your pleasure until I decided to let you come."

Fuck.

"Don't go soft, Phoenix." Micah intruded, his gaze

catching Nix's in the mirror. "A succubus of her caliber requires a dominant in the bedroom."

"So says you," she shot back.

"You'd eat him alive if he didn't play his part. How many times have I stopped you from consuming *all* his life-force?"

Micah had a point.

In the months since they'd married, she'd accidentally almost drained Nix at least a dozen times. Only Micah held the power to halt her.

"Maybe I'll deny your pleasure," she said, holding Micah's gaze in the reflection as she continued to rub the heel of her palm over Nix's erection.

Micah slowly shook his head. "Won't ever happen, kitten." His look said he *always* remained in charge. Nix couldn't see the fallen angel ever submitting to another. "Phoenix, the spell will utilize a great deal of her power. She'll need to feed a lot afterward."

Nix turned, hugging Mads to him. "I can join you for the spell, that way I'm already there when it's over."

"The Kings won't tolerate your presence."

"And I apparently don't get a vote." Mads rolled her eyes. "Zen is on Amos-duty, squirreled away to only God and Zen know where. Petra is camping out in the radius where the opening is to Hakara, so she can warn off any encroachers who try to stop us. I've been forced by the Kings to command Kur and the other dragons to remain here." That last seemed to irritate her most.

The King of Hell stepped into their space, sandwiching Mads against them. "Trust is earned."

"I *own* the dragons, they wouldn't betray me and fuck up our plan." She huffed. "Nix and Petra would never betray me. And Zen just confirmed his loyalty to me, at the expense of his own near pretend-death."

"In all those you listed, I trust only Phoenix." She went to argue, but Micah talked over her. "Dragons are a shifty lot by nature and while they cannot directly betray you, there are ways around any ownership. Petra has already betrayed me once. I don't think she wants to betray you, but if she thought it'd protect Amos, she'd turn on you in a heartbeat. As for Zen...." He sniffed as if something reeked. "I've known him for eons, and I've yet to understand what motivates him. That alone triggers my distrust. You'll play it safe because it pleases me *and* Phoenix. Agreed?"

She ignored Micah, lowering to her knees between them. "I'm going to blow you before we go, Nix."

Beliel chuckled. "Watching you get him off is no punishment to me, kitten."

Chapter 30

MICAH'S SIBLING'S WATCHED with intensity in their gazes as Madison drew a symbol in the air.

"This is the design for the doorway between domains." She ignited the etching with her hellish-blue flames.

Zero hesitation in her voice, no questioning of her powers, or how she knew this specific design would work. Her confidence tugged at Micah's pride.

"It's similar to a Demon Lock, with minor deviations." Raguel traced the design with his fingertip, the flames having ill effect on him.

Hielel—better known as Lucifer in the human realm—ran his thumb and forefinger along his chin a long moment as he studied the design. "How'd you know this was the correct pattern?"

Madison shrugged. "Innate."

The answer explained a lot. Magic could be compared to breathing. It came naturally to those born to it. Hielel's dark gaze flicked to her, and she jutted her chin slightly, challenging him to interrogate her knowledge. She'd been to Hakara, that meant she'd become one of them—albeit briefly—but that scant moment gave her leverage over the domain none of them held. Because of her brief time there, she'd always feel an affinity to the locale.

"Little Queen, are you ready for this?" Hielel again.

"Are you kidding?" She tipped him a cheeky grin. "I was born for this."

Her cockiness spawned a chuckled from Hielel and a grin from Raguel. Micah winked at her.

Like always, Elias taunted Madison with, "But will you be all you can be? Or fail us like always?"

For once, Madison shrugged off his twin's baiting.

"What do you have to say for your actions?" Shifting through his ever-changing facades, Hielel faced Elias, confronting Eliel for the first time since his near murder of Madison.

"I answer to no one." His twin nodded at Madison. "The princess requested my aid, I'm giving it. That speaks for itself."

"What it says," Raguel piped in. "Is that she's securing our future."

"As did I." Elias elevated his eyebrows at the insinuation that his actions hadn't secured Hell's future. Even Micah couldn't dismiss that they probably had. Despite that, Elias wasn't entitled to a royal pardon. It wasn't in Micah to be that forgiving.

"Let's focus on salvaging Hell. Eliel shouldn't divide us until afterward." Micah wanted to rip into him worse than anyone, but Hell must take precedence.

"Finally, some wise words out of your mouth, *zkihtak*." His twin's sarcasm didn't go unnoticed.

He burned to remind his brother only the privileged could call him brother, but Madison interrupted. "I gave y'all the words to bind the doorways together. I'll draw the design the moment we arrive at the opening to Hakara."

"You remember the words to bind them in Hell, Madison?" Hielel returned his attention to her.

"Yeah." Her intelligence had intrigued Micah even in her youth. Thanks to a photographic and audiographic memory, Madison outsmarted most.

"Is everyone ready?" At everyone's nod, Micah portaled Madison to Hakara's fissure.

She went to work immediately. The moment she completed the drawing, she smacked her palm toward the air-hieroglyph and it burst into blue flames. Residents of the monster domain could be seen through her design. He could sense their curiosity, and more than a few recognized him and Elias.

"Stay back!" Madison yelled when it appeared as if a few would charge the opening, he suspected to seek revenge on him and his twin.

At her words, the Hakarians halted and glanced at one another, a clear show of uncertainty. Aramayis was the male equivalent of Madison, and he'd run Hakara. It wouldn't be implausible for them to worry she'd iron fist them the way the incubus had.

With her palm pressing against the center of the symbol, Madison said to the abominations housed inside Hakara, "Hakarians know this doorway opens to Hell. Coming through the portal is a covenant with me, your Queen of Hell and Hakara." Eliel shot a hard glare in her direction, and for a second Micah thought Elias would go for her. Not having noticed Beliel's astonishment, Madison went on. "The moment you breach the doorway, I own your soul and will use and rule you as I deem necessary." She quickly etched her own sigil over the one she'd just drawn. Pink flames mixed with the blue. "This makes it a legally binding contract."

Raguel gave Micah a cagey glance. The unexpectedness of her claim on Hakarian souls stunned even Beliel. It was one of his classic moves, but to have Madison sell the rest of them out never crossed his mind.

Hielel's features remained blank, indicating he'd expected this outcome. Or had foreseen it at the very least.

Beliel's twin laughed, and his words filtered into

Micah's head, *Seems like our princess learns fast.*

"Impressive," Elias remarked aloud, eyeing Madison with a new critical eye.

Micah took a deep breath and released it, as Madison went on without acknowledging any of the Kings. She chanted the words that solidified the doorway in its location permanently. Micah and Hielel were the first to repeat the words, before his other two brothers joined them. Power coursed through him, scratching up his spine, as they implemented the spell. The intimacy of the shared magic delivered his twin's bitterness to him. Micah had received all his dreams, while Elias lost everything. Micah would've been more empathetic if his wife's life hadn't been part of his brother's strategy.

Instead of the incantation tiring her as he'd anticipated, the magic amped her up. He'd known Madison would get off on the power of working in tandem with them. Eliel even knew she'd relish deciding the fate of the lives of others. She'd just claimed monsters as hers, so how much more would she enjoy helping Elias destroy the soul he was set to claim?

A twinge of jealousy bristled along Micah's skin, almost short-circuiting his focus of magic. He glanced at Elias. His twin had convinced Madison to break a soul before Micah had, and that was galling.

The moment the door locked into place the flames fizzled out with a hissing and popping noise.

"Join me, my pets." Madison smiled at the monsters hanging out near the portal. She turned to Micah and extended her arm, palm up. "Take me to my chamber so I can ready it to house my minions."

Chuckling at her drama, he took her hand and opened a seam. "After you, kitten."

She went through it without a word. He glanced at his siblings. Hielel nodded at him. Raguel just gaped.

Elias grinned. "A kitten with minions, what *is* Hell turning into?"

"A powerhouse," Hielel replied in a solemn voice. A one-sided smile tilted the corner of his mouth as his mental voice slid into Micah's head. *She protects her humans by claiming the Hakarians so we can't use them against humankind. It's a ballsy move, Beliel. One a true Queen would make.*

Micah let that sink in before turning and going through the portal. By the time he arrived in the chamber created to cage any Hakarians, she'd already worked the spell to house them. Pink and blue magic weaved together to create a home, rather than a cage, for the monsters.

Madison leaned against the wall, her left knee bent with her foot anchored against the wall. Arms crossed over her chest, with her pink eyes rimmed in yellow, she watched him as if she expected him to explode. From the moment she'd entered Hell to craft the spell, she'd allowed her Lynx complete freedom. He could see the evidence in her eyes and in her pink-and-red interlaced aura. A calculating demon stared at him now.

He walked straight to her, clasped her face between his palms, and kissed her, plunging his tongue into her mouth. She grasped him in return, her hands fisting his shirt. Breaking the kiss, he Eskimo kissed her. "Do you have any idea how your duplicity affects me?"

She laughed against his lips. "I believe I have some idea." She wrapped a leg around his hip, and rocked her pelvis against his hard-as-fuck-cock. "You're not angry?"

He shook his head and ground his dick against her. "Should we join Phoenix and feed you?"

"I'm not hungry."

Micah could see that. Instead of draining her energy, performing this magic with the Kings lent the opposite effect of what he'd expected...it'd fed her. "But I'm hungry for you."

Chapter 31

ELIAS GRINNED AT Phoenix's pacing. He'd rankled the Ark of Heaven, and that pleased him. The Jesus-toy asked Madison not to go along with their agreement to claim Eliel's soul and torture it until it broke.

He pitied his twin having to endure Phoenix's naivety.

They'd brokered a contract. His sister-in-law must uphold her end of the bargain. Agreements among royalty were more binding than the covenants they used to bind the souls they bartered for. Not that Madison balked once at the idea of aiding Elias. He liked that. A lot. It indicated her succubus held a strong position inside her. He knew her demon craved doling out torture. He hadn't met a demon, pureblood or made, that shied away from tormenting others. Most relished meting out suffering.

Micah leaned against the brick wall with his arms crossed, watching and waiting as Madison entered the building across the street. A few minutes later, the princess exited the structure with a magical pink rope looped around the human's neck. She led him toward them with a skip in her step.

Goddamn. Finally. It'd taken her long enough to embrace her demon. The wicked glint in her eyes reminded him of the naughty child he once adored, cossetted with his devotion, and helped deliver misery to mortals.

She offered the rope to him, a glimmer of mischief in her eyes. "For you, my disadvantaged King."

Disadvantaged! Ha! The princess bitch obviously required another demonstration of his musical instruments—*my talons*—to show her the lack of his shortcomings. He'd gained what he wanted from her by using them on her. Being ousted by his brothers the price he paid for aiding in her Fall from her condescending piousness. A price he'd pay a thousand times over to gain her submission. She'd required his unprincipled guidance to illustrate the gift she shunned.

Declining her offer of the rope, he said, "He's yours to tame, princess." Elias turned his back on her and stepped through the portal he crafted.

He could feel Madison's presence and once she entered his hellish room, she directed the soul to the center of the chamber.

Micah's expression remained passive, but Elias could feel his eagerness to watch his girl torment a soul. It'd be like foreplay, or the very least an aphrodisiac. Phoenix nipped at their heels, glowering, but even though the Jesus-toy abraded his nerves, he wanted the holy-heir to witness the depth of Madison's depravity.

"Why'd you sell your soul?" Madison asked.

Elias angled himself so he could watch the Ark of Heaven while ogling Madison. Without instruction, she'd strung up the male with bright pink magic.

Zero tears from the mortal, he answered her question with an oddly strong voice. "The devil cured my daughter's cancer."

"How long will her remission last?" She toyed with

the end of the magic-rope as she turned only her gaze to Elias.

"Remission is remission," the soul said.

Elias shook his head. The mortal hadn't brokered a deal for the span of his daughter's lifetime, but simply for her remission. He'd given the man what he wanted, and not one second of time more.

"How long Elias?" she demanded.

"It ended the moment you took him."

The mortal visibly crumbled by that reality. "You bastard!"

"You have no idea," Madison said in a singsong voice.

Elias shrugged. "I can't be blamed for your lack of negotiation skills."

The human victim wept. "Please save her."

Eliel ignored the soul's plea.

The princess took the time to explain. "It's too late, you've got nothing to barter with."

Evidently the human believed Madison would sympathize with his daughter's suffering. "You could save her."

"Here's the deal, human." She smacked him on the cheek and caught his chin. "You want her saved, then you must break for Elias."

She dragged her thumbnail along his jaw, creating a thin cut in his flesh. Elias peeked at his twin. Micah adjusted his growing erection. His gaze slid to Phoenix who pinched the bridge of his nose.

"Once broken...." Her thumb pad swiped over the man's blood, smearing it along his cheek. "You can act as Elias's liaison and offer her a deal to save her life."

Elias liked the way she thought.

"Never," the soul vowed.

We'll see about that.

Unable to see her face with her back to them, she cocked her head to the side as if she contemplated the male. A few seconds later, she palmed his shoulder and pushed him to his knees. She circled him a few times, rubbing his blood between her thumb and fingertips, and sniffing the substance. She paused behind the soul. "The big fella over there"—even though the former mortal couldn't see her, she indicated Elias with a tilt of her head, and the soul peered straight at him with fear in his eyes—"with the brown hair. That's your new master, and he wants me to torture you until you become a good and biddable demon."

The human whimpered.

Pathetic.

The scent of the soul's fear leeched from him and infiltrated Elias's nostrils, increasing his eagerness to defile and maim his newest acquisition.

"The hottie with the spiky hair"—she tangled her fingers in the man's ginger hair and forced his head around to face toward Phoenix—"he doesn't want me to torture you." She ran her finger down the side of the soul's cheek. "What say you, Micah?"

Elias saw the gleam in his brother's eyes. He wanted Madison to persecute the male. He'd get off on it as much as Elias would.

Before his twin could reply, Elias spoke up, "I say get on with it and quit toying with him."

Her gaze shot to him and a predator smile curled her lips. "Don't you mean quit toying with you, Elias? Haven't you ever heard the longer the foreplay the bigger the climax?"

A chuckle jerked from Eliel. Micah elevated his eyebrows, a grin stretching across his face. Phoenix continued to look squeamish, like he might puke any moment. As if the man hadn't once tortured souls alongside them.

Pansy motherfucker.

The Jesus-toy had committed worse acts during his Fall from grace at Micah's side. Actions much, *much* worse than Elias requested from Madison.

"Princess, my idea of foreplay is choking my victim while I stick my dick in it."

Madison grimaced. "No imagination."

"You're stalling."

Holding Elias's gaze, she called his bluff by dragging her nails across the mortal's cheek, leaving long lines of flesh gouged from his skin. Blood oozed from the wounds. In a heartbeat her eyes ignited into a pink glow as she kissed the track marks she'd created in his skin.

Red marked her lips, and she swiped her tongue along them. Her eyelids fluttered closed, and she breathed deeply, exhaled slowly, as if rapture swelled through her system.

When she opened her eyes yellow rimmed the pink, and her ember colored pupils showcased her royal status. She ran the back of her fingers along the man's entire cheek. "I've tasted your soul."

Fuck me. Did she do what I think she just did?

Micah went from slouched against the wall to spine straight and striding toward his wife.

Madison ignored him, but kept her focus on Elias instead. "I've enthralled you, my pet." She stroked the male's hair with an affectionate air, like she would one of her Hellhounds. "Agony like you've never known will devour you over and over again. Worse than crushed glass moving through your veins, worse than the pain of your daughter dying repeatedly. You will scream and cry, soil yourself, tear the flesh from your bones." She pressed her lips to his ear, but locked her gaze on Elias. "And that's just a start. You'll beg for amnesty. None will be given. You will be broken over and over again," she murmured low and breathy, as if on the cusp of an orgasm.

For once in their acquaintance Elias respected her by not fine-tuning his sudden erection in front of her.

"The pain will arouse Elias like I am arousing him now."

He felt Micah's jerk and knew his brother narrowed his gaze on him even though he never looked in his sibling's direction.

"He'll torture you *his way* while you suffer *my* brutality. Double the agony. *You will suffer*. A lot.

Because I command it. Because Elias will get off on it. Your suffering will last years because I desire it. Because Elias craves it. Your shrieks will anoint Hell until you finally open your mind to *what you can be.* You'll accept your new master, Elias, first, and then you'll accept your new self and all the diabolical impulses that come with the new you. Do you understand all that is expected of you?"

"Yes," the male's voice trembled.

The sweet smile Madison gave Elias was the most horrific thing he'd ever witnessed because it contradicted the beauty of her features. He shivered. The darkness of her demon had claimed her. It was a matter of how far she'd go with it.

"Let it begin." She released the male. Immediately his body bowed in her pink restraints and he shrieked, fighting against his bonds, but they held as solid as her gaze held Elias's.

Goddamn, he could finally say he was proud of her. Respected her as one of Hell's sovereigns. *About time she accepted her destiny.*

He glanced at Phoenix. The Jesus-toy ran his palm down his face. That one needed to *go* or once again be hellishly redeemed before she could embrace all of her darkness. He would hold her back.

You won't touch him, his twin's voice slithered into his mind.

Elias's gaze shifted to his twin and Eliel smirked at him. Answering to no one was liberating because he'd do whatever-the-fuck he wanted.

It is liberating. Micah verified he heard his thoughts. *I own his soul once again, bartered to me to save Madison from you. You can try to get rid of him, but you know the routine.*

Narrowing his eyes on his sibling, Elias damned his bad fortune. Yeah, he knew the routine well. He could slaughter Phoenix every day for an eternity, and the Jesus-toy would always return to Micah whole. The only way he could be destroyed was if Micah desired the outcome.

"We're outta here." Micah clutched Madison by the back of the neck and yanked her against his chest. He knew his twin well enough to recognize the lust in his eyes. "Next time...."

Elias required no explanation. Next time he saw his twin, he knew Micah would attempt to put his *Scepter of Spirits* through his heart.

Bitterness churned his gut. Releasing a breath, he stared at his soul as memories of the child Madison had once been flittered through his mind...

Elias tolerated the Earthly realm for Micah's plan. Even though skeptical over his sibling's plan, he'd gone along with it anyway. He would do anything for his twin, even suffer the stench of mortals. On a good note, it broke up the monotony of immortality.

The little hellion Micah created with magic from the Pyxis, along with DNA from Celeste and Bruce, worked hard at owning his fucking heart. A dangerous emotion for a King of Hell to feel.

The she-devil perched on Micah's lap stared at Elias. She treated Beliel like her property, and vowed she'd wed him when she grew up. There was still time to change her mind, but for now he knew the minx was serious for the simple reason that she seemed to already know her young mind. Even now, a gleam twinkled in her blue eyes.

I know that expression.

No sooner had he thought that, she piped up, "Uncle Eli, I want ice cream."

That was code for she wanted to play succubus style. Madison never asked for tea parties, dodge ball, or even to cuddle with him the way she did with Micah. Oh, no, the five-year-old coming into her latent powers possessed an uncanny taste for enthrallment and blood. Micah neglected to teach her these things. Eliel was the one who helped her fine-tune her skill. It was the least he could do for a girl that had the capacity to be Queen of Hell. So far all his sibling had done was squelch her gift.

A grave mistake. *That the little imp recognized Elias mastered mayhem and chaos better than his twin warmed his icy heart. That she knew he answered to no one, even her maker and his brother, was the single reason she managed to coerce him into aiding her treachery. Of course he allowed her to railroad him because he enjoyed encouraging her diabolical behavior. Her rebellion would benefit Hell.*

"Ice cream sounds yummy, princess." Feeling protective toward her frightened him because to date his siblings were the only ones deserving of his emotions or protectiveness.

"You two are eating a lot of ice cream lately," Micah mused, brushing his fingers through her blonde hair.

"I love ice cream better than dead kittens," she vowed, which was a delightful analogy to Elias.

"I warned you about torturing animals," his twin's voice darkened, and she visibly deflated at his stern tone. If Elias didn't know Beliel better, he'd think his sibling was an uptight prick with no aptitude for bedlam. How did curbing Madison's appetites help her?

"I've been good!" She flung herself against Micah's chest and wrapped her arms around his neck. "I promise I've been good for you. Don't leave me. Please, please, please, please don't leave me."

Elias could hear the tears in her trembling voice. The last time she misbehaved Micah had threatened to depart her life as punishment. Her reaction had been dramatic and full of waterworks, and not in the theatrical sense. The concept of him not being in her life had devastated her.

"Shhh...." Micah rubbed her back and hugged her tighter against his chest. "I'm going nowhere, kitten. I'm proud of your control. Run along with your Uncle Eli and enjoy some ice cream. You deserve it for

obeying me."

She sniffled and nodded, her small hand touching his brother's cheek. "You still my Micah?"

"Yes and you're still my girl." His twin thumbed the tears from her cheeks.

Elias stood and approached them. "Want to join us for the treat, Micah?"

Beliel shook his head as Elias lifted Madison into his arms. "Have fun, Madison."

You're making a mistake depriving her of her skillset, *Elias sent the telepathy to his twin.* It makes her stronger to hone her magic.

Micah replied in like kind, It's not your decision to make. She's too young and doesn't understand limits. In her mortal world drawing attention to herself would be a bigger mistake. She'll have time to learn her magic when she's older. We'll teach her then. Just show her a good time like you always do.

Elias was certain his sibling's decision was a mistake. Even if hunters knew about her, there were ways to protect her from them. But this was Beliel's pet project. Eliel was just along for the ride.

Twenty minutes later they entered the ice cream parlor in the sleepy Alabama town. Being a Sunday afternoon it was full of family, which meant Madison had lots of victims to play with.

Neither of them spoke as Elias passed her a small blade. She took it, skipped over to a woman seated at the same table as a brown haired boy about Madison's age. A quick flick and the blade nicked the mother's hand.

"Momma!" the boy cried as the mother gasped. But a second later, Madison had smeared her finger through the blood and brought it to her mouth.

"You will do everything I say." While giving succubus commands, Madison always sounded older than her age.

Goddamn, I almost love this child.

Elias flipped the sign hanging on the door from 'open' to 'closed' and twisted the lock. He pulled a chair from a nearby table and straddled it so he could watch Madison work her magic.

"Bobby Ray pulled my hair in school Friday," she told the mother.

"Your big-fat head was in the way of the whiteboard!" Bobby Ray yelled, which snagged the attention of a few curious onlookers.

The hate in Madison's gaze should've cowed the boy, but he was a stupid child like all children his age that weren't lucky enough to possess demonic blood.

"Slap him," Madison instructed the mother.

Tears streaked the cheeks of Bobby Ray's mother, but she smacked her child across the cheek as coached. The room silenced when the boy cried out, and all eyes turned on the scene Madison instigated.

"Harder," Hell's princess instructed, her voice becoming a low growl of excitement.

The next strike knocked the boy to the floor.

Madison giggled and clapped her hands. Her curls bobbed as she looked over at Elias. "I made him cry like a baby, Uncle Eli!"

"Please, stop this. Stop her," the mother begged Elias with her tone, while her eyes and expression asked how Madison's influence was possible.

A do-gooder exited his booth from the back of the café and approached. Before he could interfere, Elias extended his claws and allowed the Kingly fire of his eyes to glow. Alarmed cries echoed in the room. The benefactor's steps came to an abrupt halt. The good patron's eyes widened, and his Adam's apple bobbed with a nervous swallow. Some began to pray, while others wept. Frightened children crawled into the protective embraces of their parents' arms. Today those 'protective arms' would be ineffective fortification.

Elias tapped a claw against the back of the seat. "There'll be silence and order while she plays, or I'll make all of you bleed."

Madison smiled. "You're my favorite uncle."

He grinned. She was his favorite creature, with hopeful potential that he planned to cultivate until she was a heartless, killing machine.

An infant began to squall. Probably squeezed too hard, he surmised.

Madison turned in the direction of the racket, located the baby, and in a cool as cucumber voice informed the mother, "You make it quiet or I will."

Eliel shook his head, clearing away the fond recollections of chaos reigning for hours at the hands of a cherubic face with demonic ideas.

Reality was a harsh bitch to harbor though. Existing on the edge of a domain he'd helped build, while his twin despised him and sought his death, it might seem like he had nothing to live for, but there was a season for everything. A biblical truth. Madison's rise as Queen was a birthing process, one that would benefit Hell, and in time, his problems would be smoothed over. It might take longer for his twin to come around, but so long as Madison forgave him he felt certain his brother would eventually follow in her footsteps.

Micah has turned into her lapdog.

A bitter snort echoed in the cavern. Love ruined his twin. Thankfully that malady would never assault him.

What galled him most was that all those years ago he'd recognized Madison's potential before Micah had. And still today he understood her needs better than his twin. Elias knew she'd needed to maim a soul to feed her demon. Her succubus sustained off sexual energy, but her demon required different things, and would always thrive on chaos and mayhem.

Am I the only King remaining with common sense?

"Eliel," Lucifer halted at the entrance to Elias's section of Hell.

"You may enter." He watched his sibling approach. Humans acquainted Lucifer—Hielel—as the devil out for the souls. While he owned a few, he was more the physician of the group, working his magic from a different angle. It was Beliel and Eliel who'd bartered

286

for so many souls for Hell's realm. The other King, Raguel, attacked mortals through their dreams. "You've done great work." Hielel pointed at the soul Madison tortured with her succubus enthrallment. "Getting her to participate in Hell's design is wise." "I know."

A slight grin hit Hielel's lips, even while his appearance was ever-changing. "Yes, well, this was a smart move on your part."

"Did you come to tell me things I already know or do you have something else to say?"

"Beliel will never forgive you for almost killing her." Elias waited for Lucifer to continue while his brother studied the damned. "If Beliel succeeds in killing you, the outcome will be detrimental to Hell. There can be a merger between you two. I suggest finding an alternative path through Madison to penetrate his hatred of you."

Elias smirked. "Nothing kinky sounding about that."

His brother frowned at him.

"Forget it." Eliel shook his head. "Thanks for the advice, brother."

"While I might not agree with your methods, I thank you for sacrificing yourself for the good of Hell."

"No problem." Bitterness burned Elias's gut, but he said nothing else, just walked away from his fellow King.

"Time has a way of healing old wounds, Eliel," Lucifer called after him.

Not soon enough.

Maintaining his brisk stride, he descended deeper into his section of Hell. He'd given up *everything* for his twin, not once, but twice. His twin thought Elias betrayed him. But Micah had betrayed Elias too.

The acrimony of his loss burned like white-hot lightening through his system. His claws curled into his palms and he allowed his wings to expand.

Fucking a succubus while he made her bleed and

beg would soothe his indignation at losing the one person who meant everything to him.

Chapter 32

MICAH LAY ON his side with Madison sandwiched between them, Phoenix at her back. The Ark's hand rested over her baby bump with Micah's knee wedged between her thighs. They'd taken her several times, sometimes together, and other times separate while the other watched. He loved making his succubus Queen purr.

He'd anticipated Madison being squeamish over harming the soul Elias offered up, but her demon had risen to the challenge. The way she'd relished the moment, taunting Elias, had aroused him. Until today, he'd only fantasized about watching her demon toy with a victim. Phoenix had flinched at her demonic tendencies, and that worried her enough that her thoughts kept seeping into his.

You were forced to torture the soul, kitten, that's why Phoenix hated it, Micah sent her the telepathy as he kissed her forehead. *He wanted you to make that choice, not be forced into it.*

Opening her eyes, her blue eyes honed on him. "I wish...." She cleared her throat and reverted to telepathy. *I wish I believed that.*

"Wish what, baby?" The Ark rubbed her baby-bump in a circular motion.

She laced their fingers together over her belly and squeezed. "I wish every woman was as lucky as me."

Nice save. Micah trailed his fingertip across her jawline. *Your double standards are cute, kitten. My secrets pissed you off, but you're going to keep this one from him.* He mentally *tsked* her. *Just say the word when you're ready to kick him to the curb, and I'll do the dirty work.* Because if she started keeping secrets it wouldn't take long before Phoenix grew tired of the duplicity.

The pink of her demon flared in her eyes. She smacked her palm to the center of his chest, shoving up onto her knees. "What the hell does that mean?"

"You two doing that mental shit again?" Phoenix skirted his fingers along her thigh to her hip. "I detest your top-secret chatter. I feel left out."

Micah taunted her with a grin. "Telepathy is useful in dangerous situations, Phoenix."

She glanced at the former Sherlock who remained on his side facing her. "Micah was invading my private thoughts. There's a difference between that and secret chatter."

"Then tell him what you were thinking." Beliel challenged rolling to his back and getting comfy with his arm over his head. "Be honest with him."

Her eyes narrowed on him, and he challenged her further by elevating his eyebrows.

Phoenix slid his palm down her leg. "Tell me, baby. I can't help if you don't trust me."

"Why did it bother you when I tortured Elias's soul?" She called Micah's bluff. He'd been so sure she wouldn't address her concerns.

"It's not your style, baby."

Micah snorted at that bullshit. The capability of her breed and the gruesome natures of succubi could terrify even him.

"It is me, don't forget I'm a demon." Her frustration

chafed Micah mentally. "I liked it, Nix. The power to do whatever I wanted to him was liberating, and every much as addicting as stealing the power of others."

They both knew how much she craved ingesting the magic of others.

Her former Sherlock abruptly sat up and palmed her nape. The aggressive move caused Micah's cock to twitch. "I understand the allure, baby. I've been there, but it'll break you in ways you're not prepared to deal with."

Madison yanked out of his hold as if he struck her. "I held back, tortured him with my succubus to make *you* happy. I'm always holding back so I don't disappoint others, and I'm sick of it."

"Mads—"

"Save it, Nix." After cutting him off, she crawled off the bed with a huff and conjured clothes out of thin air. Micah loved watching her in action.

As she pulled on the jeans and shirt, her Ark of Heaven tried to engage her again. "Don't walk away mad, let's talk about this, baby."

"Talk? Micah got off on it"—*fuck yeah I did*—"and you were disgusted." *Wouldn't go that far, kitten.*

"I wasn't disgusted."

She ignored the Ark. "I don't want to talk about how it hurts me that you can't accept what I am." Micah felt Phoenix's flinch more than he saw it. "I spent too long ignoring my demon. No longer will I pretend to be something I'm not. Had that soul been a living breathing human, I would've done everything in my power to save him. He damned his soul long ago. I hold no culpability in that choice. That's on him. I'm not going to seek out evil, but I'm not going to walk away from the influence my role gives me either. My status and power will keep my children safe, and I won't apologize for that." In an adorable huff, she stormed off. She paused at the exit. "You're mine, Nix. You marked yourself as mine with my sigil. Get with the program or I'll enthrall you to get with it."

Madison flounced out of the room. Micah chuckled at her feisty exit.

"She's pissed off. I don't see anything funny about that, Micah." Phoenix glared at him.

"I have always found her testiness amusing. Not sure why." He thought about the time she'd scorned him in the café when she was fifteen. She'd walked away from him, and he'd chased her down the street in his car. She'd been testy that day too, sassed him, and as a result, he'd been a goner, determined to have her even more.

"Should I go after her?"

"No, I think she needs to be alone." Taking a stand for herself was something she had to work out on her own. "You'd enjoy being enthralled." Micah knew she wouldn't follow through with that particular threat though.

Phoenix sent him a sidelong frown. "I don't know why she thinks I don't accept her the way she is. I love everything about her, even her demon."

Micah rolled off the bed and pulled on his jeans. "Do you really, Phoenix?"

"After everything you doubt me?"

"I've no doubt you love Madison, but her succubus is a very different side of her you might not have prepared yourself for. I couldn't fault you if that were the case."

"I'm not listening to this bullshit. I love—"

"Don't make the same mistake I did and let your pride get in the way. You *will* listen if you want to be right with our woman." At Micah's statement, Phoenix leaped off the bed and dressed, his irritation evident in his jagged movements.

"Don't make the mistake thinking I'm anything like you." The former Sherlock's icy tone contradicted the heat in his stare.

Beliel snorted. "As if I'd ever make that blunder. You're too pious for my tastes."

"You liked me well enough when we were fucking."

"You were Fallen and at your best then." *The good*

292

ole days. Too bad Madison insisted on putting Phoenix back together and reverted him back to holier-than-thou-Phoenix. At times he could be as pretentious as the uptight immortal. With *Fallen* Phoenix as part of the package deal, they would be an amazing threesome, inciting havoc and mayhem. He sighed at their loss. "Even then we were different. You consider Madison's wants more than I do. I just *do* what is best." *I know what's best for her. She just hasn't figured that out yet.* "We both know *I know* demons." He'd created the first of them, so he knew them inside and out, what motivated them and what made them tick. "A demon's nature is to torment others. I'm an angel so I do it out of revenge because I'm a sadistic fuck and I want to destroy Father's creation, show Him how weak His favored are. You're an heir of Christ, and you did it to gain power for revenge against Zennyo Ryuo for a perceived wrong against Madison. Demons don't torture out of any compulsion other than it just *fucking feels good.* Remember how you felt when you were torturing souls with me?"

"Yeah." The Ark of Heaven smoothed his fingertips over his brow. "The power went to my head. Felt great. I was a sick and twisted motherfucker, high off their screams."

"Exactly. You and I come from a devout breed. Madison was spawned from the worst lot of demons Father ever created. He didn't lock them away and throw away the proverbial key for no reason. I stole it from Him for that very reason because the genetic markers in the Pyxis gave *me* power."

"He let you steal it." Phoenix swiped his fingers through his spiky locks.

Micah refused to consider the likelihood. He preferred believing he'd given his parent the middle finger in the biggest way with Madison's birth. "What I'm getting at is that means her desire to give in to her demon is stronger, and something she cannot contain without imploding. Her need to torture, steal powers, and suck us dry sexually is an ingrained part of her. It's as basic as hunger. I hate Elias for what he did to her, but after today I realize he sees her more clearly than I do."

"If you tell me you forgive him for hurting her, almost killing her, I'll carve your fucking heart out and eat it like I did the other one."

Ah...yes. They'd entertained a damned soul during Phoenix's time in Hell. Micah had ripped the heart from the soul's chest and uttered, *"Huklejtax jioq vkulh oj mifak." Tarnished soul grant us power.* The heart gave the most power so long as it was consumed before it stopped pumping. Micah'd taken a bite of the organ before offering the remainder to Phoenix. The Ark of Heaven had initially been aghast at the idea, but when he discovered it'd give him strength to defeat Zennyo Ryuo, he'd ingested the body part as it jerked in his hand, squirting blood from the ripped valves.

Ignoring Phoenix's threat, Micah focused on savoring the memory. "Elias *knew* she needed to torture that soul, *knew* it'd appease her basic demon desires, just as I knew that heart would kick start your power like a jolt of steroids. Neither of us recognized that rudimentary requirement of Madison's, but Elias did." Too late he realized Elias had given him sage advice numerous times about Madison and he'd disregarded the counsel each and every time. "I only fantasized about watching her toy with a soul, but the reality was so much more erotic than I envisioned. You're the only one that blanched over it. The question, is can you accept her demon's necessities without falling out of love with her?"

"You're going to exploit this requirement of hers, aren't you?"

"Fuck yeah, I am. To ignore it would be unhealthy in the long term."

"I loved her enough to forfeit my mortality. I'm not going to get squeamish now." Phoenix pinched the bridge of his nose. "Anything for Mads."

Micah'd heard that before right after the Ark Fell in Hell and tortured his first soul. This time when the former Sherlock said it, they knew Madison was alive rather than dead. And because Beliel had an excellent memory, he repeated the same words he'd said to the Ark of Heaven that day too, "I like your attitude, Phoenix."

Chapter 33

MADISON COULDN'T DECIDE if she was more hurt or pissed off by Nix's unexpected attitude. Even though she threatened to enthrall him, she would never follow through with the threat. He accepted her enough to make a stand against his family. Thankfully they'd come through for him. So she knew he wasn't as disgusted by her demon as a normal Sherlock would've been or even as revolted as the Birminghams would be. Maybe she expected too much from him.

Baby steps. This was a new part of her demon life, and she couldn't expect Nix to understand every change she made. Micah was right about her coercion. At first she'd balked at the idea even though she agreed with Elias's deal to torture the soul. By the time she followed through with their pact, she'd been eager to participate. That she'd enjoyed taunting the damned should bother her, but instead she'd relished the power over him. It'd fed her demon somehow.

No point in fighting my inner demon.

She shook her head when she realized where her feet had guided her. Aramayis's cell. The incubus had threatened her Ark of Heaven, and she still remained unsure about the incubus's future. He'd been deposited in Hell for her to make a decision once the fissure to Hakara was closed. *Well, it's closed now,* her demon muttered. *And we're still not sure how to handle him,* she shot back. *Maybe we can find some way to use him to our advantage.* Madison figured that was as easy as strapping a toy-sized collar around an elephant. Squaring her shoulders, she breezed into the cell unannounced. She leaned against the wall, the damned souls cradling her frame while the ones in her line of sight portrayed macabre acts of violence on the opposite wall.

Not noticing her, the incubus reclined on a cot. In silence, she watched him. One knee was bent, his foot resting on the bed. His wings were MIA, probably pulled tight to his body. His pitch-black hair cascaded off the bed and draped on the writhing floor.

It took a moment for him to notice her sudden appearance, but when he spotted her she smiled as he sat up.

Aramayis's scrutiny slid along her body, and she could feel him undressing her with his eyes. "You have been well fucked." His voice was like liquid silk over her body.

"My men take care of me."

"Lucky bastards."

She was the lucky one, but she kept the thought to herself.

"How did you acquire the loyalty of a Zennyo Ryuo and archangel?"

"The way I hear it, my Zennyo Ryuo and archangel are responsible for putting you in Hakara."

"Ah...you have both my jailers in your pocket." Aramayis's displeasure bloomed around her as potently as his charm had in the kitchen. "How?"

"I don't share trade secrets."

"Beautiful and mysterious." He rose from the cot,

and prowled toward her, his swagger a combination of sultry and predator.

She noticed the burns she'd given him on his chest had healed. "I'm also your mistress."

Aramayis grinned and went from good looking to drop dead gorgeous. "Remains to be seen, bride."

"I'm not your bride."

"We shall see."

Clearly, he underestimated his predicament.

He is a fine piece of ass. Usha sized him up like a piece of jewelry.

The incubus folded his arms over his chest. "As a united couple, we will be notorious."

"*Li.*" No. "Together, at full capacity and no morals— "

"Morals are overrated and not for our kind."

"—the world would flame out sooner. That outcome benefits no one."

He tsked her. "You are being gratuitously melodramatic. What good are humans if not to play with?"

"They're *my* humans, Aramayis."

"Yours?"

She nodded, while he seemed entertained by her claim.

"All of them are yours, love?"

"The entire lot."

An inky black eyebrow elevated upward toward his hairline. "Is that protectiveness or possessiveness I hear in your voice?"

"Does it matter?"

"No. Stingy is stingy either way even though there is enough of them to share. Gluttony is unattractive."

She felt a blast of sensual spell roll from him. Only royalty's magic worked in Hell, but his mojo still packed an annoying punch. She couldn't fault him for trying even though it ticked her off.

Madison pushed away from the wall and stalked to him. She halted in front of him and pinched his chin between her finger and thumb. "Try to enthrall me again and I'll have you chained up and acid dripped on your wings for a thousand years or until you learn to respect me."

"I respect you, love. You have managed to master me somehow, at least for the time being. I do not enjoy your mastery, but I respect that I have been vanquished." Aramayis jerked his chin from her grip. "Where am I? What is this place?"

"Hell."

His black eyes narrowed. "Is that supposed to mean something to me?"

"Well, you're trapped in Hell, so I'm speculating that means a whole helluva lot to you. And this place"—she made a swirly motion with her finger indicating the room—"neutralizes you, turning me into your magical governor. But here's the important part, incubus. I am Queen of Hell. My archangel is one of the Kings."

A confused frown rippled across his brow. "His Father built another domain for him?"

Madison gave him a quick rundown of Micah's Fall and how the Kings created Hell. The slight widening of his eyes detailed his awe, and maybe a little respect as well.

"Amusing that my jailer's obedience to his father held no value in the end. I can aid his cause."

"Like I'd ever trust you after you threatened my husband and forced your enthrallment on me."

"Cannot fault a man for trying."

"That's where you're wrong. I hold a grudge, and my memory is long."

"This...." he tapped his foot on the floor, and she got the notion he struggled to take her seriously. "Impressive framework. It has a nice flair to it."

I'm sure the Kings thank him.

Aramayis lifted a hand and captured a lock of her hair. Staring into her eyes, he fingered the strands and lowered his voice to a seductive purr. "What are your diabolic plans for me, mistress?"

"Leave you stripped of your powers unless you teach me how to enthrall the way you do." Where'd that entreaty come from? Didn't matter, she wouldn't rescind it. If she could enthrall without ingesting a person's blood, the advantage would be huge, and she'd take the knowledge in a heartbeat at almost any cost.

"I require a boon before I consider your request." He sniffed the lock of her hair that he fingered.

That's creepy in a psycho sort of way, Usha pointed out.

Madison smacked Aramayis on the cheek just enough to garner his full attention. "You're in no position to negotiate with me, Aramayis. You're in Hell, which means I already own you. I could command you to obey me, and you'd be obliged to comply. I also took your Hakarians from you as I promised for failing to return Petra to me" His nostrils flared, detailing his displeasure with the information. In truth, she wasn't so sure of her magic over him because Hell hadn't managed to conquer all of his. "But I won't command you because when you yield to my requests freely, the reward will be that much sweeter for me. And you *will* surrender."

"What you detail sounds a lot like seduction, bride."

She gave him a nonchalant shrug. Let him decipher it however he pleased.

"You are a tease. I like that, but you should be warned I am the master of seduction, love." Hell had not dimmed Aramayis's arrogance.

The incubus was cocky because he'd never met an equal that challenged him or bested him. Starting tomorrow, she'd rectify that long-standing problem. "I'm the mistress of thwarting even the best laid plans. You'll surrender."

"I eagerly anticipate witnessing your best efforts."

His conceit told her a thousand different things. At the top of that list she knew he'd be hard to break, if not impossible. If he ever surrendered he'd be the most loyal creature in her servitude. Probably more steadfast than Zen. She wasn't opposed to enthralling him for real to gain what she wanted. She stood close enough now to snag his blood and enslave him. For the moment she rejected that path. Madison desired his voluntary allegiance because, as she'd told him, his willing surrender would make her victory all the sweeter. "Be a good bride and provide me with a meal. I prefer blondes." He tugged on her hair in a not-so-subtle hint that *she* was the blonde he fancied.

"And I prefer any kind of power." Madison buried her nails into his wrist and guzzled his magic.

Aramayis attempted to jerk out of her hold, but his sudden movement put him on his knees and wheezing for air.

"That's how fast I can incapacitate you." She slowed the consumption of his mojo, noting his elixir wasn't as tasty as she'd anticipated. Total letdown. "Big mistake forgetting my genealogy. You asked if I knew how to use it, do you have your answer?"

A leer sufficed as his reply.

Madison caught his chin in her palm and dug her fingers into his jaw hard enough the half-moon imprint of her nails would leave a mark on his skin. She shoved his head back so she could stare into his eyes. Lust burned hot in his gaze. No way she imagined that. "Disrespect me again, and I'll take everything you have just because I can."

Chapter 34

Five months later

ZEN SURVEYED HIS surroundings. A youth league baseball game was in progress. Parents cheered from the stands. Humans were odd creatures, engaging in sports their children played as if they were professional athletes.

"What are you doing here, Madison?" He stopped beside her where she sat on the end of one of the bleachers.

She nodded at a male gripping the chain-link fence with white knuckles and screaming so loud his face was red. "Trying to decide if I should kill him or enthrall him."

A few people around her peeped at her. One parent seated in front of her slid down the bench away from Madison.

Zen wasted no time in entering their minds and swiping their memories.

The father she indicated took that moment to yell, "Conner, get your head out of your ass and get into the game!"

Zen perused the players. None had their heads in their anal canal, so he classified the statement as a crude euphemism.

"He's abusing the boy. He's not playing well because he's hurting."

How long had she been watching him to know that?

"Abusing the mother too. He's a bad man." Madison rubbed her swollen belly.

Anticipation to meet his nieces had him softening a bit, relaxing against the bleacher as he joined her in rubbing her tummy. Baby-Trouble as he'd dubbed the infant, kicked his hand like always when he touched her momma's stomach.

"What would you have him do if you enthralled him?" He blew the babies a mental kiss and felt their warmth over his affection.

Madison shrugged and looked at him for the first time. "You told me when I accepted my demon"—that comment received several double takes, so he took care of her infraction again—"that being one didn't make me evil, but what I did with it was what was important."

"Not my exact words."

"It's the general gist."

He nodded, agreeing with her.

She went on without his need to prompt her, "So, if I enthrall him, I'd demand he be a good dad and husband."

Sometimes she surprised him. This counted as one of those times. "This is how you want to use your Lynx? To better the world, make it more peaceful?"

She blew out a weary sigh. He knew how much she struggled with her new identity. Her succubus was technically *her*, just that side of herself that demanded sexual sustenance, but her husbands micromanaged that well and kept the demon sated. The Pandora entity she'd been forced to ingest to survive, along with her Lynx, wanted to gorge on everything and consume power. Instead of amassing figurines like a normal hobby, it wanted and demanded a more macabre collection.

"It seems like a good way to utilize my Lynx." She glared at the father they discussed when he began to curse at his child once again, kicking the chain-link fencing this time.

Zen worried for Madison, but her resilience continued to astonish him. She was not a normal woman. "Have you considered their struggle now hones them for greatness later?"

"I did." She opened the palm of her other hand, exposing her pink Azura stones. "The mother will be dead in a year, the child will become his father and end up a prison-lifer after he murders his wife."

There was no way she knew all that from the stones. "Those stones are meant to guide you not give prophecy."

"Amos gave the prophecy. The stones kept leading me to them."

Now he was getting the rest of the story. "What else did Amos say?"

"The boy could have a good life if his father wasn't abusive." At his dead stare, she went on. "He'll be a genetic physicist if the cycle of abuse stops."

As Amos would say, the decision was a 'no brainer'. "Your decision was made before I showed up."

She slid off the bleachers and hugged him. He wrapped his arms around her, Baby-Trouble kicked him in the gut, and Baby-Sweetness grazed him with her palm. Both were fond of him, their actions from the womb their way of showing him affection.

"Your opinion matters to me, Zen."

He squeezed her harder. *She* mattered to him. Madison and her children were all that mattered. "I don't have all the answers."

"You have more than I do."

She shifted a little. The ache in her lower-spine slid along his senses, so he rubbed her back with his thumb.

Everyone thought he'd given up everything to save

her when the angels came to kill her. What no one but Madison seemed to understand was that she'd filled the hole in his heart created when he lost his family during the times of Atlantis. Thanks to Madison, he'd gained a family he cared about and a reason to *live* rather than exist.

Zen was blessed because of her and their sibling-like bond. He was almost certain she and her family was his gift from his Creator. But he would never confess that suspicion to Micah because it would mean their father still meddled in Beliel's life. The King of Hell would rebel again if he suspected his father's involvement. This belief was the only reason why he'd forged an alliance with Beliel.

Yes, he was certain God still held plans for them. Those plans may not become clear for millennia or more, but He *was not* done with them.

Chapter 35

Two weeks later

MADISON RECLINED ON the sofa, the logs in the den's fireplace snapping and popping, as she reread the same paragraph for the third time in her ebook. Unable to concentrate, she lowered the reader to her chest and closed her eyes. Nix sat on the floor beside her, and she ran her fingers through the short strands of his hair, taking delight in the soft texture. Sitting on the opposite end of the sofa, Micah rubbed her feet with his fingertips. Even before he'd walked out on her, he'd given amazing foot rubs.

The babies were restless, and she suspected they'd arrive soon. She'd been having contractions off and on all day.

As if Nix could sense her thoughts or the girls' irregularity, he swiveled on the floor, palming her belly and kissing the mound.

"You'll get to do that to them soon, Nix."

He smiled at her, his love for her and the girls in his eyes. "I can't wait to meet them."

Madison feathered her fingers through his spiky

306

locks as he rested his head on her belly. She glanced at Micah.

"You tired or hungry?" he asked.

"Tired." No amount of food would alter that. Only giving birth to the twins would alleviate that dilemma.

A slash of pain whiplashed across her abdomen, stronger than the others she'd been getting. Wincing, she gasped and rubbed the offended region.

"What was that?" Nix sat up, worry gouging his forehead with creases. "Your belly just tightened up."

"Another contraction?" Micah ran his hands up her calves, kneading as he went.

"Yeah." She skimmed her fingertips along the furrows on Nix's forehead. His concern for her always warmed her. "Told you you'd meet the girls soon."

"You knew?" Nix shot Micah an accusatory glance. 'And didn't tell me' remained unspoken.

"I can feel them when she does. The contractions aren't coming consistently, and I figured she'd tell you when she was ready."

"Mads—"

"I wanted to be sure they weren't fake contractions before I said more." She ran her thumb along his bottom lip.

"And now?" He caught her hand and kissed her wrist.

"I think they're the real ones." Her water hadn't broken, so she couldn't be certain. "If they're not, they'll probably kick start the real ones soon."

"We should take you to Hell, let Hielel check you out." Micah swirled the pads of his fingertips against the soles of her feet.

Before she could comment, Zen teleported into the room, his rainbow orbs disturbing the air mere seconds before he appeared. He said nothing, just stepped to her, placed his hand on her shoulder and teleported her to her bed.

"The guys are gonna kick your ass for that."

Zero emotion. "They're welcome to try."

"Goddamn it, immortal!" Micah bellowed when he and Nix came through a portal into the bedroom. "If you—"

Before Micah could finish what was probably a threat, orbs hit the air and a moment later a squalling, messy baby girl was in Nix's hands. Nix sucked in a gasp of surprise before clasping her protectively to his chest. Seconds afterward the second infant was delivered into Micah's arms.

Both of her men seemed stunned into silence as they stared at the crying babies. She caught Zen's eye as he ran his palms over her abdomen. Her adopted brother winked at her.

"You did that to them on purpose," she accused.

His telepathy oozed into her head. *No point in discussing the method of delivery. Micah would've debated the need to return to Hell. Sometimes it's easier to remove the choice from him.*

Zen teleported her shirt away and before she could demand an explanation, he said, "Give the girls to Madison. Skin-to-skin contact will help them bond."

Nix's eyes were wet when he settled the first one into her arms. He kissed her and she could taste his tears. "Thank you, baby, you're amazing. They're...." he shook his head. "There aren't words for how perfect they are."

Madison understood his overwhelming emotions. She'd felt them with Amos and knew she would with the twins once she had a moment to process Zen's hijacking of her delivery.

Thank you, Zen. She hadn't planned that quick of a delivery, but she was thankful for the ease of it.

From the foot of the mattress Zen nodded. *Couldn't watch you suffer to birth them. Didn't give you a heads-up because you can't lie to Micah.*

Micah sat beside her on the bed and adjusted the other infant to lay belly down on her chest. "I vow to protect them with my life, kitten, as if they are my own."

Madison peered at her newborns. The one Nix had

returned to her squinted up at her. Instantaneous love blurred her vision as she kissed the infant's forehead. "This sweetie is Jaclyn. And you, my precious girl," she smiled at the one Micah had lain facedown and had begun to root for her breast, "are Jaelyn."

Wearing a goofy grin, Nix swiped at his eyes. "I can't believe this is real. That I'm a daddy."

Nix had never planned to marry or have children, but had predicted an early and bloody death. He'd been honest with her about that since shortly after she met him. So she understood the gift the twins were to him. "Y'all help me adjust them so I can nurse them."

Her guys assisted, positioning the twins so they could latch on.

Nix gave her a smooch that would've curled her toes any other time. "Didn't know you could get sexier, baby."

She laughed as he kissed each of his daughters on the forehead, before relaxing beside her on the mattress.

When Micah glided his finger along Jaelyn's hand, she curled her fingers around it. "They're identical."

"I can sense their personalities." Madison nodded at Jaelyn. "This is the one Zen dubbed 'Trouble'."

"She liked to kick me," Zen defended his nickname.

"Smart girl." Micah grinned at Madison, so she knew he teased.

Taz somehow worked his way into the room and made a beeline for the bed. Zen caught him by his tail and the mini-dragon squawked as if her immortal brother plotted Taz's murder.

"Allow him to come, Zen." Only she understood the mind of the dragon she'd accidentally crafted from a photo Amos had drawn. He could sense the newness of the babies, recognized they belonged to his mother, and he craved knowing he was still loved.

"As you wish, but one wrong move by Taz and I'll vaporize him."

"He'll be good." She watched Taz as he sniffed at

each of the girls, before painting both of them with a claiming swipe of his tongue. He curled up around her neck, his head hanging over her shoulder blinking at the girls. She kissed his scaly head. "I still love you, sweet boy."

From the corner of her eye she could see Nix shaking his head. He scratched the dragon behind his ear. "What a messed up family we have."

"Fuck no." Micah snatched up both Hellhounds by their scruff when they jumped onto the bed.

"The hellhounds will resent the twins if they're off-limits. That could be worse than allowing them to meet the girls now." Nix's sage reply surprised Madison, since he'd been so vocally against her keeping them.

She blew her Sherlock a kiss over Taz's head.

"Devlin and FiFi," Nix snapped his fingers at them. "No touching the babies, but you can sniff them and protect them like you do your momma and brother."

"I got sisters!" Amos bolted into the room with Petra on his heels. Her demon stepdaughter's grin was as big as Amos's.

Her son bounced onto the bed and crowded their space. Micah remained standing beside the bed with the squirming Hellhounds in either hand.

Madison glanced around the room. A giggle escaped. When had her life become a circus?

I love every minute of it.

Chapter 36

Two years later

"DO YOUR HUSBANDS know you're stalking me again?" Elias met her gaze as she took the seat across from him in the Sherlock bar.

"Hide better, and I'll stop." Not that she really stalked him. She found him when she needed something. Otherwise she left him to his own devices. Keeping her clandestine meetings with Elias a secret from her husbands wouldn't hurt them, even if her skulking came with complications on occasion. Almost three years since Elias tortured and tried to kill her and Micah still sought vengeance by way of spilling Eliel's blood. After all the years of Beliel's vendetta against his Father, she feared he'd never forgive his twin. "Why are *you* stalking Sherlocks?" It was a matter of time before one of them got up the nerve to approach them.

"Stalking is beneath me."

She snorted.

He tipped his shot glass at her and downed the

contents. "I'm taunting them."

That she believed.

She surveyed the bar's patrons. Many of them watched Elias, and had tensed the moment he put the shot glass to his lips. "I'm pretty sure they spiked your drink with something."

"Holy water," Elias confirmed, a sneer in his voice.

"Morons." She motioned to the waiter. "Another for him and one for me. What?" she asked when she caught his grin.

He leaned forward, anchoring his forearms on the table. "Princess, you know they'll lace your drink too and it'll burn like a motherfucker because you *are* a demon."

"Nah...I suck down so much of Nix's messian and Micah's seraph, nothing holy hurts."

"Except for when they want it to hurt, eh?" Elevating his eyebrows he sat back in his seat.

Madison stared at her brother-in-law, hating it when he turned their conversations lewd. She'd decided his goading was a test to see if he could provoke a response. Many times during their relationship she had lashed out at him, hated him, but now she thought she understood him better than Micah did. Better than Elias understood his motives. She still had the urge to see him bleed a little, to beg her for clemency. If the opportunity was granted, she'd take it...or maybe she wouldn't. She understood his actions, that he protected Hell, and his loyalty to give Micah all his dreams.

Elias has paid enough for his loyalty. Yeah, her Lynx was right.

She also realized Elias was as broken as Micah. His father had made him choose between mankind and Him. He'd Fallen, become an outcast from the rest of his brethren, except for the Kings, and all because of humanity. His daddy issues were as enormous as Micah's. Eliel needed a woman. A woman that could show him the mercy he'd never been given or shown to others. Just the idea of subjecting any woman to his ungentle ways...she cringed.

"Thank you," she said on autopilot when the waiter plopped their order on the table. She ran her fingertip along the rim of the shot glass as she studied Elias. "I need someone killed—"

"Fuck you. I'm not your servant boy. Bloody your hands like a real Queen of Hell."

"—and someone protected."

"*What?*" He paused with the glass halfway to his mouth. "I believe I misheard you."

"Nope." She touched his glass with hers. "To partnerships." She downed the spirits, and it burned as bad as Elias predicted it would.

"How does the holy water feel, princess?"

"Great." The sting didn't touch her tongue like it did when she lied to Micah. She'd learned a while back she could fib to the other Kings, but not Micah. Sometimes it was a damned nuisance, but neither could he lie to her so it all came out in the wash.

His chuckle called out her lie. He replaced his shot glass on the table, the liquor untouched, refusing her toast.

"Look...." She motioned to the waiter with her shot glass, requesting another for the simple delight of knocking the Sherlocks off kilter. "I can't kill him or I'll gain his power. And this isn't a power I want or need. He'll kill the girl if he doesn't die, but others will come after her too if she's not protected."

"She's mortal?"

"Yes."

"You've lost your goddamn mind if you think for one fucking minute I'm going to babysit a motherfucking human."

"Gee, Ellie, could you pack any more curse words into that sentence."

"Stop calling me that sissified name!"

She grinned at his explosion and slid his liquor closer to him. She'd taken to the nickname the moment she realized it rankled him. "I wouldn't ask you to do this if she wasn't important."

"Madison—"

Whatever he would've said halted when she dropped her Azura stones between them on the wooden table. The room silenced like all noise had been vacuumed from the space. "That's how important she is. Keeping her alive protects Hell."

"A human protecting Hell?" He scoffed. "Bullshit."

"You know the Azura stones don't lie."

"They're vague. You misread them."

"No."

He glanced around the room, and she knew the moment he realized she'd cast her power around them.

"At least one realized what the stones represented and was about to commit suicide by coming after us," she explained as she retrieved the prophetic rocks and tucked them into their bag.

"How?" He indicated the Sherlocks.

"I learned a while back I could stop time for short periods of time. It's a convenient gift."

"Too bad you didn't utilize it the night the angels killed you."

She shrugged. "Or when you tried to kill me." As a reply, he grinned. "But would I be where I am now had I?"

Elias took her measure for a long while. Finally, he nodded his head, grasped the shot glass, and swigged the liquor. "To royal partnerships, princess." The chair scraped against the floor when he pushed to his feet. He set the glass on the table. "Give me the human's name, and I vow to you no one will harm her so long as she's an asset for Hell."

Her heart beat like a sewing needle. Could she really give him the name? Could she damn the poor innocent girl?

Yes, Usha said with conviction, *because without her in his life,* he *is damned, and Hell will suffer.*

Without an ounce of guilt, Madison gave him her name. "Andrea Kozari."

314

Chapter 37

Two and a half years later

"HELLION, DO YOU have permission from your mom to do that?" Micah bit the inside of his cheek to terminate his grin from surfacing.

Jaelyn added pressure to the mini-dragon's neck when he attempted to squirm from her hold. Once Taz was compliant again, she resumed applying bright pink paint to his scaly backside. That little monster of Madison's created a funny sounding clicking noise that might've passed for growling. It was evident the creature was very displeased...and the look in his eyes said he'd get payback at the first opportunity.

"He likes it," his mischief-maker said as Taz made a high-pitched yap noise that no self-respecting dragon should ever make.

"Then why are you holding him down?"

She blinked at him, offering him the sweetest expression, before ruining her angelic appearance with a devilish grin. "He's ticklish."

Micah barked with laughter. Jaelyn giggled with

him.

"What do you think your Uncle Zen would say?" Not that he really cared what the uptight immortal's opinion was, but the little one idolized him, and Zennyo Ryuo seemed to have more sense when it came to discipline than Micah did. Phoenix's idea of correction resembled letting her run wild rather than any form of chastisement Micah recognized. Left to Micah he'd let Jaelyn and Jaclyn run roughshod all over him. He would've never thought these complacent years would've fulfilled him, but he'd never been happier.

Her eyes widened in alarm. "Please don't tell my Uncle Z."

"You can't hide it from him when he'll see your artwork on Taz."

She considered the dragon a long moment. "I'll risk it," she finally said with a minor shrug.

He made a 'come here' motion with his hand. "Give me the dragon, Hellion."

"But MicDaddy—"

"Now." He put his Kingly eyes on display along with the command so she'd know he meant business.

The devious child poked out her bottom lip, and it wobbled right on cue. She played him like a seasoned diva. With a huff, she deposited Taz into his hand.

"Let's go confess all to Momma."

"You're not playing fair," the five-year-old complained in a tone that made her sound wise beyond her years.

Taz hissed at her, proving he always understood what was said, but only Madison could make out the winged creature's mind.

"When do I ever play fair?" He even cheated at board games.

They walked side-by-side down the hall. "We could work out a deal. Momma ain't gotta know."

"Momma's going to notice Taz has a sudden color change."

"We could tell her he has a rash." The humor caught

him unaware, and he laughed before he could bite it back. She must've mistaken his laughter for weakness because she said, "I promise I'll be good for three days if you're up for the deal."

What five-year-old talks *like this?*

Shaking his head, he halted at the library door, where he knew Madison, Amos, Ginnie, and Jaclyn had been a few minutes earlier. He peered down at the hellion that owned his heart as much as if she were his own blood. "Ready to get this over with?"

She gave a melancholic sounding sigh and said, "Only if you insist on being disagreeable, MicDaddy, but it's gonna be a *looooong* time before I forgive you."

He doubted it'd be all that long, but he appreciated her efforts at negotiation.

At least a hundred butterflies fluttered about the library. Madison had brought them to life from Amos's drawings, only as a means to entertain Jaclyn and to add something beautiful to the world. The way she saw it, giving them life kept her craft honed, and it gave humanity a gift from the hellish region. They flitted about in an array of colors, some even glowing with varying phosphorous shades.

Jaclyn giggled and chased after one that caught her eye, but unable to catch any. Winded, her daughter flopped down on a chair, her smile infectious as her rapt gaze remained on the ceiling. Soon Madison would open the window and allow them to fly away, to live out their life however it panned out.

"Jae's gonna be jealous she missed this, Jac," Amos said using Nix's nicknames for the girls, and handing over a final drawing to his sibling.

"She will," Ginnie agreed. "It was odd she elected to take a nap instead of join us."

Anytime Jaelyn's behavior turned 'odd' it usually

signaled trouble.

Madison strolled to Jaclyn and peered down at the picture. Pink wings, tipped in sapphire blue, it was a simple design, but appealing.

"Momma, can I have it as a pet like your Taz?" Jaclyn turned hopeful eyes up to Madison. "I promise to treasure it."

"I'll help her care for it," Ginnie said. The Baltic pleased Madison, and who knew such a dangerous creature would make the perfect nanny?

"Speaking of Taz...." Micah's deeply accented voice interrupted them from the doorway.

Madison looked their way and, "Oh, good gawd!" she screeched when she caught sight of her defaced dragon. "Jaelyn Birmingham!"

There was no question where the blame rested.

Taz fled Micah's arms so fast he was a blurred pink arc through the air. Micah chuckled.

"I don't know how he got that really bad rash." Jaelyn blinked, the sweetest, most concerned expression on her face. If Madison didn't know better she'd have fallen for her child's antics.

"You really wanna add lies to your crime?"

"Sowwy, Taz. Sowwy, Mommie." Baby talk surfaced from Jaelyn anytime she plotted to wheedle her way out of mischief she'd caused. Which was much too frequent.

"Did you consider Taz's feelings?"

Right on cue, big crocodile tears streaked her cheeks. That was a clear 'no' Taz's desires hadn't been factored into Jae's monkey business.

"I'm not falling for that, young lady. You're grounded. Gawd, he's getting paint in my hair." She groaned as Taz burrowed under her hair and wrapped himself around her neck like a tight shawl, his body vibrating with his outrage. "We'll work out your punishment, Jaelyn, after I talk to Daddy."

Micah rolled his eyes, and said telepathically, *Daddy-Phoenix is going to take one look at her sweet face and cave. We both know her punishment will be too light.*

Not this time, she said back. *She's gotta learn boundaries or she'll become Hell on Earth.*

Madison popped a gummy bear in her mouth and chewed slowly. Taz blanketed her shoulder and neck making a moody, snuffing-purring noise that displayed his continued displeasure with Jaelyn. She understood his displeasure since she wouldn't want to be held down and painted either. No idea what she was going to do with her child, she shook her head, but seriously Taz needed to learn to let offenses go, move past them. But he was as big a kid as her twin daughters.

Jaelyn had been punished, her favorite ice cream removed from her daily schedule for two weeks. The only trouble was she never seemed to learn from her punishment. Zen had taken her off alone and when they returned, her child had been solemn. Disappointing Zen hurt Jaelyn most.

Thinking of the pink paint trapped between the grooves of the mini-dragon's scales, she wondered how long it'd take for the color to wear off. At least Jaelyn had picked a decent color to use, but sheesh after an hour of bathing him and scrubbing his scales with a toothbrush, Madison still had no luck in removing all of the paint.

As if his weird agitated noise wasn't enough, the tip of his tail twitched back and forth like an agitated housecat. "You need to let it go, Taz." She held a green piece of candy to his nose. He executed a cautious sniff before curling his tongue out to receive the treat.

The irritated dragon smacked on his candy as she placed the next three pieces of the jigsaw together. With the puzzle spread out on the table, Zen entered the room as she fitted a piece into its groove. He sat down in the chair opposite her.

"You're back early." He'd gone Elias hunting with Micah earlier. She could've told them they'd be unsuccessful, but if wasting time made them happy, then who was she to take away their happiness?

She dug a handful of gummies out of the bag, and took the time to sort them by color in the palm of her hand.

Back ramrod straight, Zen's dark-brown hair cascaded over his forehead, and his steely silver eyes gauged her. "You and I know we went on a wild-geese chase."

Unable to bite back a full-blown grin at his screwed up saying, she let one corner of her mouth tilt up. After ten years he still couldn't get basic sayings correct. "Micah know?"

"Not yet."

"What about Nix?"

As an answer Zen gave her a headshake.

"How'd you figure it out?" She studied the pieces spread out across the table. "Get it from my mind?"

"Does it matter how?" Madison shrugged at his question and he went on. "Why are you protecting Eliel?"

"I'm protecting Micah, *not* Elias." At her statement, his eyebrows elevated upward and disappeared beneath his bangs. "Think about it. They're twins, connected since their life began. That's a huge bond. I realize how big of a bond thanks to the girls. If Micah kills Elias, he'll eventually regret it. I can't have him living with regret for an eternity." *That is too long to regret your actions.* "In time he'll forgive his brother and be glad he never caught up with him."

"You ever think he needs to feel the satisfaction of revenge in order to be whole again?"

Madison snapped her gaze off the puzzle and onto Zen. "If I let him have his revenge, Micah will descend into a self-destructive phase we won't be able to control. I don't control him now, and only you can conceive of how much worse he can get. Besides, Hell can't afford to lose Elias anyway." She ran her fingertips over Taz's snout. "And you know what? If anyone has the pleasure of killing him, it should be me. I was the one injured. Only Micah's pride suffers."

Zen nodded, his focus drawn to the dragon. "He's still angry."

"You have no idea." She rolled her eyes. "He takes everything too personally."

"Such a hard life the monster lives."

Madison snorted at Zen's sarcasm.

"That you know how to locate Elias disturbs me." That comment came from nowhere and since it wasn't a question, she didn't reply. "How often do you meet him alone?"

"He doesn't pose a threat to me, Zen, if that's what you're worried about."

"Why would I worry? It's not like he tortured you and tried to kill you, or anything sadistic like that."

She grinned at his dry tone. "Seriously, you've gotta stop hanging with Amos. His sarcasm is rubbing off on you."

"Elias is dangerous."

"No kidding. He's a King of Hell, but he's no longer a threat to me." She leaned back against her seat and fed Taz more candy.

"You're playing fast and loose with your life, Madison."

Surprised he got that euphemism correct, she nodded. "Yeah, like I said...Hell needs him."

"Why now, when he's been out of Hell's business for five years?"

Madison picked up the pouch next to her on the sofa, opened it, and turned it over so her pink Azura stones dropped out into the palm of her other hand. "Those tell me Hell needs him. About two years ago they pointed me in Elias's direction." She took a moment to consider what information to impart, and decided to divulge as little as possible. "The Kings believe Hell can be sustained without Elias's powers, but they're wrong. It's doomed without him."

Zen stared at the prophetic stones that were connected to her soul somehow. "I thought those only showed your future."

"Hell's future affects me." The rocks knocked against one another as she wiggled her fingers. "You ever wish you had a significant other, Zen?"

He frowned. "I had a wife. She died. I'm happy with my life the way it is."

Not what she wanted to hear. "You don't sometimes wish you had what I do with my guys?"

"What are you getting at?"

Madison sighed and returned her stones to the pouch. "I know two things about your future, Zen."

"I don't want to hear it."

"Whatever makes you happy, big brother." She scratched her dragon's head. "We'll pick up this conversation after War comes for you."

"Madison—"

She cut him off before he could chastise her further. "I talked to Alessa today."

"I'm sorry."

Tears burned her sinuses, but she somehow managed to hold them back. "Me too. I haven't told Nix yet. I offered her a deal. She declined."

"It's her life, her choice."

"Yeah." She leaned her cheek against Taz's head, his pointy ear twitching against her hair. Just by Taz's presence she gained comfort. "The cancer's terminal. They gave her a month at most."

Surprisingly the outspoken woman had become one of Madison's best friends. Alessa wanted to die on her own terms. Madison wanted to provide her with options.

"No, Madison."

Sometimes his ability to snag her thoughts was a hindrance. She met her brother's gaze, his silver eyes bright in the dim lighting, and she challenged him with, "What's wrong with me wanting her to live?"

"Many reasons. It's not what she wants, and you

should respect that. You know what it feels like to have your life micromanaged without your consent. You have to accept that you can't save all your family. They will die eventually, and you'll live forever. That's part of immortality." Madison snorted, disliking his reasoning even if it was sound. "Alessandra rejected your offer, respect her and allow her to die on her own terms. To take the choice from her is selfish on your part."

Silence decimated the friendly air. Sometimes she despised Zen's shrewdness.

Madison inhaled, and released it. "I'll miss Alessa. She makes me laugh when my days are dark."

"She's a special mortal."

Yeah, even I like her, Usha piped in, and her demon rarely liked humans. They'd miss her when she passed, leaving a hole in her heart, and she could imagine how much worse it'd be for Nix.

There were too many dark days ahead. The Azura stones revealed there were even darker days coming. Being the Queen of Hell wasn't always what it was chalked up to be.

And now I have a trusted immortal deceiver to worry about.

Blanking her thoughts from Zen, she pondered him and their diverse relationship. He was her brother, her best friend, and she couldn't imagine an eternity without him. Often he was all that kept her focused and moral. She prayed he wasn't the 'immortal deceiver' the Azura stones foretold would darken her future sooner than she'd like. If that was his role, she'd cross that bridge when the day came.

"What's wrong?"

She shook her head. "Nothing."

Zen rose from his seat and sat beside her. Taz chuffed his disappointment at sharing her, but her brother ignored him. She leaned against him when he pulled her to his side.

He's not the immortal deceiver. He can't be. Zen

demonstrated his loyalty and love through his actions. She would be devastated if he deceived her.

If he is the prophecy...

I'll probably set the world aflame with my sorrow at the betrayal.

THE END

Other Books by Gracen

About Gracen

Gracen is a hopeless daydreamer masquerading as a "normal" person in southern society. When not writing, she's a full-time basketball/lacrosse/guitar mom for her two sons and a devoted wife to her real-life hero-husband. She's addicted to writing, romance novels, watching paranormal movies, Alabama football, and coffee...addictions are not necessarily in order of priority. She's convinced coffee is nectar from the gods and blending coffee and writing together generates the perfect creative merger. Many of her creative worlds are spawned from coffee highs. To learn more about Gracen or to leave her a comment, visit her website at:

www.gracen-miller.com

98482939R00187